Summoner Mage

Tarren Guy

Books by Tarren Guy

Veritas Rerum Novels
Power of Will

Written in the Stars Novels
The Earth Beneath Us

Novels From Earth
Hail Atlantis

This book is dedicated to anyone who has experienced the darkness of this world, who have looked into the void and found their lives corrupted.

TRIGGER WARNINGS

From beginning 1st chapter there is a young character dealing with abuse. If you find you need to put this book down then please do so. Your strength is still building and I look forward to the day you choose to step out into the light once more, to share your brilliance and worth with the rest of the world.

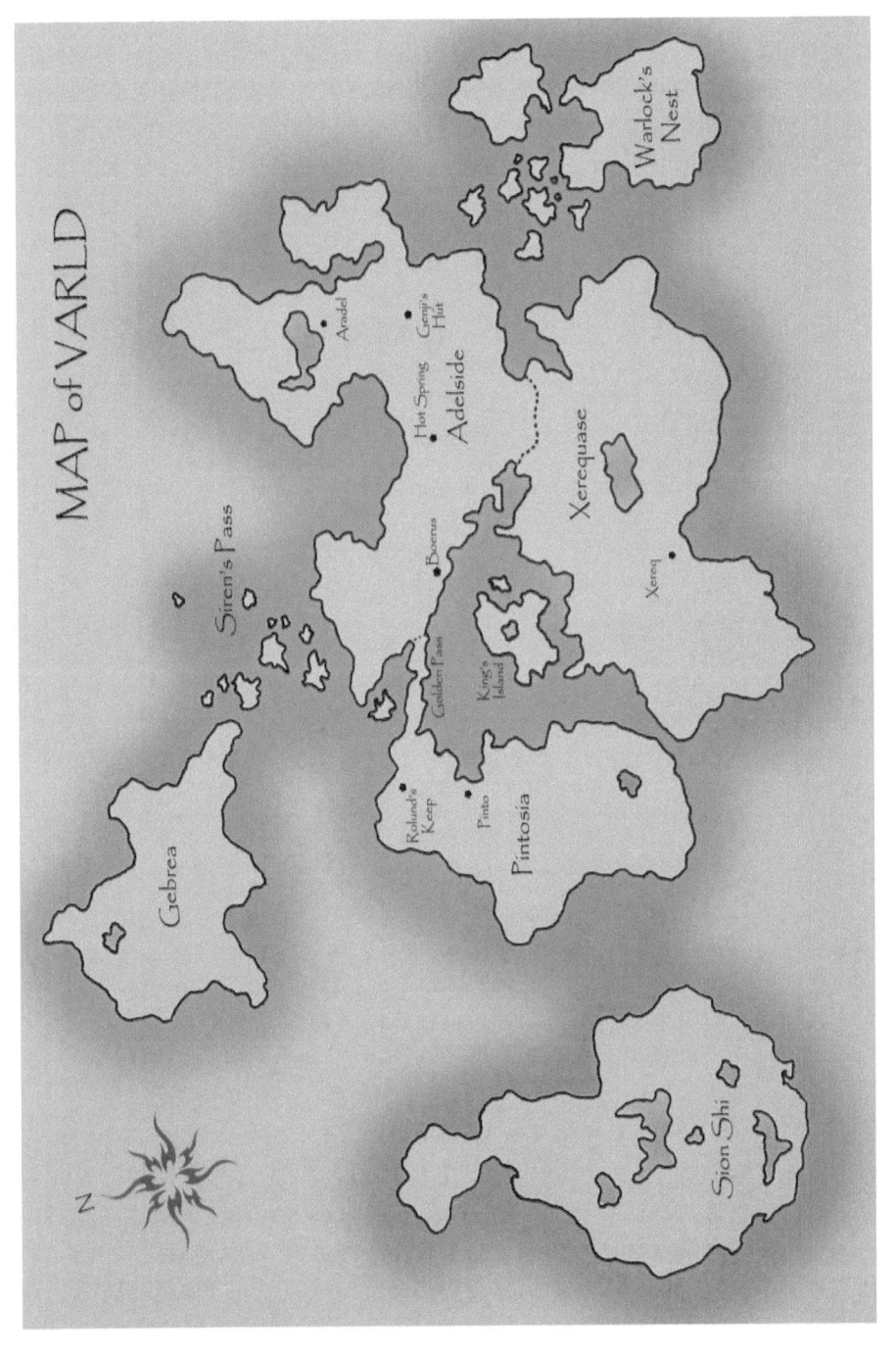

MAP of VARLD

Warlock's Nest

Aradel

Genji's Hut

Hot Spring

Adelside

Xerequase

Xereq

Siren's Pass

Boerus

Golden Pass

King's Island

Gebrea

Roland's Keep

Pinto

Pintosia

N

Sion Shi

Prologue

Ancient bone dice danced across the table to determine the fate of the onlookers. Many would come to this tavern to gamble away their hard earned coin for two reasons. The dice were provided by the tavern keep so no arguments about cheating could occur. And so was the axe that would split a head or two if a fight did break out.

The axe was always on display, wedged into the wall outside the kitchen. Just the sight of it was enough to calm any rising anger. Double winged, the battle axe fanned out like a butterfly sitting atop a polished ebony pommel. For those who called the bluff, the sight of the blades cleaving through their head warned all others that the grizzly Sir Galis meant what he said when protecting his tavern.

Twice honoured by the king for his gallantry in past wars, no guard would ever call into question Sir Galis's actions if a body or two rolled out the door. They knew he did only what was necessary and it made their job easier in the long run having ill-tempered miscreants off the street.

As the dice settled, Galis let out a sigh of relief. He knew the losing streak wouldn't remain forever. The game had kept him tense since the players entered his doors and not for the first time. Those rolling were the only ones he feared he could not hold true to the code of his hall. To allow a fight between the dice players would lead many others to question his authority. To stop it would mean his tavern doors shut for good.

'*Leave the dice,*' Galis silently prayed.

The Crowned Prince Atalis couldn't hear his prayers, however, and reached once more for the ancient bones. With a dramatic shake on each side of Atalis's head, the dice danced once more. This time the numbers read a more favourable result.

"BARTZAR!" Atalis cried Pintosia's victory cry. He grinned. "Looks like my lucks starting to turn around, boys." Reaching for the coins, Atalis stopped as a razor-edged dagger bit into the table between his fingers.

"I've heard a few rumours about you, my young Prince," the man with the dagger said. Pushing the hilt towards Atalis he pinned the Prince's hand in place.

"I wouldn't know what you mean." If Atalis seemed worried he didn't show it. Recognising a Page Boy who was standing at the entry way staring back at him in shock, Atalis waved to him with his free hand. "Jiven, come join us."

"He wasn't invited," the other man said shooting Jiven a dangerous look.

Jiven just stood unsure how to proceed. By now, many of the patrons had paused in their gambling to watch the exchange. Some glancing at Galis to see if he would step in.

"Nonsense, Hern" Atalis flicked his free hand at the man holding the dagger. "If he's here it's official Castle business and therefore has access to anywhere." Atalis turned his attention to Jiven. "Come on, spit it out boy. You can see I'm busy."

Jiven remained frozen, eyes transfixed on the dagger still pinning Atalis's hand.

While Atalis tried to get anything out of Jiven, Hern studied the dice rolling them a few times. His face darkened and he sat waiting for Atalis's attention once more.

Galis swore.

Atalis, however, took advantage of Hern's distraction and removed the dagger throwing it at Jiven. With the hilt hitting the boy in the shoulder it brought him back to his senses. More importantly it removed the weapon from Hern.

Jiven stepped forward. "My Prince, the King requests your presence in the throne room immediately."

"Tell him I'm busy," Atalis waved him away settling his eyes back on Hern. He shot the man a confident grin.

Hern was about to speak when Jiven cut in once more. "It's important..."

"It always is with him," Atalis replied giving Jiven a sideways glance.

"There is a shell," Jiven said unsure.

Atalis's eyes narrowed. "A shell?"

Jiven nodded.

"Go to my room and gather my sword. Bring it to the entrance of the throne room. I'll meet you there," Atalis ordered. Watching the boy leave, Atalis pushed himself to his feet. "Our game ends here."

Hern's arm shot out to grip Atalis's wrist.

"Sorry but I'm just not into holding hands," Atalis tried to drag his arm free but found it was held tight.

"You cheated me," Hern said. "Nobody cheats me."

"I've been losing til now."

"The dice have been swapped. You won't lose from here."

"Hern, if you want the coin, keep it. I'm needed elsewhere," Atalis got an edge to his voice.

"You're going to be late, my Prince." Hern's muscles tensed as he readied to attack.

A loud thump echoed through the tavern. Hard pressed against the Prince's arm and wedged deep into the table was Galis's axe. "You will both leave the tavern immediately." Galis's voice was like ice.

"Stay out of it, Galis," Hern said. "He disgraced your tavern. He deserves everything he gets."

"It is for me to deal out the punishments. Continue against my orders and you will be meeting, Lillian," Galis said patting his axe. "Now take the Prince's *gift* and leave."

Hern held Galis's gaze a moment longer before grunting. "Keep it. Just remember we are far from done." With a sweep of his arm, Hern scattered the coins and left.

"My Prince," Galis's voice still held its edge.

"I'm going," Atalis assured him, turning for the door. "Take the coin as an apology."

"Take the back," Galis said. "They'll be waiting and your summons was urgent."

"Still don't miss a thing," Atalis smiled shooting

Galis a wink. Atalis left out the backdoor into an enclosed alleyway. No one from the front could get in here without swinging up close to the castle where the guards were thickest.

It was another half hour before Atalis emerged near the castle. The guards seemed to be expecting him and ushered the Prince through the gates. Atalis wasted no time, heading straight for the royal entrance behind the throne and paused. Jiven hadn't made it back with his sword. Without it, his father would have a fit expecting him to wear it everywhere outside his room. Even now.

Bouncing from foot to foot with impatience, Atalis cursed the Page Boy. The mention of the word *shell* meant danger was imminent and they had no time to lose. Now, he was stalling for a Page Boy and fear of getting reprimanded. Taking a deep breath, Atalis prepared to enter.

A large commotion sounded from behind the doors and Atalis reacted. Bursting in, he passed into a static haze. Electricity surged over his limbs causing Atalis to falter a moment before he was through.

Now by the throne he saw three orcs crossing the room away from him. As he was about to react, Atalis's knee bumped something solid. Looking down, Atalis's face drained of all colour. Propped in a sitting position, the king sat in a pool of blood. His throat had been opened and his lifeless eyes were staring back at Atalis.

"Father?" Atalis gasped. Anger started to grow in his chest fuelling Atalis's next moves. Taking up his father's sword, he chased the orcs into a rift that opened across the room stepping over another casualty as he went. Atalis didn't have time to note it was the court Mage.

Inside the rift a dark, ebony staircase spiralled away from him into the deep void.

Chapter 1

She lay in the dark on her brother's bed. The soft mattress and warm blanket the only thing that would bring her comfort since her brother left home. Her mum was always working late and her stepdad... he was a drunk.

Crickets sang in the autumn air lulling her to sleep. She fought it though. It was dangerous to sleep in the open. The front door creaked open.

'No.... it's too early for mum to be home,' she thought her spirits dropping. The girl rolled from her brother's bed straightening the blankets. She didn't want anyone to know she'd been there. Heavy footsteps on the stairs alerted her to someone's approach. More than one.

'Hassheell,' came a rough, slurred voice. Hazel dove under the bed and scrambled to the back corner. She could see the slither of light from the hallway outlining the door. 'Come out.... Hashel.' Hazel heard a large thump against the wall as someone stumbled around. The footsteps walked into her room and she heard rummaging as the man her mother married searched for her. Hazel heard him growl "Where is that little slut," as he stormed back out into the hallway. The door to her brother's room was thrown open and Hazel saw two sets of feet enter the room. Her breath caught in her throat and she clamped her eyes tight. The room remained quiet and after what seemed like minutes Hazel chanced opening her eyes just a little. She whimpered seeing the face of her step father. The sunken bloodshot eyes sporting dark bags beneath. The dirty, unshaven features evidence that he didn't work. Stale, gross ale drifted along on his breath. "Zere jou are... Hashel,' he said with a yellow toothed grin. 'Come on out... and... meet my ffvend.' Hazel shook her head and retreated far into the corner. His face changed immediately and she could tell he was angry.

Reaching a grubby hand under the bed, her step dad grabbed for her leg. At ten Hazel was still small and was able to avoid being caught. She felt safe under her brother's bed but her safety was relative. Hazel's step dad slammed his fist into the ground and scrabbled back. She hoped that tonight he would give up and leave her alone. That he wouldn't touch her again. The bed shifted slightly and then was thrown across the room hitting the small television and exposing Hazel. Her step dad stepped in and grabbed her by her shoulder length autumn hair swinging her back into the room. Her mum made her grow it back out after Hazel cut it short. She would not have her daughter act like a boy. Hazel tried to tell her that it was for her own protection but her mum wouldn't listen.

'You little bish,' her step dad yelled. Too quickly, he was upon her pinning her down. Hazel started to struggle, tears coming to her bronzed eyes. She looked to the second man. A skinny, little weasel with a lustful grin shaping his lips.

'Daddy,' Hazel cried. Her step dad punched her hard in the stomach. He would never hit her in the face. The continuous bruises would obviously point to abuse. All the wind burst from Hazel's lungs and she couldn't breathe for a few dizzying moments. Pain was rippling through her side.

'I am jour... daddy now and you are going to keep me... and my fvend... company. Don't worry. Jour shlut of a mother will be home very late,' the step dad told her. He reached down grabbing the collar of her pyjama top and started to wrench it from her. There was a small ripping noise coming from the clothing.

'Noo!' Hazel screamed thrashing from side to side trying to get free.

The Academy of Mage Craft had stood for eight hundred years. Founded in the times when magic was reintroduced back into the world after the Mage Killer's massacre wiped it from the land. The doors were open to anyone showing signs in any magical discipline for knowledge, growth and development. The grounds itself was fashioned like a regular college or learning centre with multiple levels. Each discipline of Magic had its own separate rectangular building so there wouldn't be any distractions from the more erratic and dangerous practices.

A Mage chose the time they spent in any given area. Some excelling in certain fields while coming up short in the disciplines of others. Everything came down to the ability and patience a Mage held within themselves. Those who could master all nine disciplines were rare and normally went on to do great things in the world. The highest honour given to those Mages that could master the cruel and draining art of summoning along with all other disciplines. These Mages would henceforth be known as Summoner Mages.

One likely candidate was pacing the halls of the Academy awaiting his final exam to commence. Genji was worrying, talking to himself about the different elementals and beings that he could call upon. Reminding himself of all the things that could go wrong and the counter measures to stabilize the summon. Darkness... Darkness... Genji's mind came up with a blank as he thought about the types of demons that lived in the depth of fear and despair. Tests had a troubling effect on his mind. In the field he could create a simple fireball within moments and without thinking. He couldn't believe that he had to take that basic test three times.

Genji knew the information for summoning dark beings this morning but he couldn't conjure the information now. If he was asked to summon a being of darkness he would fail and it would be another month before he could retake the test. Turning in his long blue robes he almost tripped stepping on the material. He would not spend another month wearing these ridiculous things. His dark ponytail wouldn't get caught in the hem of the neck either. The vast library would have the answers he needed and so that was his destination.

Walking out of the hallway and into a large open area Genji stopped to look at the beautiful architecture.

A handful of students had to walk around him but he didn't care. They were going to be left behind at the end of today. The ceiling was domed and made of glass to let in natural light. The walls going up to the dome six storeys above, did not meet smoothly at each of the eight edges. Instead, each panel overlapped the panel to the right and was slightly angled up. This gave the viewer a visual affect like they were in the eye of a tornado looking up. This was Genji's favourite room in the entire Academy.

On the floor was a symbol that spanned from wall to wall. It was circular in design with lines like thorns arcing out around the circumference. Four lines like taloned fingers hooked around from behind the circle to cut in from north, south, east, and west. The centre of the circle remained white except those four lines almost meeting in the middle. This circle was used in all summoning of light beings and Genji thought it had the perfect setting with the domed roof. Genji was told that this symbol had history in all of magic and was responsible for magic's return to this world. He didn't know how true this was but he trusted the Mage masters.

Continuing on to the library, Genji didn't want to get called up before he refreshed his memory. The library was very basic as libraries go. There was seating areas randomly around the room near different sections of study. Between and around these seats were the many rows of books that were solely on the discipline of summoning. Other areas in the campus held their own libraries specifically for those disciplines. There was no one to lend out the books as there were multiple copies and students were given a lot of trust with returning them in a timely manner.

Genji found the section on darkness and was dismayed that there were no general purpose books sitting on the shelf for a quick refresh. Feeling cursed and about to search for numerous books that would hold similar information Genji saw an old faded book titled simply *"Darkness"*. The book was lying on its side and other books stood upright upon it as if the book was part of the shelf itself. Removing these, Genji picked the dusty book up off the shelf and blew upon the cover. The layer of dust didn't disperse and Genji used a sleeve to wipe it away.

Confused by what he saw Genji reread the title. He was not wrong as the book definitely said Darkness but the symbol on the front was the same one he had just been admiring in the hall which dealt with light. Genji opened the book randomly to determine if it held the information he was after. He read:

"In the darkest reaches of the steps there came a demon of great evil known as Aragaranatan. It marked the last Mage of the Mage Killer Massacre with a summoning circle. The circle that has commonly been associated with the circle for light. This it tried to use to summon itself into the world of man. If not for the..."

'Genji, I knew I'd find you here,' A female voice interrupted him. Genji's brow furrowed as he looked up at possibly his only friend in the Academy. Beverlin was shorter than most of the females on campus. Her black hair was curled up at the ends and just sat upon her green robes. The rich blue of her eyes were a striking contrast against the colour of her hair. Genji saw that her face was full of mischief. Though she was his only friend she was also a thorn in his side at times like this. He had to get rid of her fast if he was going to get any studying done.

'Beverlin,' Genji said sternly. 'I'm studying. I have my final test today and I want to be completely ready for it. I don't want to be stuck in these halls for another month.'

'You know it all, Genji,' Beverlin replied smiling. 'I'll miss you if you leave. Another month won't hurt.'

Genji grabbed her by the shoulders, turned her around and with a playful slap on the butt sent her on her way. She jumped and feigned shock at his actions. 'You would have me stay for the two years you'll be here if you could.'

The petite girl smiled and, with a wink, ran away. Genji shook his head and turned his attention back to the book. He'd just finished reading the same lines once more when a bell sounded inside his head signalling his attendance was required in the exam hall. Genji swore and placed the book back on the shelf. He couldn't get the image of a darkness circle in his mind and prayed the exam would be on any of the other seven circles.

It took Genji no time at all to reach the exam room only around the corner from the library. The room was a big empty space with black walls and dark grey floor. At the far end was a raised desk that held four examiners. Three men and one woman would sit at the desk watching everything Genji did critically and mark him a pass or fail. If the result couldn't be agreed upon, it was an automatic pass. Genji stood before the examiners as he had done for other disciplines and waited to be addressed.

'Genji, you have asked to be examined in the discipline of summoning,' an old, greying man, Boris, said. His voice was raspy and he had a harsh cough that happened randomly. 'This exam, should you pass, will be your final exam at the Academy of Mage Craft. Are you ready?'

Genji was nervous and his mind was spinning but he was determined. 'I am,' he said with a nod.

'Good,' the woman, Tilia replied. She was a lot younger than the other three judges and her voice drifted along like a melody. 'Today, with the new moon present, your exam will be how well you can summon a being of darkness.' Genji's lips pursed cursing his luck. He knew this would be the case. 'You may begin.'

Looking to the left, Genji found bags of salt. He collected these and brought them back to the middle of the room. The first step he knew was to draw the circle of the given force in salt. He just couldn't remember what he needed to draw. Standing with his head bowed and eyes closed, Genji pleaded with his brain to conjure the memories of his training. The examiners looked on saying nothing. They would leave him alone until he either finished the task or resigned.

The words of the book he just read ran through his mind. "*Commonly been associated with the circle of light.*" Did this mean the circle could represent other forces? Genji thought to himself. With nothing left to lose he picked up the bag of salt and started walking out the pattern. Salt pouring to the floor as he moved. When the rough design was laid he started to sharpen the edges and correct the angles and algorithms of each line until everything sat perfectly before him.

Looking at the judges, Genji could see nothing written on their faces as to whether he was going to pass or fail with this circle. Resigned to his decision, Genji pushed forward. Choosing a demon wouldn't be hard. Succubi were simple to control and easy to find in the demon realms. He focused his mind like a portal and pictured the humanoid being with his mind's eye. Genji used a technique learned in the Academy to silence the other parts of his mind and when all was in place directed a pulling force from the demon realm, through his mind and into the circle. The circle started to glow a dark purple.

'Tenebris Adducere,' Genji said in a strong even tone. His head started to ache and the strain of holding his focus was almost over bearing. Genji's whole body tingled with pins and needles that grew in intensity as the summoning proceeded. A dark purple twister rose up from the circle to the height of Genji whipping the salt around. A small part of Genji's mind celebrated as the summoning couldn't fail from this point. He only needed to control the succubus produced.

As the twister died away a scream reverberated around the room. No one was prepared for what they saw in the centre of the circle. A young girl with torn clothes and bruises over her body was thrashing and crying, struggling with some imaginary being.

The succubus was smaller than Genji had wanted but without missing a beat he stepped forward forcing his control over the demon. The thrashing and screaming didn't subside. Worried, he moved closer to increase the intensity of his force. The girl opened her eyes and Genji saw that they were human in nature. Forgetting the exam, he walked in close and knelt beside her. Instantly, she rolled away from him and tried to hide in the corner where the raised desk met the wall. Her clothes barely holding to her skin let alone covering her. Genji didn't move any closer seeing the fear in her eyes.

'What have you done, Genji?' Genji looked up to meet the eyes of Gerard, an examiner known for his harsh marking. The man didn't look pleased.

Genji could only stand with his mouth hanging loose looking from the examiners to the girl then back to the examiners again. No one in the history of the Academy had ever summoned an actual human. He wasn't prepared for this and was starting to sweat.

'Well?' Gerard demanded once more. All eyes were on him except Pendar, the last of the examiners. He was staring intently at the girl. Without taking his eyes from her he reached back and grabbed Gerard next to him after missing a few times.

'Wait, Gerard, look at her,' Pendar said.

The voice above frightened the girl, who didn't realize they were there. She fell back and crawled to the far wall huddling up in a ball. Her short hair lying in a tussled mess over her face. All four examiners leaned forward to look at her.

'This can't be real,' Tilia exclaimed.

'Either she is a being of darkness or Genji has done an impossible act.'

'The girl is human,' Pendar confirmed. 'But the amount of darkness that surrounds her is incredible. She has suffered terribly. Genji?' Pendar addressed the young man.

Genji snapped out of his stupor. 'Yes sir?'

'Explain your actions and the choice of circle you made.'

Genji stumbled for the right words so decided to start from the beginning. He admitted to his absent

12

mindedness before the exam and the quick refresher in the library.

'I haven't seen that book,' Boris said. 'Who is it by?'

'There was no name on the front. Just a title,' Genji replied before explaining that he'd been interrupted by Beverlin and then the exam had begun before he could go any further. 'My mind still couldn't penetrate the clouds that filled it but the line from the book really stuck up there. I interpreted it as meaning the circle for light wasn't always thus and with the book having the title *"Darkness"* I felt I had nothing to lose.'

'It's is a preposterous notion but you did manage to accomplish the task,' Gerard said. A touch of hope lit Genji's face. 'However I am still deliberating on whether this outweighs the use of the wrong circle,' Gerard said to Genji's disappointment. The examiner continued to eye off the young girl huddled by the wall. 'Can you send the girl back to where she came from? She's starting to get on my nerves.'

The young girl was listening to the conversation for anything that could be an invitation of harm upon her. When they said that she needed to be sent home a picture of her drunken step dad with his full weight upon her crashed into her mind. Her emotions ignited against the idea and she silently mouthed no over and over again. Genji raised his pointer and middle finger straight up together and with a sweeping motion from left to right he spoke the words of release. She remained.

'Emundetur a fluxi seminis,' Pendar said rising from his chair and mimicking Genji's actions. Still she remained. 'It seems that the girl's will to stay is greater than our ability to release her.'

'Then take the bloody girl outside, Genji,' Gerard said. He was getting fed up with the whole situation. 'We shall deliberate now on your fate.'

As Genji moved towards Hazel in an attempt to obey Gerard she quickly got to her feet and moved towards the door. Genji paused watching her before following her out of the room. Passing the door, Genji lost sight of her. He looked around frantically but there was no avenue she could have taken to get away that quick. The thought that she had returned to whence she had come crossed Genji's mind but he knew that was untrue. He would have felt the severing of the connection between them.

There was a rustling behind a small table and Genji saw the girls toes sticking out from underneath. He smiled and squatted near the table to look at the frightened girl. She was trying to squeeze as far back as she could.

'Hi,' Genji said trying to build some rapport. He had no experience in these sorts of situations and didn't know what he should be saying. 'My name is Genji. You don't need to be afraid of me. I'm not going to hurt you.' Genji waited for a reply but nothing came. 'Do you have a name?' He asked.

Hazel looked as though she was about to say something then the moment passed and she dug her head further into her arms.

'I know you must be scared. You are in a new place with no knowledge of how you got here and not knowing if you could ever go home,' Genji told her trying to be empathetic. 'Just know that I will do everything I can to help you find your way back.'

This only caused Hazel to sink further away. Genji wanted to say more but he was asked to come back to the exam room.

'I know that it's hard to be brave at the moment but you need to return with me to the room,' Genji said. Hazel didn't move. 'I'll tell you what. I'll go in first and leave the door open. When you are ready you can follow me inside.'

Genji walked into the exam room leaving the door open for Hazel to come through. He studied the faces of the examiners and didn't like what he saw there. Each one was serious reminding him of the times he had failed exams about to be given hard news. Standing before his fate Genji awaited his verdict.

Tilia cleared her throat. 'It has been discussed in

depth and an agreement has been reached. Not all here are happy with the outcome,' she glanced at Gerard. 'But we feel it is the correct choice. For your use of the light circle alone when asked to summon a being of darkness, you have failed.' Genji's heart faltered its next few beats but Tilia continued. 'That being said there is more to be considered in this exam than just the technical side of things. A young girl has been displaced from her home. She is shrouded in darkness and in that sense you have completed the task at hand. We have been divided as to your result. The deciding factor was the girl herself.'

At that moment, Hazel walked cautiously just inside the door and slid up against the back wall.

Tilia paused for the girl to settle then continued again. 'She does not want to go home and it falls upon you, Genji, to care for her until the summoning is dispelled.'

'No,' Genji protested. 'I don't know how to look after a child. I'm about to get true freedom and you want to chain me down? I won't accept that.'

'Genji!' Pendar said harshly. 'You were the one who summoned the girl. You are linked to her. It is your responsibility and no one else's. If you do not accept you will fail the task and still you will have to look after her. Only by accepting this outcome will you gain the votes needed to pass. Tell me your answer now.'

Genji had a strained look on his face as the ultimatum was placed upon him. Looking back at the girl, he knew she was going to be a hassle but he had no other choice. Either way he'd be looking after her. What he was really choosing between was living at home as a Summoner Mage, the highest honour one can get, or on campus as a student.

'I accept,' he relented. 'I will care for the girl at my home having passed every course a Mage can.'

'Congratulations Summoner Mage Genji. You may practice any form of magic outside this campus at your discretion,' Boris said clapping his hands. The other examiners congratulated him in turn. When it got to

Gerard he just grunted and looked away.

Genji bowed to the examiners. 'I joined the Academy of Mage craft when I was nineteen. All the staff at this campus have treated me with respect and patience over these last eleven years. I have learned a great deal here and will strive to uphold the reputation of the Academy. Thank you all.'

With that Genji turned and started to walk out. Pausing at the doorway he turned to Hazel. 'Follow me and I will take you to a place of safety.' He didn't say anything more before walking out the door. Genji didn't look back to see if she was following. Part of him hoped she didn't. As he was walking past the Library Beverlin popped out from around a corner.

'Congratulations, Summoner Mage,' Beverlin said enthusiastically. The echoes announced your ascension.' The echoes were the primary form of communication in the Academy, feeding information straight into the receivers mind.

'Not now, Beverlin. Farewell,' Genji said shaking his head. He kept walking. Beverlin was left bewildered by the sad, almost depressed, look on Genji's face. What confused her more was the strange little girl in tattered clothing that seemed to be following him at a distance.

When Genji was coming to the exit of the building he closed his dark eyes and started to concentrate without slowing down. A moment later he opened his eyes again and the doorway that led to the outside was now showing a different scenery on the other side. The world beyond was darker as if night had descended in an instant. The only thing visible beyond was an ebony staircase. Genji turned to look back at Hazel only once.

'Don't be afraid but do be careful on the dark stairs,' He told her before continuing into the rift. It didn't take long to traverse the stairs. Genji was adept at time magic and could create stairways that led to the exact point in time, past or future, he wanted with the least amount of steps.

The world that Genji stepped into was nothing like the Academy grounds. It was a small clearing that was surrounded by trees. Though it wasn't too far passed midday the shadows were growing long across the area, created by towering cliffs to north and west. Close to the base of the cliff was a small log cottage with straw roofing and a stone chimney. It looked crudely built. Genji saw the smoke was still drifting out from the top of the chimney and was glad that he almost got them back to the hour he last left.

Turning back, Genji saw Hazel peering out from just within the portal. 'You're going to need to come through as I will not be able to hold it open much longer,' he lied.

Wide eyed, Hazel ran out into the clearing moving to the far side away from Genji. He wasn't fussed and let the girl do as she pleased. Around the edge of the forest a glimmering haze sat and Genji walked alongside, periodically tapping it. The haze reacted as if it were a liquid wall, sending ripples far across its surface. Satisfied with the strength of the barrier, Genji finally turned his attention to Hazel.

'Girl,' he called not knowing what else to call her. She jumped and turned towards him cautiously. Genji sat upon the ground hoping that this act would prove more comforting. 'Please, come take a seat with me.'

Genji indicated to a position some metres away and Hazel slowly walked over to the where he said but didn't sit down. She wanted to be on her feet if she needed to run. Genji understood the logic behind her behaviour and let her be.

'You and I are going to be living in this house together,' Genji said tackling the situation head on. 'This was an accident on my part and I hope that one day you will forgive me for taking you from your home. The home behind you will have a room for you and a room for me. I will never enter your room while you are in there and the door is closed. This is the sanctuary every person should be granted. Therefore I would expect the same courtesy from you. When I am in my room with the door closed I don't want any visitors.' Genji thought for a moment. 'Unless it is extremely important. Understood?'

For the first time the girl nodded slightly.

Genji smiled. 'Good. Also, don't run off into the woods looking for your home. You may not believe me but this place is around one thousand two hundred years in the past.' Hazel looked confused but remained quiet. 'Now, I don't want to keep calling you girl. Would you give me your name?' She shrunk back again. 'Then I had best give you one. How about... Beverli... No, let's forget that one. Helen.'

Hazel shook her head. It was too close to her own name.

'I liked Helen,' Genji said with a frown. 'How about... Mayvin.'

Hazel's face contorted in disgust.

'Guess that one's out also,' like in the exams Genji's mind didn't supply any female names. He started sounding words together. 'Jes... Jus... Lin... Adi... Ask... Aski,' rolling the last one around on his tongue again he tried it out. 'Aski?'

Hazel thought for a moment before a small smile tried to reach her lips. She stopped it instantly but not fast enough that Genji didn't see. After a long moment Hazel finally nodded keeping her eyes downwards.

'From this moment forward you will be referred to as Aski. Welcome to my home, Aski, but I do need to ask you one more question and I am not going to be able to help you with the answer. If you could choose any location on the house for your room where would it be? Know that it doesn't even need to exist.'

Aski looked at the old, single storey cottage. She didn't know the layout inside but that wasn't an issue. Pointing to the roof, Aski looked back at Genji who smiled. This smile looked different to her step dad's. She couldn't help but feel comforted by it.

Kneeling down, Genji placed his palms on the grass. There was a pattern of long and short grass that ran in a big circle around the house. Aski retreated as the lines started to glow a soft blue not sure what was happening. The home started to rumble and to her surprise a tower grew from the side of the home. Numerous trees behind her shrivelled away to nothing as the tower continued into the sky. Finished, Genji got up and looked at the conical room.

'I've always found alchemy taxing,' he said cracking a bone in his neck. 'Do you like it?' Aski nodded smiling. 'I'm glad. Now take your clothes off and ill conjure you something new.'

Aski went pale white as the blood drained from her face. Unconcealed terror could be seen in her bronze eyes and her body started to shake.

'What's wrong?' Genji asked noticing the change. 'Nobody is going to see you. There is no one for miles around. I would use your old clothes but I'd thought you would like a clean start and I want to give you a gift.'

Aski was shaking her head and she started to back away. Genji traced a symbol in the air and uttered a single word calling the element of air. The tattered clothes concealing Aski's body tore away. Genji saw more bruises over her body along with small scrapes and cuts. A horrible scenario started to grow in Genji's mind. He crafted a red dress over her body using the same alchemy circle and a smaller tree as the exchange. Aski only screamed and ran for the house. There came the sound of feet running up steps and a glimpse of the girl as she passed the window of her tower.

Genji knew the time ahead was going to be far harder than anything the Academy threw at him.

Chapter 2

Screams flooded the house jolting Genji from his sleep. He cast aside the blankets recognising Aski's voice rebounding around the walls. The possibility that a demon or creature of the fey had broken past his barrier was unlikely but not impossible. He knew that he had yet to peak in his power. As Genji ran through the house to the closed door of Aski's room he was preparing himself for a fight with a beast more powerful than himself. Passing the fireplace he grabbed two small vials of blood that he prepared for such an occasion. They would give him the ability to do extreme enchantments and even the odds. As Genji reached for the door he hesitated. By entering the room he knew he was breaking the only rule he set with Aski but this was an emergency and he believed that her life was in danger.

Throwing caution to the wind Genji flung the door open and raced up the circular staircase. There was no door at the top and he burst into the room rolling along the carpet. Looking around rapidly Genji couldn't find a threat. He glanced at Aski in her bed and realized she was having a terrible nightmare. Her body was thrashing from side to side and she was still screaming. Genji sat down beside her and placed a consoling hand upon her.

The thrashing calmed down and Aski's eyes shot open to find a figure sitting on the bed touching her. She pushed out with her arms while twisting to get her legs around. Screaming louder than before Aski started kicking Genji as hard as she could causing him to move back.

'Calm down, Aski,' Genji said feeling a little more than annoyed. 'You were screaming in your sleep. I was only consoling you.'

'Get away from me,' she cried. Her feet were pulled back ready to defend herself if needed.

His limits reached, Genji grabbed both of Aski's legs. This brought forth more screams as she struggled to get

20

her legs back. Using magic from the healing discipline Genji put Aski into a deep sleep that she wouldn't wake from for a number of hours. It was more commonly used on patients in extreme pain but he saw no other way to settle the situation.

Fuming over the incident, Genji stalked from the home and created a portal with a staircase that would link to a time in the future a month or two after he'd taken the exam. He didn't want anyone thinking he didn't give the situation a chance to work. The Academy was the same as it had always been. The grass was rich and soft. Gardeners channelled nutrients through the earth to feed the grounds. Keeping it lush even in the harsh winter months.

Genji walked into the Summoners section intent on finding his examiners. He would demand that they combine their ability and send the girl home. That or at least find someone more capable to look after a young girl. Checking the exam room first he found only darkness inside. Determined, Genji made for the personal quarters of the examiners. It was forbidden for any student of the Academy to do so but he was not of the Academy anymore. There could be no consequences.

Getting closer, Genji heard hurried footsteps behind him getting closer. Turning to the side, he looked back at who was in such a hurry only to find Beverlin running straight at him. She jumped into a tight embrace that Genji tried to escape but found was too strong to break. When she finally leaned back a little she saw the angry emotions written across her friends face.

'I've missed you, Genji,' she said. 'But what's wrong? You look upset.'

Genji changed his expression quickly but he couldn't fool Beverlin anymore. She was going to keep pushing until she got all the details. 'I need to see my examiners. There was a mistake made in my exam and I want it rectified.'

'That was over a month ago,' Beverlin replied

shaking her head. 'Why are you still stewing over it? You passed, didn't you? You've already reached a height that so many will never achieve. Why not talk it over with me? Maybe I can help.'

Genji bit his upper lip and rolled his teeth back and forwards as he thought. Coming to a decision he tilted his head back the way they had come for Beverlin to follow. Smiling Beverlin kept the harsh pace and they entered a room where a person could have peace while practicing mage craft. Finding a seat Beverlin sat as Genji paced with a hand to his mouth. She could see he was stressed knowing all his little quirks.

'Well?' Beverlin asked Genji interrupting his line of thought. He looked her in the eyes and she saw him become determined.

'It has not been months for me. It has been hours at best,' Genji told her about the events in the library leading up to the exam and his summon going terribly wrong.

'That small girl,' Beverlin said answering a question that had been gnawing away at her mind.

Genji nodded and continued to tell Beverlin about his reason for passing and the actions of the girl since. 'I was left no choice but to put her into a deep sleep and seek out the examiners so that we may send her back with our combined power.'

'I understand now,' Beverlin said softly. She thought through the situation carefully before replying. 'I think you are wrong in this decision.'

'How could it be wrong,' Genji said frowning. 'The girl couldn't be more than ten. She would have a family that misses her and friends with whom she must miss.'

'Then why haven't you sent her back?'

'I told you already,' Genji said becoming impatient. 'Aski stopped me.'

'And therein lies the problem,' Beverlin replied. 'Think about it. If she was in such a loving family with friends and happiness around her why would she not want to go back? Clearly, she isn't comfortable around you.'

'She can't stay with me, Beverlin,' Genji told her firmly.

'Let me talk to her before you make a rash decision after only a couple of hours. There is always going to be teething problems in the early stages when you start living with someone.'

Genji was about to object but Beverlin's blue eyes pleaded her case. 'Alright, come talk to her,' Genji said and Beverlin threw her arms around him. Genji tried to push her away but like every time she had hugged him he was locked tight. 'But if you don't get anything of value out of this talk, I'll be sending her home.'

'Agreed,' Beverlin said with a smile releasing the hug. 'So, I get to see your house? This is going to be awesome.'

'Is that the only reason you're doing this?' Genji asked.

'Just a bonus,' she replied with a wink. 'Lead on.'

Genji didn't bother walking to a better location. Focusing, he opened a portal. 'We shall be using the stairways to cover the distance required. Have you had experience?'

'A little,' she lied. 'Well... I haven't gained the ability to use them myself.' Genji smirked and walked past the threshold of the swirling vortex. Beverlin hesitated at the entrance peering inside. The area was dark with an ebony staircase spiralling downward. It wasn't the type of dark that blinded a person. More, a bright dark. She saw Genji getting far ahead and she entered the stairway with speed almost tripping down the steps. Grabbing the railing, she stabilized herself before continuing.

'Don't fall over the edge or you will be falling for a long time,' Genji warned. He smiled as Beverlin moved to the centre of the stairs reaching out a hand to hold tight to the rail.

They made it out safely and Beverlin was in awe of the area she walked into. With her trained eyes she saw all the Mage craft that had gone into the area. A barrier, like a dome, protected Genji's home from any intruders. An Alchemist's circle was dug into the dirt, which she guessed was to change his home whenever he needed. Different scorch marks and disturbances in earth and forest was evidence in the practice of Mage craft. Not only this but the natural aspects of the trees and mountains. They created a magical scene under a sky full of stars. The crescent moon sinking below the western landscape.

'I am blown away by your home, Genji. It's beautiful,' Beverlin said. Genji looked for signs of sarcasm but found none. The comment bolstered his self-indulgent personality. Everything that he did was to make himself look better to the people around him. He didn't acknowledge the comment, however.

'This way,' he said getting Beverlin's attention. Genji showed Beverlin to Aski's room and let her enter first. As he was about to come through Beverlin blocked the doorway.

'We are going to have a little girl talk,' Beverlin told him. 'We don't need you standing around making things awkward.'

'Whatever, the sleeping spell is light so you won't need me to dispel it,' Genji said flicking his hand in a dismissive way. He was more than a little annoyed at being treated this way in his own house. Wandering outside, Genji felt a strange tingle in the air. Something was near his barrier and possibly trying to get in. Ducking back inside, he retrieved a retractable staff, the size of any good cooking utensil. A small quartz crystal rested at the top and as he got outside again he quickly jolted the staff downward. Mahogany slid out locking into place at the staff's full length, as tall as Genji. The staff was used for any magic performed in the shadow discipline. Though hollow, another layer was hidden below the surface giving the staff weight. Genji made the effort to reinforce the inside of the staff with a metal of his own design, stronger than any other known to man. Should someone be swinging a sword at his head and this staff was his only defence, Genji wanted to be sure the staff would withstand any impact.

Holding the staff near the top Genji raised it high above his head. The quartz started glowing in a soft orange haze which was mirrored by Genji's now glowing eyes as he looked out into the forest. He had to get close to the barrier so that it didn't obstruct his vision. Just inside the woods a green ball could be seen floating between the trees. Realizing that he was holding his breath Genji released it sharply.

'Only a forest spirit,' he said aloud.

As if hearing him the ball grew in depth of colour and size. Genji knew his assumption was wrong and as the being sped at him, he stumbled backwards. The green light could barely be contained in the canopy of the trees now racing straight at Genji. When it hit the barrier, the light washed over it like a wave upon rocks, before dispersing into nothingness. A rush of air passed through ruffling Genji's clothing and losing his ponytail.

Tying his hair back up, Genji turned to find Beverlin standing before him. The light of day touching her skin. Genji looked around quickly and saw that it was indeed day time. Hours had passed in the moments he had witnessed the green light.

'Did you just see that?'

'Yeah, it was funny,' Beverlin giggled. 'It's not often I get to see you stumble.'

'No, the light,' Genji said seriously. Beverlin looked around before shrugging her shoulders. 'Never mind. What did you find out about Aski?'

'Her name isn't Aski for starters. It's Hazel.'

'I knew it wasn't Aski but she kind of helped me choose it,' Genji said. 'Until she tells me otherwise, it is what I'll call her.'

Beverlin nodded. '*Aski* mentioned that also...' Beverlin had trouble determining where to start but once she did the words just stumbled out. Genji listened patiently, his emotions reaching dangerous lows at times. Beverlin spoke of the abuse from Aski's step dad and how her mother didn't believe what she said. Her mother neglected her a lot and the only times Aski was acknowledged was when she was getting yelled at. Even the kids at school picked on her because she never had clean clothing or tidy hair. Only one person ever made a difference in her life, her brother, and he left home.

Genji closed his eyes, fighting with strong feelings of sadness and anger within himself. 'She can stay as long as she needs,' Genji said with a nod. 'How can I send her home now?'

'I'm glad I could help her,' Beverlin said. 'Now I had best be getting back to the Academy. I didn't realize so much time had passed and I'm supposed to be taking the Healing exam today.' Genji just laughed. 'What's so funny?'

'The test you are referring to is set sometime next millennium.'

'What are you saying, Genji?' understanding dawned on her. 'How far back are we?'

'We are 1,162 years back in time. When you arrive home only minutes will have passed.'

'You can do that? I knew you were talented and all but you can really get it that close?' Beverlin took a few deep breaths to calm herself as Genji nodded. 'Well, my friend, any time I'm in trouble I'll be counting on you to save me,' she laughed. 'You're going to make a huge difference in that girl's life. Just be gentle.'

'Geez, get out of here,' Genji said opening a portal to the stairways that would lead Beverlin back to the Academy. He wasn't any good at showing emotions. Beverlin just hugged him once more and stepped inside the portal. As the entrance was closing Beverlin heard Genji thank her.

'Soon they would come once more,' he thought to himself. 'Soon he would need to fight once more.'

The young Prince Atalis stumbled on gasping for air as he held the ebony rail. In the darkness before him three figures rose up. He didn't need to look at them to tell they were orcs. Their muscles bulged with green, crusty skin. Drool dripped in long tendrils from the openings created by large elongated teeth in the lower jaw. One orc clashed his sword against his leather armour and the two in front charged.

'How many of you have I killed already?' Atalis said as he swore. Raising his sword he brought it down into the neck of the lead orc wedging it in the process. A strong heart beat was evident in the spurts of black blood hitting the stairs.

The second orc swung a crude, heavy axe at Atalis's chest. Sweat dripped from his forehead as he moved backwards dodging suddenly. Sparks flew into the air as the axe scraped perfectly through the ugly gash in Atalis's armour, not going any deeper.

Atalis took the moment the orc was off balance to retrieve his sword. Grasping the hilt sticking out into the air he kicked the blade free. Spinning on his heel Atalis sunk the blade deep into the orcs side. Grabbing the blade the orc fell over the railing into the abyss below. Atalis looked over in time to see the third orc making for a newly opened rift.

The deep shadows grew below the thick canopy of the forest. The difference between day and night was minimal. Animals had already fled the area due to the large numbers of humans present and now there was only an eerie silence accentuated by the creaks and groans of tree limbs.

The tents within the forest had been erected anywhere that space could be found. Normally, they would be perfectly lined in fields in groups of twenty. The erratic setup irritated the Field Organiser to no end and he needed to sleep away from everyone so that he didn't continually view the mess. The tents were all made from white canvas with a blue circle painted on the side to symbolise Mage Killers. The men that wandered the camp getting breakfast and chatting quietly amongst themselves also bore this symbol. Over their armour was a mantle of black that held the blue circle. It was a requirement that Mage Killers always wore this mantle either in everyday life or going in to battle.

Outside the edge of camp one man sat alone watching a small clearing in the distance. He sat with his back against the curved base of a tree, hand and a half long sword resting with the tip in the dirt against his shoulder. The opening to the clearing was bright against the dark of the forest and little could be distinguished. That didn't matter to his task. He was looking for discrepancies in the light to show groups of people passing through.

'Anything moving, Tristan?' A small, weasely looking man asked. He was the type of man you would never gamble against. Tristan flexed his broad shoulders, having not moved for a few hours and turned to the new comer.

'Nothing yet, Shard,' Tristan advised him. 'The time is getting close though.'

'How can you tell?' Shard said looking around. 'This forest is all consuming. I've lost all sense of time.'

'Just a gift I have.'

'Sounds like magic to me,' Shard laughed nudging his friend in the side.

Tristan's expression turned dark. 'Don't even joke about it, you fool.'

'How long have we been friends, Tristan? Four years? Five?'

'Five,' Tristan confirmed. 'Just before Old Durin created the Mage Killers.'

'Then you should know I won't let anyone know about your magical ability,'

Shard ducked under a swing from Tristan and bounced back a few metres. 'Get out of here, Shard,' Tristan said pointing a metal plated finger at the smaller man.

'Can't do that. Durin wants to see ya,' Shard said scratching his unshaven cheek. 'I'm here to replace you.'

Tristan got to his feet and stretched his tired limbs. Lying still for hours on end was hard work but he never let the team down. He nodded to Shard, who had taken up a position from where Tristan rose, before heading into the camp to look for Durin. He wasn't hard to find in the main tent looking over plans with a number of Mage Killers. Deciding to wait until Durin called him, he stood to the side of the entrance with hands behind his back. Tristan watched the Commander studying the land surrounding the camp. He was large, larger than Tristan at six foot and had long orange hair that blended into the thick beard. Only his dark eyes below bushy eyebrows could be seen on his face. He looked up and those eyes met Tristan's own blue eyes.

'Ah Tristan, come over here,' Tristan obeyed standing opposite the commander. Durin pointed to a bare patch on the map. 'You grew up in these woods. What is located at this point?'

Tristan saw where he indicated and shivered. 'That's the location of a large fire. A huntsman lived in a hut with his wife and three children. They all perished and the cabin is just charred remains. Many of the villagers won't venture there. I did once as a child and the scene touched me with fear. It wouldn't affect me so now but it's been left as it was to remind people to be weary of fire. No one ever did determine how it started.'

'Magic probably,' Durin stated. 'We should cleanse the area after the next battle.'

Tristan pursed his lips struggling with the decision to say anything before Durin saw the expression and bade him talk.

'I believe that the area should be left as is,' Durin's eyes narrowed but there was no more hesitation in Tristan. 'Some villagers already planted the seed to suggest it was the work of Mages. The story spread and because this area remains the villagers are united against Mages. It is something physical to keep the feelings strong.

'Fine. It stays,' Durin said after a moment. Ignoring Tristan he went back to the maps. Shard ran in moments later with news that the group of Mages they were tracking were now passing through the clearing.

'Finally, some fun,' Durin said with psychotic ecstasy in his eyes. 'Round up the men and be quiet about it. These Mages have ways of hearing things that are unnatural. Let us cleanse these demons.'

Tristan left the tent with the generals to move into skirmish position. He felt the same way Durin did about all mages except he didn't have the psychotic tendencies as he could see their leader possessed. It didn't worry Tristan as the man was a brilliant strategist and could counter any magical attack with natural manoeuvres on the field.

Tristan remembered the first time he'd seen Durin on the day the Mage Killers were formed. Two Mages were about to execute a man for reasons Tristan never found out, having arrived late. Before the deed could be performed Durin walked in wielding a large double winged battle axe. He blocked a ball of fire with the weapon before dispatching the caster. As he approached, the second Mage stopped what he was doing and started to retreat. Durin's axe slid cleanly through the man's shoulder and out the stomach of the opposite side. The Mages body holding together by small strands of tissue.

The speech Durin gave was moving but not once did the maniacal look leave his eyes. He spoke of the corruption running through the ranks of Mages since the times of the Elven King. Durin finished by asking people to unite under a single banner to save the lands. The banner would be the circle the second Mage was crafting in the dark sand. It would symbolise this moment. Tristan knew that to follow this man, there would be fighting and death but the Mages were a blight and needed to be stopped. He stepped forward with Shard not far behind.

Now, he had made a name amongst the ranks of the Mage Killers known to friend and foe alike. The safest place on the battlefield, if one could be found, was beside Tristan. He would protect his comrades with his life while striking deep into the Mage lines.

Today's battle was going to be tough. Normally,

Mage Killers would take on groups less than twenty. Tristan counted more than fifty in the clearing and knew the odds were against him and his comrades. Glancing back he saw the last of the Mage killers moving into position. Once they were there the attack could be sounded.

A young man to Tristan's right crept further forward to get a good look. Tristan recognised him as Feldran. This was his first battle with Mages and had little experience with fighting in general. Tristan tried to indicate the man to get back but Feldran didn't see. A Mage paused in his steady march and looked towards where Feldran hide in the undergrowth. His eyes went wide. Tristan knew they were found out and rose.

'Forward to glory,' he yelled signalling the chaos to begin while they still had some element of surprise. Mage Killers rose at various locations in the woods and soon a flood of the blue circle on black was pouring into the clearing.

The Mages didn't act surprised at all as if they had been expecting them. Tristan knew that it would happen eventually with the continual attacks but hoped there was still more time before they put up a real fight. The Mages broke off into groups tracing different symbols in the air or chanting deadly spells. Others were busy creating intricate salt circles that could be used to summon ferocious creatures. These they would need to deal with quickly. There were four mages that used a staff to bend light around themselves becoming invisible. Tristan had learned to watch for footprints in the sand Durin pours over battlefields on the eve of battle. They would be easily dispatched always thinking they can get around with little defence.

Tristan and Shard ran in always fighting back to back. A rogue fireball was knocked off course by Tristan's sword inches from Shard's face. No time for thanks they continued straight at the enemy. Lightning crackled from the fingers of Mages, attracted to the armour of the Mage Killers. Handfuls of men went down across the field. Noticing the symbol used for lightning, Tristan threw his sword at the ground ahead of him. Lightning burst forth from the Mage ahead of Tristan and was drawn into the sword earthing out before it could cause any damage.

Collecting his sword, Tristan spun after three more strides and took the head of the elemental Mage. All along the line the two forces clashed. Durin had archers start peppering the back lines aiming for the Summoner Mages. Some were dispatched with arrows protruding from them while others fell to sword, axe, and mace of the Mage Killers. Tristan was having trouble with a nimble Mage as the Summoner Mage's voice reverberated out.

'Ignis Adducere,' the Summoner Mage said. Flames started spinning over the salt circle gaining both height and momentum.

'Shard, take him down before whatever beast there is comes out of that inferno,' Tristan yelled as he leaned back and away from an assault of ice daggers.

Shard sidestepped and rammed the first of his dual short swords into a particularly slow Mage before dodging past and into a clear line to the Summoner Mage. Too late though, the flames died away to reveal a wolf the size of a horse. It's limbs were like tree trunks and it had fur of billowing smoke. Within the mighty maw flames were curling around. They leapt forward on every breath creating a fearsome enemy. The Summoner Mage started to utilise the circle once more but an arrow appeared from his chest and he dropped with a shocked look upon his face.

The wolf like beast charged straight at Shard grabbing the man with it's sharp fangs. Shaking Shard from side to side the beast threw him, knocking over two fighters grappling each other. The flaming wolf found a new target and charged once more, leaping upon three Mage Killers and sinking retractable talons through their armour.

'Shard!' Tristan yelled witnessing his friend being mauled. Swinging clumsily the Mage caught Tristan's sword in his hand and with the use of a transmutation circle upon his gloves changed the steel blade into brittle graphite and flimsy iron pieces. Tristan discarded what was his blade and punched the Mage in the face with his gauntlet. While the Mage was holding his face Tristan got the man in a headlock and snapped his neck.

With haste he ran to his friend's side. The body was lifeless having already breathed his last breath. Through cloth and armour, great holes could be seen where the teeth had sunk in. He closed his friend's lifeless eyes and gathered up the two short swords. They were not Tristan's ideal weapon but by all that was good and just, he would use them to make the Mages suffer.

Turning away, Tristan found himself looking into the fearsome eyes of the flame wolf. 'Well, come let me send you off to your master, you horrid mongrel,' Tristan said eyes locked to the beast. As if understanding the Wolf charged in ripping up chunks of dirt with every stride. Tristan ran forward watching for the opportune moment. When it came, he flicked a wrist sending a small throwing knife into the wolf's left eye. The beast twisted its massive head in response to the pain allowing Tristan to side step and ram one sword into the wolf's throat, the other into it's chest. From each wound flames billowed out scorching Tristan's hand. The beast tried to cry in pain but the sword had torn through it's voice box leaving it to die silently.

Tristan faced the Mages once more ignoring the pain in his hand. Many stepped back having seen what he had done to the flame wolf. A young Mage of mid-teens, however, did not shy away. Only just mastered the basics of elemental magic he believed he was invincible. Tristan watched him trace the symbol for earth having learned what each symbol meant through countless battles. He also knew through experience the best ways to counter the elemental forms of magic and started to prepare his defences.

Suddenly, everything around him slowed almost to a

halt. Tristan found that even his own movements were in real time and not the time that his mind found itself. Time magic was something Tristan had little experience in but he felt that if he concentrated on what his body was doing he would still be able to move in the way he wanted. A large green light appeared ahead and to the right of him and Tristan noticed that no one else could see it. At least they didn't react to it. It grew to the size of a small tree before rushing him. He was unable to avoid the green mist like substance that seemed to glow like the moon and he felt the full force of it entering him.

Time resumed its regular pace and a strong gust of wind rumbled past his ears as if the green light had produced it from the movement. All to late he remembered the young Mage who said a command for his earthen magic. A great pillar erupted from the earth taking Tristan in the middle of his chest and burst out his back in a rain of blood. Tristan was punched from his feet and dragged into the air to hang as the last of his life drained from his body. Darkness and cold were the last things he remembered.

Chapter 3

In the days following the visit from Beverlin, Aski adjusted to her new home. She was still weary of Genji after her first impressions but Beverlin assured her he was a good man and would protect her. Aski tried to ease her fears and change her view of the man.

Normally, she kept herself locked up inside her room. Genji didn't try to enter again or even acknowledge her as she crept around the house on trips to the toilet. She was happy that he gave her the space she needed. At meal times a knock would sound at her door indicating food was outside. Aski gave it a moment before going to retrieve what had been left. The second meal included a letter asking if there was anything that Aski liked to eat and she wrote down a number of different things that she enjoyed including breakfast meals and desserts. There was never any expectation that Genji would go out of his way for her but from that day on the meals all reflected something that was written as a reply. This moved Aski more than any other had in her life but she told herself she didn't trust him yet.

A surprising addition to her room that was not originally available came in the form of a tap and handles sitting over empty floor. When Aski first noticed them she had stared at them for a long time trying to work out what it was that they would be used for. After a day she decided that she would test the tap to see if anything actually came out and as she touched one of the handles the floor started to rumble. Aski jumped back as a bath tub rose out of the floor. A bath tub in her room! Genji was very considerate and Aski's barriers were chipped away at the edges. That night she spent more than a few hours in the water that didn't seem to cool down but remained at a perfect temperature.

A week went by and still Genji and Aski had yet to say a word to each other. Aski was comfortable to call this house home and she was happier now than she had been living with her mother. Lying in bed watching the sun creep into her room a movement caught Aski's eye. In a dark corner behind a small table were two funny looking ears. They were large, green, fluffy triangles with white fur on the inner ear. There was no Animal Aski could think of that had those sort of attributes. She confirmed that it was not something she had ever seen when the creature popped its head up for a moment to look around the room before ducking down again. The head was also green furred and triangular in shape. The large ears, creating a v shape, sat awkwardly on its head. The eyes were also overly large and oval in shape. They were ruby red in colour with no whites or blacks that any other animal had.

Aski threw back the blankets wanting to get a closer look at the small creature. Peering over the top of the dresser the creature became scared and let out a long screech showing little fangs. Aski stepped back not wanting to disturb it too much. She saw that it was the size of a hamster she once owned when she was four, with a long tail. The green fur covered the rest of the body with patches of white covering the feet and tip of its tail.

A knock at the door indicated breakfast was sitting outside and Aski thought maybe the creature would be happy to share. She raced down the stairs and flung open the door. Genji had still been setting her plate down at the time and she froze, eyes wide, having forgotten about her housemate. Genji gave a forced smile, nodded and moved away. Watching him go, Aski slowly picked up the plate of food and ran back into the room.

The plate held a stack of pancakes with maple syrup and bacon. The smell was making her mouth salivate and she ripped off a small piece of the fluffy pancake. She could see the creature below the table when she lay on the ground and she got its attention calling 'hey'. The creature let out a small screech watching Aski below the table. When Aski threw in the food the creature calmed and sniffed the morsel. Twitching its nose the creature moved away without touching it.

Aski thought for a moment and decided to try the bacon next. This time the creature let out a different noise and took the piece of meat happily. Over time Aski was able to coax the creature out from under the table by throwing pieces at shorter and shorter distances. Finally, Aski was able to feed a piece to the creature by hand. Risking a pat, the creature retreated a little with a screech at her touch. It settled quickly and this time when it came to get the bacon it allowed for Aski to pat it behind the ears.

'You're a cute, little critter,' she said in a soft, friendly voice. 'Shall I give you a name?' The small rodent didn't make any objecting movements. 'How about Paws because your little feet are white? Will that suit you, Paw Paw?'

Paws continued to nibble on the small chunk of bacon while Aski scratched behind it's ear. For the rest of the day Aski built up a strong bond with Paws until it was comfortable to sleep in her arms. When the sun was setting and the shadows were growing in strength Aski felt the need to go to the toilet. She placed Paws in a cave made from her blanket and tip toed down the stairs.

Peering out of the door she noted the location of Genji in the living area by the fireplace. She hurried past the room hoping as always that he didn't call out to her. On the way back from the toilet she looked into the living area to make sure that Genji was still inside and she saw him doing something odd.

Genji was holding a stick and drawing a triangle on it in charcoal. The tip of the triangle was facing away from him. Aski didn't understand why he was doing this as Genji would only be burning the stick in a few moments anyway.

'Krak!' Genji said the word with force and it resonated around the room as if alive. Fire leapt from the stick Genji was holding and he tossed it into the fireplace catching onto the pre-set wood stack. Flames licked the surface of each bit of wood savouring the taste before biting deep into the stack growing in intensity.

Aski's breath caught in her throat. So frightened and confused was she on the day she arrived that all the magical events going on around her passed without making an impression. Now, since she had settled this one small act shocked her to the bone. She couldn't remove her eyes from the flames born of magic and didn't notice that Genji was now looking straight at her.

'Are you okay, Aski? Can I help you with anything?' Genji asked the stunned girl.

Aski realised that he was now talking to her and made a little squeaking noise before dashing back into her bedroom. She sat on the ground against the wall and tried to calm her breathing. Her heart was almost punching through her chest and everything was shaking. She jumped when she felt something soft rubbing against her hand.

'Oh, Paw Paw, thank you,' Aski said relaxing at the touch of the little rodent. She sat contemplating if what she saw was real magic or the trick of a light.

Aski watched in terror as the walls of her bedroom started to buckle and twist. The furniture and paintings swayed with the movement of the room and Aski started to freak out. Diving onto her bed, Aski drew the blankets up to her mouth. Her two little eyes peering over the top. The window folded out and away from the house leaving a large hole and as the walls flexed it grew in size. Aski screamed as the bed sped forward towards the crude hole and launched her into the air.

Wind whistled passed her ears as a weightlessness caught her. She looked out over the trees and noticed smoke plumes coming from the south. Gravity kicked in and Aski started to fall again, arms flailing wildly. She closed her eyes and let out a shrill scream not understanding why this was happening to her. She landed with a jolt but it was softer than the ground should have been.

Genji looked at the girl in his arms. Aski was far lighter than he imagined her to be but then again maybe all children this age are light. Genji was ready for a struggle when she opened her eyes but she was too distracted by the house literally turning inside out. Slowly, he lowered Aski to the ground and as he tried to tilt her off himself Aski realized what was happening. Her whole body tensed and she pushed herself away rolling across the grass to watch Genji. Backing away, Genji sat on the ground with hands out in front of himself to show he meant no harm.

'What's happening?' Aski asked suddenly. It was the first time she'd talked to Genji since they'd come to his home. Holding back his surprise, Genji wanted to answer as if it was the most normal thing in the world.

'I'm just cleaning the house a bit,' he explained. 'You may not have noticed but it's gotten rather dirty this past week. The house will eject all dirt, dust, rodents, and scraps that have accumulated since the last clean. It won't take long.'

A memory of soft green fur, ruby red eyes, and funny, oversized ears came to Aski's mind. 'Paw Paw,' she cried out. Genji saw that she was distressed over the tropical fruit and he couldn't work out why. She didn't even indicate she liked it.

'What's the matter Aski?'

'Paw Paws' still in there,' she cried

'All the food will be there when we go back in,' Genji assured her.

Aski shook her head. 'No, Paws is my friend.'

'Paws?' Genji started to get the idea that they were not talking about fruit. 'Tell me about Paws, Aski. I can ask the house to let it out.'

Aski described the little creature to Genji whose brow furrowed. If what Aski described was correct he was about to see the first recorded Lazurian Mouse in over nine thousand years. Fully grown it would stand almost as tall as Genji with a body mass that would only just fit through the front door of the home. They were both rodents and parasitic creatures that bonded

39

with their host and shared the combined energy and magical ability. The fact that Aski could befriend such a creature when any Mage could only dream of doing so was beyond him.

The house shifted on a random course as it looked for the rodent inside. After a few moments a small green blur was ejected in much the same manner Aski was. Trying to follow the curve of Paws's flight Aski ran around with her arms outstretched before falling over herself. Paws landed gently and ran over to snuggle into Aski who scratched it behind the ears.

'Can I see him?' Genji asked crouching down close by. Aski pulled Paws closer to herself. Whenever she had been asked such a question the person asking would always steal the item. Paws was something she didn't want to lose. As if reading her hesitation for what it was Genji sat down on his hands. 'I don't want to take him. I just want to see... Paws. I've never seen a Lazurian Mouse before.'

With hesitation Aski brought Paws out from the folds of her clothing. 'Paws, I want you to meet Genji. He is giving us food and shelter,' she told him pointing across at Genji. As if understanding Paws regarded Genji with its ruby eyes. Bouncing across the space, it started to sniff Genji. Aski made to retrieve Paws but stopped seeing that Genji hadn't moved.

Genji didn't believe it before on the word of a child with no background in magic but now with the creature sitting before him he was in awe. It was indeed an infant Lazurian Mouse and by the way it acted had already bonded with Aski. Letting out a soft chirp, Paws started nuzzling the back of its neck into Genji's knee. Stunned by this action, Genji looked up at Aski and saw the jealousy in her eyes.

'Best be getting back to your bonded, little one,' Genji said motioning his head towards Aski. Paws listened and ran back to where Aski was sitting. She scooped up the creature and placed it within her clothing where it would sleep. For a bonded creature to acknowledge and then listen to another was unheard of and Genji would need to think more on this.

'I want to keep him,' Aski said defiantly seeing Genji's tense expression. Genji focused on the girl, his mind coming back to reality.

'Of course you may,' Genji assured her. 'I would not discard a new member of our family.'

The words were unexpected. 'Family?' Aski queried. Behind her, the house made a loud noise as it expelled a large ball of waste that was thrown miles away over the land. Aski jumped but settled back quickly.

'Beverlin told me of your circumstances, Aski,' Genji said gently. Aski's mouth shut and Genji could see that she had locked herself up. 'Everything you told Beverlin, she told me. We don't need to speak of it again and your past does not make the person you choose to be. I offer you a place in my family which right now consists of myself. Paws is welcome to join also. Before you answer I want you to know that being part of my family means we look out for each other, protect each other and never harm each other. Is this something you would like?'

Numerous emotions ran through Aski. It was true that Genji had never actually tried to harm or abuse her. He had only ever taken care of her. But it was hard to trust a man and Genji was still clumsy with her feelings.

'I have never lived with another person as an adult,' Genji told her feeling uncomfortable in the silence. 'My parents passed away when I was about your age and I have been able to fend for myself since that time. What I am saying is I am not good with people but I would like to learn to be good to you if you would help me.'

This was enough to sway Aski's emotions. With tears of happiness she didn't know she could shed she nodded. 'Me and Paw Paw will join your family, Genji... But I want you to promise me something. If you can't then this family will not work.'

'Anything,' Genji replied.

'If I ever tell you to stop or leave me alone, you will obey,' there was a shake in the young girl's voice and

Genji knew the courage she possessed to even talk to him.

'I shall, without hesitation,' Genji told her. 'You are strong Aski. You push through your fears and don't...'

'Stop,' Aski said and Genji went quiet wondering what he'd done. Her little lip quivered with emotions and fresh tears rolled down her eyes. 'Thank you, Genji, for giving me such a gift.'

Genji understood why she told him to stop. She was testing him. 'Welcome home, Aski... And you too, Paws.' Genji saw indecisiveness in Aski. 'Is there something you would like to talk about?'

With head down, looking away, Aski spoke. 'Yesterday as the sun was fading I saw you...'

'Stop,' Genji said suddenly, Aski lifted her head to look at Genji, her mouth frozen in mid-sentence. She didn't expect for him to do as she had. Genji used two fingers to point at his dark eyes. 'Look me in the eye when you speak. By lowering your head you are saying you are lesser than I am. We are equal and whatever you say will be discussed rationally and without judgment.'

Aski smiled. For a person with no people skills, he was doing a good job, she thought to herself. 'Last night when you were by the fire place you created fire from nowhere,' Aski said keeping eye contact. This act alone felt empowering to her. 'And just now with the house. That wasn't natural.'

'Is there a question behind these statements?' Genji asked knowing where the conversation was going.

'How did you do it?'

'I am a Mage,' Genji said with a little flare trying to impress her. 'I have learned all disciplines of magic at the Academy of Mage Craft.'

'I'd already assumed that much,' Aski told him bluntly. 'I want to know how you did it. I want to use magic too.'

'First, tell me why you want to learn magic,' Genji said becoming serious. He was dismayed by her lack of amazement but the topic of magic was a serious matter to him. 'With your answer I will say whether you are worthy to learn about magic.' Aski was about to answer but Genji put up a hand. 'Just know that if you answer and I find you unworthy, you will never get a second chance and I will never speak of magic again. Do you still wish to answer?'

Aski hesitated for only a moment considering her options. 'I want to learn magic so that...'

'Thank you, Aski, that will be enough,' Genji stopped her once more.

Aski became concerned that she said something wrong. There was fear evident in her eyes. 'How can you assess me on those few words alone?'

'I like you, Aski. You are smart and address me in a manner beyond your years,' Genji said smiling. 'To learn Mage Craft, as we put it, is a choice only you can make. Every novice who seeks admittance into the Academy is asked the same question and given the same terms. Those who walk away not ready to risk everything on their answer feel deep within themselves they are not ready. Those that answer regardless of the consequence prove they have the strength and determination to succeed. You could have told me you wanted to learn magic because you didn't like the colour of grass and still you would have been accepted. It is what is in your heart that counts.'

Aski's face was beaming having passed the first test. 'So you will tell me how you did it?'

'I will begin your lessons tomorrow at a time convenient to you,' Genji assured her. Aski's face lost a bit of spark. 'But I see you want to take away something today so I'll give you an idea of what to expect. Elemental magic such as fire has both a symbol and a word that will activate the magic. You need to picture what you want in your mind and focus that picture out through the word and into the symbol. If your mind links everything just right the magic will work.'

'That's all there is to it?' Aski asked and Genji laughed.

'That is the bare bones of it but you will find putting

it into practice much harder than it sounds. Now, let us retire to the house and celebrate this new family with a feast.'

Aski was smiling as she walked behind Genji. She may not be completely trusting as some walls are hard to knock down but she had never felt like she belonged in all her life. This life was going to work after all.

Atalis looked at his father's lifeless face lolling to one side. The blue eyes were cloudy and void of the spark that usually lived there. No more would this honourable man, who loved all his subjects, walk the streets of Pinto again. No more would he be seen tilling the fields alongside the farmers under his protection. No more would he speak a word of kindness where others would have chosen abuse to a son who had failed him in so many ways.

Anger welled up in his chest and he looked around. The orc was creeping up behind the court Mage, his axe about to come down. The Mage had just succeeded in opening a rift to what he believed to be a new world. This was the pinnacle of years of research and he could not be more proud. Electricity crackled to life around the dark portal and mesmerized the Mage. Atalis tried to call a warning to the man but too caught up was he in his creation that the words fell on deaf ears. The court Mage turned with a great smile upon his face to view the king's reaction. He went white as a ghost however as he took in the devastating scene. He did not hear the whistling of the axe but became confused as his perspective flew to the floor. The body followed the head soon after.

Mage Killers would not touch a body killed by magic or those that used magic as they were now tainted. All across the field, bodies lay to rot under the burning sun or to be picked apart by the carrion birds already descending. The Skirmish was a success as almost all the Mages had been destroyed. The rest were being hunted through the forest until every last one was taken care of. Durin would stop at nothing to see all Mages wiped from the face of this earth.

This was not a concern of Tristan anymore. His body hung metres above the ground, suspended by the jagged spike running through his chest. Blood had ceased to run and was now dried up along the ridge of the spike and in a round stain at the base. A large crow sat just above eying the body for any signs of movement. It bounced along the curve of the spike to sit upon Tristan's back seeking the juicier parts of flesh. A pulse through the body sent the crow into the air to seek other food sources.

Tristan's body started to glow a soft green seemingly from within. Soon the veins could be seen through the skin. They were a rich green that became so bright; anyone watching would need to cover their eyes. A flutter came from Tristan's heart before the body convulsed three times and Tristan opened his eyes. The green glow subsided to the screams of Tristan as the pain of impalement rippled through his body again and again, never giving him rest. Soon, he couldn't scream anymore, his mouth hanging in soundless agony.

Somewhere inside his mind, Tristan's rational thought told him the pain was coming from the earthen spike. He tried to break it, his hands hitting it with the force of a child, and soon he gave up that idea. Gripping the spike in front of his chest he pushed back. As his body slide backwards towards freedom a fresh round of agony tore through Tristan's chest causing him to lose his grip and fall back to his original position. This idea had merit; he just wasn't prepared for the fresh crippling pain.

Breathing was hard as with every breath his chest would slide back and forth along the spike. Tristan kept his breathing to a minimal. Preparing his mind he closed his eyes tight and using a hand over hand method started to slide himself back over the tip a metre behind. He didn't stop or think about what he was doing but kept forcing himself backwards until he folded over the tip and free-fell to the hard dirt below.

His landing created more pain than the spike through his chest but it was a quick pain and slowly subsided to settle around the gaping hole where his sternum would be.

A whole night and part of a day passed by. Tristan longed to black out or pass away but neither of these luxuries were granted to him. He couldn't adjust to the pain and, therefore, couldn't move. Those long hours lying on his back gave him time to contemplate what led him to this moment. The only explanation was that he had been cursed by a Mage and would need to find one to lift the curse.

'*Of all the intelligent beings, humans are the most daft*,' a voice sounded in his mind. Tristan got the impression it was ancient beyond time. '*I will do this only once so make the most of it.*'

Green light started to pulse in Tristan's chest around the wound. Muscle, sinew, and bone started to materialise, building within the wound and tying together. Soon the wound was closing up with skin carpeting the area. It wasn't the same tone as the rest of his body but with a little sunlight the pale area should go back to normal. All pain ceased within Tristan and he sat up feeling his chest.

'What are you demon and why do you steal my honour in death?' Tristan said out loud but there was no answer.

Getting to his feet Tristan walked the field looking for a new set of armour that may fit him. The putrid smell that hung in the air was almost making him gag but he steeled his stomach and continued on. Tristan found what he was looking for on a corpse that was burnt to a crisp. Both the black mantle and armour survived whatever gave these wounds and Tristan started to retrieve them for himself. Burnt skin that was stuck to the material of the mantle near the neck tore from the body. Annoyed with this small event, Tristan tried to dislodge it as best he could. In the end he had to accept a part of the man that wore this armour would always be with it.

Dressed now and feeling once again like a knight of the Mage killers, Tristan set off into the forest to find the rest of the band as the sun was hanging low in the sky. He kept Shards two short swords not wanting to forget his friend. It was a sad moment living with this curse and Tristan would make the Mages pay. Movement ahead made him pause drawing the slender blades.

'Fuck, Gendal, It's Tristan!' the man ahead said. Tristan saw that it was the young man, Feldran who messed up the skirmish. He couldn't believe the young man actually survived his first real battle.

'Feldran, it's good to see you,' Tristan replied moving forward and sheathing his weapons. 'Where is Durin? I need to speak to him.'

'Stay back, monster,' Gendal said coming out from behind a tree. 'Any closer and I'll be taking your life.'

'But Gendal, it's Tristan,' Feldran said incredulously.

'I saw Tristan get impaled through the chest by an earthen spike bigger than your leg. That is not a wound someone would be coming back from,' Gendal said before turning to Tristan. 'You've been cursed or brought back by necromancy. Either way you are a threat to everything we stand for and are Mage Touched.'

The term was one Tristan knew well. Anyone who was Mage touched was said to be tainted and unworthy of being alive. If Tristan was standing where Gendal was he would of said the same thing. Especially knowing that something had specifically used magic on him to bring him back from the dead and heal his wounds.

'You're right, Gendal,' Tristan said accepting what he knew to be his fate. 'I have been brought back to life by some unholy magic. I vowed my revenge but know I would never be accepted back into the ranks of Mage Killers. I just ask that you make it swift.' Tristan got to his knees and opened his arms awaiting his cleansing.

Feldran was in disbelief. 'We can't do this Gendal. It's Tristan. Tristan. The one who has saved countless numbers of us in battle.'

'And killed countless other Mage Killers who were Mage Touched,' Tristan told the young man. 'You have much to learn boy. This will be a good place to start.'

'You want me to kill you?' Feldran asked. He looked to Gendal who wore a serious expression.

'No. I want you to cleanse me of this curse. Only a brother can do so to someone willing,' Tristan said. 'It is a final gift.'

Saying no more Tristan spread his arms awaiting the sword stroke that would take his life. Feldran looked to Gendal one last time hoping the man would stop this.

'Strike true,' Gendal said with a hand upon Feldran's shoulder. 'Don't let him suffer.'

Feldran's shoulders sank as he accepted his task. Standing before Tristan he drew his sword. 'Know peace, brother.' The sword entered cleanly stabbing Tristan's heart. Pain lanced through Tristan once more and he fell back with a smile. Darkness descended and there was nothing of this world left.

'Come on Feldran,' Gendal said. 'Tristan has moved on.' As the two men started to walk away a cough came from the body. Gendal turned to examine him closer. The chest was moving with each breath and there was a pained look on Tristan's face. 'You idiot, you missed his vital point.'

'I'm sorry,' was all Feldran could say in reply, his face turning ashen grey.

Gendal drew a blade and approached Tristan's body. 'It may not be swift but this method has always worked. Be at peace, brother.' Gendal knelt down drawing the sharp blade across Tristan's throat. Life blood began pumping from the wound and Gendal sat with the cursed man until all breathing had ceased.

'Don't dwell on it, Feldran,' Gendal said walking away. 'As Tristan said, you have a lot to learn. Take it as experience and do better next time.' Feldran became shocked and Gendal saw the man was looking past him. Turning back he saw Tristan half raised and swore. 'This is why you don't trust those that are Mage

Touched. Let's see him live without a head.' Gendal drew his sword.

'*Good luck to him,*' the ancient voice echoed in Tristan's mind once more. '*If you wish to carry your head around be my guest and wait.*'

Tristan could feel the pain from each wound inflicted on him and he didn't want to know what a severed head would feel like. 'Wait Gendal. It won't work,' Tristan pleaded. Gendal didn't listen but continued towards him. Everything happened too quickly but Tristan knew that it was by his own reflexes that Gendal was dying. As the man had aimed his blow Tristan blocked it with one of Shard's swords burying the other in the man's chest.

'You are a monster,' Feldran said. Becoming emotional he ran in with killing intent in his eyes. A sloppy overhead cut was slapped away easily by Tristan's gauntlet.

'I don't want to kill you, boy,' Tristan said blocking two more swings.

'You deserve death for what you've done,' Feldran said with anger in his voice. He didn't stop the assault.

Getting annoyed Tristan grabbed Feldran's blade and held it tight. 'You have two options, boy, and you would be wise to take the second,' Tristan said with an edge to his voice. He got right up close to Feldran's face. 'First, you and me fight to the death. You've seen I cannot die so it's a rather foolish choice on your behalf. Otherwise, you can leave with your life and inform the commander of what has happened. He will have a better solution than repeatedly killing me and having me resurrected.'

Feldran's face was full of anger but he wasn't stupid. Tristan saw the choice was made and let the sword go. 'We will chase you, Tristan.'

'May you learn of a way to kill me for good,' Tristan called to the back of the man as he ran off into the dark forest. Dropping to the dried leaves covering the dirt Tristan clutched the two wounds. They were paining him terribly. 'Heal me, Demon,' he called but nothing happened. 'What do you want from me?' Still silence. Tristan tore two shreds of material from Gendal's mantle. Tying one around his neck, Tristan stuffed the other one into his chest wound before setting off into the forest. He cursed whatever fates befell him that he now needed the help of a Mage. Tristan decided the best place to start was the burnt out cottage in the north.

Chapter 4

A dread feeling hung in the air making it thick and hard to breath. Slowly the feeling grew in intensity as the night rolled on as if the source was getting closer. Genji didn't like this feeling at all and worried whether his barrier could hold up to whatever approached. The second thought was that the barrier would be ineffective regardless. It was designed so that birds and other creatures that didn't seek to harm him would pass through with no negative effects. If a creature of darkness had possessed an innocent than theoretically it could get through.

Looking up at Aski's room in the tower, he saw the light turn off. With Aski tucked away for the night Genji decided to investigate beyond the barrier so he could better discern what was coming. He gathered a few vials and crystals that could grant him different affects and hid them away around his person. Before walking out the door he grabbed his retractable staff, a cloak and his necklace of night sight. The necklace was of leather braid that held a small, spherical, crimson stone in place near his throat. He looked at the thin rapier on a mantle across the room and decided against taking it. Genji had never been too good with a blade and if things went south he'd be fleeing to the sanctuary of his home.

Ready now he crossed the threshold of his barrier and turned to take one last look at his home. The image he saw was not the same image everyone saw. To those who wished him harm or would report him should they find out the truth, the burnt remains of a home were all that could be viewed from outside the barrier. It was a last defence and took one tenth of Genji's energy to keep it active but it was worth the safety. None wanted to enter the area where a family was burnt to death by Mages, a rumour Genji himself started.

Happy with the strength of the barrier, Genji drew one last charm symbol into the earth and focused enough power into it to last the night. Anything that crossed the barrier threshold wouldn't be able to see Aski for the next ten hours. Genji walked into the forest, a soft red glow coming from his throat. The trees before him looked as if the sun was out on a clear day. Nothing got by his gaze. Creating sight that would be able to see in the dark was easy with magic and took only a little focus to hold but Genji believed the focus could be better used elsewhere. He would imbue stones and other objects with magical abilities that operated autonomously while worn and left him free to use his full strength.

Following the growing feeling Genji walked for almost an hour. He couldn't believe how strong it was getting as he thought the source close by when he felt it at home. He couldn't make an accurate judge of distance now not knowing how strong the source could potentially be. Movement alerted him to something on his left. Genji couldn't see anything through the shrub and changed the way his necklace worked so that he could see heat signatures.

He looked around to make sure there was nothing else nearby before giving the noise his attention. The hairs on his arms and neck rose as he saw the red and yellow shape of a Wrathwood Drake. The creature was kin to the dragons of old that scorched the world in the first terrible cleansing, millions of years ago. Only the bones of those magnificent creatures were evidence of their existence. Now the lesser drakes walked the earth. They were the size of Genji if he was to lay on the ground with a tail that length again. The body mass though was four times the size. When that thing charges Genji knew he would be dragged down under the beasts weight alone. He knew he only had moments left and transferred the necklaces energy to night sight once more.

Slowly drawing his staff, Genji crafted a ball of light with his other hand by tracing the specific symbol of a circle with a dot in the middle in the air and using the word 'Luysay'. The area lit up and Genji used a jolting movement to extend his staff. The movement was enough to set the Wrathwood Drake into a charge and Genji acted quickly. The crystal upon the staff started to glow and soon four illusionary Genji clones were standing randomly around him. They were perfect replicas in every way. The drake faltered in it's charge before leaping at the closest figure and finding nothing but air.

As the Drake landed, it circled back slowly. It's tongue flicking in the air to get scents from around it. Locking eyes with it, Genji knew the beast had found him out and now he would have to fight or lose his life. Genji's mind raced to think of something that may be strong enough to take on the beast. He'd never out run it so far from home and illusions wouldn't work again. Pulling a small purple phial from a leather pouch on his belt Genji saw the beast charge once more.

Rolling below as the Drake pounced Genji smashed the phial against the creature's skin. Purple smoke enveloped it as Genji looked for sanctuary but found nothing. The Drake bounded out of the smoke screen with tendrils of purple trailing it. Genji's only thoughts went back to the rapier as death closed the distance. He could have imbued it with lightning creating a blade with enough force that it could pierce the skin of the Drake no matter his skill. No other form of magic has ever been good against a Wrathwood Drake.

As the Drake pounced for its prey a dark figure rushed the area to knock the creature off its course. Genji recognised the attire immediately as that of a Mage Killer and could only assume the man hadn't witnessed any of the fight until this moment. Otherwise, he would of left Genji to die getting as far from the Drake as possible. As they tumbled, the creature ended up on top of the man. Genji knew that the Mage Killer was about to die but he couldn't look away. One of the Drake's claws pierced into the armour of the knight barely entering the skin. It was enough for the poison that laced each talon to start it's work.

The man hadn't given up. With a short slender blade he was able to move his arm enough to ram it up the inside of the Drakes mouth and into its brain. It slumped down instantly becoming dead weight.

'Help me,' the man choked barely getting the words away.

Genji was in two minds about this. If the Mage Killer recognized Genji to be a Mage he would definitely try to kill him. A fight Genji could easily win but one he still didn't want. Genji decided that with the poison in his veins the man wouldn't be a threat. Tracing an upwards triangle with a line through the top Genji called forth the power of air with 'Ody'. It took vast concentration and energy to lift the weight of the Drake but finally the man was able to wiggle free. He was breathing heavily and Genji started to take pity on him.

'Sir Knight, come here and I shall treat your wound,' Genji told the man. Genji saw the man would be a formidable foe if he decided to turn on him but would deal with him should it happen.

'You are a Mage of great strength?' Genji noticed the question was not to determine if he was a Mage but rather whether he had any talent.

'Please sir, there is poison running through your veins,' Genji tried to explain. 'I need to neutralize it quickly.'

'That isn't an issue here. And stop calling me sir. My name's Tristan.' Genji noticed the pain on Tristan's face but didn't understand why the man wouldn't accept his help. The banner on Tristan's mantle flapped in a sudden gust of wind and Genji remembered he was a Mage Killer. It explained enough.

'Well Tristan, you choose your own destiny,' Genji said not worried now if the man was to die. His act of kindness complete, Genji moved to the Wrathwood Drake and started collecting bits and pieces from the corpse. Never before had he gotten such a treasure trove of ingredients. Claws to be ground to dust, teeth to enhance charms and procure poison from. He even got a few scales and a small vial of blood for various arcane practices. Tristan stood waiting patiently. 'In answer to your question, I am the strongest Mage across all the lands. No form of magic is too hard to perform.'

'You looked to be having a lot of trouble with the Drake,' Tristan said critically. 'If not for me you'd be dead by now.'

'Apart from your crazy heroics, a Wrathwood Drake is weak only to electrified steel. Having left my sword at home I was at a loss as to how to proceed.'

'All that ability but no common sense or experience,' Tristan taunted before clutching the wound where Feldran stabbed him.

'What would you know about it, *Mage Killer*? Your kind has no knowledge of magic or the strength one needs to cast. You didn't look to comfortable yourself wielding those toothpicks,' Genji spat pointing at the slender blades.

'You say you can use all forms of magic? Alchemy and elemental magic is all you needed.'

'And how do you believe that would help?' Genji said his mind turning blank as he tried to think of a way he could have won.

'Alchemy to change the elements in the ground to steel. Lightning to charge the steel and then alchemy once more to stick the Drake with sharp spikes. I have experienced a similar move before.' Genji was surprised by the thought out answer and calculated it would have taken 1.3 seconds to complete once he had the circle set. Far shorter than the time it took the Drake to cover the ground between them. He didn't acknowledge the answer. 'And these swords aren't my own. A friend died in battle and I couldn't save him. I lost my long sword but honour him now by using his weapons.'

'May I see them,' Genji asked holding out his hands.

Tristan wearily passed across the short swords. 'Just don't destroy them.'

'Why would I destroy them?' Genji asked. Genji reached into a pouch and drew out a piece of cloth with an alchemic circle drawn on it and one of the drake teeth. He placed all three together and they started to

55

glow.

'What are you doing?' Tristan's eyes bulged when he saw the light. Before he had a chance to stop Genji the two blades and drake tooth merged together to take on the form of a long sword. The hilt and guard kept a similar shape to the short swords though crafted to suit the longer weapon. The blade shone like silver and was honed to a perfect edge.

'What the fuck did you just do? I told you not to destroy them!' Tristan raged. If not for his need of the Mage he would have killed Genji then and there.

'I didn't destroy them,' Genji said knowing Tristan didn't understand. 'I've used alchemy to make a sword that you can wield more comfortably. The weapon is made entirely of your friend's blades so you can still...'

'I know what alchemy is, you bastard. The blades are now Mage Touched and therefore useless to me. You have tainted the memory of my friend.'

'But the blade has been strengthened by the drake tooth never to dull or break. The weight is lighter than a regular sword as well due to my mastery of all elements...'

Tristan grabbed Genji by the throat with his left arm. Fresh pain coursed through his body from the wound over his heart and Tristan dropped Genji to the ground. 'I don't care for your magic or your knowledge,' Tristan growled as he held his chest and talked through the pain.

'Than what do you want?' Genji asked, casting the sword aside in annoyance. Tristan hadn't attacked or asked for assistance.

'I need you to kill me,' Tristan said bluntly. Genji was surprised by the answer knowing any Mage Killer would loathe being Mage Touched in death.

'If that is your wish,' Genji knelt to the earth placing the cloth with the transmutation circle. 'How about I use the suggestion for the Drake?'

'That won't work. As I said I have had experience with such a move. Took me a long time to push myself back off the spike.'

Genji didn't understand or like the implications of what Tristan said and stood confused. 'Tell me what's going on.'

Tristan reached up and pulled the material from around his neck. The cut was still open but blood had ceased flowing. Genji's eyes went wide and he took a closer look. He could clearly see that the veins in Tristan's neck were severed and wondered if some sort of Necromancy had been cast on the man.

'Emundetur a fluxi seminis,' Genji said throwing all his ability behind the discharge spell. Finding no form of magic to dispel the words dissipated into nothing. This troubled Genji as it wasn't magic causing Tristan's status. 'You need to explain it all to me from when you first noticed the affect to this very moment.

Tristan told the story of the raid on the Mages. Genji's face became hard but he said nothing. He told Genji about the earthen spike taking his life before he woke up and had to pull himself off it. When Tristan mentioned the voice and the healing of his chest wound Genji stopped him.

'What did the voice say exactly?' Genji asked.

'I don't quite remember as I was in a lot of pain. It said something about human intelligence and then it would only do this once.'

'And that was when your chest was healed?'

'Yes,' Tristan confirmed. 'After that I came across brother knights in the forest and allowed them to kill me. Thus the wound in my neck and this,' he said pointing to his chest wound over his heart. 'You can see the poison hasn't killed me either.'

'Did you try speaking to the voice?'

'I did but it never replied. The only time it spoke again was to tell me if I was beheaded I still wouldn't die. The pain will not leave me and as the Mage Killers weren't going to stop trying to kill me I had to kill them. I decided from that point I needed a Mage so here I am.

'You have been possessed,' Genji said casually. 'It is the only thing that makes sense. The being will keep you alive until it's energy has been drained. You will die after that.'

'How long?' Tristan asked.

'Hard to say without knowing what the creature is that possessed you. A lich could keep you alive maybe... two hundred years,' Genji estimated. Tristan's face dropped. He didn't want to be alive for so long. 'Are you sure nothing else happened before you first died?'

'Yes... No,' Tristan corrected. 'Someone slowed time and there was also a green mist that rushed me.'

Genji's eyes narrowed remembering the Green light that became a mist as it charged at him outside his barrier. 'Glowing green covering an area about the size of a tree?'

'You know of it?' Tristan asked hopeful that Genji may know how to release him.

'I saw it once at night,' Genji said. 'It rushed me like it did you. A barrier kept it from getting to me. I don't know what it was but the strength I sensed was beyond anything I have felt before. You may be alive for a long time.' Remembering the reason he was out in the forest Genji felt out for the power he had followed. As he thought it was located within this man now suppressed. Suddenly a burst of power pushed Genji's mind back and physically knocked him from his feet.

'Are you okay?' Tristan asked surprised.

'Yeah, your passenger didn't like me snooping around,' Genji replied. 'Come with me to my home. I'll help you, Tristan.'

Genji Looked back at the sword he'd crafted and knew it wasn't something that should be so easily thrown away. Lifting the light sword he set of towards his home with Tristan keeping pace.

Aski laughed as Paws came out from around the table. He would rear up on his hind legs before continually stomping down again. With each stomp Paws let out a squeak and Aski would retreat a little before rushing back and chasing Paws around the table. She was having so much fun now that Paws trusted her completely.

The sound of the front door opening filtered up the stairs. It was too late for a visitor to be coming over and Aski moved to peer out the window. The reflection of the light was making it hard to see so she turned it off and was surprised to find Genji walking outside.

'He must be going to do some magic,' Aski said to Paws, wiggling his ears. 'Why don't we follow him and watch?'

Paws gave a little squeak Aski took as an affirmative so she grabbed a cloak and made her way outside. Paws was resting on the back of her shoulders just inside the hood. His fur tickled but Aski enjoyed the warmth he gave. Catching the shadow of Genji disappearing into the woods Aski made for the opening but stopped just before entering. She noticed that her body, clothing and Paws had vanished from sight. She could still feel everything in its place but couldn't see anything. It was an odd sensation but Aski had seen people become invisible on TV shows and when she became comfortable she actually started to enjoy the feeling of not being seen. Paws on the other hand didn't like the visual manifestation of invisibility and started to move around on Aski's shoulder.

'It's okay, Paw Paw,' Aski said as she stroked behind his ears. 'Once we find Genji we can get him to turn you back.'

Paws settled and Aski tried to hear for movement to indicate Genji's position. With no noise reaching her ears she decided he couldn't have gone far and started moving in the direction she last saw him. Almost instantly the woods grew dark having lost the light of the moon and the stars above the canopy but Aski wasn't afraid. Being invisible gave her bravery she couldn't conjure otherwise. Forward she continued keeping her ears open for any sound Genji could be making and eyes open for any light. It was the latter that she came across first. Starting as a small dot at the edge of her vision, Aski moved towards the glowing light between the trees.

At the tree line surrounding the source of light Aski could see that it was a camp fire and her little heart stopped as she saw what sat around it. Three large, green, muscle toned men... no not men, Orcs, she noted. Their heads were round and small compared to their bodies. The eyes were tiny, black circles and a large tooth stuck out on each side of their lips. As she calmed from the fright of this confrontation she noticed that they weren't moving at all. She remembered her invisibility and realised they didn't know she was there.

Her confidence grew and she stepped out from the tree line, taking a few cautious steps. Paws was rustling in her hood and making hissing noises as if trying to warn her but Aski knew that she was safe. When the Orcs didn't move, Aski closed the final metre to stand by them. The rush of adrenaline with exotic and she moved about the creatures looking them straight in the face. They didn't acknowledge her in any way until she got to the third.

As she looked into the ugly oaf's eyes they looked straight at her for a split second before looking back at the fire. Aski saw the look and understood with no self-disillusion that she was not as safe as she previously believed. Fear registered on her face and she started to back away. The Orc in front of her got up and swung one of its long arms trying to grab at her. Aski jumped away but was snatched up by a second Orc who took hold of her ankle and lifted her upside down.

'*You gave us away, Drishbak,*' the Orc holding Aski said. Aski didn't understand the noises that they were making but knew they were talking to each other when the first Orc that chased her made noises back.

'*She got right up in my eyes, Groktire,*' Drishbak replied, drool rolling down his mouth and falling from his chin. '*Even you couldn't have stayed still.*'

Aski started to scream wildly as the Orc squeezed her ankle to hard. The Orc lifted Aski higher and growled in her face shaking her from side to side. Taking this as a warning to stay quiet Aski gritted her teeth whenever the grip was too tight. The breath smelt

60

like rotting flesh and she hoped she wouldn't be adding to it soon.

Aski couldn't understand how they could see her. She still couldn't see herself, yet they were able to catch her so easily and accurately. Deciding this wasn't what she should be focusing on; Aski pushed the thought from her mind and started trying to think up an escape.

'It was still clumsy,' the final Orc, Brogda, critiqued. *'At least we know Groktire's idea works.'*

'I was watching a moth around the candles last night and thought of how we always find humans around fires. I knew if we made one and sat still enough they would come,' Groktire said proudly holding Aski up like a trophy.

'Yes, yes, build it and they will come. You've told us how many hundred times?' Drishbak said impatiently. *'Let's just get her back and roast the juicy little thing. She will be cooked through ready for the morning meal.'*

'Fine, but I get these juicy legs,' Groktire said running his long, wet tongue up the calf of the leg he was holding.

Aski's mind suddenly turned to terror as thoughts of her abuse came flooding back. She'd gotten the wrong idea from the action and started thrashing around erratically trying to get free. Brogda walked up behind her and cracked her across the back of the head. Bright lights flashed before her eyes as she lost all consciousness.

When Aski finally came too, she didn't know what was happening. Her mind was groggy and she felt like she was suspended by something. It took some time for her mind to reboot and feed her memories of the trip in the woods and the run in with the Orcs. She could feel her arms brushing against small shrubs and rocks as the Orc still carried her by the leg. It was dark as they moved through the woods and Aski could only assume she hadn't been out long or they would have made it to the Orcs lair by now. It would be stupid to travel to far from their home.

Pushing all her fears and anxieties away she told herself that to survive she needed a clear mind. She took in everything from the grip of the Orcs hand to the arc his arm swung. Seeing no weakness, Aski looked around trying to find a weapon in arms reach but nothing stood out. She didn't even know how far her arms could reach, still being invisible to her. Then Aski remembered Paws. She could feel his warmth in her hood and was thankful when a small movement came from him. Reaching up Aski drew Paws from the hood and brought him close to her face.

'You need to find Genji and bring him to me where ever I end up,' Aski whispered into the creature's ear. Groktire heard her voice and looked down to see her holding Paws. Reaching down he made to grab the rodent thinking it would make a great treat for the trail. Seeing the hand reaching down, Aski threw Paws awkwardly into the shrub nearby. As Paws left her hands, Aski saw colour and body come back to him while she still remained unseen. Brogda dashed over to try and catch him but he came back empty handed with a growl.

'Please get through to him,' Aski whispered a silent prayer.

A few minutes later and Aski found herself dangling at the entrance to a cave. If she thought the Orcs breath was bad whatever was billowing from the darkness made Aski's nose wrinkle and eyes water. Not wanting to enter but knowing she had no choice Aski steeled herself against the smell and didn't resist being carried inside. She couldn't afford to be knocked unconscious at this moment when she may only have minutes left.

The walls of the cave were damp, emphasized by the torches reflecting upon the surface. Aski saw three open areas leading away from the central tunnel she assumed must be the private quarters for each Orc. The Tunnel opened into a large area with a small hole in the ceiling leading outside. Smoke from a nearby fire was drawn up and away by the natural vent. The smell in

62

the room was terribly over powering and Aski put a hand to her noise to try and stop the smell getting through. It didn't work. She saw piles of old rotting flesh and bones and knew this was where the smell was coming from. Maggots were crawling all over the waste and Aski forced herself to hold back throwing up, her stomach convulsing at the sight.

With a swing of his arm, Groktire tossed Aski to the corner of the room while he started to prepare for the roast. Brogda had moved to the doorway, keeping an eye on her and Drishbak had moved out to another area. Desperately, Aski looked around for something to help but there was nothing that would work. The only things that resembled a weapon were the few bones scattered around her, the size of her lower leg. Her mind looked at the bones once more, echoes of something familiar pushing at Aski's mind. She stared a moment longer when she noticed the triangle shape the bones made. Instantly, she remembered the triangle Genji used to create fire. There were doubts it would work but it was her only chance.

Picking up a bone, Aski drew a triangle into the earth before her making sure the point was facing away. She placed a hand over one edge and tried to remember the word Genji spoke. Karc, Kerk, Kert, Krok... Krak! That was definitely the word. She could hear Genji repeat it over and over as her memory played back. Groktire turned to face her holding a large metal spike. Aski's face drained of colour as she remembered the family BBQ with the pig on a spit. Now, this was to be her fate.

'Krak,' she said hurrying the word. Nothing happened. 'Krak, Krak, Krak,' Aski repeated with the same result. Genji's words invaded her fear like a survival mechanism. *You need to picture what you want in your mind and focus that picture out through the word and into the symbol.* Groktire was almost over her now and she pictured pillars of flames all around her blocking any access. Putting all her emotions behind the word, Aski spoke. 'Krak!' Aski felt the power of the word ripple through her and embed itself in the triangle. Flames rose up all around her and the Orc jumped back in surprise. Brogda swore and approached the flames. From down the tunnel, Drishbak came running out wanting to know what the commotion was about. Seeing the flames, his eyes went wide and he also moved closer to inspect them. Reaching out a crusty, green hand, Drishbak touched the flames before crying in agony as they bit into his skin. It was hotter than natural flames and the skin had flayed from Drishbak's fingers.

Aski felt safe once more behind the magical fire, locked in her own little world. She was extremely proud of herself with what she had accomplished. But the smile didn't last long as the flames started to dim.

'No,' Aski cried but she couldn't deny the fire was losing its strength. The Orcs started to smile a terrible, cold grin.

A hazy, predawn light gave everything around a dull, grey look. The temperatures started to change and Tristan shivered, reminded that the night was colder than his body told him. When Genji offered to create heated air to surround him, Tristan almost spat. He would never take aid of magic no matter what he was feeling. He would only accept magic if it meant his release from life. Even the wounds that didn't heal were starting to become numb, the pain only flaring if he moved in certain ways. Genji smiled knowing that would be the answer and had fun teasing the Mage Killer.

Suddenly, Genji stopped in front of Tristan with a serious look on his face. 'My home isn't far from here and there are some things I want to go over.'

'I won't be touching anything,' Tristan assured him. 'I will remain only long enough to learn how to reverse this curse upon me.'

'That's not what I wanted to talk about,' Genji replied. 'I have a house guest staying with me. A young girl of about ten.'

64

'You don't seem old enough to have a daughter. A sister maybe?' Tristan surmised.

'She isn't a relative of mine.'

'You two aren't..?' Tristan said. Genji shot him a dangerous look.

'Nothing of the sort,' Genji grunted. 'Her background has been hard though. She's been abused and mistreated by almost everyone in her life. Circumstance brought her into my life and I shall not see her come to harm.'

'You think me cold hearted because I am a Mage Killer, *Mage*. She has nothing to fear from me.'

Genji could tell that the sentence implied he did have something to fear but he wasn't worried. He could defend himself against the man. 'Not what I was trying to say,' Genji expanded. 'She's had a hard life and is now weary around strangers. She may not come near you or even talk to you regardless of what you do. I want you to be prepared for that and not try to push things. I would say the same to anyone I brought home.'

'Understood,' Tristan nodded. 'If that's all let's continue.'

Moments later, they walked into the clearing where Genji's house stood still cast in shadow, the sun being blocked by the forest. Morning light was almost upon them and Genji was feeling weary after spending the night out. He reached the point where his barrier stood and paused when Tristan started talking.

'How far to your home?' Tristan asked looking at the burnt out home. 'It is ill luck to travel so close to these ruins.'

Genji's eyes narrowed as he regarded the man. 'You still wish me harm even though I have promised to help you?'

'With every fibre of my being but I'll be patient and wait until after you kill me,' Tristan said with a wink. 'What's that got to do with the hut? Were you the Mage that did this?'

Genji laughed. 'Of course I was. Wait here a moment

or you won't get much further.'

Tristan's face hardened as he thought of the Mage in front of him committing such a heinous act. Genji on the other hand held the smile on his face and reached out a hand. A shimmer occurred in the air like a semi translucent curtain in the shape of an arched doorway.

'When you walk in walk through this point only. Anywhere else and you'll turn around and leave the area after a few metres?' Genji told him before stepping through himself. A soft purple light flashed at Genji's feet and he stopped kneeling down. 'Whoa Tristan, I almost forgot,' Tristan observed the Mage place his hand on the dew covered grass. 'Emundetur a fluxi seminis,' Genji whispered and the charm he placed to render Aski invisible to any who crossed the barrier dissipated.

'What was that?' Tristan asked feeling uncomfortable with all the magic that was being thrown around.

'Just a charm to hide my guest while I was absent. If anyone got past my barrier they wouldn't be able to see her.' A funny thought struck Genji at that moment. 'It'd be fun to see Aski's reaction if she herself crossed over the charm and her body was rendered invisible.'

'I don't see the humour in alarming little girls,' Tristan said with a less than impressed face. 'You talk like the house is close. How far have we to go?'

'Just come inside,' Genji said, his good humour gone. He was starting to feel dizzy like a first year Mage over extending himself. That couldn't be the case here as Genji had used very little magic to what he was capable of.

Genji turned his back and walked towards the home. After hesitating a moment longer, Tristan followed through the shimmering air. He wasn't quite sure what to expect as he passed through. A rush of cold maybe, one could never be too sure with Mages afoot. What he didn't expect was the vast change in the area around him. Where once a ruin of ash and coal stood with grey dirt over the vast area, now there was an established home with grass and flowers, shrubs and birds. The whole area had become a beautiful, liveable home.

'What is this?' Tristan asked confused. 'What have you done?'

'Nothing, Tristan,' Genji replied evenly. 'There is a barrier around my home. Any who may intentionally or unintentionally cause me harm will see the ruins of a hunter's family shack. The image and the rumours were started and passed around by myself. I enjoy my privacy and my safety more than anything.'

'But what did you do to the family that lived here?' Tristan asked still getting his head around the scene.

'There was no family, Tristan. Only a story I created about them. I set everything up to seem like a family home was burnt to the gro...' Genji paused looking serious.

'What is it?' Tristan asked recognising the look. Looking around, he assessed the area for danger.

'Something isn't right,' Genji said before racing into the house and throwing Tristan's sword just inside the entrance. He knocked on Aski's door to her room and when she didn't open it he forced the lock. 'Aski, I'm coming up okay.' There was no answer and Genji bounded up the stairs, Tristan not far behind. There was no sign of life within the bedroom. Even the blankets looked as though they hadn't been slept in but Genji couldn't be too sure with the way Aski made her bed.

'Your house guest run away, did she, *Mage*?' Tristan said with a smug look. Who would want to stay with a Mage anyway, he thought.

Genji ignored the remark and focused on following Aski's life force. The connection they shared as summoner and summoned gave him a far stronger link to the girl. When the initial search in and around the immediate facility of the barrier came up short he started to really worry. Expanding the spell over a much larger area, a small blip drew his attention to the west. Whatever it was had the same energy signature as Aski but was far too small. Finding nothing else, Genji focused on the object and immediately got an image of Paws in his mind. He would not go anywhere his host didn't. Genji also realised the reason Paws listened to him was because he was connected to Aski in a similar way. Putting the thought from his mind Genji pinpointed the location and his heart froze.

'Hurry,' Genji said to Tristan and raced out of the room before shouting back. 'Take up your sword and follow me.' Glancing back Genji saw that Tristan didn't have the sword he crafted and came to a halt.

'I told you. I'm not touching that thing,' Tristan said stubbornly.

Genji became annoyed and fetched the weapon. 'Keep up and save some strength. We're going to be fighting orcs.'

'Orcs? She would be dead by now if she were taken by Orcs. You must have gotten it wrong.'

'Trust me Tristan. I was wondering why I was getting such bad head spins but now I know it was Aski.'

'You're not making sense, Genji,' Tristan called to the running man.

'It's magic. That's all the sense you need,' was Genji's reply.

Neither man said any more as they raced through the forest. Though it was a quarter of the distance Genji had already travelled the night before he was still feeling drained for what he hoped was Aski borrowing his energy. He somehow knew that she was still alive but couldn't get a read on her energy signature. How she got caught up with Orcs was a completely different matter entirely. She was supposed to be asleep in her room, not gallivanting around in the woods. Young girls are supposed to be scared of the dark.

Leaving his troubling thoughts behind, Genji exploded from the tree line and almost ran head first into the cliff face. He paused a moment to get his bearings but Tristan motioned in the direction of the cave. It was only a few yards away and Genji could already see the small, Lazurian Mouse.

'Paws,' Genji called and the rodent ran to him climbing up onto his shoulder. It was hissing and shaking as the bristles on the back of its neck were standing up. Genji reached up to scratch Paws behind the ear. 'Don't worry, we'll save her.' He turned to Tristan. 'Are you sure you won't take this sword?' Genji asked holding forth the blade. Tristan just shook his head. 'Then let's go kill some Orcs.'

As they entered the smell of the cave washed over them. Genji put an arm over his nose and mouth trying to adjust to the shocking smell while Tristan seemed unaffected. He'd smelt far worse on the victorious battlefield and believed his sense of smell had dulled over the years. Pushing on, Genji could see light coming from the far end of the tunnel. A roar of frustration came from the same location and the two men gave caution to the wind before running deep into the Orc cave. Past the open rooms leading off the main path they entered the central hall.

Genji looked past the three huddled Orcs and saw a small girl he recognised as Aski kneeling behind a fast dying fire. The girl looked terribly drained and before Genji got the chance to call to her he saw her eyes roll into the back of her head, her body collapsing upon the hardened earth floor. The fire died away completely and one Orc stepped forward to claim the long awaited prize. Genji spied the well-used symbol for fire directly under the orc.

'Krak!' He screamed and fire erupted upwards into the Orc above. The flames ate at the skin, blistering and melting the flesh. The Orc flailed about as the fire took hold, crying in agony, before toppling over dead to burn upon the floor.

The remaining Orcs turned to face the intruders and upon seeing only two men charged. They split off and crossed the floor quickly. Genji had no time to create any more magic. Instead he lifted the sword before him. The Orc slowed, advancing cautiously. Genji didn't have the best sword skills but he did know enough to protect himself. It would all depend on the experience the Orc had fighting. No doubt enough to match him.

Tristan got into a fighters stance waiting for his opponent to come to him. As the Orc threw a punch, Tristan grabbed the arm and rolled the Orc over his shoulder using the beast's momentum. The Orc sailed through the air to land heavily against a wall, the wind being knocked from his lungs. Looking back Tristan saw that Genji was in trouble once more. The Mage was blocking like a farmer who had just been given a weapon for the first time. The Orc saw this as well and seemed to be playing with Genji, allowing the inexperienced man to gain some confidence before destroying him. Tristan came up behind the Orc and rammed his palm into a soft spot where the base of the skull met the spine. The Orc fell to the ground growling in pain while holding the back of his neck.

Tristan turned back to his own opponent, having given Genji a major advantage. The Mage need only ram that sword he was so fond of into the beasts green chest and it would almost be over. Tristan was suddenly bowled over and dragged to the ground. The Orc who was his opponent recovered faster than expected and was now grappling with him. The strength in the limbs above were almost inhuman and Tristan felt his muscle strength waning. The Orc was right up in his face and Tristan could definitely smell something terrible living in that mouth, not to mention the drool now moving down Tristan's cheek.

'Help me, Genji,' Tristan called, disappointed that he asked a Mage for help.

Genji saw the predicament and threw over the sword Tristan so openly refused to use. It slid within reach. 'Use that. Ill dispatch mine with a little magic.' Genji said before starting to etch a symbol in some soft earth.

Tristan swore being forced to take up this sword but he had no choice. Releasing one hand he reached over grabbing the hilt while tilting his head away. The Orcs face fell head long into some stones as Tristan couldn't hold the beast up anymore. A strong grunt sounded beside Tristan's ear as the blade tore into the Orc's. With little effort Tristan pulled the sword up through the body exiting just behind the Orc's neck splitting the creature in two. Rolling out from under the creature, Tristan turned to see the remaining Orc crumble to ash under an intense energy ray.

Genji dropped to a knee as the adrenalin left his system and a wave of fatigue washed over him. He was about to reprimand the Mage but chose to leave it for now. Feeling okay to move once more Genji made his way to where Aski was. Paws jumped out from somewhere in Genji's clothing and snuck into Aski's hood. The girl slowly stirred looking up at Genji above her.

'Is this real?' She asked. 'Did I make it?'

'You made it,' Genji said. He was having trouble understanding the emotions that were running through him and drew the girl into a hug. Aski was too tired to care about the human contact and burst into tears, happy to be alive. As her vision cleared and Aski saw past Genji she noticed another figure in the room. A man dressed in armour holding a sword. Aski's breath caught in her throat as the man looked her in the eyes

'Brother?' she whispered.

Chapter 5

As the flames died away, terror crawled across Aski's skin and the small hairs all over her body stood on end. The smiles that the Orcs shared only cemented the fact she was about to die. She knew the blaze was hot like she wanted seeing the effect it had when the Orcs stupidly tried to test it but it was dying away faster than intended. As the flame was about to die off completely Aski said the word she had learned spying on Genji, once more. Brogda had been preparing to jump the last licks of fire when new fountains of flame shot into the air. He fell back with a growl having his prize taken from him once more. These spires had been tempered with less heat and, Aski hoped, more longevity. She surmised that if the flame was eating away the oxygen around it too fast it would suffocate. Aski let out a sigh of relief seeing the theory bear fruit. Her brother had shown her one time how fire needed to breathe to survive. He placed a plate on top of a glass with a candle inside. Aski was very intrigued watching the flame burn out.

Now though, her smile died away as the second round of magical flames started to die down. The flames lasted about three times longer than her first attempt. She repeated the process again and this time started to feel it. A small niggle at the back of her mind that she ignored at first but was hard pressed to deny it now. With each use of magic she grew more weary. Her head became foggy and her limbs grew weak. Sitting on the ground to save energy helped only for another hour.

The Orcs weren't helping either. They would continually throw stones and other objects over the flames causing Aski to waste energy trying to dodge them. Not all she escaped successfully. Aski never dreamed she'd be even slightly thankful to her upbringing but she was now. The tolerance for pain Aski displayed was at an extremely high level. Thinking about her step dad made Aski angry and she used the anger to fuel her body. To be more aware and react faster. Just in time too. The dumb one, Drishbak, had made it within the circle of flames from the far edge and was approaching fast. Aski cried the magical word and closed her circle locking the Orcs out once again.

While resting between casts, Aski saw the sky was starting to lighten out the natural hole in the roof. She had no concept of the length of time she'd been casting. Her mind was working on autopilot, repeating the same steps over and over, fighting her eyes to stay awake. Aski had started casting a small fire right next to her. She knew it would drain her stamina faster but it became a requirement. Holding her hand over the small flame she felt safe. If she fell asleep her hand would fall into the flame waking her instantly. The burns would heal and for the two times already she'd been saved this way she was happy for the blisters.

As the cave became brighter, Aski held one thought in her mind above all else. Paws will find Genji. Genji will save me. She kept repeating it holding to the hope of life. She did so right up until darkness fell. Having forgotten now to light her safety fire, Aski didn't wake this time. She didn't even know she'd passed out.

The first sensation Aski felt was something small moving around the back of her neck. There weren't any uncomfortable feelings like the Orc's dry, calloused hand. This sensation was warm and... furry. Aski willed her eyes slowly open and saw a dark figure standing over her. Allowing her eyes to adjust she saw Genji and a lump started to form in her throat and slowly tightening in her chest.

'Is this real?' She asked. 'Did I make it?'

'You made it,' Genji replied.

Aski saw the worry in his eyes and was surprised when he hugged her. No terrible memories came bubbling to the surface. This hug felt different. It was one of love and life. The first time she ever knew a hug to be good. Tears welled in her eyes and she cried unashamedly until there were no more tears to be shed. Still in an embrace, Aski looked passed Genji and saw the other man for the first time. A knight by the look of his worn armour. He looked strong like someone you never had to feel scared if travelling with, someone that would lay down their life to protect you. When she looked into the man's eyes, her breath caught in her throat. Her last memory of her brother came to mind and she could see no difference between the knight and this memory. The blond, wavy hair growing over the ears, the arch of the nose, even the small freckle under the chin were all identical.

'Brother?' Aski whispered under her breath.

The word was audible enough next to Genji's ear to grab his attention. He looked back at Tristan confused. Pushing herself away from Genji, Aski approached Tristan. He saw her coming and remembering Genji's words, smiled. Aski's face light up and her eyes became teary once more.

'Brother,' she cried before running up to Tristan and leaping into his arms.

Tristan on the other hand mirrored the look on Genji's face. He didn't know the girl or even have a sister.

'Brother, I've missed you so much,' Aski said with such joy in her voice. 'You have no idea how horrible it's been at home since you left.'

'I'm sorry, I,' Tristan was trying to let her know he was not who she thought he was but Aski cut in.

'You're hurt!' Aski just noticed the wounds beneath Tristan's armour and the bandaging around his neck. Looking back at Genji there was genuine fear in her voice. 'Genji, can you fix him?'

'He's not your brother,' Genji said bluntly. 'He isn't even from your time.'

Aski couldn't believe what Genji said and looked between him and Tristan. Tristan gently lowered her to the ground and knelt down to be at her level.

'What he says is true,' Tristan said. He saw a flash of jealousy in Genji's eyes but didn't say anything. He saw how fragile this girl was and if Genji cared that much it was a good thing. Tristan knew she would be protected. 'I've never had a sister.'

Reality sunk in and Aski retreated back a ways watching the man. She didn't know what to say or how to act feeling embarrassed with how she had just acted. 'Can you still help him?' Aski asked Genji coyly.

Genji didn't understand the emotions he was having with the girl. She'd just started to trust him after a hard start and just like that, the Mage Killer was already making strides in gaining her trust. 'I can't help the man,' he said more harshly than he wanted to. 'The man is a killer anyway. He murders people for being different.'

'Genji!' Tristan growled. 'You may not like me but you don't need to infect anyone else with your hatred.'

Watching the two men bicker backward and forwards, Aski became overwhelmed and ran out of the cave. Sunlight washed over her and already tired she sat back against the cave mouth. The warmth felt like heaven not realizing how cold she truly was in her fight to stay alive. Soon the fatigue of the night caught up with her and she was fast asleep. Paws's little head poked out from her hood and rested on her shoulder as he also slept.

'All I'm saying is leave the girl out of our fight,' Tristan said as he and Genji walked from the cave. They paused seeing Aski sleeping peacefully in the sun. Genji softened at that point.

'Okay,' Genji replied. 'I will leave my own feelings out of it for her sake. Let's go back to my home. We can recover from the events of the night there. Once refreshed I will look into ways I can kill you.'

Tristan nodded. Reaching down he gently picked Aski up, cradling her in his arms. She moaned and adjusted herself a little but continued to sleep. Paws objected to Tristan touching Aski. The hairs on the back of his neck rose as he made hissing noises at Tristan from the edge of Aski's hood. Genji laughed and put Paws mind at rest.

'At least you're on my side,' Genji said to the little rodent, scratching it behind the ear. Paws settled back knowing there was no danger.

'A curious little creature,' Tristan said. 'I haven't seen any like it.'

'Lazurian Mice are extremely rare and you could say the Mage of the animal kingdom. Aski befriended it and they have been inseparable ever since,' Genji said. He looked to Tristan's belt. 'I see your still carrying the sword. Thought it was tainted?'

Tristan glared across at the Mage. 'The sword embodies everything about my situation. I will wear it until I am cured.'

'That's what I've been saying all along,' Genji replied.

'Don't push it Mage,' Tristan growled low. He didn't want to wake Aski. 'The sword is still an abomination. Get me to your home.'

Genji smiled and walked into the woods. It was a tedious walk back to the house with little to make the trip faster. Genji opened the barrier for Tristan before letting him know there was a lounge in the living area he could sleep on.

'That is not an issue at the moment,' Tristan replied. 'Whatever has changed me has given me no need to sleep. Rest maybe at times but my mind will not shut down.'

'Make yourself at home but be careful of anything that looks magical... or are near magical objects... or that shouldn't be where they are placed,' Genji thought for a moment. 'Maybe, just leave everything where it is.'

'I will wait out in the garden if it's all the same to you,' Tristan replied shaking his head. He entered the house and took Aski up to her bed, placing her down gently and pulling the blanket up. When he returned downstairs Genji had already retired to his room so Tristan walked out to bask in the sunlight.

Atalis was raging now. He drew his father's sword from the king's side. It was created by a master craftsman and gifted to the king for the birth of Atalis. The king wore it every day with pride.

With a murderous roar Atalis charged the orc. He

swung as the orc sidestepped away. Bringing the sword around again, Atalis was blocked by the orc's axe. A small chip became evident and Atalis went berserk. He hacked down the orc's defences and cleaved his head in two. Not thinking clearly he raced into the rift searching for more enemies. With every step he took his head started to become light. His breaths came in great rasps. His lungs burned and a great weariness took over. Atalis took a knee to allow himself time to find his centre.

Genji hated the fact he had to return to the Academy so soon for matters in magic he didn't have answers for. He knew a whole year would have passed by now for the students and staff but that didn't change the fact it was barely over a week for him. No one else would know, but he would. When Genji passed the final exam to become a full-fledged Summoner Mage he believed he was a master of his craft. The truth was quite the opposite. Nothing had changed. He was still a student to the ways of magic. Even a Mage Killer understood the essence and tactics one could use in battle and life better than he.

'Don't look so down. We are all students to the ways of magic,' a voice said. Genji looked up to see the examiner, Gerard, walking into the entrance hall.

'Are you reading my mind, old man?' Genji said dropping all the formalities he upheld as a student.

'Gerard,' the man stated.

'What?' Genji asked.

'You called me old man. I assumed that you had forgotten my name in... What? The month or so you had left here. The disciplines we teach at the Academy of Mage Craft are not just in the use of Magic. Manners and respect were also disciplines of this learning centre. You may not be a student anymore and therefore don't need to use terms like sir but the use of my name is expected.'

'Yes, yes... Gerard,' Genji said to satisfy the old man. He was worried about the month comment. 'How did you know it hadn't been so long for me? Did I miss my mark?'

'Vanity,' Gerard said simply. 'You seem to have a lot of it. I have felt your energy very little this past year. I had assumed you were jumping in time as many Summoner Mages do after their final exam. Most will return within days with more questions. The extremely vain put some time between when they complete their training and when they return. So how long has it been?'

Pursing his lips, annoyed at having been read so easily. 'A little over a week,' he admitted.

'When are you visiting?' Gerard asked. 'The time of the Elven King perhaps?'

'I'm about 15 years shy of the lost era.'

Gerard's eyes widened. 'You know the dangers of those years. There are Mage Killers roaming the lands and if you leave it too long, you may lose all magic completely. Darius's curse was to powerful, even for you.'

'I will be fine,' Genji replied stubbornly. He didn't want another lecture from the old man. 'The day I passed my Time exams I jumped back and created a home for myself. There are protections around the house so that no one who wishes me harm could find it on their own. As to the Lost Era, I would not have stayed so long.'

Gerard was actually rather proud of Genji's insight into the matter but he wasn't about to say anything. 'The girl giving you trouble?'

'Aski's not the reason I 'm here. Beverlin, a friend of mine, helped me through the hardest parts. The girl has even shown promise in magic having already produced flames.'

'She is using your energy and ability. While she is linked through the summoning she has access to your strength,' Gerard said dismissing the remark. 'I reckon she had to put in a few hours before she could perform it though.'

Genji smiled. 'No, I believe she spied me lighting my

78

fire place, hearing the word and seeing the symbol for fire. She asked how I did it but I only told her it was a link between the mind, the word, and the symbol. She produced numerous flames for half a night continuously to ward off the Orcs that kidnapped her. It was just long enough for me to find her and free her... Oh, and she has bonded with a Lazurian Mouse.'

To say Gerard was surprised was an understatement. He was unable to hide the astonishment from his face, his mouth hanging low. 'A lot has happened in a week. If you ever do work out how to release her, bring her here. We would be happy to train one so talented.'

'Dismissing her is the least of my worries,' Genji said. He told Gerard about the Mage Killer and his immortality, along with the reason he was here.

'I have heard of the Immortal Knight, Tristan,' Gerard admitted. 'Many here believe the stories to be myths but you have come here saying you met the man.'

'I have met him and am now seeking a way to make the story just a myth. He wants this as he is now Mage Touched. Tristan has been possessed by a green glowing mist that is sentient and has even spoken to him. It is keeping him alive but is not healing any wounds. The being even suggested decapitation would not end his life.'

'Probably true,' Gerard said off handed. 'There have been many theories regarding immortality. None we can rightly test ourselves. Possession could only last until the being that possessed him runs out of energy.'

'I told Tristan as much,' Genji said nodding. 'But I also encountered the being before he was possessed. The power within was one of the highest I have felt. He would be alive a very long time.'

'I was curious when you mentioned that book on darkness. So curious in fact that I found it and read it cover to cover. An interesting read.'

Genji shook his head confused. 'What has that to do with the matter at hand?'

'It spoke of a sword strong enough to destroy any being. A sword that was lost about the time you have found yourself in. Look into the book. It may give you some ideas on where to start.'

'Thank you, Gerard,' Genji said genuinely.

'You are walking your own path now,' Gerard said walking up beside Genji and placing a hand on his shoulder. 'Don't be afraid to ask for or accept help, young sprout.' Gerard started to walk off but paused. 'I believe your friend, Beverlin, of whom you just mentioned, borrowed it recently.' With that, the old man walked off leaving Genji to himself.

Beverlin. Genji didn't know whether to curse the fates for the distraction their reunion will bring or thank his luck for having someone as smart as she is already having read the book. Deciding to do both Genji sent out a probe to track Beverlin's energy. It wasn't long before he found her recognizing the dorm rooms. He'd not bothered to visit Beverlin in her room before today and knew she was going to make a fuss over the occasion. It was that fuss that Genji was agonizing over.

Finding himself standing outside her door, Genji reached up to knock. His hand hovered above the wood stalling for time as he weighed his options. It took a great deal of will to finally tap on the door twice. Waiting but a moment, Genji turned and started to walk away.

'Genji,' Beverlin squealed. Genji turned as the girl pounced, catching him in a big embrace. 'I've missed you dearly. The people here are so dull compared to you. How have you been?'

Genji struggled free. 'This past week has been rather troublesome.'

'Only a week?' Beverlin looked annoyed. 'You've got to visit in shorter periods. Are you treating Aski well?'

'We are actually starting to bond,' Genji said proudly. 'This isn't the time for that, however. You have something I need.'

'Why Genji, it's so sudden,' Beverlin joked, feigning

80

coyness.

'What? No. Why would I want that?' Genji said.

Beverlin's face suddenly became hard and she walked back to her room. 'Whatever you want, you can learn to be a bit nicer before asking again.' She made sure to put a bit of force into closing the door to emphasis her statement.

Genji just stood with a blank look on his face trying to work out what just happened. He didn't have the patience to be playing to the whims of women. Taking out his retractable staff and extending it, Genji decided it was finally time to test his theories in reshaping the molecules of the body to become invisible. Though, he would need to change the invisible part to pass through walls.

Feeling the surface of Beverlin's door, Genji noted that it was crafted from natural hardwood with no enchantments or charms within. This was going to be easier than he thought. Placing the staff ever so gently against the door so as to balance on its own, he positioned both palms on the woods surface. He focused deeply on this form of magic. If he misplaced any of the molecules on the other side the results could be catastrophic. The feeling of the magic shifted and Genji felt the moment everything was ready.

The quartz atop his staff started to glow as he began with the particle manipulation of both himself and the door to allow him to sift through. He put emotion into the magic with his body physically moving against the door. The small amount of force swung the door open sending Genji flat on his face.

'What are you doing, Genji?' Beverlin asked, amused by her friends acrobatics. 'I made sure the door didn't latch so that you could follow.'

'How was I supposed to know that?' Genji stormed picking himself up. 'You were yelling and carrying on like a demented harpy, it didn't enter my mind you meant *please come in*. Women!' Genji threw his arms up in the air in frustration.

'Firstly, close the door,' Beverlin said calmly.

'What? No. Do it yourself,' Genji's pride had come to the front after the spill.

'Close the door and we can talk,' she said more sternly.

Genji held her gaze, stubbornness not allowing him to look away. As the battle continued, his anger became predominant until finally he turned back closing the door. He made sure that it latched properly this time.

'Thank you, Genji,' Beverlin said with a smile. 'Onto business. What you had to say sounded important. I was bringing you someplace private giving no reasons for sneaks to be listening at the door. You wouldn't want every Mage Craft Adept finding out your secrets and possibly going after them yourself do you?'

'No Mage could.'

'Be that as it may, I am more comfortable talking here than in the hall. And honestly, you think way to highly of yourself. Did you really believe that I would get so worked up over a little unrequited flirting? I've known you long enough to know it's not your thing. Also, this may come as a surprise to you but we are just friends. You aren't my type.'

'Well, you're not my type either,' Genji said weakly.

'I don't believe you even have a type, unless you count someone wearing dirty pants and shirt with black hair tied into a ponytail, going by the name Genji.'

'Well what's your type then?' Genji asked lacking any other line of thought.

'You remember, Bran.'

'Spindly legged dope.... No?' Genji was surprised.

'He always had a handsome face,' Beverlin replied. 'When he passed the healing discipline he used it to buff himself up. Healing arts are quite useful with a bit of knowledge behind you.'

'You didn't offer to... Buff him up with your healing arts?' Genji smirked.

Beverlin threw a pillow at him bouncing off his shoulder. 'Why have you come to see me?'

'You have a book I need to read,' Genji once again told the story from when Beverlin left until he found himself outside her door. Strategically, he left out the fact Tristan was a Mage Killer. He wasn't ready for a lecture into how dangerous it was. She sat listening with a concerned look on her face.

'Why would the man wish to die? A cure maybe.'

'The pain he feels is with him always. I have tried to help him but nothing works. This may be his only release,' Genji told her. 'Could you watch a loved one slowly die in agonizing pain knowing there was no possible way to help them. All the while they asked for release. It is a harsh reality but he knows himself best.'

'The book does mention the sword,' Beverlin told him. Genji brightened. 'The sword is a weapon crafted to kill a demon named Aragaranatan, an ancient and powerful being. There was little that could match this demon so therefore, whatever has possessed this man should be killed by this sword.'

'Did it mention where the sword may have been found?'

'There was a rumour only, listed at the back. A Western prince inherited the sword from his late father but from that day the blade never had the same presence of power.'

Genji quietly deliberated over the information given. He was chewing the tip of his thumb nail as he did when deep in though. 'The Western prince could come from nowhere other than Pintosia. A king has reigned there for at least twenty years so we should still have time. The sword may have passed into the Lost Era and therefore lost it's magic.'

'Well, let's go find it then.'

'Let's as in you and I?' Genji asked, one eyebrow raised. Beverlin nodded vigorously. 'No. You and I will not be looking for the sword. I will be looking for the sword.'

'There is a lot more information in the book I haven't told you yet,' Beverlin said. 'And an extra Mage couldn't hurt in a world full of Mage Killers. Apart from Necromancy and summoning, I have mastered all other magic disciplines.'

'I'm not going to wait for you to pack,' Genji said thinking she may back out. 'You can come as you are or not at all.'

'Yay,' Beverlin's face was glowing. She reached down beside her bed and through a dusty old backpack over her shoulders.

'What's that? Genji asked pointing at the backpack.

'Knowing where you lived I always thought you would go on an adventure someday. This has sat here ready packed since I returned home a year ago. I will be coming with you.'

Genji growled. 'Fine,' he said before turning and walking out of the room.

Out in the hallway, Genji opened a rift to the stairways leading back to his home. Beverlin was fast behind him not wanting Genji to deliberately leave her behind.

'Look, it's Bran,' Genji said. Beverlin saw her crush walking up the hall. Not a bad way to leave seeing him once more. 'Hey Bran,' Genji called out waving. He thought it was the perfect time to get back at Beverlin for earlier. Bran stopped moving as he tried to recognize Genji. 'Beverlin wants to have your babies.'

Bran's eyes went wide as Genji stepped into the rift. Beverlin knew Genji was about to be a prick and so was ready. Catching his eyes, she gave him a sexy little smile and a wink before exiting into the Stairways herself. She stared hard at Genji's back deciding how to retaliate. He didn't like spiders much. Part way down Genji paused in his walk straining to listen. Beverlin followed his lead having little experience in the stairways. The sound of steel on steel echoed around the unending darkness.

'What is it?' she asked.

Genji looked concerned. 'Trouble. Someone's fighting on another flight of stairs. A Mage possibly came across a monster of some type that was trapped here by another Mage. Let's hope that's all it is.'

Genji continued slower now keeping watch for anything that may come their way. Happily, he saw the

84

opening to his home clear of any problems.

Chapter 6

Aski spied the steel armoured boots just outside the door. They belonged to the Knight that looked like her brother lying against the house. Finding herself staring at them for too long she forced her mind onto something else. Paws was close by so she started to play with him. She would drag a scrap of material across the floor that Paws would chase in cute little pounces. After a few minutes, Aski scooped the mouse up in her arms and started stroking the soft fur.

'Do you think that he is dangerous?' Aski asked Paws not realizing she'd come back to the subject of the Knight. 'I mean, he did help save me and is traveling with Genji.'

Paws let out a soft hiss

'They did argue but I've seen many people who are great friends argue,' Aski was looking at the boots again. 'I think that if Genji is happy to have him around than he is safe. Genji wouldn't bring me into harm's way. We are family.'

Paws chirped a high pitch tone. It was sharp and to the point.

Aski looked down at the mouse now lying in her lap. There was sadness in her eyes. 'True family doesn't hurt you. Those people that I lived with, they weren't family. A cruel twist of fate meant I would share the same blood but they weren't family. Genji is different. His smile is different. He doesn't want anything from me and yet is doing his best to care for me. You like him too, don't you paws?'

Paws whistled an agreeable note.

'Thought so,' Aski smiled. Putting Paws down beside her, Aski rose and walked to a nearby window. It was opened outward and she could see the Knight near the doorway through the hazy glass. She raced back to get a chair.

Tristan felt a mixture of feelings sitting in the sun. Pain was pulsing in his neck and chest from the wounds that wouldn't heal. Time had made him accustomed to the pain but it was still almost overbearing. Conflict between the heat of the day and the coolness from the walls of the house overrode some of the pain and he was thankful for this. Hearing bards sing stories of the quest for immortality as a child Tristan had always wondered what it would be like to live forever. Now knowing the extent of it, like anything Mage Touched, it was a far greater curse than a boon.

A low rustling came from across the house and Tristan shifted his attention. Two small legs had sprouted from the open window and were thrashing about. He was about to get up and help when they started to slide further out and bend towards the ground. Soon the form of Aski could be seen looking at him cautiously. There was also a curiousness to her that drove her on. Tristan glanced at her from time to time but embellished the movements when he looked away.

Looking once more, Tristan saw that Aski had sat against the building on the opposite side of the door. As he watched from the corner of his eyes, she started to wiggle closer with a grin on her face. It was almost like she was waiting for him to pounce but his embellished movements usually had that effect on younger people. He waited until she was just edging past the door before he feigned an attack letting out a sound almost like a bark. Aski let out a squeal as she stumbled trying to get up. Jumping from the doorway, Paws put himself between them, hissing at Tristan.

'It's okay, Paws,' Aski said recovering from her surprise and scratching the mouse behind the ear. 'We were only playing. I actually used to play this same game with my brother.' Paws became quiet but still watched the knight carefully.

'Tell me about your brother,' Tristan said trying to make conversation. 'Was he good to you?'

Aski looked up at Tristan seemingly in two minds on what to say. She took the side of caution. 'Genji said that you killed people because they were different. Is this true?'

Tristan took a moment to gather his thoughts. He didn't like talking about the topic to a child but he felt honesty was a requirement with this girl. 'You should be able to tell by my armour that I am a knight. Normally, people recognize me by the mantle as a Mage Killer but I see you do not. The Knights I am with hunt Mages and, yes, kill them.'

Aski was shocked by this confession and she took a step back. 'Why?'

That one, innocent word almost made Tristan question everything he stood for. An image of a Mage and an old man crossed his mind and he steeled his will. The girl was too innocent, that was all. 'There is much in life you have yet to experience. Mages are corrupted by the power they wield and become bloodthirsty themselves. I wish only to protect those who cannot fight against the power they wield.'

'You won't kill me will you?' Aski held her breath awaiting the answer.

'You are too kind a soul to kill,' Tristan said perplexed by the girl's line of thought. 'You aren't even a Mage.'

'But I can do magic,' she whispered.

'No one so young has been able to perform magic,' Tristan said surprised thinking he didn't hear her correctly. 'Would you show me?'

Aski was hesitant at first but decided to be brave. Drawing a triangle tip up in the dirt, Aski steadied her mind and spoke the word of power. A small flame came to life and danced over the triangle for a few moments.

Tristan's heart sank as he witnessed her ability. It explained how she lasted so long in the Orc cave. But how could he kill a child. Even in his mind he played out the scenario and couldn't complete the task.

'*Let her live, you don't belong to the Knights anymore,*' the ageless voice said from the depths of his mind. '*She will be vital before the end.*'

'It will be your end,' Tristan said aloud.

Aski had been watching the emotions play across

Tristan's face after he witnessed the magic unfold. She could not guess as to what he was about to do. When he spoke all her fears came rushing in and she started to retreat. Tristan saw the movement.

'No, not you. There are voices that speak to me in my head sometimes,' Tristan said quickly taping the side of his forehead. 'You have nothing to fear from me.' The words sprung so easily to Tristan's lips but he found that he meant them.

Aski paused.

'My name is Tristan.' A strange look crossed Aski's face but she didn't have a chance to reply.

Within the boundary of Genji's protection a rift opened in the air. Tristan was already on his feet with sword in hand before Aski even noticed it was there. The speed at which Tristan moved startled her and she found the Knight standing in front of her protecting her from whatever came through. When Genji stepped out he had his full attention on a woman dressed in an odd garb. Tristan relaxed and lowered his weapon, turning to apologize to Aski for the fright.

The sound of pain reached Tristan's ears and he looked back to find Genji doubled over. He was about to help him but stopped as his body started to contort and rip apart. It was almost as if he was splitting down the middle into to perfect copies of himself, combining before the two parts separated completely. 'What's happening?' Tristan demanded but was ignored. The woman was kneeling close to Genji with a look of concern on her face. Genji continued to writhe in pain as random parts of his body tried to separate only to come back together. As quickly as it started, the convulsions ended and Genji was left Gasping for air. 'What was that?' Tristan tried again.

Glancing up, Beverlin noticed the Mage Killer for the first time standing before Aski with a weapon in hand. There was no hesitation in Beverlin as she traced the symbol for lightning and spoke the word of power. With the experience of years fighting Mages, Tristan's body reacted on his own. Throwing his sword before him, all the lightning was attracted to the large chunk of metal and Tristan dashed in. Retrieving the sword, he swung it in a turning arc towards Beverlin's neck. The shock and fear in her eyes was evident knowing she was about to die.

'Yerkiry,' Genji said in a strong voice and a spire of earth rose from the ground between Tristan and Beverlin. The sword dug into the spire with the strength of the swing halting only centimetres from cutting cleanly through. 'Both of you stop at once,' Genji commanded. 'This is my home and I will not have guests fighting each other.'

'Guest? He's a Mage Killer, Genji!' Beverlin was incredulous. 'He deserves death.'

'And that is why we are here,' Genji replied.

Beverlin stood with a dumb expression on her face before something clicked. 'This is your immortal?'

Genji nodded.

'Apart from everything I have come to adore about Mages,' Tristan said sarcastically. 'You would be?'

'Helping Genji get rid of your sorry arse,' Beverlin replied. Her study on the history of this time told her Mage Killers weren't to be trusted under any circumstances.

'And what just happened to Genji?' Tristan asked still concerned about what he'd witnessed.

'Why don't you tell me? You're the Mage Killer.'

'You think I had something to do with that,' Tristan stormed

'Please don't fight,' came a small squeak from near the house.

Everyone looked at Aski, forgotten and scared by the way things had turned out. Both Beverlin and Genji had helped her escape and transition and the Knight, Tristan had shown he had a kind soul. She didn't want them to fight anymore. Tristan laid down his sword and knelt by Aski.

'I had reacted only in your protection,' Tristan said. 'If it shall make you happy, from this day forth until our quest is complete I shall be your Knight.' Tristan lowered his head before her.

Aski didn't know how to respond having never been in a situation like this. Genji watched on closely. He could feel the jealousy rise again as it had in the Orc cave but he pushed it away. He knew that this would mean Tristan would be close to Aski, closer than even he was.

'Don't do it, Aski,' Beverlin called out. 'He is a murderer and can't be trusted.'

The hesitation Aski felt cleared upon hearing those words. She knew immediately Tristan would protect her above himself. He had shown that moments before when Beverlin had attacked. He was honest about his past and seeing how Beverlin acted not even knowing the man she was more inclined not to trust her.

'I trust you, Tristan,' she said. 'If you would be my Knight I would accept your service so please don't fight these people anymore. They have both helped me so much.'

'These two I shall protect as if they were you,' Tristan replied smiling softly. 'Until the day they leave or turn on you yourself.'

Beverlin threw her arms up with a grunt. 'I'm gunna regret this,' Genji heard as she stalked off into the house. He too, made for the home.

'Come, Knight,' he said, disdain in his voice. 'We have much to talk about.'

Tristan followed Genji into the house with Aski in front. Genji offered the man a seat opposite him in the living area. Beverlin was standing by the fireplace watching the fire, her back to the two men.

'Did you need to bring her?' Tristan asked indicating Beverlin. Aski made herself comfortable in the final chair and listened intently. She was unsure exactly what was going on and wanted to be enlightened.

'We may have found a way to... cure you,' Genji said conscious of Aski's presence. 'Beverlin holds all the information so it will be five times faster than if I had to study up on it myself.' Tristan nodded for Genji to continue after a moment. 'There is a sword that is supposed to be able to kill one of the most powerful demons there ever was. We believe that it is in the possession of the King of Pintosia. Our records show that it will lose it's power soon but we have no accurate accounts as to when or why. Only a rumour.'

'And you believe this sword will complete the job?' Tristan said following Genji's lead and watching his words.

'If you have been possessed by anything of lesser power than the demon it was designed for than yes. Otherwise, you are going to live far longer than I could even imagine.'

'If you're willing to start into this venture for the sword, I will also,' Tristan said extending a hand. The gesture was surprising to Genji and he was moved by the strong meaning behind it. No other Mage would have ever gotten a similar gesture from a Mage Killer. He saw the stern look on Tristan's face and knew the man was having trouble with the gesture himself. Genji took his wrist in a grip sealing the pact.

'And I meant what I said to Aski,' Tristan continued. 'If you or...'

'Beverlin,' Genji offered. Beverlin turned back for the first time.

'...Beverlin, find yourselves in any danger, I will protect you. Any who travel with me I extend this offer.'

'Hmph,' Beverlin grunted before turning back to the flames. Genji smiled.

'We had best pack for the road then,' Genji said rising. 'It's about four days to the desert town of Boerus. From there we can catch a ship across to Pinto and the sword.'

Aski popped her head up with an excited expression. 'A real adventure?' She squealed. Paws mimicked the sound.

Genji laughed. 'Yes. A real adventure. It is going to be very dangerous. What do you think, Tristan? Should we leave her here?' Aski's mouth dropped and her attention turned to the Knight.

Tristan caught the sly look in Genji's eye. 'I don't

92

know, A road isn't a safe place for a young girl,' Tristan said before letting the silence linger a while. Seeing Aski was struggling to find words to say she could do it he couldn't let it linger anymore. 'But I am Aski's Knight after all. I couldn't very well go running off leaving her unprotected now could I?'

Seeing her opportunity Aski spoke up. 'Yeah, where he goes, I need to.'

Genji feigned weighing up his options. 'I guess we have no choice than. You had best go pack. We leave in thirty minutes.' Aski almost burst out in joy as she ran off to prepare.

Beverlin just shook her head.

Aski was running wild around her room grabbing clothes and items she thought she would need and crammed them into a backpack. The bag was well constructed without stitching or joins of any kind. Genji had conjured it up somehow with one of his circles. Someday, she would be able to create anything she wanted. Aski dreamed of that day while she continued to pack.

Caught up on Aski's shoulder, Paws was having a terrible time trying to hang on. So much so that he decided to abandon his perch for a more stable spot on the bed. Curling up in the messy blankets, he continued to watch Aski with one ruby eye as she ran around the room. He was happy with the choice he made.

Soon, Aski picked up one last item and tried to cram it into the top of the bag. She knew nothing else would fit and as she dragged on the zipper Aski had to force the edges to meet each other. Finally getting the zipper closed she heaved the bag to her back almost falling over from the weight and momentum. Adamant nothing was coming out Aski raced downstairs with Paws close behind. She burst from the room full of excitement but the mood in the living area killed the feeling. Aski started to become worried.

On the floor by the window, Beverlin and Genji crouched, cautiously looking over the sill. Tristan was also peering outside from the doorway as if he was playing hide and seek while watching the seeker. The tension in the air started to scare Aski and she moved to where she could see the yard outside. All along the line of the forest were hundreds of men dressed in the same armour as Tristan. As groups approached the house they would slow to a stop before turning and walking back to the tree line. This confused Aski.

'Aren't they your friends, Tristan?' she asked. Tristan, Genji and Beverlin all turned to look at her, eyes wide. 'They have the same armour as you.'

Genji motioned for Aski to be silent as Tristan studied the men. Durin was on the yard and moments after Aski spoke he stopped and looked sharply in their direction.

They know, Tristan mouthed and Genji nodded gravely. Beverlin's face had gone pale and she sat visibly shaking. Moving to where Aski stood he put his finger to his lips so she would remain quiet. 'You know the type of Knight I was. I would chase and kill Mages,' he whispered. 'I have now become your Knight. I will kill only who you tell me to. These men will not follow my lead. They believe this place has magic and they want to kill any Mage inside along with anyone who are found with them. Nod if you understand.'

Aski nodded furiously, fear still evident in her eyes.

'Don't fret for I am by your side,' Tristan continued. 'I won't let anyone get to you.'

'You won't need to,' Genji said casually. Tristan gave him a questioning look. 'I have constructed a smaller barrier around the four of us. They won't be able to see or hear us for possibly twelve minutes. We need to move now while I can still hold this. The other barrier is starting to wear away. It may only last twenty minutes at most.'

Tristan nodded. 'Than let's move. I know how their trackers work so I'll take point. Genji, you and Beverlin,' he looked across to ensure she was listening. 'I want you both to remove traces of our passing until I can find a tree to climb. You should drag a tree branch behind you. Aski, climb upon my back. You may need to lose the backpack. It'll only hinder us.'

Sadly, Aski shrugged the backpack off her shoulders. Genji was surprised by the loud thud as it hit the ground.

'Did you get your whole room in there?'

'Only the essentials,' she replied as she vaulted to Tristan's back.

'Ready?' Tristan looked around.

'Wait,' Beverlin said approaching the Knight. 'Raise your right foot.'

'What do you mean, woman? Tristan asked. Even Genji couldn't guess at her reasoning.

'Woman?' Beverlin demanded dangerously. 'How dare you address me in such a manner. I have a name.'

Genji stepped in between them. 'Beverlin let it go. Men don't have the same manners as they do in our time. And honestly, we are running short of it.'

'I'm sorry, Beverlin, isn't it?' Tristan said as he looked away and raised his right foot, keeping perfect balance.

Beverlin rested her hand below his foot. 'Ody,' she said.

Tristan looked at her sharply hearing the word of power corresponding to wind but said nothing.

'Other foot,' Beverlin commanded. Her look challenged him to disobey. Slowly he placed his foot down and lifted the other. 'Ody,' she said again touching the bottom of his metal plated boots. Slowly, Beverlin repeated the process with Genji and Aski before quickly doing herself. 'Now we will leave no tracks.'

'Can we leave now, there are minutes left in this smaller barrier,' everyone nodded. 'In case it fails, do not make a noise at any point until we have at least ten minutes between us.'

The group filed quickly out of the house keeping an eye on the Mage Killers surrounding the area. The hardest part was weaving through the ring without touching anyone or letting them into the protective enclosure. Genji was sweating profusely as he struggled to hold the barrier and as they crossed into the tree line the barrier finally broke. Trees blocked them from view as they silently moved westward.

The flight through the forest was harsh and full of peril. Though Genji had taken to leisurely strolls through the woods, he wasn't prepared for how rough the terrain could get. While under speed, branches reached out to lick his face or rocks and the roots of trees looked to grab him by the ankle. Twice his foot snagged on something in the undergrowth threatening to pull him down. Righting himself just in time, Genji looked back to where Beverlin was leaning on a tree. Her breathing was coming in sharp, tortured gasps. There wasn't much more endurance in her.

Doubling back to where she rested, Genji started to rub her back. As he rubbed, he used his healing arts to sooth tired muscles and encourage the body to draw in more oxygen. The magic ensured Beverlin would be able to run for thirty minutes without the need to slow down. Genji had set it so that there were stages to how the magic would be released.

'Thank you,' Beverlin said. Her voice was ragged but they didn't have the leisure of stopping. Mage Killers still walked the woods.

Genji knew it was partly the fault of Tristan for their current predicament. Having let the Mage Killers go after discovering he was immortal ensured pursuit. It was now only a matter of time before they closed in. He knew Tristan would live a horrible life after they killed Beverlin, Aski and himself but Genji couldn't decide which would be better. Looking at the man carrying Aski, he wondered how the girl could feel comfortable enough to sleep with only a scrap of fabric between her and Tristan's armour. He didn't understand how the girl could be comfortable so quickly with a stranger.

'Tristan, why are we using such rugged terrain?' Genji asked climbing another small rise between the trees.

'It's the best course to stay ahead of the Mage

Killers,' Tristan replied scanning the forest ahead. Every move he made was cautious yet precise.

'How will they know which way we have gone? Beverlin took care of the tracks. We could be following parallel to the main road and they won't even know.'

Tristan stood dumbstruck. 'Forgive my complacency. I forget that I am leading a band of *Mages* at times.'

'We aren't all bad, Tristan,' Genji said. 'Don't let a few misdeeds by some unnamed Mages condemn us all.'

'I am still waiting to meet a Mage who could change my perspective.'

'You probably kill them before giving them the chance,' Beverlin said levelling her eyes on the Mage killer.

Glancing at Beverlin, Tristan's eyes took on a dangerous look. Quickly dislodging Aski, He made a mad dash towards the young Mage drawing his sword with his left hand. The sudden movements sent Beverlin's body into overdrive. Her breath caught in her throat as adrenalin pumped through her veins. Everything slowed for her and the threat of harm made her move without thought. Tracing the symbol for Earth in the air, she was about to speak the word of power when she found Tristan already upon her. His agility was incredible closing the gap between them in an instant. Knowing she couldn't produce any form of magic in time to stop the immortal Mage Killer, Beverlin closed her eyes to the imminent pain.

Tristan got his hand around the back of Beverlin's head just in time to take the knife through his wrist. He grunted as fresh pain lanced up his arm. The noise was not what Beverlin had expected and upon opening her eyes she saw Tristan spin around her throwing the sword with his good left hand. Tracing the line of his throw she was shocked to see a Mage Killer standing inches away from where Tristan's sword was lodged in a tree.

'Yerkiry,' Beverlin's voice vibrated around the

earthen symbol still fresh in the air. Roots sprung from the ground all around the attacker reaching up to grab at ankles and shins. With terrible slowness they crept up the screaming man's legs, crushing bones as they went. Trying to cut the roots away caused tree limbs to swing down and take hold of his wrists. More screams came from the man.

Dragging the blade from his wrist Tristan closed the gap to the Mage Killer. Placing a hand over the man's mouth, Tristan rammed the knife into his throat. Whispering hushed tones to the man that was Feldran, his life blood ebbed away. Finally his eyes rolled into the back of his head and Tristan let Feldran hang, suspended by the tree limbs and roots. Retrieving his sword, Tristan walked back to the others.

'Why did you kill him?' Beverlin asked. Her anger rolled through her body like a trembling volcano. 'That was my kill. He deserved to suffer.'

'And while the man *suffered,* his screams would have brought every Mage Killer nearby down upon us,' Tristan retaliated producing the same guile in his voice. 'As it is we need to move quickly. Many will have heard Feldran.' Tristan glared at Beverlin who looked deflated. 'Yes, the man had a name. Feldran. He was inexperienced in our ranks and had only two months ago ran away from his family's farm so that they had one less mouth to feed. He only joined and followed command because he got fed every day with us.'

'Why are you telling me this?' Beverlin asked, eyes almost tearing up.

'Hate is a curse when placed upon you by others,' Tristan said more calmly. 'If you need to hate make sure that you understand the feelings and the reason you hate. Don't just steal reasons from a history book.' Leaning down, Tristan gently picked up Aski once more. 'We aren't fighting. Just debating our beliefs,' he said to Aski who was becoming more worried with each word. This calmed her once more and she rested her head on Tristan's shoulder.

Beverlin was insulted by Tristan's words. 'Well, why

do you hate Mages then?' She called trying hard to find something better to say that may hurt him. Tristan didn't answer or turn back.

'If we've had enough fun let's move,' Genji said. 'From now on we follow the main roads from just within the forest.'

Chapter 7

Beverlin couldn't help but watch the Knight sitting across the camp, back against a tree. He was an enigma to her. History told her that Tristan was dangerous and would do anything to kill a Mage but from what she had seen it was the complete opposite. The flight through the forest gave her plenty of time to dwell on Tristan's words. They had sounded harsh and insulting even, when she was angry but now she'd had a chance to calm, the words were only direct and held actual merit.

Her mind whispered the Mage Killer had killed before and only allowed them to live because he was cursed and needed them. If this was not the case, would he have still shielded her from the throwing knife? Beverlin knew she would even now be lying dead and forgotten in the forest, her adventure only just begun. So, therefore, did the man deserve a thank you? Beverlin shook her head dislodging the thought from her mind. She wouldn't be thanking a man who had killed maybe hundreds of her kin for no real reason and then demanded help now that he needed them. Genji nudged her on the shoulder, the move causing her to jump. Too lost in thought was she to hear his approach.

'You don't need to be on edge, Beverlin,' Genji said smiling. 'I have a barrier up and Tristan is on our side. Do you still not trust him after saving your life?'

'He is a Mage Killer, Genji. He has killed before. How can you forget that?'

'I haven't forgotten but the man needs our help,' Genji said. 'The being that possessed him intrigues me. To my knowledge, no record exists that describes such a creature. I want to know about it. And don't forget, our quest is to kill Tristan.'

'What?' A small voice behind them sounded. Genji's shoulders dropped as he turned to look at the girl who only moments before was sleeping. 'You can't kill Tristan.'

'This was at the request of Tristan,' Genji tried to

say.

Aski's face puffed up. 'You can't kill him,' she yelled. Overwhelmed with emotions Aski fled into the forest. Tristan was quickly to his feet.

'No, wait,' Genji told him. 'I'll go. We have some things to talk about, anyway. I'll craft a small movable barrier for us so we'll be safe.' Tristan was about to argue but Genji raised his hand. 'Beverlin, make sure he doesn't leave.' Knowing Beverlin was definitely about to arc up over being left with the Mage Killer, Genji made a quick exit. He could hear Beverlin calling out that if Genji came back and she had been brutally murdered she would kill him.

Alone with the Knight, Beverlin slowly turned to look at the man. He was staring straight at her with a serious look on his face and she gave a brittle smile. Time seemed to pause around them as their eyes remained locked, Beverlin in a desperate battle to remain on top. Her strength broke and she looked away before glancing back moments later. Horrified, her eyes went wide seeing Tristan on his feet, walking towards her with the same serious look on his face.

'N... No, you don't need to get up,' Beverlin stammered slowly moving backwards.

With Tristan a metre away, her back came up against a tree. Still, the Knight didn't stop. He moved to within inches of her face, at the height of Beverlin's unease, before pausing.

'You think me only good for lying and killing?' Tristan said.

Beverlin had a hard time trying to determine if it was a statement or a question. 'Everything I have read about Mage Killers is just that. Death and terror on Mages.'

'That's just it,' Tristan's eyes looked disappointed. 'You *Mages* get all your information from books. You never break out into the world beyond to learn for yourself what is of true value.'

'And you know, *Killer*?' A flame was growing in Beverlin's stomach fuelling her courage to take on the man. 'The time I come from, long after today, Mages are an accepted part of the world and Mage killers can only be found in books. Be glad I even know of you at all.'

'What does it matter who is around today, tomorrow or a thousand years from now? In 10,000 years, the world may topple and all that we know could be dust.' Laughter sounded inside Tristan's mind. A laughter so ancient there could be only one source. 'And what is your problem?' Tristan said aloud.

'*Nothing at all,*' came the calm reply. '*Carry on.*'

'Noth...ing?' Beverlin said confused.

'Not you. Genji told you about the being that possessed me. Sometimes it talks. Right now it was laughing at me.'

'Because it knows you're wrong,' Beverlin smirked.

'Let me tell you a little story about why I am the way I am,' Tristan's tone became deadly. The close proximity only helped to enhance it. 'When I was but a child, younger than Aski, my parents and I were traveling down the main roads outside of Aradel in the north. I was riding in the back under the furs we were carting when a man hailed the cart down. Being friendly, caring folk, my parents stopped to help the man. One hour later, they had been strung up in the forest to drain their blood. The Mage, as it was, needed the blood to experiment with and learn more about blood magic. The man never knew I was there.

At the age of 14, the village I came to live in, after being orphaned, was destroyed by a Mage. He had been roughed up by some drunks after being caught cheating at knuckle dice. Feeling humbled and mistreated, he set loose a fire demon on the village. It killed without mercy. Over half the villagers died that day and nothing was done about the Mage. He just left the villagers to pick up the pieces as if nothing happened.

Two years later and the village didn't exist anymore. No one wanted to live in a village that was full of such terrible memories. The following years were hard. I found my way back to the capital city Aradel and

102

fended for myself. I was alone, vulnerable to the weather and hungry all the time. Soon I got to watching the coming and goings of a nobleman's daughter. No matter where she went or what she did she always drew attention. Gathering my courage I stole into her room late one night...'

'You stole into her room?' Beverlin was disgusted. 'I had expected no less from you. Let me guess, you had your way with her and a big, bad Mage chased you away.'

Tristan smiled shaking his head. 'The girl was well known for her wasteful nature. Every morning, large bowls of uneaten food were thrown to the dogs to fight over. I snuck in only to get a share before they did. The big, bad Mage as you called him was also the nobleman himself. He bound me in rings of pure energy and tortured me for almost a month. He used his craft to constrict my insides inflicting agonizing pain until I blacked out only to have me healed and start again. When I was finally set free, I had not been healed of the last wounds. I was cared for by a priest of the old religion. It was almost a year before I was back to myself again and almost another before I had expressed my thanks to him, minute for minute.

Mages had a strong strangle hold on the population since the reign of the Elven King. It was almost a general consensus that there was nothing anyone could do to even the odds. Imagine my surprise when I saw a man take down two Mages who were about to execute another man, in a matter of seconds. I was in awe of his strength and maybe even a little scared of his character. Durin, leader of the Mage Killers had inspired in me the strength to fight back. I know where my anger comes from and why I cannot fully trust a Mage.'

'We aren't all this way,' Beverlin said. She was feeling foolish for her comments a moment ago and sorry for the life Tristan had lead. 'The time I am from, Mages have integrated into every day society. Sure, you will find a rotten apple or two and there are laws that protect the populace against them but on the whole,

Mages are good.'

'You asked what I believe is of true value. I believe it is all around you. Joy and laughter, love and bonding. Life should be enjoyed and the good times shared with everyone. I believe things like hate, fighting, insults, and corruption are not necessary.'

With a smirk, Beverlin thought how hypocritical Tristan's beliefs were. She started to laugh with such mirth, tears filled her eyes. Tristan saw the amusement for his inner most feelings and thought a little retaliation was in order. As Beverlin started to calm and tilted her head back down, Tristan moved in. His first kiss was warm and slightly moist, Beverlin's lips soft. The two sets of lips felt as if they had melded together and Tristan couldn't believe he left it 28 years to try. Realizing his eyes were shut he opened them to find Beverlin looking back at him. Her body had gone stiff and her rich, blue eyes were wide with shock. The sting of the slap that followed was another feeling Tristan wouldn't forget, the memory to be stored with fondness.

'How dare you!' Beverlin almost screamed. Her rage was starting to take over.

'I thought it was something you *expected* of me,' Tristan replied smugly. 'You were so busy laughing at my beliefs that I thought I should honour yours.'

Beverlin was still fuming but Tristan's words cut her intensity down. 'That still doesn't give you the right.' With a dirty look she moved to the other side of the camp and made sure he knew she wasn't going to be giving him attention. Tristan smiled once more and turned to see Aski running back from the forest. She wrapped her small arms around him and cried into his mantle. Tristan started to stroke her hair soothingly.

'Did we miss anything,' Genji asked walking into the camp.

Tristan shook his head before looking down at Aski. 'You going to be okay, little one?'

Aski gave him another strange look as she did back at Genji's house when they last spoke. Tristan couldn't grasp it's meaning or what must be running through the young girl's mind after such news but he would help her through it any way she needed. Finally, Aski nodded her head with a smile.

'I'll be strong for you,' Aski told her Knight.

The camp was quiet as the cool breeze of twilight coursed through the trees. The first day was now behind them and Genji was glad to see it go. On numerous occasions, he had skirted the camps of the Mage Killers, watching them, learning their ways. History books were nothing compared to firsthand experience and if ever he was in a tight spot Genji wanted to know his enemy. He knew it couldn't get tighter than it was now.

Looking to the Immortal Knight, Genji wondered, not for the first time, what he had gotten himself into. A possibly futile venture to find a sword that falls from existence which may or may not have the power to kill a creature not listed in any book anywhere. To make things worse, the Knight had goaded the nastiest group in the realm to hunt him down. Genji knew they wouldn't give up. Tristan, however, looked as calm as ever, sleeping against the roots of a large tree, hand resting on the blade of his longsword leaning against his shoulder. Genji couldn't understand how he could portray such a sense of calm with all that was going on.

Shifting his gaze to Beverlin, Genji saw the polar opposite to Tristan. A dark aura surrounded her spewing forth a sense of malice and hostility towards the Knight. Genji knew that she didn't hold Mage killers in the highest regard but this was going far beyond that feeling. Slowly, her gaze shifted to stare straight at Genji, the same daggers pointed at him. This gave him a sense that he had done something terrible to upset her going well beyond a simple matter of dislike. Fighting the look for only a moment Genji turned away.

Rising from his spot by the fire, Genji walked over to Tristan. Tucked in behind the knight at the side of the tree was Aski snoring softly. The girl hadn't left Tristan's side since she found out he was to die. Genji was about to speak when Tristan raised a finger to his lips, motioning to the sleeping girl. At least the knight was caring for the girl. Kneeling, Genji placed a hand on the girl's brow. Warmth rushed through his fingertips putting Aski in a deep sleep. Her breathing changed, getting stronger.

'She won't wake now,' Genji told the knight.

'What did you do to her?' Tristan asked frowning.

'Do not fear. You may be her knight but she is still in my care. I put her into a deeper sleep allowing her body to relax and recover after the long day. We still have a long way to go.'

'She seems calm after learning my fate?' Tristan said, a question hidden within.

'What is your relationship to her?' Genji asked ignoring Tristan's question.

'I am her knight,' Tristan replied. 'I met her when you brought me into your home and offered my services because of her history.'

'She believes you to be her brother,' Genji said. 'You share the same looks, name and call her the same pet name.'

'We've been through this, Genji. You aren't even from my time. There is no way it could be me. You know this.'

'I know, I know,' Genji replied. 'Still, far weirder things have happened throughout history. I needed to be sure.'

'My life has been a hard one but never have I had a sibling,' Tristan said softly. Genji could see the emotion in his reply but didn't push it.

'You wanted to know what I said to Aski that made her accept your fate?' Tristan nodded. 'I asked her if she was put in a situation where she was always in pain, always wanting to escape, would she not do everything she could to free herself. When she went quiet and reflected on her recent history as I knew she would I told her that is your situation right now. I

106

explained what happened to you. She knows your struggles and will be there for you. That is the type of person she is. Make sure you are someone who deserves it.'

'What's that supposed to mean?' Tristan became defensive.

'Calm down,' Genji replied putting his hands out in a calming manner. 'I left you with Beverlin for a matter of minutes. When I came back there was an unease in the air and she's worn a terrible look on her face since. You're lucky you're immortal because the daggers getting thrown from her eyes would have lain a normal man low.'

Tristan smiled. 'She was rude to me so I thought to teach her a lesson.'

'What did you do,' there was dread in Genji's voice as he pictured all the cruel things the knight could have done.

'I kissed her,' Tristan said shrugging his shoulders.

'You kissed her?' Genji blurted out louder than he meant to, eyes wide. He looked back at Beverlin to see she got an idea on the topic of conversation. Her cheeks puffed out and she looked away annoyed. Genji laughed. 'You kissed her. How did that come about?'

'I told her a little bit about myself and how I came to be a Mage Killer. She laughed in my face so I kissed her. There is a little more to the reason behind it but that was the trigger,' Tristan told him.

Genji suddenly grew serious. 'So how are we going to solve this?'

'I was just going to let her stew over it a bit then possibly apologize when she calmed down.'

'I mean you and I,' Genji said. 'You kiss my woman and you expect me to just let it go?'

Tristan's face drained of colour. 'I didn't realise and never would have dishonoured anyone that way.'

Genji could only keep up the facade for moments longer. His face cracked up and laughter rang out through the camp. Tristan looked confused. 'I jest, Tristan,' Genji smiled. 'Beverlin is a free woman. It was still a dangerous move. How did she take it?'

'She slapped me,' Tristan was breathing easier. 'Now she is in a mood.'

'She may be for a long while. I'm starting to like you more and more, knight.' Tristan was stunned by the comment as Genji walked over to Beverlin. 'I just heard what happened,' Genji said trying to conceal a laugh. Beverlin levelled her eyes on him. 'Don't worry, Bev. I won't tell Bran.'

Beverlin's mouth dropped and her eyes became wild. 'Energia,' she growled as she drew a quick circle in the air. A strong pulse punched Genji in the stomach, knocking the wind from him and sending him tumbling across the dirt. He lay there unmoving. Tristan made to get up. 'He will live,' Beverlin told Tristan giving him a look that challenged him to intercede. Tristan laid back and spoke no more of it.

Two more days travelling saw the group to the edge of the forest. There had been little trouble from the Mage Killers that were hunting them having kept to the high roads and unused pathways. On occasion, Tristan would hold up a fist, signalling everyone to be quiet. They would hide 20 metres off the main road and watch as caravans and travellers, entertainers and rogues passed by. Some Mage Killers who were putting in as little effort as possible passed on the main roads also. They were not alert for the fugitives within arm's reach and therefore posed little threat.

Save for Aski, no one was speaking to each other after the first evening. Paws, for the most part, slept within her hood, barely stirring at all. The young girl wandered along beside her knight looking for things to talk about. Anything to break the unease that had descended upon them. She brought up the creatures of the woods, the variety of leaves, the different colours in the stone and dirt compared to Genji's home, and how hard and boring it must be only using carts and horses to move things. Normally she would get a rather vague answer always resulting in a failure to continue the line of conversation except for the carriage. Tristan had been intrigued by what else people could possibly use that wasn't derived from magic. Aski had been happy just talking about her childish understanding of science and the power of automobiles, motor boats and planes. She was even more delighted when Tristan continued to show genuine interest and ask even more questions.

Too soon the trees started to diminish and Aski gazed in wonder at the sea of sand. School had been the only place she'd seen a desert and even then it was only in pictures. The breeze that blew across the yellow, hazy landscape was warm to the skin and smelt of salt. Teetering at the edge of the forest and the start of the desert, Aski felt the two opposing environments clashing against each other. Sweat had already started to bead upon her brow even though it was late in the day. Genji saw the wonder in her eyes and smiled.

'The Great Desert of Adelside spans from here to the Northern coast at Siren's Pass,' Genji informed her. 'It is hard to imagine that you grew up in Boerus at the western coast line of this desert.'

'I didn't grow up in a desert,' Aski argued.

'No, you didn't,' Genji admitted smiling once more. 'The Boerus you know is full of flora and fauna. A lot will happen over the next thousand years that will change this landscape and that of our ultimate destination, Pintosia. They will inevitably swap landscapes. Desert for grasslands, grasslands for desert.'

Stunned by this new bit of knowledge, Aski wanted to know more. 'What caused the lands to change so much?'

'Adelside was for natural progression,' Genji told her. He realized just how much he sounded like the lecturers at the academy. 'A large underground river system fed the forest. The sand as well is rich in nutrients that gave strength to the forest. If you think of the forest that you passed today, that has only existed for the last hundred years. Nature is magnificent that way.'

'And Pintosia?' Aski asked enthusiastically. 'Where did the desert come from?'

Genji was filled with sorrow at the question. Even Beverlin looked down. 'There was once a seer in the castle city Pinto. He had a prophecy of war and the battle of good and evil. It was important in the history of Mages but a sad event none the less. The land never recovered.'

'Would you tell me about the prophecy?' Aski asked, her little mind imagining many different events.

'Not right now,' Genji replied to her dismay. Aski turned to Tristan.

'He speaks of events that haven't come to pass,' the knight replied. He was feeling ill at ease about the topic and sought to change it. 'We make camp here tonight. The desert is a cold place to be stuck in after sunset and we still have a good day's travel ahead of us.'

Aski knew the night was going to be another boring waste of time. No one communicated with each other and she was starting to grow tired of the silence. Seeing Genji setting up a barrier for their protection, Aski decided to accompany him.

'Is it very different from when you cast an elemental spell?' Aski asked coming up behind him.

Lost in concentration, Genji almost missed the question all together. 'What was that?'

'The barrier,' Aski started again. 'Is it very hard to cast?'

'It is a similar process to elemental magic but vastly different up here,' Genji tapped his forehead. Genji then pulled out his retractable staff. 'There are two ways someone could conceal themselves. The first is in the Shadow discipline using a staff as a catalyst.' Genji raised the staff and a small light enveloped him turning him completely invisible. Aski giggled and clapped her hands. 'The only problem with this as a group,' Genji continued while invisible. 'Is that any noise made will still be heard around you.'

'So you use a different spell to hide both form and sound,' Aski said hearing a little squeak.

'You're very intelligent, Aski,' Genji remarked. The wording even sounded like one of his lecturers. 'Many people learning Mage Craft wouldn't jump to that conclusion straight away.'

Aski enjoyed the praise and decided to keep to herself the fact Paws supplied her with the answer. 'Thank you,' she said with a smile. 'So what... umm... discipline do the barriers come under?' Aski asked finding the right word after a moment.

'It doesn't quiet have a discipline of its own,' Genji said falling into the role of a teacher. He wanted to show off more than answer Aski's question. 'Barriers are an off shot of the elemental discipline. Instead of a known element, though, barriers feed off the Mage's will power thus there is no need for a symbol or word of power. It is a very complex and very dangerous form of magic if used wrong.'

Two more squeaks came from within Aski's hood and the dawning of understanding spread across her face. Closing her eyes she started to move her hands slowly in front of herself. Genji was shocked as lines of a barrier started to weave around Aski. She started to fade from view and Genji lounged forward without thinking. Grabbing her arm he almost pulled her from the ground.

'What are you doing? I said it was dangerous,' Genji said with heat in his voice.

Aski started to grip at his fingers trying to tear herself away. Her whole demeanour changed and she fell back into her shell, desperate to get away from Genji's touch. Seeing her distress Genji let go of her arm and Aski scrambled back.

'I'm sorry, Aski,' Genji said dropping to his knees to show he wasn't a threat. 'You scared me and I reacted hastily.'

Aski didn't respond. She was still processing the events moments before and calming down. Her body was trembling softly, rolling out from her stomach.

'You don't understand the dangers involved with barrier Mage Craft,' Genji continued. 'You could have cast yourself out of this plane.'

'I had instruction,' Aski said, still not wanting to give up the fact Paws was explaining it to her. Paws had watched Genji over the time of his stay. He had also read the Mages thoughts using the link Genji had with Aski and had learned a lot.

'No, the information I gave you weren't instructions into the depths this magic needs. It isn't like real elemental magic that you picked up within a matter of moments,' Genji sounded harsh but was worried and knew the consequences of magic better than most. 'I only want what is best for you. I want you to be safe.'

'I know you do but...' Aski stopped mid-sentence, her mouth slightly ajar. There was fear in her eyes.

Genji followed her gaze to find a Mage Killer standing barely metres away looking around and shaking his head. Placing a finger to his lips, Aski nodded and remained silent. Genji then gestured for her to inform the others. As Aski crept away Genji got lower to the ground. The interruption by Aski meant the barrier was not fully erect. Partial sounds, though barely audible, could still get through and there would be patches where the camp could be visible. This would be the cause for the Mage Killer's confusion. Genji drew the symbol for water and waited. Should the Knight find them Genji was ready to fill his lungs with water, drowning the man without a sound.

A pat on the back caused Genji to jump. Tristan had snuck up behind him and was now crouched alongside. Tristan indicated to the man and spoke in hushed tones. 'Let me deal with him.'

'I'm already prepared,' Genji replied thinking Tristan to believe him useless.

Tristan shook his head. 'He is like a brother,' Tristan said sadly. 'I must be the one.'

Narrowing his eyes, Genji looked hard at Tristan. He understood the depth of the decision he was making and with this action trusted the ex-Mage Killer completely.

Tristan watched Giri hoping that it wouldn't come

down to violence. If Shard was his longest friend in the Mage Killers, Giri was a close second. He was Shard's cousin, though quite opposite in personality. Where Shard was loud, Giri was quiet. Where Shard joked, Giri was serious. They were the only two friends Tristan could need.

'Don't turn around,' Tristan pleaded.

As if in defiance to the plea, Giri turned and caught sight of the camp, Genji and Tristan. His eyes went wide and he hesitated. Tristan looked away sadly cursing under his breath.

Watching the scene play out and seeing no movement from either side, Genji decided he needed to step in. He didn't want the Mage Killer to come to his senses first and giveaway their location. 'Ju...'

Before Genji could get the full word out to cast his spell, Tristan was charging at Giri. With his sword parallel to the ground, point forward, it punched through the stunned man's chest, erupting in blood from Giri's back. Tristan cradled the back of the man's head lowering him gently to the ground as blood pumped from his mouth.

'Rest, brother,' Tristan said softly. 'You die untouched by magic in the line of duty. I will dine with you soon.' Giri's eyes closed and his body slumped to the side. Tristan left the sword where it was, standing above his friend and turned on Genji. 'I told you he was mine!' Tristan growled.

'I made a decision in the moment when you failed to move,' Genji replied with an edge to his voice. 'The outcome was always going to be the same. Mourn your friend and let me complete this barrier.'

Tristan gave him a lasting glare before turning to tend to Giri. Continuing with the barrier, Genji completed it quickly so that there were no more intrusions. He did make sure to weave into the barrier access for Tristan to return once he had buried his friend.

Aski watched the events as she held to Beverlin. She was frightened of the man seeking to bring harm down upon her and her family as she saw them. Beverlin smiled for the first time in days as she placed an arm around Aski. When the fighting was done, Aski let out a sigh of relief. She continued to watch Genji fortify the area and found it strange that Tristan treated the man so gently, giving him all funeral rights. When Tristan was saying his final goodbyes, he poured a small amount of liquid from a hip flask on the unmarked grave.

'Why is he treating the enemy so kindly,' Aski asked Beverlin.

Beverlin pursed her lips before answering. 'He told you that he was once allied to the enemy. He still has feelings of loyalty to them and therefore he will always give a part of himself to them. You can't trust him completely.'

Aski looked saddened by the comment. 'He vowed to protect me.'

'And he most likely will never break that but somewhere in his heart there is still a Mage Killer. Don't turn your back.'

Sitting silently, Aski just nodded.

Chapter 8

The dawn mist hovered at the edge of the desert like a barrier into the unknown. Little could be seen beyond the first metre outside camp, different shades on the surface of the mist tricking the eyes into thinking things were moving inside. It started to set in only two weeks prior for more extended periods as the days rolled by becoming cooler.

Beverlin shivered and shifted closer to their small fire. The mediocre warmth she gained felt like heaven. It was like those first moments sliding into a hot bath, letting the waters soak deep into the skin. She already noticed the men were up and moving about but she had no wish to interact or even allow them to know she was awake so she continued to feign sleep. Listening to their conversation she couldn't understand how Genji was so taken by the Mage Killer. They were natural enemies but right now acted as though they were lifelong friends. Beverlin knew the truth though. The man was arrogant, abusive and a murderer. It didn't matter that he was nice on the outside. It was all an act to accomplish his own goals. Beverlin made a point to watch him closely in the future.

A flash crossed her mind of the kiss. No one had ever kissed her like that before. No one had ever kissed her before. Always too busy with study to have time for boys Beverlin was still a young woman and dreamed of romantic rendezvous and stolen kisses in passing. She had not once thought the person to steal her first kiss would be someone who hunted and killed her kind. *It was warm, soft... nice even,'* Beverlin's mind stated running the kiss through her thoughts once more.

'Argh, No it wasn't!' she said aloud slamming a fist into the soft earth. Genji and Tristan looked around and Beverlin knew she was found out. Rolling over she levelled them with a deadly gaze. The men didn't question her but looked away once more. She listened in on their conversation to ensure they weren't discussing her.

'Going to be a long winter, this one,' Tristan said to Genji looking for a subject to discuss. He offered the Mage a chunk of dark bread and cheese.

'Thank you,' Genji took the food. 'Hopefully, this quest will be over by then and I can lounge by the fire in my home.' Genji started eating not pursuing further conversation. He'd spent a restless night thinking over the events of the night before and knew he had done wrong by Tristan. The man had done everything he could to show he was trustworthy and for a moment only Genji believed he trusted him. This was only a false belief as within a moment of Tristan not acting towards an enemy he stepped in, no trust at all. 'I'm sorry.' The words were spoken so softly Genji doubted Tristan heard them. From Beverlin's vantage, she missed the fact Genji said anything at all. The Knight took another bite and Genji looked forward again, his courage gone.

'The man was a brother to me in everything but sharing the same parents,' Tristan said breaking the silence. His eyes were on a point beyond the mist he couldn't actually see. 'The man whose weapon I carry was his cousin. They were my only friends in the ranks of the Mage Killers. It has been circumstance alone that brought me to this point. We all chose our own outcome.'

Happy that they weren't talking about her, Beverlin couldn't believe Tristan's spite for Genji. It hadn't been Genji's fault the enemy had shown up and it certainly wasn't Genji's fault the man now lay dead. Yet why was it so hard for Tristan to let the matter rest. He told Aski that he wasn't a Mage Killer anymore but Beverlin saw the truth. The fact he couldn't let such matters as the death of an enemy drop showed it all. Beverlin just hoped Aski would be safe.

Looking at the sleepy eyed girl as she started to stir, Beverlin saw that a wardrobe change was in order. A desert was no place for a tattered dress. The forest wasn't the place either but the need for haste forced the situation. The branches had torn small holes in the

116

dress and dirt and grass stains could be seen covering the fabric. Rising to her feet she looked at the men once more.

'If any of you follow us I will see to it you die slow and painfully,' Beverlin stated.

With Genji and Tristan now looking confused, Beverlin motioned for Aski to follow her. Curious, the young girl did as she was bid. Paws following close behind. Beverlin waited on the other side of a screen of tree and Bush and as Aski entered she smiled.

'Has Genji told you anything about Alchemy, Aski?'

Aski shook her head.

Alchemy is the discipline in magic that allows you to change something from one form into a different form. It involves breaking things down on an elemental scale and building things back up again piece by piece.'

'Like how Genji built my room on top of his house?' Aski asked.

'Exactly,' Beverlin confirmed with a smile.

Paws chirped three times and Beverlin noticed Aski leaning in as if she were listening. Watching the small girls expression change from intrigue to enlightenment almost cemented the idea that Paws was talking.

'So, using a transmonation circle as a chrysalis...' Aski started.

'...Transmutation circle as a catalyst,' Beverlin corrected.

Aski thought for a moment. 'Yes, a catalyst for the magic to pass through you can change things into other things as long as they're of equal matter.'

'That's correct... *Paws,*' Beverlin said. She giggled watching the small girls face compute what she had just said, Aski's jaw dropping. 'Does Genji know you have this connection with Paws?'

Aski just shook her head.

'He always was slow to catch on,' Beverlin told her. 'Don't worry, I won't tell him. Have you ever been to a hot spring?'

'No.' There was sadness in Aski's voice. 'West of where I live is a really famous hot spring in the forest.

117

It was said to have strong healing properties. My dad... My real dad wanted to take me and my brother there but he passed away suddenly. After that I never had the opportunity.'

'I've been to those hot springs and they were very refreshing. How about we recreate them right here? There's a good half an hour before the fog fully lifts and we can move on.'

Aski's grin was beaming at the thought. 'That would be fun,' she said enthusiastically.

Beverlin quickly drew two small transmutation circles in the ground. Through trial and error she realised that a large circle was never needed when working with big objects as long as you accept the boundary of the circle doesn't always go straight up and down. She was able to fold the energy into a tube like shape that encompassed a larger area encircling back underneath. With this she could work with any area she wanted. Touching the first circle, she pictured the hot springs in her mind and willed them into existence. The circle started to glow as grass and dirt, rocks and trees, all started to disappear and the hot springs took shape. Drawing oxygen from the air and hydrogen from the trees, Beverlin filled the springs with water. For a final touch, Beverlin manipulated the dirt and rock underground to form a tunnel system for molten lava to pass through and heat the water to a perfect temperature.

Aski's eyes were full of wonder watching the magic take effect. Though she had a foot in the door she was still so innocent to all of it. Racing over she felt the water and immediately pulled her hand back. 'It's cold,' she detested. 'I'm not getting in that.'

Beverlin laughed once more. 'The water will be warm soon enough. Until then take your clothes off and place them on the second circle. I'll change them into something more suitable for the desert crossing.'

Aski was hesitant at first to remove her clothing but after Beverlin had placed her clothes in a pile on the circle, Aski done the same. Beverlin felt sorry watching the inner turmoil of the girl play out. She knew it was a risk to ask Aski to disrobe with her past but knew that if the girl lived forever in the shadows of her demons she would never be free. Best to have it occur in a safe environment to encourage the small flame inside to chase the shadows away. When Aski had removed her clothes, Beverlin was touched by a completely different type of sadness. All over the girl's body, normally hidden under the clothing, were small scars and even the remnants of healing bruises from her turmoil. Beverlin couldn't think of anything to say at the time so stayed quiet.

Reaching down, Beverlin changed the pile of clothing into light coloured, hooded robes, long sleeved shirts and pants. She looked over the material and assessed the weight of the cotton, as well as thickness. Happy, she placed them back down.

'That'll be too hot for the desert,' Aski complained. 'I don't want to wear that.'

'The most important thing in the desert besides water is staying out of the sun. The clothing needs to cover your whole body or you will get sunburns and dehydrate faster. Also the cotton material will help keep sweat on your body longer so it helps regulate your body's temperature. These clothes may be a little uncomfortable but they will help keep you alive. You'll find I added an extra cooling effect to the material as well.'

Beverlin walked to the springs and tested the water. It was just the right temperature and she started to get excited, not having been able to wash these last few days. Placing both hands on the surface of the water she imbued the hot spring with strong healing affects. Aski won't realize while she's in the water but the scars across her body will be gone by the time she got out.

'Come on, the water's perfect now,' Beverlin called to the younger girl. She felt a rush of pleasure ripple over her skin as she slipped into the warm water. Instantly, she felt her tired muscles rejuvenating.

Aski didn't completely trust that the water had

heated up enough to be warm but dipping her toes in she was pleasantly surprised. She slipped in quickly and reared up straight away. The heat seemed far hotter as it touched Aski's cold skin. Paws stayed cautiously away altogether.

'Ease into it, Aski,' Beverlin told her. 'You will get used to it quickly.' Beverlin watched the girl slide into the water. A strong motherly instinct had started to grow within her and watching the girl float around a while longer, called her over.

'Let me wash your back and get the tangles out of your hair,' Beverlin said.

Aski blushed as the older woman started to wash her. Her own mother had never done anything like this with her and she started to feel sad. Tears formed in her eyes and ran down her cheeks.

'What's wrong,' Beverlin asked worried she'd done something.

Aski voice quivered as she spoke. 'Why didn't my mother love me?' Fresh tears now coming in great sobs.

A knot formed in Beverlin's throat and she pulled the girl into an embrace. 'I'm sure she did in her own way.'

'Then why didn't she stop him?'

The words were so full of sadness; Beverlin couldn't help but tear up with her. She thought about the question but couldn't find a suitable answer. She didn't know how to ease the girl's emotional pain so thought to distract her. 'Want me to show you another magic trick.'

Aski slowly brought herself back from her emotional outburst. Wiping her eyes she nodded.

'Then dunk your head under the water and get your hair wet,' Beverlin instructed.

Aski did as she was told and came up with her short, autumn brown hair plastered to her face. Beverlin giggled as the girl tried frantically to wipe it away.

'Oh this will never do,' Beverlin said. She traced an upward facing triangle in the air with a line crossing over the top third of it. 'Ready for the magic... Ody.'

Beverlin said the word of power for air and instantly gusts of wind started to circle through Aski's hair, drying it and removing the knots. The air started to tickle the top of Aski's head and small giggles burst from her mouth as she shook her head to get away from the invisible tickler. As the air started to die away Beverlin used the last of the magic to smooth her hair and set it into a bob. She noticed that Aski's hair had grown almost to her shoulders. 'Did you like that?'

Aski grinned. 'It was fun. Can I try it?'

'On me?' Beverlin was worried the girl didn't have full control and may rip her hair completely out.

'Please. I'll be gentle,' Aski said. Her eyes melted Beverlin's will and finally the older woman gave in ducking her head under the water for a moment. With a squeal of excitement Aski drew the same triangle formation into the air. '...'

'Ody,' Beverlin supplied.

Aski pictured just what she wanted to happen and focused the same way she did when producing flames. 'Ody.' Winds stronger than Beverlin's engulfed the woman's hair. She tried hard to keep a straight face but the wind pulled at her hair as if someone had grabbed a bunch of it and was dragging it back. A soft squeal sounded from Paws. 'Ody,' Aski said once again and the winds died back in power. 'Paws just gave me better insight into control. Sorry about that.'

The feelings that now ran over Beverlin's scalp were like a massage soothing the pain from a moment before. She could almost fall asleep to it. A commotion from camp interrupted the feeling and a little annoyed Beverlin came out of her relaxed state. 'Best let the wind die off now. Sounds like the boys are starting to get impatient.'

Aski broke her focus on the air and soon the wind dissipated to nothing more than a soft breeze. Beverlin started to climb out of the water just as Tristan ran into the area.

'We have Ma...' Seeing Beverlin naked before him caught Tristan off guard. His mind went blank as his gaze traced her smooth, womanly curves to rest on the soft pelt at the beginning of her legs. Beverlin too, stood frozen on the spot.

'Morning, Tristan,' Aski said seemingly at ease that a man stood so close while she wore no clothes. Aski still saw Tristan as her brother and she was always comfortable with him.

Aski's greeting brought Beverlin out of her shock. With cheeks flushed she traced a circle with two lines in the centre that quartered it. 'Khavary,' she invoked the power of darkness. A black mist settled over Tristan's eyes rendering him blind. 'How dare you enter while we were taking a bath!' Beverlin Screamed.

Lowering his head, Tristan continued what he was going to say. 'I apologise. While you were getting ready I had a scout around. We have a large group of Mage Killers heading our way. They will be going to Boerus. Genji doesn't believe the barrier will hold so we need to leave now. We will move in an arc around the desert. They won't chase a Mage in these conditions without proper supplies and will beat us to town but we'll be safe.'

'Give us a moment to dress,' was all Beverlin said. As she moved towards the clothes she paused. Walking up to Tristan she slapped him hard in the face causing Aski to flinch. Tristan reached out to defend himself as Beverlin started to walk away and still blind managed only to slap Beverlin on her butt. A small yelp escaped her lips and she turned on Tristan once more. 'I so hope that I'm the one to find the sword. There won't be any time to say your goodbyes.'

'You and me both,' Tristan replied.

The girls got dressed quickly and started to walk away from the hot spring. Beverlin took one last look at it knowing that she didn't have time to dismantle it. She will have changed history by leaving the hot spring which was one of the most fundamental rules to avoid. Still reeling from Tristan's intrusion and thinking of the conversation she was having with Aski in the water she turned to the girl.

'One day you will have the chance to kill your demons,' Beverlin said. 'Make sure to never back down. Me, Genji... even Tristan, have your back. I know it's expected but a parent may not always have the ability to love a child. That's not on you. We love you. You are truly special.'

Aski forced a smile.

The trek across the desert was tiring and Genji forced a stop during the midday hours. Erecting a tent through the use of alchemy, the group settled in the shade to wait out the worst of the heat blazing down from the sun.

The Mage Killers missed their departure by fifteen minutes. So that they didn't attract any attention while moving over the warming sands, Tristan had the group hide behind a large dune and watch the Mage Killers ride by. At least 70 of the enemy rode from the forest with a number of pack animals carrying water and supplies. Genji knew they would have a hard time securing a boat at Boerus with the enemy bunkered down in the harbor town.

Genji changed his clothing into the same set up as Beverlin and Aski but he felt more affected by the heat than the girls looked. A heat rash had started around his neck area that irritated him. Reaching up, Genji tugged at his collar to expel excess heat that was building around his body. Genji offered to do the same for Tristan but he refused the help of magic once more. Said he often travelled the desert in full armour.

'Aren't you hot under all those clothes, Aski?' Genji finally asked the girl.

'No, the clothes Beverlin made for me are rather cool,' Aski replied with a smile.

Genji turned to Beverlin questioning her with his eyes.

Beverlin just shrugged. 'I made them out of cotton as you did. The quality of your fabric mustn't be up to scratch.'

Grumbling Genji looked away. He didn't see the sly

wink between the two girls. As the sun passed its zenith and moved an hours more towards the west, Genji deconstructed the tent. The heat pulsing from the sand was hotter than before. It soaked in the sun's rays building its reserves to make the second half of the trip more uncomfortable than the morning. Genji continued to tug at his collar, much to the amusement of the girls.

Now with the sun partially covered by the distant sea, Boerus was in sight. The journey through the desert had been uneventful though a close call almost ended them. Walking along the top of a dune Paws had spied a small group of Mage Killers resting out of the sun. With a warning to Aski they were able to backtrack and avoid the danger.

'What's the plan,' Genji asked Tristan as he watched the city from a safe vantage. At the gates to the town Mage killers were checking anyone that entered trying to locate the fugitives.

'We go through the front. You and Beverlin will be my captives. Aski will be free to wander as she is still a child,' Tristan replied casually. Beverlin scoffed at the thought of being Tristan's captive but said nothing. There was no point trying to argue with the knight.

'You do see the guards right?' Genji shook his head. 'I'm sure you were known well enough to be recognized.'

'That's why I...' Tristan looked to be having difficulty forming the words.

'Spit it out. We are all too invested to hold anything back now.'

'I want you to craft me a Mage Hunter helm,' Tristan said seriously.

Beverlin's breath caught in her throat. 'I don't know what's more alarming. You asking for help through magic or you wanting to impersonate a Mage Hunter.'

'I haven't heard the term used,' Genji admitted causing Tristan to give a grim look.

'You never did care much for the histories,' Beverlin shook her head. 'Here you are gallivanting across the countryside with a murderer and a child and you don't know the strengths the enemy holds.'

'Then tell me what's needed,' Genji demanded. He was starting to get agitated always feeling useless in these situations.

'It will take too long,' Tristan said. 'Beverlin. You'll have to craft them.'

Beverlin looked concerned. 'Do you really believe you can pull it off?'

'It's all we have. Don't forget the hand restraints.'

Beverlin pursed her lips. No one moved for a minute before she finally gave in. 'If you get us killed, I will kill you, knight.' Tristan just smiled. Bending low, Beverlin drew her third transmutation circle for the day. Sand was a wonderful substance to work with as the fine grains made it easier to shift protons and electrons around to create different elements. She visualized one of ten helmets she'd seen in a history book and started to transmute the material. Like vines creeping out of the ground, steel tendrils started to grow and weave together. They melded into one another to create a perfectly smooth surface.

Genji was intrigued by the mystery surrounding the Hunters and the significance of the helm that he watched on intently. He wasn't impressed with the final result. Cylindrical in shape with a slight wedge where the nose would be. The helm had two slits for vision and a gold ring that ran around the top like a circlet. Almost taking up the whole front of the helm, a ring of blue coloured steel indicated it was made for a Mage Killer.

Tristan looked dismayed. 'Barung is going to be a tough role to play.'

'They're all evil,' Beverlin said kicking the helmet over to Tristan. Next she created two sets of solid iron gloves, tossing one set to Genji. 'Put these on,' she told him before doing so with her own. Looking up from the gloves, a shiver ran up her spine, spying Tristan in the Mage Hunter helm.

Tristan had a short chain he attached to a cross bar

that held each pair of gloves together. The gloves were designed to take away a Mage's ability to move their hands and draw symbols. It made Mages easier to transport. After both sets of gloves were secure Tristan gave the chain a small tug. 'Come along now. Your torture awaits,' Tristan's voice had become deep as it echoed around the helm, almost demonic. Beverlin didn't entirely trust it was in jest. 'Come along, Aski. Keep close and I'll keep you safe.'

Aski bounced along beside the knight. 'You look funny in that helmet.'

Tristan stopped for a moment to kneel beside the girl. 'You can't talk to me for a while. The people that showed up at Genji's house are guarding this city. We need to get inside and we all have to pretend that Genji and Beverlin have been captured. You have to pretend to hate me. I may do or say things that aren't true but it is all to keep us safe. Okay?'

Aski looked worried but understood what was about to happen. 'I watched a movie where something like this happened. I know what to do.'

'Whatever that is, I hope it spoke true. Now, get back with Genji and Beverlin.' Aski hurried to Genji's side, clutching at his arm. This made Genji feel closer to the girl for choosing him over Beverlin.

As they started to move towards Boerus Genji leaned in to Beverlin. 'How bad are the Mage Hunters?'

'They were the worst of the Mage Killers beside Durin. Only 10 ever existed. Their soul occupancy was to hunt down hard to find or highly skilled Mages and subdue them. Sometimes they tortured them for information but mostly they killed on sight. There was no equal in the ranks of Mage killers for skill and experience.'

'They do sound bad,' Genji smiled. 'Glad we have one on our side.'

'Don't mock, Genji. They're dangerous. Even for someone with your skill.'

'Shut yer holes,' Tristan bellowed as they approached the gates.

126

Instantly, the Mages went silent. Upon seeing a Mage Hunter approach, the two guards held fists to chest in salute.

'We had not expected you, Barung,' the first guard stated.

Tristan thought back to his only meeting with the Mage Hunter, trying to remember attitude and mannerisms. 'If I didn't shag yer pig rootin', whore of a mother, don't presume to use my name.' Tristan got up close to the guard. 'You look more like a pig than my spawn.'

'Y... Y... Yes,' the guard fumbled then looked around wanting to change the subject. 'Your prisoners?'

'Yes, they are mine. Keep those fuckin' little trotters of yours away from my prize,' Tristan grunted ignoring the real question.

'We've been looking for some Mages such as these and one of the Mage touched,' the second guard stepped up when the first hesitated too long.

'Now they have been found. They are to be tortured to learn the location of the Mage touched swine. Durin has set me this task personally.'

At the mention of torture Aski let out a growl and ran at Tristan kicking his armoured shin. Without hesitation, though it pained him to do so, Tristan backhanded the girl across the face. Aski flew to the cobbles and started to cry.

'You bastard!' Beverlin screamed in rage. She crouched over the girl but couldn't console her due to the cuffs. Genji just stood glaring at him.

'The girl?' The second guard asked.

'Fuck's wrong with the Mage Killer ranks these days? Are you all inbred swine of his mother,' Tristan pointed at the first guard. 'The mother is standing above her, that's for certain. As for the father, the bitch was probably so full of cum no one could know whose swimmer won out. I'm tired of this shit. I'm going in.'

Tristan started to walk through the gates, dragging on the chain. Aski had gotten to her feet to follow. Tears still streaming down her face.

'Hunter,' the second guard said as Tristan walked by. Tristan stopped to look at him and froze, a sword protruding from his front. The first guard had run him through while he was distracted.

'What is this?' Tristan coughed as new pain lanced through his body.

'You were quite convincing but Barung is already inside with Durin,' the second guard whispered. 'Thank you, Tristan, for bringing us these Mages.' As the guard looked up at his prize he was shocked to find them breaking out of the fake iron gloves with ease.

'I got left,' Genji called while drawing the symbol for energy, a plain circle. 'Energia,' he voiced and the guard on the left was propelled into the air by a burst of pure energy. He continued high into the clouds and out of sight with no promise of coming down.

'Yerkiry,' Beverlin said, bile dripping from every syllable. The earth opened up below the guard on the right like a great maw. A short scream like a dog yelping escaped his lips before the earth once more closed over him. 'We need to find somewhere to hide. There will be more guards along before too long and I don't think they'll stay quiet.' Beverlin jabbed a thumb back towards the common folk who had lined up behind them on the bridge but were now running back into the desert dunes.

Genji nodded his agreeance. 'Into town then.' Looking around for Aski, Genji found her leaning over the fallen knight.

Aski looked back at him. 'We need to help him,' she said, tears still in her eyes.

'Leave him, Aski,' Beverlin sneered. 'He hit you. He can't be trusted.'

Aski became stubborn. 'Take him inside or I'll stay here with him. Either way I'm not leaving him alone.'

'Ody,' Genji said after drawing the symbol for air. There was no time for arguments now. He lifted Tristan with the help of the spell and they ran into the city and down an alleyway.

'A dead end,' Beverlin said looking back. She heard

an alarm go up as the guards at the gate weren't found.

'Get in close to the wall,' Genji told her as he placed Tristan down next to Aski. When Beverlin complied Genji pulled out his retractable staff and unfolded it. The crystal on top started to glow and a wall materialized a metre in front of them across the alley. Happy with the look, Genji then created a sound barrier around them. 'That's better,' he finally said.

'I'm sorry,' Aski sobbed over Tristan.

His eyes were closed tight and he was slowly rolling off the sword hilt. He tried to reach back but couldn't get a grip. Smiling Beverlin stepped in grabbing the sword. She wreathed it out of his back causing a grunt to escape Tristan's lips. His body going tense. It was minutes before he could breathe easier. The pain numbing faster now that he was getting used to great intensities. Reaching up Tristan wiped a tear from Aski's eye.

'Why do you apologise, little one,' Tristan asked.

'It's my fault they found us out,' her voice quivered.

Tristan shook his head. 'No, they knew before we even reached them that it was all fake,' Tristan told her gently. His lips pursed. 'Did I hurt you when I hit you? I never wanted to but I had to stay the part. Can you forgive me?'

Aski gave a soft little smile. 'It's what happened in the movie also. I was ready for it.'

'Wait, you knew he was going to respond by hitting you, Aski?' Beverlin was incredulous about what the young girl had just said.

Aski nodded. 'I only wanted to make it more real.' Beverlin just shook her head.

'Still, I'm sorry,' Tristan said again. 'It shouldn't have happened.'

'I made it happen,' Aski replied. 'If it's forgiveness you seek for something I orchestrated you have it.'

Let me heal your cheek, Aski,' Genji said moving the conversation forward. 'It's going to produce a large bruise and will soon start to ache.'

Aski contemplated letting Genji heal her but nuzzled

her head into Paws lying once more in her hood. The mouse picked up on what she was after and chirped multiple times. With the information from Paws, Aski now had all the information she needed to heal herself.

Aski smiled. 'No, I'll heal myself.'

'You haven't been taugh...' Genji paused as Aski reached up to the top of her head with both hands. Her mind set, she slowly rubbed down over her face. As she moved the blemished, hurt skin, muscle, and bone, mended itself. Aski giggled from the warm sensation the healing caused.

Genji looked sharply at Beverlin who just shrugged. 'Who taught you to heal, Aski?'

'You did,' she smiled again. Aski ignored any more probing questions and Genji gave up frustrated.

'So what are we going to do now?' Beverlin asked. 'We can only hide here for so long.'

'Give me some time to rest and get used to this new wound,' Tristan told her. A cough racked his body sending spasming pain to all extremities. He allowed himself to calm again. 'I'll go into town to get information and try to organise us a ship.'

'If needed, I'll craft us one,' Genji replied.

Tristan nodded before rolling over to sleep in a position slightly more bearable.

Chapter 9

'...I cannot last much longer,' he gasped, taking a moment to catch his breath. His father's sword dragged his arm to the ground. A small chip marred the otherwise perfectly honed edge. The ugly, jagged cut in his armour poked at his skin. This was causing an almost unbearable irritation to which he couldn't scratch. He pushed the numbing pain from his mind as he got to his feet once more.

Crowned Prince Atalis dragged his foot down the next step. The dark spiral stairs that ran from the rift in the throne room ate at his soul. It bit almost as hard as the idea he may be king at this moment. No, his father yet lived just up ahead. He need only make haste. He need only be faster next time.

'Soon they would come once more,' he thought to himself. 'Soon he would need to fight once more.'

Tristan woke to the feeling of small hands on him. Opening his eyes, he found Aski kneeling beside him, eyes full of tears. Immediately, he sat upright bringing fresh pain to the recent wound. His face clenched tight with the pain as he waited for it to subside. 'What's wrong, Aski?' Tristan asked before looking around making sure the others were safe. Genji and Beverlin were resting against a wall, the barrier still in effect. A wet cough caught in Tristan's throat, forcing it's way out. Looking at his hand, he realized he'd coughed up a small amount of blood. Must have clipped a lung, he thought.

'It just won't work,' Aski told him. She was looking at her hands as she talked. 'It won't work.'

'What won't work, little one? Tell me what worries you.'

'I wanted to heal your wounds,' she confessed, tears still in her eyes. 'I wanted to take away your pain so that you didn't have to leave us at the end of our journey.'

Tristan was moved by the gesture. As a Mage Killer

he would have reprimanded the girl, killed her even but the girl before him was kind, loving, caring, he felt nothing but love and sorrow for what was to come. 'I wish I had more time to know you, little one, but this body will not provide what I need. You get me through the hard times. You have shown me for the first time that someone with magical ability can have a kind soul. With these small gestures of love you have put me on a path I cannot return from, a path that wills me to protect you and forsake everything I thought I knew previously.'

'But I can't help you,' she told him softly.

'Aski look at me.'

The young girl looked up into his determined eyes. She felt how important what he was about to say was.

'You save me every day just by being you. I think of you when I am in pain or feeling like I can't go on and you give me the strength to continue. Don't feel sad that you can't heal the physical wounds. They don't worry me when I think of you so no more crying or worrying, okay?'

'Okay,' Aski sniffed deeply.

'Good,' Tristan said ruffling the girl's hair causing her to giggle. 'Now, I need to go out into town to find us a boat. Can you let the others know I'll be back before morning?'

'I will.'

Tristan smiled at the girl before trying to leave. He found that there was no exit for him and remembered even with Genji's home he needed to have a hole crafted when he wanted to pass through. Looking around, Tristan saw that the wall they backed onto was clear at the top. Taking a step back to stand against the barrier he took a deep breath readying himself to make the 2 metre jump. Out of the corner of his eye he spied Beverlin watching him through the slits of her eyes but he ignored her. She would have heard the conversation and knew where he was going. He didn't feel like getting into an argument at this time. With two broad steps he leapt for the top of the wall, pulling himself up with momentum. He was able to get himself part way over before needing to rest. He was having trouble breathing. A series of coughs raked his body and he noticed the blood splatter on the wall below after each. At the end he was feeling better and was able to breathe easier now that there was less fluid in his lungs.

The town was quiet with the night aging quickly. Taverns were closing doors and drunken stragglers were getting thrown out on the streets. As Tristan made his way slowly along the dark alleys, he spied a few pockets of Mage Killers marching the main thoroughfares, likely looking for him and the others. A single man in Mage Killer armour didn't attract any attention from these groups. It was going to be hard getting Genji, Beverlin and Aski out, Tristan knew. He needed to find the safest path to the docks.

Tristan's breathing grew ragged. He wasn't getting enough air on the inhale and as he exhaled it felt like bubbles were trying to creep up his throat. He knew his lungs were starting to fill with blood once more and he stopped by a short alleyway, leaning heavily against the wall. Tristan felt like he wanted to throw up and his stomach lurched struggling with the horrible sensation of drowning on dry land but nothing came up. The location of his discomfort being in a different organ.

'Demon, are you listening?' Emptiness filled Tristan's mind. 'I know you're there. You're always there. Speak!'

'*And what would you have me say?*' A familiar, ancient voice echoed in his mind.

'I knew you were there,' Tristan started coughing. As he pulled his hand away he noticed blood covering it. 'Heal me!'

'*No,*' the voice said calmly.

'Then make it so my friends can heal me,' Tristan told the being.

'*No,*' the voice told him once more.

'You would have me suffer? Why take over a body to run it into the ground? Free me, demon!' Tristan demanded, his anger rising.

'No... I need you to suffer,' the voice continued. 'It is too big a risk to heal you. Now, I have more important things to do.' With that Tristan's mind became empty once more.

'Don't run away from me,' Tristan growled. His aggression brought on a strong bout of coughing, dragging out a mouthful of blood. Spitting it onto the sidewalk he breathed easy once more. 'My life will not be full of pain and suffering, you hear me demon? My life is my own.'

When no response came, Tristan growled and continued down the street. Coming to a corner he peered around to determine the coast was clear and he froze. Moving towards the cross road was a group of Mage Killers lead not only by Barung but by Durin himself. Word had reached the Mage Killer's leader that Tristan and the Mages were somewhere in town.

Tristan looked around sharply, trying to find a place he could hide. He didn't want to come up against Durin in his current state. The man would probably take pleasure in torturing him as long as he could if he got his hands on the immortal knight. Spying a window that sat slightly ajar, Tristan rushed to it. Testing it, he found it was not latched and swung freely. Clambering inside, he knocked over a clay pot holding a small fern. The sound echoed around the house but Tristan couldn't worry for that just yet. He closed the window just as Durin and the group of knights came into view, pausing at the crossroad.

The shadows of the home enveloped Tristan like a protective father, obscuring his view from the outside. The torches the knights carried only enhanced this effect. Watching as Durin barked orders, Tristan saw the knights split off into different directions. Durin remained at the crossroad seemingly in thought. The large commander turned and started to walk along the street where Tristan stood moments before. Even alone, Tristan would not risk ambushing Durin. The commander had come through every battle unscathed and his psychotic streak was unpredictable.

Tristan found he was holding his breath as Durin moved along the street. Letting it out slowly, he shivered with the bubbling of blood. Ignoring the torturous feeling, Tristan watched Durin intently, willing him to move on. This was not to be. As if sniffing the air, Durin had come to a stop only metres away. Tristan couldn't smell what caught Durin's attention but he was shocked to see the commander move to the alleyway Tristan had rested at and bend down where the blood splatter was.

Durin looked around sharply, seeking the source of the blood. As he looked up, Tristan's soul turned icy, a shiver running up his spine. Durin's eyes were intense, their focus piercing everything they looked at but the gaze alone didn't frighten Tristan. A deep orange glow had taken over Durin's eyes with dark slits like cat's eye within. As the commander searched for Tristan, the orange glow left trace lines along the path they moved. Looking directly at him, Tristan ducked below the window sill.

'Shit! The man is possessed. Warn me when your friends are close,' Tristan directed at the being within him. He hadn't expected a reply and was surprised when one came.

'*It is no friend of mine,*' the voice commented. '*That man has been taken over by a Shade.*'

'A Shade?' Tristan asked searching his memory for any reference of such a creature.

'*A creature of shadow and ash. They cause those they possess to seek death and destruction. They thrive on the large amounts of energy a creature creates as it passes into the afterlife. They are commonly referred to as Liches.*'

'Durin is a Lich? How do we combat it as it just saw me?' Tristan said hastily.

'*Do not fear,*' the ancient voice was calm. '*Look again. While I am within your body lesser beings of darkness will not see you. Only their physical host could.*'

Tristan frowned as he looked back at the form of

Durin still searching. Finally the man gave up and moved on.

'And if you believed I could be taken down as easily as they could you would be mistaken,' the voice said reading Tristan's thoughts. 'I am not of darkness.'

'You still seek to inflict pain. How are you any different?' Tristan argued.

'I only said I need you to suffer. I do not wish it upon you.'

'What do you want from me, Demon?' Tristan became frustrated once more.

'You will know in time,' came the answer. 'And trust me, we have plenty of it. Our hosts name is Sianna.'

'What?' Tristan asked confused. Emptiness greeted him once more.

Looking around, Tristan saw only a glimpse of the cooking pot as it cracked against his temple. Tumbling to the floor, great aching coughs coursed harshly through his throat, expelling excess blood from his lungs. There was not as much as previous times but the pain was just as harsh. Tristan hoped the wound was starting to decrease in the amount of blood it let out as his throat and heart wound had. Rolling slowly, trying to ignore the pain, Tristan found a woman standing above him, a copper pot raised ready to attack. Tristan was surprised to find she was petite as the impact from the pot gave the impression she would be much larger or stronger.

'Your kind aren't welcome here,' the woman said. Her voice quavered as she spoke. 'You must leave now.'

Tristan smiled. It was not uncommon for someone to hate or fear the Mage Killers. It was, however, very rare that one would act out against a Mage Killer and risk incurring the full force of the knights to come down on them.

'You and your friend have nothing to fear from me,' Tristan said trying to stay friendly. 'I have as much to fear from the Mage Killers as you do.'

'You are a Mage Killer,' the woman said edging the pot back further. Then as an afterthought. 'I live here alone.'

'Former Mage Killer,' Tristan corrected her. 'I have been Mage Touched and am being hunted. The reason the knights are in town is to find me and my two Mage friends.'

'I don't believe you.'

'Your name is Sianna, correct?'

Sianna dropped her guard at hearing her name then raised the pot once more. 'You must be hunting us or how could you know my name?'

'Us now, is it?' Tristan asked catching her mistake.

Sianna's hand came to her mouth as she realized what she had said. From another room stepped out a man. To look at him you wouldn't suspect he held any secrets. Short, dark hair sat atop a plain face. A simple, grey shirt and leather leggings dressed the medium frame. There was no muscle mass or fat but he wasn't thin either. Just average in every way.

'You have skill in finding information,' the man stated.

'When I was with the Mage Killers, I had taken many missions seeking out Mages who blended into the regular folk. I can see the signs. Next time have Sianna offer aid to any Mage Killer. No one has courage enough to attack a knight unless they were hiding something.'

'We will take it on board,' the man said. 'It doesn't explain how you know Sianna's name...'

Tristan saw the man was waiting for him to provide a reason. 'I have been possessed. The Demon keeps me alive but also stops me from healing properly. It provided me with the name.'

'Sounds rather far-fetched.'

Tristan slowly got to his feet keeping his hands where Sianna and the man could see them. Moving his mantle aside he showed them the fresh wound he received at the gates. 'They clipped a lung and now it has been filling with blood over time causing the coughing fits you witnessed earlier. It's hard to breathe and there's no way, magical or otherwise, to heal it.'

The man thought for a moment processing what he saw and the knight's predicament. 'I could make you more comfortable if you wish.'

'How?' Tristan asked sceptical. He could feel the wetness of blood on each exhale.

'I could create a small cut at the base of your lungs. The blood will drain into your body. I have the ability to redirect the blood back into a vein. It's not a cure and will still pain you but you won't continually...'

'Do it,' Tristan said cutting in.

The man looked into Tristan's eyes and saw the determination there. 'Give me a moment,' the man said.

Tristan watched as he closed his eyes, concentrating hard. After a moment the man placed a hand where Tristan's lungs were and the other further down near his hip.

'Ready?' He asked and Tristan nodded.

Warmth flowed into the open wound and towards the base of his lungs. The heat grew in intensity until it felt like a burning fragment of the sun had been placed within him. He was able to hold against the pain after having plenty of practice and the surgery continued. The sensation scorched through Tristan's body as it travelled to the Mage's second hand exiting his body back into the Mage. Tristan immediately felt air filling his lungs once more to full capacity. He felt a warm line in his stomach where the blood was now draining. He noticed it wasn't as painful as the Mage lead him to believe.

'Wow,' the Mage whistled. 'Normally, people pass out half way through.'

Tristan just smiled. 'Thank you. You have given me a great gift. My name is Tristan.' Tristan offered his hand.

'No Mage Killer would offer gratitude to a Mage. You are welcome, Tristan,' the man took Tristan by the wrist in a traditional handshake. 'My name is Darius. Is there anything more we can do for you?'

'I need a safe route to the docks for me and my

friends currently in hiding. Would you happen to know any?'

Darius started thinking of the many streets around Boerus. Nowhere was better than any other street. While he was thinking Sianna stepped forward.

'You could use the sewerage lane between the houses if you don't mind a little smell,' she said. 'It was designed to take our waste straight to the sea without being in plain sight. The lane is thin but you could move sideways along it just fine.'

'Show me,' Tristan said, glad he fell through this window.

With a yawn, Genji's consciousness slowly flitted into life. As it did so an awareness that something small and furry was on his face grew. Thinking of the furry spiders that lived along this coast line and grew to the size of one's fist, Genji tried to slap it away. Waiting for this moment, Paws jumped off Genji causing the sleepy Mage to slap himself in the face. This caused Beverlin and Aski to erupt into peals of laughter.

Genji shook his head, coming completely awake and glared at the three pranksters, Paws having retreated back into Aski's clothes. He was starting to get to big to ride in Aski's hood, dragging her backwards more than anything.

'And whose idea was this?' Genji asked, one eye raised, unimpressed at being the butt of a joke.

'Don't know what you're talking about,' Aski giggled.

'Your face must be comfortable and warm,' Beverlin supplied, her eyes tearing up as a new wave of laughter burst forth.

'Well I don't appreciate it,' Genji said sulking in the corner of their small space. 'Where is Tristan anyway?' He asked changing the subject.

The girls started to calm down and catch their breath when a small squeak came from inside Aski's clothes. She started to make a grinding noise in the back of her throat as she held back her laughter but it all came rushing out in a flurry of giggles. This reignited Beverlin's laughter and once again the small area contained uncontrolled howling.

'Fine be immature then,' Genji said, annoyed by the noise.

After a moment Beverlin calmed down once more. 'Come on, Genji, we were only having a bit of fun. There's very little time to just be ourselves right now.'

'I didn't ask you to come along on this journey, Beverlin,' Genji snarled. 'You could have been back at the academy having fun with Bran.'

Beverlin's face grew serious. 'You can close your mouth now or you can move to the other side of the barrier with the Mage Killers.'

Genji considered the option of leaving the safe zone, fuelled on by his pride.

'Please don't go out into the streets,' Aski said worried at what may happen.

Genji took one look at the girl and all his pride faded away. 'Sorry, Aski, I'll stay in here with you.'

The little girl smiled, happy once more.

'Good, I'm glad someone can bring you round to your senses,' Beverlin said before answering his earlier question. 'Tristan jumped the wall behind us to seek out safe passage to the docks.' Beverlin shifted closer to Genji looking back at Aski who was now occupied with Paws. 'I think that last injury done some damage and he wanted to get some space so that Aski didn't worry so much.'

'It's a hard thing to carry wounds that would kill a man, feeling the pain of each constantly. His nerve endings would be flaring non-stop. I don't know anyone else that could go through that much pain and still be in a sane state of mind, let alone care for others,' Genji paused watching Beverlin look away. He thought she must be feeling guilty for the way she had treated him until now. 'You really should lay off him and give him a chance.'

Beverlin's face tensed once more. 'The first time I thought to give him a chance he forced himself on me.'

'A simple kiss because you were being arrogant

doesn't sound like such a big thing,' Genji shrugged.

'It doesn't matter how big or small the act. There was no consent.' Seeing the lack of sympathy she got, she tried again. 'He also barged in on me and Aski, completely naked while we were getting out of the bath. He has no boundaries.'

'The Knights of this age are rarely allowed to mix with women. Especially the Mage Killers as they never know which whore may have magical abilities. You probably scared the poor man more than you know.'

Having heard her name, Aski had gotten a rough idea of how the conversation was progressing. 'Tristan also slapped Beverlin's bare butt,' she said with a giggle.

'Aski!' Beverlin cried, her cheeks burning up as she flushed with embarrassment.

'I take it back,' Genji replied with a smile from ear to ear. 'The Knight must have a lot of pent up frustrations.'

'Don't say another word or I'll...' Beverlin started but Genji shushed her holding a hand up.

He was looking for something out past the barrier. Beverlin noticed him reaching into his pockets producing a small vial of blood. Aski also picked up on the desperate need for quiet.

'What's happening,' Beverlin asked keeping her voice low.

Genji continued to look forward ignoring her. A strong foreboding sense of dread filled the air like the night he first encountered the being of green mist. This though felt somehow more threatening.

At the end of the alleyway, orange glowing eyes traced around the corner looking straight at him. The man behind the glow was easily over 6 foot tall and wearing Mage Killer armour. Genji knew things were about to get far worse as the barrier wouldn't conceal them against a man possessed. Whatever demon lay inside would be able to sense the magic in the air if not see it.

'Found you,' the man growled in a low tone.

This sent a shiver coursing over Genji's skin. 'Get over the wall with Aski,' Genji quickly told Beverlin. We're about to have company.'

'I can fight,' Beverlin said holding her chin up. She couldn't see outside of Genji's barrier and didn't know the odds but she wouldn't back down regardless. 'How many are there?'

'Not this time,' Genji said firmly. 'There is a Mage Killer, taller than Tristan, who is possessed by a demon. By the looks of the eyes I would guess the creature to be a Shade.'

'A Shade!' Beverlin remarked. They should have all been wiped out with the Elven King.'

'That was only 70 years ago. One could have easily slipped through the net and lived without a host 5 times that long.' A thumping noise came from the Barrier and Genji looked to physical pale. 'He is too strong Beverlin. You need to go now.'

'But.'

'GO!' Genji yelled.

Nodding, Beverlin helped Aski up over the wall before Genji done the same for her. Another thump on the barrier had Genji stumbling, his head swimming as he tried to keep focus on it.

'We'll come back for you,' Beverlin called as both she and Aski dropped to the other side of the wall.

Genji knew that he couldn't take another hit from whatever possessed the man so timed the barrier shutdown for greatest affect. As the man moved to strike once more Genji dropped the barrier throwing the man off balance. With a flick of his wrist Genji threw the vial of blood at the ground below the Mage Killer and started chanting a line of incoherent syllables.

The man possessed, started writhing in agony as tendrils of blood grew from the ground, wrapping themselves around the man's limbs and body. Red smoke poured from the Mage Killer where each tendril touched him. The blood magic ate at his skin like acid.

Genji actually began to believe he was going to make

142

it through when his hopes were dashed to pieces. Emitting a loud growling noise the being possessing the Mage Killer absorbed the blood magic into the skin. He stayed still kneeling on the ground as the creature healed all the wounds Genji had inflicted. This gave Genji precious moments only.

Guessing the creature to be a Shade, Genji thought to fight the creature of darkness with elemental light magic. Tracing a circle with a dot at its centre in the air, Genji waited for the man to right himself.

'Luysy,' Genji said, his voice emanating power.

Balls of light burst force, entering the man's chest and growing in intensity. It started to glow with such force the skin was becoming a translucent pink tone. The Shade inside the man was struggling to combat the light and was causing the body to thrash around erratically. Finally, the orange glow in his eyes faded and the man once more had clarity. The wicked, maniacal grin on the man's face made Genji feel even more afraid then before. Reaching a hand behind himself, the man unlatched his gruesome battle axe.

'My friend may have trouble in the light but if you think your little magic tricks can work against me, you're sorely mistaken. I have killed far more adept Mages in my years as Commander of the Mage Killers,' Durin said. His eyes were psychotic. Taking the few steps to close the gaps, Durin brought his axe around in an arc aimed at Genji's neck.

'Luysy,' Genji said once more hoping the symbol he drew in the air was still fresh enough. He had no time to produce any other forms of magic. He'd been put off by the fact the man in front of him was the Commander of the Mage Killers himself and wanted nothing more than to flee.

A burst of light, brighter than a solar flare, before Durin's eyes sent the axe off course and had the Commander clutching his eyes with both hands. He started rubbing his eyelids and blinking rapidly trying to dissipate the temporary blindness.

Seeing his opportunity, Genji made to run out the

alleyway but a small whistle had him find Tristan lying atop the wall offering a hand. Taking one last look at Durin, Genji took a running start and with the help of Tristan made it over the wall. The sound of a hastily swung axe bouncing off the stones echoed behind him.

'We have to get away quick,' Tristan stated. 'Durin will never give up the chase.'

Genji saw Beverlin and Aski close by, both looked relieved. 'The man is possessed.'

'I just found out myself. Come on we can talk on a ship.'

Tristan turned and started leading them through Boerus, stopping at corners to make sure the streets were clear. Genji followed trying to keep himself moving. Happy to be away from Durin, his body started a series of internal tremors from the adrenaline used that made his hands shake. The constant movement kept this from getting to him.

Soon, Tristan stopped at a home and knocked on the door. After a moment they were given access and the group moved off the street. Warmth from an archaic bread oven, hit Genji the moment he stepped through the door. Passing the lavender by the door, the smell of freshly baked bread caressed his nose making his mouth water. He realised in that moment just how hungry he was.

'Sorry to intrude once more and thank you for your kindness,' Tristan said to their host. He introduced both Aski and Beverlin to their hosts and as he was about to introduce Genji, the mage stepped forward extending a hand.

'I'm Genji,' he said to Sianna first.

'Sianna,' she replied taking Genji's hand. Sianna turned motioning to Darius. 'And this is Darius.'

Genji hesitated as he offered his hand upon hearing the name. He gave Beverlin a quick look before he fully extended his hand for Darius. 'A Mage?' Genji asked.

'As much as you and Beverlin,' Darius raised an eyebrow. He was reading Genji's body language and knew there was far more to the question than

144

determining whether he could perform magic or not.

Genji's eyes lit up and he shook Darius's hand more enthusiastically prompting Darius to pull back. 'It is an honour to meet you,' Genji said before looking at Beverlin once more. 'It's Darius!' He exclaimed in childlike wonder.

'You're scaring our guest, Genji,' Beverlin replied calmly. 'Remember yourself and what we are here for. We need to keep moving.' She turned to Darius and Sianna. 'Sorry for my friend. He gets a little too excited meeting new Mages.

Darius was still frowning, watching the wide eyed Mage as Beverlin pushed Genji passed and to the back door. Aski followed without a word not understanding what was going on. Tristan remained a moment longer.

'I'm gunna have to hit you,' he said bluntly to Darius.

'You what?'

'Durin, Commander of the Mage Killers is after us. He will pass through here and I am sorry for exposing you to the danger but he will not look twice if you've been knocked to the ground and a pot or two smashed,' Tristan confessed while tipping the lavender pot at the door over.

Darius pursed his lips and nodded gravely.

'Thank you for your help, Mage,' Tristan spoke as he punched Darius as hard as he could sending the man across the room and into a small cupboard breaking some shelves. Small pottery cups smashed across the floor. Sianna reacted as was necessary without prompt. Her hands had come up to her mouth and she was frozen in shock.

'Farewell and be safe,' Tristan said racing out the back to catch the others. He came hard up against the wall and started sliding sideways down the narrow passage.

As Genji came out into the passage the smell almost made him throw up. It was the complete opposite of the rich smells inside and he was having a hard time adjusting. Forced to move by Beverlin and Aski behind him he saw a glimpse of the sea a few hundred metres away and started moving in that direction. A gasp came from Beverlin behind him and Genji was happy he didn't need to suffer alone. He noticed Tristan took his time coming out but there was no stress on the man's face and this relaxed Genji a bit.

With the docks just ahead, Genji exploded from the narrow passage taking in great gulps of fresh air. A Mage Killer nearby saw him and thought it odd someone was walking the sewer paths. As Beverlin and Aski exited, he realised they were the group everyone was hunting. Taking up his sword the man shouted an alarm up the streets and started moving on the group.

Both Genji and Beverlin stood ready to fight, plans forming in their minds. Aski hid herself behind the Mage pair in relative safety. As the Knight was closing and The Mages were now tracing their symbols, Tristan entered the streets. Without hesitating, his sword was in hand and he was past the Mages.

'Get a ship and prepare to depart,' Tristan called over his shoulder, eyes fixed on the knight. 'More will come and Durin is in the passage.'

Tristan engaged the knight as Genji traced an inverted triangle. He'd decided the night before to craft his own ship as there could be complications from ones they stole or got passage with. 'Jur,' he said invoking the element of water. Ice started to form in the sea, growing in the shape of a large sailing ship.

As Genji was still concentrating on creating the vessel, he called out to Beverlin. 'Set fire to the other ships. We don't want anyone following us.'

Beverlin nodded, tracing an upright triangle in the air. Facing up the docks, she called forth the element of fire which coursed from her hands in multiple balls of heat and rage. Aski had to step back a pace to shield herself from the heat. Turning in the opposite direction, Beverlin repeated the process with the rest of the ships. A number of fireballs hit every vessel ensuring the sails and wood would catch fire.

Tristan dispatched his opponent surprised by the

skill the man had shown and turned back to find the ice ship ready to set sail. He was amazed at the detail that was put into the ship. All the components from sails and ropes to steering wheel where all added and fully operational. Magic aside, Tristan found something was off with the ship but he couldn't quite pinpoint what it was. Just a niggling thought in the back of his mind that made him stop and question it.

He didn't have long to think, however as large groups of footsteps could be heard rumbling along a number of streets. Running in, Tristan scooped up Aski and scrambled aboard the ice ship.

'Get on here now!' Tristan called to the Mages. 'They're upon us.'

Genji and Beverlin looked around hearing the boots and then ran up the gangplank which melted as they got safely aboard.

'Ody,' Genji boomed, tracing the symbol for air. Large gusts of wind filled the ice sails and the ship sped out into the ocean sailing itself. Looking back Genji saw almost 100 Mage Killers standing upon the docks, Durin out in front. With no ships available to give chase, they slowly turned and walked away.

Beverlin watched the knight, her mind debating whether she should approach him or not. She knew the man was hurting but still was unsure about him. Finally, she gave in and decided she would try and be friendly. 'You're looking better then you were this morning,' she said leaning against the deceivingly warm rail next to him.

Tristan seemed far more relaxed in the way he held himself than Beverlin did. Giving her a quick smile he looked out to sea. 'The wound earlier had clipped a lung. I was having difficulty breathing with blood entering the hole. The Mage, Darius, helped me. Thank you for your concern, Beverlin.' His words had genuine emotion behind them.

Beverlin became embarrassed with his gratitude, her guard coming up. 'If you're in pain Aski gets worried, is all. Don't look too much into it.'

'Thank you anyway.'

'Hey Tristan,' Genji called out. Both Tristan and Beverlin looked back. 'Slapped any more butts lately?'

Tristan looked confused but Beverlin's face grew red. In her anger she flung a fireball at the Mage who ducked away laughing.

Chapter 10

'We're gunna need to put down outside of Pinto.' Tristan said. 'We don't need the extra attention coming into port sailing a block of ice.'

The journey over the sea to Pintosia's crown city was boring. Genji had sat healing a fresh burn wound, compliments of Beverlin. Aski stood out on the bow of the ship watching dolphins frolicking in front of them or waving at bewildered fishermen as they passed by. For safety reasons, Tristan stood behind the excited, little girl ready to catch her if her excitement got too much and she fell overboard. Beverlin, too, had watched over them but her focus had shifted more and more to Tristan. Her emotions were all over the place as she tried to have an unclouded opinion of the man. It took half a day to cross the sea to Pinto, spurred on by Genji's Magic and now as the sun passed its apex, the coast was in sight.

'There's a small cove not too far from Pinto,' Genji replied. 'It'll be secluded this time of year. I'll make for it now.'

The ship turned south to make a long arcing voyage away from the city back to the cove Genji had mentioned. The cove was more like a cave that hung over a small patch of sand disappearing into the darkness beyond. Long tendrils of vines partially covered the opening making the area hard to spot from sea. If you didn't know it was there you would surely sail on by.

'How are we going to get into the cove? This ship is way too large,' Tristan stated.

'We just make the ship smaller,' it was Aski who replied matter-of-factly.

Genji smiled. 'She really does have a mind for magic.' Drawing the symbol and calling forth the element of water once more, Genji started to shrink the ship. As it shrunk, the passengers started to shift into new positions. When the magic slowed and everything came into place, the boat they were left with was no larger than a rowboat. Aski had a seat to herself behind Genji, who was smiling mischievously by the oars. In front of him squeezed onto a seat barely big enough for one large person, was both Beverlin and Tristan. Tristan had tried to turn himself in a way to give Beverlin majority of the room but Beverlin wasn't happy.

I know what you're doing, she mouthed at Genji who shrugged and tried to look innocent.

A small scream broke the moment, as Aski flew off her seat and backed up against Genji. Paws was standing at the edge of the rowboat hissing at the water. Looking over the side, Genji saw three sets of fins had breached the surface and were following the boat.

'Don't fear the sharks, Aski. The cove makes a beautiful swimming beach. The sand allows for a few groups of people, the water is deceptively deep and the cavernous landscape gives privacy. This time of the year, however, the Grunion fish use the beach to spawn new young. And where there is fish there will always be sharks. They are only interested in the fish and possibly burly that fisherman sometimes leave behind.'

'Are you sure we don't need a bigger boat?' Aski asked cautiously. 'I saw a show on the television at mum's house once that showed a shark attacking people both swimming and on boats.'

Genji smiled remembering the media hype around thrillers that used animals as the antagonist. 'They are all make-believe with over emphasised actions and attributes. They only want to scare you but it has no real truth behind it.'

'Okay,' Aski replied still unsure.

She settled back on her seat in the centre and cautiously watched the trailing fins. As the boat slid up the white sand beaching itself, Aski jumped over the front with Paws and retreated a few paces. She worried as Genji jumped off the side into the water to drag the boat further onto the sand allowing Beverlin and Tristan an easier dismount.

Tristan offered a hand to Beverlin but she ignored him and leapt the side catching the edge of her foot on the railing to fall face first onto the shore. Genji laughed and Tristan stifled a giggle as Beverlin glared at him with sand encrusted on her face like thousands of tiny diamonds sparkling in the sun.

'Not a word,' she warned the men. As she spoke, a gritty substance rolled around her mouth sending shivers up her spine each time her teeth crunched the grains of sand. Again, Beverlin ignored an offered hand from Tristan and continued towards the cave entrance muttering curses.

As the group exited the cave they found Pinto lay only a mile to the north. The disconcerting sight that drew their attention was the long line of people waiting to get into the city. Normally the gates would be open and access was free for all but the line troubled Genji.

'Something must have happened,' Tristan said confirming Genji's worries. 'We're going to have a long wait before getting the chance to enter. I'll ask around a bit to get some information so we are more prepared when we reach the gates.'

'I'll help too,' Beverlin said. 'We can split up and cover more ground that way. Genji, take Aski to the end of the line.'

Genji looked from Beverlin to Tristan then back to Beverlin again. A cheeky smile crossing his face.

'No!' Beverlin grunted reading Genji's thoughts and left them behind.

'She really explodes for no reason, doesn't she?' Tristan observed falling in beside Genji.

'I was teasing her,' Genji admitted. 'She knows me well enough to read my body language alone.'

'Teasing? You were only looking at her. You really must have a close relationship,' Tristan said astonished that a whole conversation passed by from just a glance.

'I did glance at you also.'

Tristan's brow furrowed. 'I see now. She still hates me doesn't she?'

Genji smiled and patted his friend on the shoulder.

'Quite the opposite actually. You seem to miss a lot.'

'What?' Tristan asked confused.

'Since you saved her in the forest I started noticing a change in her attitude towards you. It became more guarded, more intense. She was fighting with feelings she may not have expected to feel towards you. Just looking between you two put her on edge. It wouldn't have affected her so badly if she wasn't at least thinking of it.'

'I'll take your word for it. I admit I know little in the ways of women,' Tristan rubbed the back of his head feeling uncomfortable with the conversation. He didn't know for sure what Beverlin felt for him but all he saw was the outward anger she portrayed. He decided the moment was right to take his leave and start searching for information.

'Looks like it's just you and me,' Genji said to Aski.

Paws let out a small chirp. 'Don't forget Paws,' Aski replied.

'You two have been inseparable these last couple of weeks, you're almost counted as one.' Aski just smiled back. 'How has the journey been for you? Are you coping okay?' Genji asked. He hadn't had much opportunity to really talk to Aski. She was quiet to begin with and only started to really come out of her shell when Tristan had joined the group.

'I'm okay,' she replied happily. 'I know everyone has trouble getting along but you have all been there for me and I feel safe around each of you. For the first time in my life since my brother left I have been treated like a person and not garbage or something to be used.'

'Do you still believe Tristan is your brother?' Genji didn't want to disillusion the girl knowing that Tristan was to die. It was already going to be hard enough on her.

'No, I know he isn't the brother I grew up with,' she told Genji to his relief. 'But I still can't help but treat him like my brother. Each time I say his name or see his face, when he calls me little one and all his other random quirks, my mind continues to tell me it is the

Tristan I knew. It makes me happy to be able to spend time with him once more...'

Genji let out a sigh. It was never going to be a simple thing. Even to end the life of someone who desperately wished for relief.

'I know I have to say goodbye soon, Genji. He's in pain. I won't stop what needs to be done.'

Genji studied the girls face. There was determination in her eyes. 'You are far stronger than I was when I was your age.'

It wasn't long before Tristan and Beverlin returned from questioning people in the line. Everyone who had any clue was giving them the same story and there was no point wasting any more energy.

'So what did you find?' Genji asked.

'The King and court Mage have been killed. Both the Crowned Prince and the King's sword are missing. That's all anyone knows,' Beverlin told him.

'This complicates matters,' Genji's brow furrowed as he thought on the issue. 'The sword was recorded to have lost its power around this time, not disappear completely. I had assumed it just passed into the Lost Era. We may already be too late.'

'You can't just do your little thing and jump back in time a bit to when the King died and the Prince went missing?' Tristan asked concerned for his own fate.

'So, we are using magic now?' Beverlin raised a brow at the Knight. 'What happened to your '*I would rather die than use magic*' attitude?' Her voice had gotten deep as she mocked Tristan.

'You have a certain way of touching my heart and changing my perspective on such matters... Beverlin,' Tristan said with a smile, looking straight at Beverlin.

Beverlin hadn't expected Tristan to answer in such a way. Hearing her name alone had her struggling for words and when she couldn't find any retreated from the conversation. 'Whatever,' she mumbled turning to watch the slowly moving line into the city.

'You're starting to see what I mean,' Genji nudged Tristan before turning serious. 'I don't like to travel to times I have already lived through. Existence doesn't like for two copies of oneself to exist at any given time. We can cause great damage to the flow of time itself. The only place there is an exception on this rule is in the Time Stairways. They lay outside the rule of time.'

'*Listen to him,*' the ancient voice sounded in Tristan's mind. '*Corrections with time have been made in the past but if you make too big an impact, life itself will be reset completely.*'

Tristan's eyes grew wide and Genji became concerned. 'What's wrong?' Genji asked. It looked as though Tristan had just been stabbed, his face growing deathly pale.

'Let's just say my passenger agrees with you on this matter.'

Genji nodded his understanding. 'When we get inside, we'll get a room at one of the inns and work out a plan then.'

'Agreed,' Tristan said.

'Agreed,' Aski repeated not wanting to be left out. The two men looked at the girl and laughed breaking the tension.

It was starting to get dark as the group reached the gates. The guards looked weary from the day's work and Genji knew they would be relieved with the night's watch soon. A hand suddenly rose in front of them and one of the guards shook his head. Genji hadn't thought regular town guards would be hunting them or that word of their exploits had even reached Pinto yet but he readied himself should a fight arise.

'You will let me through,' Tristan said with great authority.

The guards grew worried but held firm. 'The gates close from sundown. No one else may enter at this time.'

'I am here on official Mage Killer business. We offer our services to Pinto to help in finding the truth of recent events,' Tristan told them his expression dangerous.

'We do not recognise your kind in this kingdom,' the

first guard said. A creaking noise came from the gates behind them as they started to swing shut. Both guards began to walk through.

Tristan caught the first guard by the scruff of his neck and dragged him back. 'It is good you don't recognise my kind,' Tristan whispered in the man's ear as he brought his sword up to rest on the man's throat. 'If I slit your throat right now no one would recognise me.'

The man squirmed to get free but Tristan held firm. As the guard watched the gates slowly closing he relented. 'Okay, you can enter the town but don't for a second think the castle guards will give you access to the castle.'

Tristan dropped the man and slipped past him through the gate. Genji, Beverlin and Aski followed before the guard slipped in sideways at the last moment, the gate shutting with a thud. With a deadly stare, Tristan had the guard retreating to the barracks.

'Well that went better than expected,' Tristan said, relieved. 'This armour does come in handy sometimes.'

'Better if you weren't wearing it,' Beverlin grunted looking at it with disgust.

'Beverlin!' Tristan looked shocked. 'I had thought you pure of mind but I see you are just as big a pervert as I am.'

'Wha... No... That's not what I meant,' Beverlin stuttered, her face going red.

Genji just shook his head and laughed. Telling Tristan what Beverlin was possibly thinking had turned out better than he expected. 'We're going to be staying at The Hedgehogs Dilemma,' Genji moved the conversation on.

'Like the popular hotels back home?' Aski asked.

'The exact same. This is one of the first that opened,' Genji told her.

'I'll meet you there,' Tristan said suddenly. 'I know someone here who may be able to give us some more precise information.'

Genji agreed. 'Make sure to get the timing of the

event down to the exact day. We need specific information this time.'

Tristan nodded and walked off.

'I'm glad we will be rid of him soon,' Beverlin said.

'Your comments seem to speak of other ideas,' Genji said with a wink. Beverlin shot him a dirty look.

The Hedgehogs Dilemma hadn't been what Aski was expecting. She remembered a time before her step dad had met her mother when she had stayed in one of the lavish, chain hotels. It had been just herself, her mum, and her brother coming home late from a holiday. 5 hours in with still 3 more before they reached their home, Aski's mum had pulled the car over, her eyes growing heavy.

Already tired from the long weekend holiday camping in the mountains and the boring car trip home, Aski had started whining when her mother said they may be staying on the side of the road for the night. Seeing a sign that indicated a town was close by her mum calmed Aski by promising a room for the night in a hotel. This had been The Hedgehogs Dilemma with its revolving door, red carpet, high ceilings, and bellboy's with their funny round hats that didn't sport a brim. The room was a large open plan area with a queen bed and two doubles. Aski had never slept in such a large bed and she made sure to stretch across the whole thing... diagonally.

The version Aski had now entered was far from the image her memory offered. Where there were polished stone floors only compacted dirt strewn with hay. Where there were bell boys to greet you and take you luggage only drunken men singing tavern songs filled the room. Even the fire place that should have given life and warmth to the inn was full of ash from a forgotten flame. Nothing about this inn made her feel special or like royalty.

Watching as Genji pushed his way to the counter, Aski stuck to Beverlin's side looking around wearily. Almost every guest reminded Aski of her step dad and she wanted nothing more than to be away from them all. Hearing Paws squeak from within the folds of her clothes, she smiled. To set everyone aflame like the small creature had suggested would make her everything Tristan hated in a Mage and Aski would never be that person.

A man stumbled towards her, causing the girl to freeze. His eyes were locked to hers and he had a similar look her step dad often had, one of desire. Physically shaking, Aski gripped tight to Beverlin's arm putting as much of the woman between her and the man. To her relief, the man's attention fell on Beverlin.

'You shouldn't bring children to such a place,' he told Beverlin, belching loudly. 'How abouts we take her to my room and while we are there maybe you and I can have a bit of fun. What d'ya say, honey cake?'

Beverlin looked the man up and down as if considering his proposal. 'And do you have all your teeth?' she asked.

The man looked strangely amused by the question, trying to figure out why it mattered. Opening his mouth wide for Beverlin to see he mumbled some incoherent words. Beverlin reached up with her thumb and dampened it with the man's saliva before drawing a line down the man's forehead with it. Falling into a short incantation the man suddenly sobered up fast, a blank expression crossing his face, and he walked out of the room.

'What did you do?' Aski asked, amazed by the outcome.

'Blood magic,' Beverlin replied. 'It's not just about the red fluid flowing through your veins but the DNA that makes it up. You can find ample amounts in saliva. I just impressed upon his mind the need to return to his home and live a decent honest life.'

'Just like that?'

'Just like that?' Beverlin told the young girl. 'When you master all the disciplines to their deepest levels, you will find there is nothing to be afraid of in this world.'

Aski thought about this for a moment. 'I want to learn everything I can about Mage Craft,' she told Beverlin.

'Then when this journey has come to an end and we have returned to our time I'll take you to the Academy of Mage Craft. There you can learn everything you could ever dream of.'

'I would like that,' Aski smiled.

At that moment, Genji made his way back to the girls. He'd seen what had transpired and was smiling openly at how Beverlin treated the situation.

'I'm glad that, even when I tease you, you don't push your will on me like that,' Genji commented.

'Do you have all your teeth?' Beverlin asked and Genji clamped his mouth shut, a stern expression crossing his face. Beverlin looked at the rather large crowd. 'Did you get a room?'

'Got the last one,' Genji held up an old bronze key. He nodded towards a door on the ground floor. 'It's the one just back there. Told them that if a Mage Killer by the name of Tristan asked for me by name, to point him in the right direction.'

Aski followed Genji and Beverlin to the room, sticking close in the crowd. She was happy to move to a more private area of the inn where she could finally lay back on a real bed. Thinking back, she realized it hadn't been since Genji's home when she last got a good night's sleep.

As Aski entered the room, her heart sank. There was only a single bed with a lumpy mattress and thin sheet that was being used as a blanket. No pillow could be seen. Looking around the rest of the room didn't help her disposition towards the inn. A small shaft of light from an outside lantern shone through a thin slit in the wall. Aski couldn't accept the slit as a window. This gave the room a soft break from the darkness allowing her to navigate the area. The only other furniture in the room was a bench against the left most wall with a single stool below it. Aski could not believe this was how The Hedgehogs Dilemma had begun.

Fed up with the room and wanting a little bit of comfort, Aski looked at Beverlin. 'Can you show me how to draw a... changing circle?'

'A transmutation circle,' Beverlin corrected. 'What did you want to change?'

'The room. It's so uncomfortable and depressing,' Aski replied. 'Genji changes his house all the time.'

'Sorry Aski but we can't do that here,' Genji said. 'With alchemy you need to give something up or have something of equal elemental makeup to change. At home I just change the house when the size remains the same or use the forest when adding elements to the house like your tower. No one misses an extra tree here and there. With commercial buildings it gets more tricky. You may destroy the integrity of the whole building and risk people's lives. It's best to just grin and bear it.'

Instead of a grin, Aski puffed out her cheeks and sulked on the bed. It was more uncomfortable than it looked and Aski considered sleeping on the ground if their stay extended too long. Getting up, she moved to the small slit in the wall giving access to the outside world. The smell of horse manure hit her square in the face and she retreated once more into the room looking for something to occupy her mind. A small squeak came from within Aski's hood as Paws reminded her of the story Genji promised to tell her about a prophecy that involved the desert and Mages.

'Genji,' Aski said getting the young Mage's attention. 'You spoke of a prophecy about Pintosia?'

Genji's expression hardened. 'Not now, Aski.'

'But we have so much time,' she pouted. Paws supplied her with three chirps almost like a bird song. 'At least tell me of the seer Perioclios.'

Beverlin narrowed her eyes at the Lazurian mouse. 'And where did you come across that name?' she asked not expecting an answer.

'That's what I want to know,' Genji said. 'Few Mages get to hear the story or learn of the Seers name.'

'You mumbled it once in your sleep,' Aski replied thinking quick. 'Please tell me about him.'

Genji pursed his lips and let out a short burst of air through his nose. 'Okay,' he replied. Taking a moment to gather his thoughts he began. 'Perioclios was a seer to King Atalis. He was not mentioned in history before this time but was spoken of forever after that. With the recent King's death and Atalis to be crowned once he is tracked down, the time of the prophecy is at hand.'

'In 15 to 16 years, no form of magic will exist. The last Mage of this era will curse the very essence of magic to return only once certain measures have been met. A magic mark, like a glowing tattoo, will form upon an individual. Should they die it will appear on another, and another until the individual is brought to a place of magic and a ceremony is performed to release magic upon the world once more.'

'Perioclios saw all this, but he also saw that the Mage Killers, the group of knights Tristan had once belonged to, the group of knights responsible for murdering all the Mages of this time, would cause problems. For centuries they hunted and killed any who bore the mark, always before magic could be returned. But cunning Perioclios set in motion a plan to thwart the knights, a plan spanning 3 centuries. He saw the point where magic was to be returned, far to the south in an area that used mountains as a natural barricade. Here he had built a fortress in the guise of a prison. The prisoners became an army to fight off the Mage killers at the final battle and as you know, magic was restored once more.'

'But that doesn't explain why the land became a desert,' Aski said frowning.

'The visions of Perioclios were accepted with almost God like faith. He was able to convince the entire nation of Pintosia to uproot all the trees so they may not be used to craft siege engines,' Beverlin said. 'Pintosia is the only nation that doesn't frown upon magic but accepts it in all forms.'

'Why did the people believe him? It was such a long

160

time before magic was returned.' Aski asked.

'Perioclios struggled for a long time convincing the people,' Genji replied. 'He held sermons on the street and for the most part was chased off. He got by on charity but when the land entered the time without magic, the lost era, they came crawling back. They saw the truth in his words and he lived a much more comfortable life in service of the king.'

Aski thought about the story. 'That didn't sound like it was the Mages fault. I don't understand why it was so hard to speak of.'

'The fact that magic or Mages were part of the reason such a beautiful land was turned into a desert saddens me,' Genji said with a fading smile.

'It's just like the king's blade,' Beverlin said.

'In what way?' Genji asked.

'It is said to be a magnificent blade with great strength hidden within yet if we were to accomplish our goal the blade will destroy itself as it destroys the being within Tristan.'

A look of shock crossed Genji's face but before he had a chance to respond Tristan burst through the door. Aski gave a squeal, startled by the knight before she lit up, forgetting her worries.

'Tristan,' she shouted pouncing into a hug.

Squeezing Aski for a moment he placed her up on his shoulders and looked to the others. 'I found out what they were trying to do,' his tone serious.

'What did you hear?' Beverlin asked.

'The King and the court Mage were working on a way to open a portal between two areas in the world. They wanted to cover vast distances quickly and move forward with a plan to invade neighbouring countries.'

'An impossible venture,' Genji remarked. 'I can see why it blew up in their face.'

'Speak plainly,' Tristan said. 'I haven't the aptitude for magic in the way you know it.'

'Even where I'm from, no one has ever opened a doorway to cover great distances...'

'Yes they have,' Aski cut in.

Genji considered the girl. 'Aski, I have researched the topic extensively at the Academy of Mage Craft. No one has achieved such an accomplishment.'

'But you did,' she replied less sure now. 'When we moved from the Academy to your home. Did that not cover a great distance?'

'I was moving around in time. We travelled over 1000 years,' Genji smiled understanding where Aski was getting confused.

'And if we only travelled 1 second in time, could we still move that distance.'

Genji's expression dropped. 'It couldn't be that simple.' He turned to Beverlin who was still doing the calculations. 'That would mean... I know where the sword is.' Genji remembered the commotion on the stairs the second time he brought Beverlin through. It corresponded perfectly when the prince disappeared.

'Well?' Tristan asked becoming impatient. 'Where is it?'

Ignoring Tristan, Genji opened a portal to the stairwell and disappeared inside closing it behind him.

'Genji!' Tristan called.

'Don't worry, he'll come back,' Aski said ruffling the short strands of Tristan's hair.

Outside in the cool air of the night a young drunk dragged himself to his feet. Looking at the dregs of his ale a sudden sickness took him. He heard the conversations of the occupants within the inn and now he couldn't look at the drink the same. A rustling of feet came from down the street and the man looked up to find a large group of knights entering The Hedgehogs Dilemma.

'What do you think is happening there, Perioclios,' another man asked the first.

'Nothing good,' Perioclios replied. 'Best we get out of here.' Glancing up the street, he gazed at the castle. 'I think it's about time I moved homes.'

162

Chapter 11

'Well that was rude,' Beverlin commented, watching Genji step into the portal leading to the stairways and closing it off behind him. 'He could've at least told us where he was going.'

Tristan still wore a concerned expression no matter how much Aski tried to comfort him. 'We'll just need to be patient,' he told Beverlin after a moment. He knew there was nothing any of them could do.

A knock at the door drew their attention and Beverlin walked over to stand by it cautiously. 'Who is it?' she called tentatively. As Genji was outside of space and time she had hoped it would be him returning though she knew it was unlikely with his ability. He would land nowhere other than inside the room.

'I've brought food for you,' a voice on the far side of the door called. If you open the door I'll place the tray on your table.'

Tristan's eyes grew wide as he recognized the voice to be a former comrade in the Mage Killers. 'Get away from there,' Tristan yelled but Beverlin was already turning the latch to the door. With no time to stop her, Tristan leapt across the room, tossing Aski to the bed and barged Beverlin out of the way. She landed hard against the wall and was about to scream her abuse at Tristan when the door burst open and a group of Mage Killers charged in. A scream rent the room as Beverlin heard Aski's cry. She had thought it only for the intrusion but as her eyes became clear, Beverlin saw that two long, slender swords had punched straight through Tristan, blood pumping from his back. He was stuck lying on the floor with his back arched up. A silent scream frozen on his face as the pain was flooding his entire body.

Aski made to help Tristan but Beverlin caught her by the scruff of the neck and dragged her back. She cradled Aski protectively in her arms as the Mage Killers advanced past Tristan with evil grins.

'Where is the other Mage?' one Knight demanded.

His face was full of scars from many battles and the eyes held a deep, pit of cruelty that gave Beverlin goosebumps. 'We know he came in her. We've been watching you for some time now.'

'Then you need to get your eyes checked,' Beverlin was thankful her voice remained calm. 'There is no one else.'

Pursing his lips, the Mage Killer looked away shaking his head seemingly annoyed by the answer. Striding across to the girls, he grabbed Aski by her hair and wrenched her from Beverlin's arms. Dangling Aski in front of her, the Mage Killer drew his sword and placed it over Aski's neck.

A darkness clouded Aski's mind as images of her abuse surfaced with unbearable realism. The hand that clasped her hair was not that of a Mage Killer but her step father's. The body at her back was unclothed ready to force it's vile nature into her soul. Her primal instincts to fight or fly took over and Aski started to buck and twist as she tried to free herself from her immediate danger. The Mage Killer struggled to keep Aski under control as the girl almost ran her own throat over the sharp edge of his sword in her struggles.

'Brother... Tristan,' Aski screamed, praying to be saved from the rough hands that held her against her will.

As the Knight's focus was on keeping Aski under control, Beverlin took the opportunity to sketch the symbol of power for water. She was preparing her mind to draw the water particles from the air and direct them into the Knight's lungs drowning him. 'You better let her go right...'

As Beverlin spoke a second Mage Killer had noticed what she was doing. With little resistance, he punched her square in the face, sending her tumbling to the ground unconscious.

'You're a fool, Ferehn,' the first Knight struggling to hold Aski under control, hissed. 'She was easier to get information out of than this little bitch.'

'Next time I'll let her cast, then,' Ferehn shrugged.

164

'You have the girl, Tobin. Do your job and make her squeal.'

Tobin just glared back at Ferehn before focusing on Aski. As he looked back down, he was just in time to see Aski's teeth sink into the soft flesh that was exposed just behind his gauntlet. Swearing profusely, Tobin loosened his grip on Aski sending her toppling to the floor. Before she could retreat any further, Tobin recovered grabbing Aski by the neck in frustration. To the sound of the other Knight's laughter, Tobin lifted Aski into the air so that he could look straight into her eyes. Eyes that were bulging as she fought to draw breath. With blood pounding in her skull she started slapping Tobin's wrists.

'You listen and you listen good,' Tobin said, a fierce calm etched into his voice. 'When I let you go you are going to answer all of my questions or you'll find yourself in the same position and next time I won't be letting go. Do you understand?'

Aski nodded furiously as she started to become dizzy. Feeling the grip loosen she fell to the floor once more. As she looked up she was greeted with something she saw in her nightmares. I large hulking figure standing over her with an unholy smile upon their face.

'Stay down!' A Knight commanded at the entrance to the room. This was followed by a blood curdling cry and the sound of steel on steel as a commotion broke out. The screams of the dying echoed out like dominoes one after the other.

Turning back to see what the commotion was about, Tobin was met with a frightening image. Tristan, thought to be dead, was back on his feet swinging one of the swords he recovered from his chest. As another Knight swung low with a curving strike, Tristan managed to block it using the sword still embedded in his chest. He grunted in pain as he brought his own sword down to severe the Knights hand. Reversing his blade, Tristan rammed it home into the neck of a second attacker.

'Swarm him,' Tobin commanded. 'Bury him beneath

you so he can't move.'

He watched as Tristan dispatched one last Mage Killer before being pinned against the floor. Happy that Tristan was taken care of, Tobin turned his attention back to Aski and his face instantly went white. The girl had just spoken the work of power for fire and Tobin saw that a soft orange glow had begun beneath his feet.

'But children can't do magic,' he stuttered.

Before Tobin had a chance to move, a large column of flame ripped through the floorboards reaching for the ceiling. The last thing Tobin would ever see was Ferehn standing with a smug look on his face shaking his head having warned him to be wary. The fire continued its ferocious swirl of flames, burning like a giant tornado fixed in the one position. The strength of the heat had most of the Mage Killers stepping back as they watched the death of a comrade. When the flames had finally died away, only a pile of ash and some glowing, red hot bones were left.

Ferehn took no chances and booted Aski in the side of the head sending her sprawling up against the still form of Beverlin. She too was now unconscious. Walking over to where Tristan was now restrained by chains Ferehn smiled. 'Seems the child has some power. I'm rather disappointed in you, Tristan. You were one of the few Knights I admired. Now your nothing more than the shit beneath our boots.'

'You've been a disappointment since the day you were born. Your mother must be feeling sorry she didn't rip you from her womb and cast you aside when she had the chance.'

Narrowing his eyes, Ferehn grasped the hilt of the sword still lodged in Tristan's chest and starting twisting it with excruciating slowness. To his great amusement, Tristan started to grunt and then cry out as the pain intensified. Getting down close enough for Tristan to smell the rot of teeth on his breath, Ferehn's eyes became pits of hatred towards the former Mage Killer. 'You are an abomination and if I could kill you now I would do so. As it is, this will not be your fate.'

166

Ferehn started rolling the blade in larger circles and watched with glee as Tristan's face contorted into a silent scream. 'Durin wants you and your Mage friends to suffer for a long time at Rolund's Keep.'

Tristan's eyes went wide at the mention of the infamous Mage Killer Keep as if the name hurt more than the blade in his chest. Even when in the service of Durin, Tristan rarely frequented the place. It was said to be a remnant from the priests of the old religion after they were wiped from Pintosia in the war of the Elven King. The Mage Killers utilized the anti-magic properties of the halls to detain and torture Mages unlucky enough to be taken alive. Tristan never slept well after spending a night in the Keep listening to the screams of the tortured. He always told himself they were Mages and deserved worse but now, after befriending some Mages, even that mantra couldn't save him.

'Grab the girls and tie Tristan behind my horse,' Ferehn commanded the other Knights. 'I want to see how long he can stay on his feet.'

Tristan struggled with the Mage Killers forcing him out the Inn's exit. Every time he became too much of a nuisance, a fist cracked him in the side of the head. He decided it would be best to preserve his energy for the road ahead. From Pinto, it would take the better part of the night to arrive at the Keep and Tristan was already weary from the recent fighting.

Checking on the girls he was happy to see they had at least been laid in the back of a rickety, old wagon. The road was going to be bumpy and they were going to be sore when they woke but Tristan was happy they didn't need to endure what he would.

With the crack of a whip, Tristan was forced into a stumbling walk as Ferehn's horse started to move. He righted himself and tried to keep a little slack in the chains to save his wrists from some of the pain he'd feel later. On random occasions outside of town, Ferehn would kick his horse into a run, pulling Tristan from his feet and dragging him along the rough surface of the dry roads. This would last a few yards before Ferehn had his fill of amusement and Tristan rose with grazes over the parts of his skin his armour didn't protect. Ferehn told him not to get used to the Mage Killer equipment for much longer. Tristan was only allowed to wear it for the journey over land as it would weigh him down more than be of use.

After walking most of the night and with the soft predawn glow on the horizon, Tristan saw the keep in the distance. He had been close to falling down and not getting back up but the sight of the Keep gave him strength to push forward. Neither Aski nor Beverlin had moved throughout the night and this was worrying Tristan. He hoped their head wounds were nothing significant. Seeing Paws poking his head out of Aski's collar at times to review its surroundings gave Tristan hope. The mouse didn't seem to be alarmed and so he hoped this meant Aski at least was going to be alright. Tristan could have sworn Paws was even making a game out of seeing how long he could stay out without getting caught. Tristan saved him once getting the attention of a Knight Paws had not noticed as he was about to see the green triangular ears of the mouse.

As the sun peaked over the horizon, shadows were cast across the uneven stone surface of the Keep walls. Vines were growing over a third of the structure as the Mage Killers didn't bother to try and maintain the grounds. When inside no one would dare try to attack a Mage Killers stronghold and therefore only a single guard stood upon the wall. It was he who shouted for the heavy, wooden portcullis to be raised.

Stumbling into the main courtyard, Tristan was glad when the horse finally came to a stop and he could rest his shaking legs. Ferehn had looked disappointed that Tristan had, for the most part, remained on his feet and walked off with a grunt. The other Mage Killers had thrown Aski and Beverlin over their shoulders before taking them inside the keep. Tristan was thankful that he was being pulled in the same direction. Inside the keep, archways were positioned along the halls to make them seem as if they shrunk when viewed from a distance. All the windows in the keep were large, round, and filled in with stained glass of many different colours. As the sun hit the windows, the rooms beyond were also filled with the same coloured glow giving an almost ephemeral effect.

Before they entered the main hall the Knights turned left, walking down a flight of stairs. This was the only area of the Keep Tristan had never entered as it was where they held the prisoners. He was getting anxious as to whether they would be separated or not but his fears were quelled when he saw the dungeon. The sub floor opened into a room four times the size of the one at the inn closed in at the end of the hallway by strong steel bars. It was here that they were all thrown in together. After Tristan's armour was removed and he was left with the simple pale green, blood spattered tunic underneath, the doors to the large cell swung shut. The clink of a key setting the lock into place echoed around the room.

'Make use of your last day,' a Mage Killer said through the bars. 'Durin will be arriving tomorrow and from then on you will really wish you were dead.'

'Have you ever noticed how the commander acts like something else at times,' Tristan asked. 'At times he seems possessed.'

The Knight struck the bars. 'You aint going to be speaking like that for long.'

Knowing he would never listen, Tristan didn't reply but rather listened as the guard walked back out of the sub floor area. Tristan then crawled across to Aski and Beverlin. Placing a hand on Aski's neck, he felt her pulse. Strong and consistent. Paws was right to be relaxed. Next he felt Beverlin's. Hers was a little fast for his liking but nothing that worried him. He felt her forehead to be sure she didn't have a temperature and jumped as Beverlin started to stir. His hand stroked down to her cheek as her eyes fluttered open.

'Beverlin, are you okay?' Tristan asked, his voice full of worry.

'Where am I?' Beverlin asked. Her mind was still a little foggy as pictures of the intrusion filled her mind. Suddenly she rose to sit up. 'Aski!'

Tristan moved his hand to her shoulders and lowered her back down. He could see that her head was swimming from the sudden movement. 'She'll be fine. Let her rest.'

Beverlin's eyes focused on Tristan and a look of sadness crossed her face. 'Why did you take the swords in my place? I was so worried when I saw those blades sticking out of your chest as you lay in a pool of blood. I've treated you so poorly ever since we met. I didn't deserve it.' Beverlin's eyes glazed over and tears started to roll down her face.

'Sleep,' Tristan told her, stroking her brow. Your body needs to recover. 'We can talk more on this later.'

Without need for anymore coaxing, Beverlin's eyes closed and her breathing became deeper as she drifted off to sleep.

Tristan watched over Beverlin and Aski throughout the day ensuring there were no complications or significant changes in their condition. He was happy that they remained normal. As Beverlin fell asleep Tristan had moved both her and Aski over to a nearby wall. Sitting with his back to it he rested their heads on his lap to give them a pillow. It was from this position that Aski woke first. Looking up at Tristan she smiled.

'Good morning, brother,' she said softly. Her eyes scrunched up and she rubbed her temple as an ache grew in the side of her head. 'My head hurts today.'

From out of her collar burst Paws. He was extremely happy to see her awake once more and started to nuzzle into the side of her face.

'Easy, Paw Paw,' Aski told her furry companion. 'I'm rather tender today.' Paws settled down and curled up on Tristan's lap between her neck and shoulder.

'You are going to be sore for a while, Little One,' Tristan told her. He had long since accepted Aski using the term *brother* for him. 'You took a big hit back at the

Inn. And as for time, it's late in the afternoon.'

Looking around slowly, Aski realized they had moved locations. She started to grow worried. 'Where are we?'

'The Mage Killers have taken us to one of their Keeps. We are currently in a dungeon,' Tristan told her tentatively. He had not expected the smile Aski now gave.

'At least it's more comfortable than the inn,' Aski giggled.

Beverlin snorted in her sleep and came awake with a start. Tristan pulled a face at Aski and they both started laughing at Beverlin. Looking up, Beverlin found Tristan's merry face above hers and overcome with embarrassment at her position, jumped away.

'What's so funny?' Beverlin asked.

'You snorted in your sleep,' Aski giggled some more.

Beverlin's face went beet red. 'I don't snort!' she said becoming defensive looking from Aski to Tristan. 'Women don't snort.'

'Sorry, but you sounded more animal than human,' Tristan teased. Beverlin's mouth fell open. 'I thought it was cute though.'

'What were you doing leaning over me anyway?' Beverlin said trying to ignore Tristan's final comment. 'I bet you were planning on doing something unwholesome to me again.'

'I was allowing you to use me as a pillow is all. I didn't try to kiss you again.'

'Again?' Aski squealed with childish delight. 'Are you two lovers?'

'Aski, stop!' Beverlin face had gone a deeper crimson as Tristan spread his hands looking innocent. 'We aren't lovers.'

Disappointed, Aski pouted. 'You would make such a beautiful couple.' As Aski spoke she held her hand to her head once more.

Seeking a chance to change the subject, Beverlin knelt beside Aski. 'Let me see,' she said pulling the young girls hand back. The skin was split and dried blood was evident around the wound. 'They got you worse than they did me. Did you want me to heal it for you?'

'You can't do that here,' Tristan casually told her.

Beverlin seemed annoyed at this. 'You can see that Aski is hurt. I don't care if the Mage Killers don't like it. I can't see any of them around right now unless you still count yourself as one.'

Spreading his arms, Tristan retreated from the argument. He didn't have the strength to argue with Beverlin when she could be so touchy on the subject of magic. Instead, he sat back and watched as the Mage tried to cast even the simplest of spells. Soon, he could tell she became frustrated as she had moved across the room and was tracing symbols of power.

'It's not going to work,' Tristan reiterated.

Beverlin rounded on him and glared. 'What is this? The Mage Killers never had this type of knowledge.'

'The room we currently reside in was previously owned and built by the priests of the old religion. They crafted these rooms to negate all magical ability. There hasn't been a soul who was imprisoned here that could break the anti-magic field.'

'The old religion,' Beverlin put her hands to her mouth in shock. 'Records show them to be nothing more than beggars on the street preaching from a book thousands of years old. There was a time when people had listened to their teachings but they were a peaceful group and were slaughtered and scattered by the powerful. How could they have done this?'

'There is more to life than what you can learn from a book, Bev,' Tristan said. 'I have said this once before that Mages don't know how to truly live outside of their tomes.'

Beverlin's eyes furrowed and Aski could see that they were about to start bickering again. She decided that she would divert the conversation and try to bring everyone back to a more pleasant atmosphere. 'So was the kiss a little peck on the cheek or was it more mushy and gooey?' Aski asked. She made two fists with her hands and was rubbing the two centres together while twisting and making a wave motion.

This definitely got Tristan and Beverlin's attention as both of them were now staring at her in shock and surprise from her question. After a moment Tristan started laughing and tussled Aski's hair. 'I'd say your hand movements caught the scene well, don't you think Bev?'

'Pfft, whatever,' Beverlin said looking away.

Aski was happy with the outcome. She could see that Beverlin was hiding from herself and her feelings towards Tristan, putting on a big show to try and fool everyone around her but Aski wasn't going to call her out just yet. Best let Beverlin accept her feelings in her own time. Anyway, it allowed Aski, opportunity to tease her. A cool draft caressed her skin and goosebumps rose up all over. Aski shivered as she noticed how fast the temperature was dropping in the cell and moved to snuggle up under one of Tristan's arms. 'It's cold,' she told him as Paws nestled under her clothing once more.

'The sun must have finally gone down. Hard to tell when you're one level underground. Any warmth you can get from me it is yours...' Tristan thought for a moment. 'Beverlin. The nights in these cells are exceptionally harsh. Feel free to share mine and Aski's warmth also.'

'I think I'll be right,' Beverlin said stubbornly. She moved to the far corner of the room and sat down hugging her legs.

Tristan watched her closely noticing the subtle changes in her demeanour as the night slowly matured. He could see her muscles tighten on occasion and she had started to yawn more as she tried to fall asleep. Small shivers ran up her body and to anyone who wasn't paying attention they never would have seen them. Tristan's eyes shifted to Aski sleeping soundlessly snuggled up to his chest. Softly, Tristan shook her awake and indicated her to remain quiet with a finger to his lips. Leaning over he whispered in her ear.

173

Leaning back to look Tristan in the eyes, Aski nodded. She was grinning from ear to ear. Getting to her feet she stumbled over to where Beverlin was trying to sleep. As Aski gently touched Beverlin on the shoulder, she jumped with a start not realizing the girl was there.

'Aski, what's wrong?' Beverlin asked concerned.

'It's cold,' she said impishly. 'I can't sleep.'

'Come here, Aski,' Beverlin said with a compassionate look. She was reaching out her arms to invite the girl in.

'No, you will only be as warm as Tristan was,' Aski told her.

'Then what?' Beverlin said frowning. 'I'm confused as to what you want from me.'

'I need the heat from both you and Tristan.'

Beverlin's mouth came open then closed abruptly as she looked across at the Knight.

'Please Beverlin,' Aski pouted. 'I'm so tired and sore from yesterday. I need to sleep.'

Failing to find an excuse not to and knowing she couldn't refuse the girl, Beverlin nodded. Secretly she was happy she was going to be rid of the cold that gripped her. She had to admit the happiness Aski showed as she bounced around already warmed her heart. Letting the girl lead her she waited for Aski to settle in before she moved to lay at her back.

'Not that side,' Aski said. She pointed to the opposite side of Tristan. 'There.'

'What? How will that keep you warm?' Beverlin said taking a step back.

'Please,' she pouted. 'It really will help me.'

'No, I don't want to,' seeing Aski's face almost break down, Beverlin pursed her lips and shook her head. '...Okay.' Hesitantly, Beverlin moved to the other side of Tristan. At least he wasn't smirking at her. Oddly, he wasn't giving her much attention at all. 'Are you okay with this, Tristan? I can go back to the other side.'

Tristan glanced up and gave her a warm smile. 'It is for Aski after all.'

174

Tristan opened his arm and Beverlin sank down next to him. She was reluctant to move around too much but found herself too uncomfortable in her current position. Giving in to the groans of her body she shuffled around until she found the most comfortable position. 'Better now, Aski?'

'You tell me,' Aski replied with a mischievous grin.

Beverlin's eyes narrowed when she realized she had just been played. Closing her eyes completely she embraced the warmth emanating from Tristan. 'Better,' she whispered.

It was another half an hour before she could settle down enough to start to go to sleep. The cold didn't worry her anymore and her breathing started to get heavier. At that moment she had thought she fell asleep and started dreaming but afterwards knew it was real. She suspected Tristan had thought her asleep but as she was drifting off, Beverlin felt Tristan lean in and kiss her forehead. Her whole body went stiff for a moment as she heard the words *'You really are beautiful'*.

Sleep was a long time coming after that.

Chapter 12

The stairways stretched for hours as Genji descended the ebony steps. Normally it would be minutes at most to get to the location in time he wanted. On this occasion, however, the location Genji was going to, resided in the stairways themselves. It was not something he had practiced before but he felt he was heading in the right direction.

After what seemed like another hour had passed, Genji decided to check his current location in the realm of time. Opening a hole in space no larger than his head, Genji peered at the world he knew and loved. The forest and surrounding mountains indicated an area close to his home. After a few more moments and catching glimpses of a number of landmarks, Genji was able to pinpoint his exact location. This knowledge troubled him for in the direction where his home should be great plumes of dark smoke were rising into the air. He didn't understand why his house would be burning until he saw the group of Mage Killers heading away from the site.

Genji noted it would have been shortly after he and his friends made their escape. This being soon after the time he needed. With a heavy heart Genji closed the tear in space. He knew he couldn't live in his home much longer with the Lost Era soon approaching and the loss of magic imminent but he did want to leave on his own terms. There were items that were precious inside and Genji wanted to return to his own time with them.

Putting the fate of his home out of his mind, Genji kept moving as he listened intently for what should have been the sounds of battle. If his theory was correct, he should come across the Prince fighting on the stairs. There would only be one exact moment where this was possible and Genji didn't want to miss it.

Though time didn't exist on the stairways, Genji felt another 20 minutes had passed him by as he pushed on down the steps. Beginning to get impatient, Genji was about to create another window to the world of time when a dark shadow passed overhead as it floated down into the empty excess of space. A fear froze Genji's heart as he watched the hulking shadow pause in mid-air as if seeking something. The darkness that oozed from this creature was all consuming and was richer and more complete even than the dark backdrop of the abyss below.

A spark of light tore through the air above where the creature floated and a new stairway formed circling downward to terminate at another portal far below. Genji had never witnessed how the stairways formed and took in the sight with great academic interest. He continued to view the event hoping this was the moment he was searching for. He didn't need to wait long when a young man in armour burst through the rift before taking a knee. He looked worn out as if stretched to the brink of breaking and there was signs of a struggle. A large jagged scar ran across the front of his armour. It must have been recent as something like that would of been irritating when worn over long periods.

Genji surveyed other aspects of the man. He was tired, for sure, but Genji could see the man carried himself with strength and confidence normally only found in nobility of this day and age. The armour the young man wore, though sporting a large gash, was polished to a mirror like sheen and had expensive gold details etched into the front. No commoner would ever be able to get such a piece and Genji was confident now that this was the crowned Prince Atalis.

His eyes then sought the prize he quested for. There in the Prince's hand was a sword of a simple elegant design. Reaching behind to a notch at his belt, he brought out his retractable staff, extending it to full length. Pulsing power through the crystal at the top, Genji's eyes started to glow in a red hue. Looking at the sword once more with his enhanced vision, Genji could see an aura of green, misty power that stretched for metres in every direction. It was more powerful than any object he had ever seen before and was left with no doubt. This was the sword that could kill Tristan and the being within him.

As he was about to let his enhanced vision fade away, Genji noted the movements of the dark, shadowy being. He could see the creature more clearly now and still felt no less anxious to be near it. Settling at different points down the princes stairs, the creature touched certain steps. A dark glow that sucked in light swirled for a moment in each spot to be replaced by three Orcs.

This must be the reason for the fighting. Genji watched on as the Prince raced down the steps to take on the creatures. Saw as he lost the sword over the side of the railing, trapped in the body of an Orc. Genji had reached out at this moment but was still inches from salvaging the blade. A sense of dread settled on him knowing the sword could not be recovered after falling into the abyss below. Genji considered the consequences of stealing the sword before the prince came into the stairways but dismissed it almost as fast as it came to mind.

While contemplating his dilemma, something strange happened. He saw the prince chase the third Orc through the exit rift and noted the dark being floating away, the stair fading to nothing, but moments later the scene started once more. The dark being came in from an impossible direction, the stairs manifested themselves and Prince Atalis appeared again at the top. Genji watched as the scene played out as it had a minute before and knew this was something that broke every law. A longing to find the answer choked all other thoughts in Genji's mind and as Atalis lost the sword for a second time Genji made his move.

'Ody,' he said drawing the symbol of power for air as he placed his staff away. This catapulted him across the void between the sets of stairs and he had to hold tight to the far rail else his momentum push him over the edge. Gaining his feet, Genji chased Atalis into the far exit making sure to remain unseen. The scene beyond wasn't what he'd expected but made absolute sense. At the back of the throne room, Genji watched the Mage succeed in a form of magic that must have taken months, if not years to master without the formal training. And to see the exit door open at almost the exact moment he'd cast his magic was amazing. The Mage had succeeded in distance magic with such a simple technique.

Genji's attention turned back to Atalis as the Prince picked up his father's sword. Genji witnessed the ensuing battle with the orc after the Mage was slain.

'No,' Genji called out but the Prince didn't hear, lost in his battle rage. Chasing after Atalis as he entered the fresh portal to the stairways, a dread pain caught him in the chest, almost paralysing him. The pain felt like he was getting ripped in two. This time Genji knew why he was in pain. His former self had just arrived at his home with Beverlin before their quest. The two forms of himself were having trouble existing at the same point in time. He remembered that it lasted only a moment and noted the portal in front of him. Pushing on he threw himself inside and the pain vanished instantly.

Taking his bearings, Genji saw Atalis charging the Orcs. 'Energia,' Genji said drawing a simple circle. As if being squeezed by giant hands, the Orcs constricted and were flung out into the darkness.

Atalis turned to see Genji standing behind him. Slumping to the railing, Atalis had tears in his eyes.

'2,981,' the Prince said. There was such weariness in his voice Genji thought he may fall unconscious there and then.

Genji face flashed between concern and confusion. 'What do you mean?' he asked.

'That's how many times I have run this gauntlet unable to change how I act in the slightest. My mind seemed to take over pushing me on through the fatigue and the dread. That's how many times I have seen my father...' The prince suddenly looked to the exit and saw the third Orc escape through. 'There was a third you fool,' he shouted, getting to his feet and giving chase.

'Atalis wait! It's already too late,' Genji tried to call out. Shaking his head, he too made for the exit.

This time things ended differently. As the prince now held a version of the King's sword, he didn't pick up the one at his father's side. Stepping into the room Genji picked up the younger version of the sword then opened a portal into the stairways before his younger self could arrive in this time. He was too late to enter; however, as he felt the same tearing feeling he did when he brought Beverlin to his home. His body started to contort and separate as the two identical Genji's reacted with each other over the vast distance. Still holding a little control, Genji took two steps before throwing himself through the portal and onto the stairway. The effect of having two Genji's in one time ended and Genji took three gasping breaths. He looked back at Atalis.

'Energia,' the words of power left Genji's lips and, having just dispatched the Orc while still failing to save the Mage, Atalis was pulled into Genji's portal by an invisible force. The portal closed tight and the ephemeral, dark light of the stairways set in.

'Why did you pull me in? I have to save my father!' Atalis screamed.

Genji watched him carefully waving around the King's blade as he spoke. 'You couldn't have prevented what has occurred. Events in both space and time cannot be altered. Only here in the stairways where there is no time can one change their fate.'

'Things were different this time. You could have helped me,' Atalis said. He was still angry but the sting had left his voice.

'I wouldn't agree to such a risky venture. You

180

weren't stuck in the time loop. This time the Orcs may have won and then where would you be. There was an unnatural element pushing you forward before. Now, I can see you are having difficulty even keeping that sword aloft.'

At the mention of the sword, both versions started to vibrate and grow warm. With great force the version of the sword that was older and should not exist anymore, ripped itself from Atalis's hands and merged with the perfect version held by Genji. Having never released the magic enhancing his eyes Genji was shocked when the power of the sword almost doubled. The density and area of the green aura spreading further than he could now see past. Pulling out his staff he released the magic enhancing his eyes. The aura disappeared instantly and Genji could see properly once more.

'Put that sword down,' the voice Genji heard was low and filled with the chill of winter. He looked up to find two of the coldest eyes levelled on him.

'You mean this sword?' Genji asked holding the King's sword aloft. With his staff Genji used his Shadow magic to make the sword invisible.

Atalis's eyes bulged from his head and his body froze as a terror gripped his heart. 'Bring it back,' his voice was almost a shriek as he spoke.

'Is it true you need the sword to prove your status and become King? Genji asked unconcerned for Atalis. The Prince was too weak to make a worthwhile attack and with the sword seemingly gone, Genji held all the cards.

'Yes,' Atalis replied after a moment's hesitation. His shoulders slumped as he understood his predicament. 'What do you want? Riches? Power?'

'Nothing of worth for I have all I need,' Genji said simply. 'All I wanted was for you to calm down so you may look over your position with an even head.'

'And what is my position?' Atalis asked. 'The King has been slain and his heir is stuck on a staircase in the dark.'

'Not stuck,' Genji assured him. 'I'm taking you to the

181

Pinto from my time. It's a week or so in the future for you. Your people have no leader and are reeling at the loss of their King and disappearance of their Prince. If I took you back sooner time would change and that would cause a paradox. I can't do that. You therefore need to make a choice. Accept you are the new King and take your place on the throne with your father's sword or deny your fate and find your own way out of this realm.'

Atalis's brow furrowed. 'That doesn't sound like much of a choice.'

'Well, if it was me I would choose option two but I know how to get out of here,' Genji smirked. He felt empowered talking down to a Prince.

'...Give me back my sword and take me to my people,' Atalis said through gritted teeth.

'Good choice,' Genji agreed. With over exaggerated movements, Genji traced the symbol for earth into the sky. 'Yerkiry,' his voice boomed. From the ground in front of Atalis, a perfect replica of the King's sword started to take shape from the very substance of the stairs themselves. When it had fully formed, Atalis gripped the hilt and held it tightly. 'Follow me, Prince,' Genji instructed. Without waiting for a response Genji started to walk up the steps. He could barely contain his glee as in his hand was the true sword, invisible to everyone but Genji. He also now knew the true history of the sword and why it lost its power. The replica would never be what this powerful blade could, even when made from the same enchanted substance as the stairs. Reaching the exit, Genji paused and stepped aside. 'One last thing before you exit,' Genji said.

Atalis moved to look out the rift. People had stopped to stare at the odd tear in the sky that formed in their city centre. 'What is it?' he asked Genji.

Genji placed a hand on his head. 'Sleep well. You deserve it.'

Atalis's eyes went wide but Genji was too quick with the healing arts placing Atalis into a deep sleep. Genji knew his body needed to recover so he made sure the

Prince wouldn't wake for at least 48 hours. Atalis toppled forward and out into the street. Following, Genji jumped out and immediately started calling for guards. The sound of the guardsmen echoed from a side street and soon they stood before Genji and Atalis who lay face down.

'What has occurred here?' the lead guard demanded levelling a sword.

'Your Prince has returned,' Genji said rolling Atalis over. Immediately the guard lowered his blade recognizing Atalis.

'How?' the guard stammered.

Genji grinned inwardly. 'The people who murdered the King escaped through a magic portal. Without fear for himself, Atalis took up his father's sword and chased them into another realm. He has been fighting a horde of enemy almost 9000 strong who were set to invade your defenceless Kingdom. He made allies in this other realm and in the end defeated your enemy. I was tasked to bring him home. Our healers have given him a strong sleeping draft to recover. It will be two days before he wakes.'

'Your story sounds farfetched,' the guard said sceptically. 'You will accompany us to the castle until this can be resolved truthfully.'

Genji spread his hands and opened a rift behind him. 'Sorry but I must return to my home world.' As the guard made to restrain him, Genji stepped through and onto the stairways closing the rift to anyone else. Looking at the King's sword, he stroked the blade. Shivers ran up his arm as he felt the power held within.

Beverlin woke from a deep, peaceful sleep. She felt refreshed and warm to her very core, not having slept like that in weeks. Her hand absentmindedly rubbed over the sheets of her bed and with a small yawn, she glanced around the room. Directly in front of her was the still sleeping form of Aski. Coming full awake, Beverlin remembered just where she had slept the night before. With a sheepish look, she spied Tristan above her and let out a sigh of relief seeing he was still sleeping.

As her nerves calmed her eyes started to wander over the sleeping Knight. His tunic was marked by several large holes that continued to sink into the skin. Beverlin knew these were hurting Tristan but with his calm, almost normal demeanour, everyone was fooled into forgetting that fact. Not realizing when it started, Beverlin caught herself tracing around the wounds. *'You could pretend you were asleep,'* the thought entered her mind unbidden and Beverlin was surprised to find herself contemplating the idea. Finally giving in, Beverlin laid back down in the position she had woken in. Emulating someone who was asleep, Beverlin closed her eyes and her breathing became deeper. As if having a restless sleep, she would move on occasion feeling the curves and muscles of Tristan's body. At one point, Beverlin's hand started to glide southwards on its own. *'No, that wouldn't be right,'* Beverlin chided herself but her hand slowly marched on. *'Aski is there. She might wake,'* Beverlin tried to argue but still she couldn't bring herself to stop. As her hand rose and fell over Tristan's strong abdominal muscles, Beverlin's breathing became ragged and rolled in trembling waves. Her hand stopped just below his stomach as she built her courage and listed off a number of excuses in her mind should she be caught. She took in a deep breath

'You do know I don't sleep, right?' A voice sounded from above Beverlin

Instantly, Beverlin's hand shot up and colour drained from her face as she stared wide eyed at Tristan. 'You were awake?' she asked horrified. There would be no chance now to spin a story for herself.

'This body of mine doesn't let me sleep,' Tristan explained. He glanced down at Aski. 'Maybe on a more private occasion..?'

Beverlin, having yet to recover, jumped up and darted across the room.

184

'Are you two fighting again?' The small voice of Aski piped up. She was wiping sleep from her eyes as she spoke.

'No, little one,' Tristan told her. 'Bev and I are starting to work things out. Our road may be a little bumpy but I think we'll build a deep friendship.'

The look Aski gave was of pure joy. Her face lit up with a warm smile and she got butterflies in her stomach dreaming up far more romantic situations than Tristan's words implied. She looked at Beverlin who instantly looked away, red-faced. Beverlin's expression suddenly changed to a more serious look and Aski watched as she reached out to rub her hand over the edge of the floor. 'What is it?' Aski called, propping herself up on one arm. Tristan, too, became intrigued.

'Runes!' Beverlin almost shouted. 'There are runes etched into the floor.'

Aski turned to paws who only gave her a quick chirp. Her brow furrowed. 'It's not something Genji has much knowledge of it seems,' Aski said.

'I can't say I know much about them either,' Tristan divulged. 'Is it something that could help us?

'I can't say for sure...' Beverlin spent a moment examining the runes, tracing each around the room. When she crossed to the other side her shoulders slumped and she turned back to the others. 'It isn't going to help.'

'What do they mean?' Tristan asked.

'The Mage Killers have unknowingly been using magic to suppress the magic of Mages,' Beverlin said with a wicked little grin. 'Runes are an archaic form of magic long since given up in regular practice. They take months to prepare and hours of incantations. The slightest mistake could see the runes rendered useless and it would only be after all the hard work that you would find out if you were successful. The priest of the old religion put a lot of time and effort into crafting these runes to block 8 of the 9 disciplines in Magic. The only magic that can be performed in this room is summoning. Either because it wasn't a prominent form of magic when the keep was built or the crafter didn't have knowledge of how to craft the runes. Summoning is all that can be used.'

'You don't sound confident in this form of magic,' Tristan observed.

'That's because I have no ability in it at all. Summoning is the highest and hardest form of magic a Mage could do. Everyone strives to reach a level to harness it yet rarely do any Mages get there. Genji was the only one here that could have done it.'

'If we put our efforts into chipping away the runes?' Tristan asked taking a different tact.

Beverlin shook her head. 'The major pay-off for using runes is that the magic isn't just reliant on the physical rune markings. Think of the rune as a doorway crafted with great care and precision to perform one task. The incantations pass through the doorway created by the rune to fill the physical form attached to it, in this case the dungeon floor. You will spend years chipping away the magical elements and that's if you actually had the proper tools.'

'So, we're back to square one,' Tristan said with a frown. 'There couldn't be much longer before Durin turns up and we're set to torture. All we can do is pray for Genji's arrival.'

'I can do it,' Aski said. She had been having a private conversation with Paws about the fundamentals of summoning. It didn't sound overly complicated when using the vast knowledge and experience stored in Genji's mind as a reference. Paws was even able to provide images and full memories, including emotions and thoughts, of when Genji had been successful. Aski had dismissed the memories when she saw one of herself being summoned. She wanted to distance herself from the girl she had once been.

'Do what?' Beverlin's eyes narrowed as she looked from Aski to the mouse. She had a good idea on what

186

had just transpired. 'If you are talking about summoning then forget it. Just knowing what you need to do won't help. It takes months of practice to get the feelings right and even when you do summon a creature it takes months more to understand and know how to control it. You lack the experience to pull such a task off.'

'It is through Genji that I have experienced summoning. Paw Paw doesn't only tell me how to do something but he provides me with the memories Genji holds so that I may experience every emotion and thought as if I was the one performing the magic.'

'A memory is a fractured being that can mislead as much as it can guide. You still need experience,' Beverlin told the girl as if that was the final word.

'It's all that we have,' Aski argued.

'What are you two squabbling about?' Tristan asked. He couldn't quite follow the conversation as there seemed to be one piece of information he was missing that would tie it all together.

'Aski believes she could use the summoning craft with no experience other than a few of Genji's memories her mouse provided to her via a rather intricate link between the three,' Beverlin told him.

'Her mouse provided her?'

'A Lazurian Mouse is a magical being and shares in the magical ability of it's host. For Paws, that is Aski and because Aski is linked to Genji through a summoning attempt, Paws is linked to him also. Paws talks to Aski through this link.'

Tristan pursed his lips as he thought about what Beverlin just said. After a moment he shrugged his shoulders and nodded. 'That makes more sense now. So how are we going to do this?'

'We aren't,' Beverlin said sternly. 'The discipline is far too dangerous and, in any case, we need salt to make it work.'

'Then scrape it off the walls,' Tristan told her simply. 'We're close to the coast. The salt in the air has dried on these walls for many centuries without being cleaned away.'

'You're not listening to me,' Beverlin said.

'No, I'm not,' Tristan replied then turned to Aski. 'Are you sure you can do this?'

Aski nodded. 'I have to.'

'Well said,' Tristan turned back to Beverlin. 'Sometimes in life we can't just play it safe. Sometimes we need to take the hard risks that could lead to our failure. I know it's hard and you are scared but put your trust in us. We need you on our side just as much as you need this to work.'

Beverlin's shoulders slumped over. 'We'll summon a fire demon to melt through the bars.' Turning away from the others Beverlin moved off to gather salt from the walls.

Tristan winked at Aski and they too, set to work on collecting salt. As they scraped of what they could, they brought it to the centre of the room and placed it into a small pile. The pile grew to be 20cm in diameter and sat 5cm above the ground. Beverlin called everyone to stop.

'That's going to be all the salt we can safely get without contaminating it,' Beverlin said. 'Aski, do you know what type of creature you are going to summon.' Beverlin decided that she wasn't going to help with the types of creatures or give hints to help make this venture a success. Though she wanted Aski to succeed so they could be rid of this place, Beverlin also held a small part of herself that hoped she would fail. She wanted the girl to learn a lesson with magic that time and effort is needed to master each discipline. Beverlin did feel jealous that Aski need only ask Paws a few questions and could perform any form of magic when she had spent years researching and learning through experience to get to where she was now.

Aski thought through all the different summons Genji had practiced on at the Academy of Mage Craft. All of them required large amounts of salt to bring forth, all except one. It was on a night when Genji had returned to his cottage for an evening of personal study. Out in the woods on a cold night the skies opened up and he was drenched in rain. With only his cooking salt to use Genji produced what would be his first summoning circle. Desperately needing a fire and with little energy to use for lasting elemental magic, Genji called forth a small salamander. With the creature he was able to start a fire, rain hissing as it hit the creatures back. Aski remembered that, though it was small, the flames were far beyond what a natural fire could burn. 'I will summon a salamander,' she said seriously. 'The creature will be small and so will need only a little amount of salt but its flames could melt through the metal bars.'

Eyes narrowed, Beverlin accepted the answer was the best course of action for the supplies they had and the situation they were in. 'Then best get to it,' Beverlin told her.

'You aren't going to help?' Tristan asked starting to get concerned. Aski had already started to sift and move the salt around to form the shape of a flame circle.

'The circle needs to be formed from the caster alone. There is magic in what you produce yourself,' Beverlin said stretching the truth just a little. 'And as I stated before I don't know anything of worth in the art of summoning. Aski has the most knowledge and as you can see, the Lazurian mouse is already helping her.'

Tristan saw that Paws was indeed standing close by chirping at times. As he did, Aski would correct a part of the circle to be more sharp or emphasise softer curves. Tristan noted the circle, though placed in a round fashion, wasn't actually a circle. It was a sequential pattern of four large and four small wisps of flame moving away from the centre point.

'*Tristan,*' the ancient voice echoed in the Knight's mind.

'What do you want? Tristan said aloud. Beverlin shot him a look but realized he was speaking to no one in particular and remembered there was another that accompanied them on this quest. A demon tucked away in Tristan's mind.

'*Beverlin was correct to cast doubt over the girl's ability,*' the voice said. '*She will bring a creature to this plane of existence but her mind is still too young to fully control it. Be ready for when the moment comes that she loses control you will have to step in and kill it. Beverlin believes that she will be able to dismiss the creature but the old priests in their infinite wisdom also set a rune to block dismissal magic. Beverlin won't be able to help.*'

'What's it saying,' Beverlin asked but Tristan raised a hand.

'Heal me first,' Tristan said. Beverlin's eyes betrayed her intrigue in the statement. 'If I am to fight a demon, I will do so at my peak.'

The laughter that rolled through Tristan's mind was maniacal. '*You seek to bargain with me. Fine. You have become accustomed to these wounds and they will do little more for you if they are left, anyway.*'

Tristan felt warmth flowing through his body. The feeling was gentle and invigorating. Lifting his tunic, he watched as a number of wounds closed and his skin became perfect again. Emotions took hold of Tristan and he had to hold his eyes shut tight lest he break down completely. A single tear escaped from his eyelid and rolled down his cheek. 'Thank you. I would have protected my friends with my life regardless but thank you.'

'*I need you to be ready. Even a moment's hesitation could be fatal.*'

Beverlin and Aski watched as the newly replenished Tristan stretched and limbered up his muscles. 'A small mercy. I'm glad for you,' Beverlin said.

Aski had a massive smile on her face knowing what this meant to Tristan.

'Thanks, Bev. Maybe on a more private occasion I will be in a better state,' Tristan said with a wink.

Beverlin gave him a mischievous smile and just shook her head. Tristan looked back at Aski.

'As you were, Aski.'

190

Aski nodded and with the circle complete set her mind to the task. She set about mimicking Genji in every way when he performed a summon. Using her mind's eye, she pictured the salamander in a fiery hell with volcanoes erupting and rivers of lava covering the land. On the banks of one such river, a small salamander was focused upon. Creating a portal like doorway through her mind and connecting to the salt circle she raised her hands in emphasis. 'Ignis Adducere,' she cried.

Power in the form of fire spewed forth from the salt circle in a swirling mass of heat. Aski didn't lose focus on the creature she was summoning and soon the dark outline could be seen within the flames. Before the flames had even died away the salamander pounced out of the fire tornado and into the room hissing at the prisoners. Aski hadn't been prepared for the sudden charge from the creature and froze in shock. Only the loud squeal from Paws brought her back into focus. Moulding her will around the fire lizard, Aski created a wall that trapped the soul of the creature within. A strong force pounded against that wall as the salamander fought back against Aski, struggling for its free will. A crack appeared in her wall as the onslaught continued but Aski had gained some semblance of control over the body. Keeping part of her mind focused on holding the creature's soul at bay, she used the other part of her mind to command the creature to melt the door away.

'Only focus on the lock,' Tristan said. He could see the struggle Aski was going through.

As sweat beaded on her forehead, Aski directed the lizard to spit fire onto the lock until it melted away, the excess liquid metal rolling towards the floor. With the command being carried out Aski focused solely on holding the salamander under her control as long as possible. More cracks ran across the surface of the wall she had crafted from her will. Large chunks had started to slip away and an eye; slitted into the shape of an hourglass stared menacingly at her. As a moment passed between the two, the salamander became more ferocious, smashing harder and harder into the wall until finally it broke down. The shock of this overpowered Aski's mind and she passed out.

'*Now*,' the ancient voice told Tristan.

Before the salamander could fully recover and turn its assault back on those within the room Tristan ran in taking the lizard into a headlock. Instantly Tristan's skin started to burn and flay up one side of his body where it came into contact with the salamander. He let out a long desperate howl as he summoned the strength to break the creature's neck. As it slumped lifeless to the ground, Tristan rolled away rocking back and forwards in the new agony that coursed through his body. Beverlin was next to him, wishing there was some way to make him feel better.

'The door,' Tristan grunted.

Looking up Beverlin saw that the area where the lock had been was glowing bright red but the door was still securely shut. She started to ram the door with her body praying that what they had done was enough. Her prayers finally answered when, on her third strike, the door started to move. Two more strikes and the lock broke cleanly away. Beverlin glanced up the stairs beyond and saw a guards head peering down. Seeing her he immediately ran out into the halls.

'The prisoners are escaping!' the Mage Killer called out numerous times.

Beverlin swore when the sound of booted feet could be heard echoing throughout the keep.

192

Chapter 13

Stepping out from the rift, Genji looked around the room. It was void of people and Genji recognized signs of a struggle. It must have happened only moments before as Genji spaced the time he left The Hedgehogs Dilemma and the time he returned by only a quarter of an hour. He knew there would still be residue from anyone who entered, around the room and decided to try his hand at a piece of magic he always had trouble with. He would try to recreate the scene of what happened using the energy left behind in the residue of the room. When Genji performed this form of shadow magic in the past, the images were always disjointed and semi formed. Arms spontaneously sprouted from the sides of heads or single legs would walk around as if they were full bodies. The animation reminding Genji of a walking stick in motion.

Reaching back, he pulled out his retractable staff from his belt and extended it. He felt odd holding both the sword and the staff but Genji had yet to create a sheath for the Kings sword and therefore had no choice. Closing his eyes, Genji concentrated on the magic he was about to perform. The room filled with a soft glow as the magic started to take affect and as Genji started to open his eyes the glow grew into a blinding light. Shielding his eyes from the brilliant light, Genji knew it shouldn't have been this powerful. He stood blinking rapidly trying to bring his lost sight back. Finally, he was able to see and he was shocked by the images before him. Perfect replicas of Aski, Beverlin and Tristan were moving around the room as they must have when Genji left.

'We will just need to be patient,' the copy of Tristan spoke.

Genji shrieked when he heard Tristan speak having never heard either his own or any other Mages recreation make any sort of noise. A knock at the door took his attention away and he put this revelation to the back of his mind for later deconstruction.

'Just a minute,' Genji called out before he was knocked down by Beverlin walking through. Genji became serious, his brow furrowed and his lips were slightly pursed. The images should be nothing more than shadows. There should definitely be no substance to them. 'Beverlin?' Genji called but his friend ignored him. Not real then, Genji told himself.

He watched as Beverlin opened the room door to a group of Mage Killers and the scene that ensued. As the group charged in, Genji was forced to the back corner out of the way. They could definitely touch him and move him but if Genji was in the way it was as if he became little more than straw getting tossed around. He didn't want to know what would happen if he got stuck between two moving objects in the wrong way.

Out of the way now, he watched the scene play out with baited breath praying beyond all that was possible his friends would make it out alive. Relieved when they were finally taken away with breath in their lungs, Genji dismissed the shadow magic. Putting his staff away, he stared down at the sword in his other hand. There was nothing to say the sword played any part in the power of Magic Genji wielded but he was still suspicious of the blade. Either way, Genji knew the only place in the area they could be taken was Rolund's Keep a few leagues from the Golden Pass. Genji also understood without a doubt they were heading for torture and a long painful death. There was no way he would let it happen.

Genji decided he would take the opportunity to test Aski's theory about moving vast distances in a moment. Feeling powerful within himself, Genji became extravagantly exaggerated and, on a whim, used the sword to carve open the door to the stairways. Peering inside a small staircase could be seen and Genji bounded up the steps two at a time. This was so much easier than jumping around both great distance and time. Diving from the exit with acrobatic fluency Genji expected to find himself on a hillside overlooking the keep but the plane he landed on was not what he expected. The realization this was his first moment alone since becoming a Summoner Mage had spurred him on to act foolishly and now as he exited the rift and closed it behind himself, he instantly regretted his actions. Genji had no way to determine where or in fact when he was.

As he started to move in a random direction, parts of the landscape began to feel familiar somehow. Coming to a clearing, Genji found himself overlooking the ocean and the Golden Pass that linked Pintosia and Adelside across the great ocean. This scene was disconcerting as; knowing exactly where he was now, Genji could pinpoint the location of the old Keep but was speechless to find nothing left except an overgrown ruin.

Lighting crackled across the sky, the thunder so loud it shook the very land Genji stood on. Turning, Genji was greeted by a frightening sight causing the blood to run from his face and his knees to tremble. In the sky across the ocean was the figure of the shadowed creature Genji found in the stairways manipulating Prince Atalis's entry and exit points. Only now, the creature took up over half the horizon. Angry storm clouds spewed out from the creatures cloak and with the sweep of his hand the creature sent large chunks of the land of Adelside hurtling into the sea. Where the land mass landed large waves, miles high, raced towards the surviving coastline to eat deep into the land.

Genji didn't wait to witness the entire worlds end and crafted himself another time vortex to take him back to the Academy of Mage Craft. Genji had a need for familiar surroundings and after finding his home destroyed, the academy was the next best thing.

Climbing the stairways, Genji jumped as seawater poured through the open portal behind him falling out into the endless void below. A shiver ran through Genji at what he'd just witnessed. Making his way to the exit he stepped out once more into a world he didn't expect. Instead of buildings, students, large, extravagant fountains and the smell of distant car fumes, all there was were large exotic trees. The rich, pure air was even more fresh than the cliff side air surrounding his cottage.

Genji had a hard time believing that to be possible in a world that man existed knowing all the ways the human race had polluted and trashed this once beautiful planet. He had a hard time believing until a creature of similar size to himself walked into the small clearing. Patches of feathers covered a reptilian textured body. The feet each had a single wicked talon that, Genji knew would only be used to slash open his stomach. The head was the most fearsome part. As the creature slowly turned to study Genji, the Mage saw a deep intelligence in the creature's slitted eyes and a terrible death in the hundreds of needle like teeth lining the beast's mouth.

'A Velociraptor!' Genji exclaimed, his breath catching in his throat.

As if some spell had been broken the raptor leapt feet first at Genji. He was only metres from death when Genji clenched his eyes shut and threw out his hands to protect himself. 'Kaytsak,' he found himself saying the word of power for lightning but knew he hadn't drawn the power symbol. He knew there was no time to act now and clenched up even further.

Time passed and nothing happened. The smell of acrid, burning flesh crept into his noise causing Genji to empty his stomach until he started dry reaching in convulsive waves. Covering his nose he looked for the raptor. At Genji's feet was the twitching, trembling body of the creature, smoke rising from all over its skin. Genji realized the creature was continually being electrocuted by some invisible force. He was in disbelief that he did this without a power circle and eyed the King's Sword suspiciously once more. Raising the blade

196

in front of him, Genji decided to test it. 'Ody,' he said calling forth a gentle breeze.

From behind him, Gale force winds passed around him and tore through the large trees ripping anything in its path from the ground. 'Emundetur a fluxi seminis,' Genji said dismissing his magic and the wind died instantly. With new eyes, Genji peered at the sword he held running his hand up it's edge. Small sparks leapt from the blade to tingle across Genji's skin causing goosebumps from the raw power. 'You are far too powerful to use for just any magic. I'll keep you safe,' Genji said to the sword.

Drawing an alchemy circle, Genji put the sword's power to work on crafting a sheath that could hide both the blade and the power it held. Sheathing the sword in the simple crafted black leather and hanging it to rest at his side Genji tested his elemental magic one last time. Nothing happened and he smiled.

This time when he created a portal to the Stairways he was confident where he would exit this time. He estimated a little over a day would be the right time to enter the Keep and this time when he peered through the exit he was no less troubled at the sight. Before him, the Keep stood tall and proud but in the courtyard Aski was fleeing from a large number of Mage Killers, held in check only by Tristan's skill. Of Beverlin there was no sign.

'Quickly, Aski, this way,' Genji called.

Looking up with hope in her eyes Aski redirected herself to hurtle towards the open portal. As she dove inside Tristan turned to make for the portal also but Genji had already started to close the rift. He held the sword aloft for a moment so that Tristan could get a glimpse of the weapon he so desperately sought as he raced to reach the portal before it shut. 'I'll keep you safe,' Genji said once more to the blade turning his back on the scene outside. He would not let it be destroyed just to kill the Mage Killer.

Mistaking the sentence for her, Aski started to cry. 'What about Tristan? We can still help him. He's right there... He's right there!' She cried pointing back.

Genji ignored the girl's tears and started walking up the stairway to their new destination. An explosion shook the grounds outside the portal but Genji didn't look back.

Tristan cried out as a hand touched his burnt shoulder. Rolling away, he glanced up with tears obscuring his vision. 'Heal me. Heal me,' he repeated over and over to the ancient being that had latched onto his body. Only emptiness replied to his whimpering.

'Tristan, we need to go,' Beverlin said with urgency. It broke her heart to watch this strong, brave man in such pain. She felt at fault that she couldn't dismiss the salamander in time.'

Tristan's eyes finally cleared and he locked onto Beverlin's. 'You need to kill me.' His voice was strained with the effort it took to craft the sentence.

The words almost broke Beverlin but she held strong. Kneeling beside Tristan, she took his right hand in her own. 'The King's sword holds the power to end your suffering. Genji has gone to fetch it and will meet us in the courtyard of this very keep,' she lied. 'You need to find the strength to move passed the pain. We need to move before the guards get to us or we are all dead.'

'I can't,' Tristan cried. 'The pain. It's too strong.'

'You must.'

Shaking his head, Tristan clamped his eyes shut to the pain. It was like a thousand knives stabbing him up his left side over and over again. A thousand knives he couldn't fight off or hide from. Suddenly, two hands cupped his cheeks and he felt something warm against his lips. The pain fled to the background as his mind comprehended this new sensation. Tristan's eyes shot open to find Beverlin kissing him fiercely. Tears clung to her eyelashes. Her expression was a mixture of sadness and pain but Tristan also saw love etched into the lines on her face. With the pain forgotten to the void, Tristan leaned into the kiss, returning it with as much emotion as he felt from it.

Neither Beverlin nor Tristan had wanted the moment to end but knowing of the pressing danger, Beverlin tore herself away. 'It's now or never. We must flee,' Beverlin said.

Pain roared back through Tristan's body but the momentary lull gave him a temperance to it. He remembered what it was to fight off pain and disconnected himself from the burn. Reaching out a hand, Tristan took Beverlin's and she helped him to his feet. Wincing, as small bursts of pain made it passed his defences, Tristan strode defiantly to the door. He saw Aski standing just outside, waving for them to hurry. Her mind was still foggy but she was recovering quick.

'Into the corner. Hurry,' she called in hushed tones. 'There is a vision barrier set.'

Trusting the girl over his own eyes, Tristan stepped across the empty air into the corner of the hallway. Beverlin and Aski followed as the first of the Mage Killers charged down the stairs. He was followed by a large group of knights who charged into the now open cell.

'No noise,' Aski whispered just loud enough for the others to hear. She placed a finger over her lips to emphasize the point.

'Where the bloody hell are they,' one of the knights shouted.

'There is no way they could have gotten by us unseen,' said another.

As the knights surveyed the empty room, one was examining the door to the cell. 'They were able to use magic in the cell,' he hissed. 'For all we know they snuck by us cloaking their bodies with invisibility.'

A growl came from the knight deepest inside the room. 'What are you lot waiting for? We need to seal the castle grounds.' Herding the group out of the cell, they ran back to the main hall. Shouts of alarm and orders to close the gates echoed around the hall and filtered back to where Aski, Beverlin and Tristan stood crammed into a corner. Tristan's breath had caught in his lungs as he clenched his fingers so hard the whites of his knuckles flourished. As Aski and Beverlin moved away, the air burst from Tristan's lungs while he took a moment to mentally fight back the pain.

When he was ready, Tristan looked from Aski to Beverlin. 'We need to move through the castle at speed. If a knight sees us, try to take him out before he can give away our position. If we stay in one location too long we will be surrounded and will have a hard time fighting off a large group of men trained to battle both magical and regular combat alike. There is a room at the top of the stairs that is used to store prisoner equipment. I'll stop in to get my sword.'

'Get my staff too,' Beverlin told him. She then spread her hands out, palms facing each other. 'It is retractable so should only be this big. There is a blue gemstone at the top. It may be useful once we leave the castle grounds.'

Tristan nodded. 'Ready?' he asked.

'Ready,' Beverlin said.

Tristan's gaze moved to Aski and Paws.

'Ready,' Aski said. She had a determined look on her face. Paws chirped his agreeance as he sat upon Aski's shoulder.

'Good, follow me and stay sharp,' Tristan said. Without waiting any longer, he turned and moved up the stairway. Pausing at the top, he peered out into the hall. Only one knight was in sight standing guard outside the storeroom. He seemed distracted by the commotion in the rest of the castle and was constantly trying to look down a hallway opposite where he stood. Timing his moment, Tristan darted out keeping away from the knights peripheral. Too late did the knight see his approach. As he tried to bring a weapon to bear, Tristan had the man's head in a lock that slowly rendered the knight unconscious.

Glancing into the storeroom, he spotted their equipment. They'd been piled into a corner on top of old, rusted weapons and armour. Around the room were remnants of old Mage robes and staffs that were becoming brittle. Tristan gave the crates full of potions a wide birth as even a small bump could set some unknown magic into action. As Tristan was setting his sword in place at his hip, he spied a silver chainmail shirt. It glittered without a mark upon it as if it had just been polished and placed here.

'*Take it,*' the ancient voice echoed in his mind. '*You will need it in days to come.*'

'Why should I listen to anything you say?' Tristan growled. 'You told me you would heal me and now look at me.'

'*I didn't tell you to jump onto a creature of fire. A creature that lives in lava flows. The wounds you carrier are of your own doing. The armour will help protect you in the future.*'

'I will not listen to you anymore,' Tristan said. There was no reply. Tristan glanced at the chainmail with brow furrowed contemplating his options. 'Argh!' he grunted before collecting the armour and quickly wiggling into it. He noticed that each small ring had a rune etched upon it but he couldn't discern what they were for. He made a mental note to ask Beverlin once they were safe.

As Tristan exited the room, Beverlin gave him a devious look. 'Just the sword?' she said seeing the glint of silver where none had been before.

Tristan eyes narrowed as he considered the remark. Throwing Beverlin her staff he decided to ignore it. 'Let's go,' he said, heading towards a hallway he believed was the exit. The others followed as Beverlin softly chuckled.

Aski's heart was racing as they turned every corner and entered each new room. Three times she had jumped as a knight suddenly appeared out of nowhere. Twice she had seen them die in a pool of blood, quickly dispatched by Tristan's sword. The third had exited a room coming out almost on top of Aski. Bringing up the rear, Beverlin drew the oxygen away from the knight's lungs and the man died gagging for air. Aski had frozen when she saw the knight and she felt more and more helpless as the seemingly endless flight continued.

Coming into a large hall with four exits, they were once again greeted by Mage Killers. The three knights had already surrounded Tristan who was fighting both the knights and the flaring pain of his burns. His left arm was held tight against his body as if paralysed. Parrying one blow, Tristan opened the neck of a second knight with a sweeping cut. As he brought his sword around to block another wild slash from the first knight, a third ran in to ram a dagger into Tristan's side. Aski could only produce a small scream as she saw the attack but was relieved to see the chainmail Tristan now wore had turned it away.

'Ody,' Beverlin said, drawing the power symbol for air.

The third knight clutched at his throat unable to breath. He died agonizingly slow as Tristan dispatched the last combatant, thrusting his sword into the man's skull. As the group recovered, the echo of hundreds of armoured boots could be heard from every exit.

'They're coming from all sides,' Aski squealed. She kept looking at each exit expecting to see vast numbers of Mage Killers coming upon them at any moment.

Tristan pointed at one of the exits. 'That is our way out. 20 metres and we'll be outside near the gates.' As he finished speaking a large group of Mage Killers filled their exit and marched upon them. Tristan felt a hand tugging at his clothes and he looked down to see a fearful Aski watching another exit. Tracing her line of sight, Tristan saw another group of knights just as large as the first. He looked to each exit and was met with a similar picture. 'Stay behind me, Aski,' Tristan said throwing her a deceptively confident smile.

'ODY!' Beverlin shouted and a large burst of air forced its way down the hallway of their escape. All the Mage Killers in the hall were sucked out of the castle as if by a large vacuum. 'Go! I'll hold the rest of them at

202

bay,' she commanded. Tristan looked ready to argue. 'We don't have time. Get Aski to safety or I'll send you flying down the hall like the others.'

Tristan looked from the advancing Mage Killers to the trembling girl beside him. There was determination in his eyes as he looked back at Beverlin. 'Don't linger to long.'

Beverlin smiled. 'I'll be right behind you. One last thing, you each need to hold your breath in the hall. The oxygen will be slow to come back. You will have another 15 seconds at least.'

Tristan nodded. Picking up Aski and Paws, he raced down the hallway. Glancing back only once, Tristan saw walls of fire around Beverlin. As Tristan broke free into the courtyard he was surprised to find a few of the knights Beverlin had expelled from the keep were recovering. Quickly placing Aski down, he drew his sword. 'Make for the gateway and see if you can find a way through,' he said.

'I'm scared,' Aski told him.

Tristan noted the quiver in her voice. 'There is nothing to be frightened of little one. You are a Mage of exceptional ability. You have saved us many times over. It's everyone else that should be scared to approach you. Now go while I sort out this lot,' Tristan tilted his head towards the small group of Mage Killers that were now advancing on them.

Tristan's words fed Aski's courage and she remembered the magic that ran through her veins. Fear made her forget but she wouldn't let it control her any longer. Turning towards the gate she ran across the grounds as fast as her little legs could carry her. As she heard the sound of steel on steel she looked back over her shoulder to see Tristan keeping the knights at bay. Her knight. She felt even more calm knowing that Tristan would always be there to protect her.

'Quickly, Aski. This way,' Genji called.

Tristan heard Genji's voice and kept an eye on Aski waiting for her to make it to the portal. When she was safe he abandoned the fight and sprinted for the slowly closing portal. He judged that no matter how fast he ran he would never make it in time but he desperately ran on. He had no time to call out as this would only slow him down. As the portal was almost too small to fit through, Tristan saw Genji flash him a sinister look as the Mage showed a sword at his side. At this moment Tristan knew he was betrayed. He saw Genji turn and start to walk away behind a portal no bigger than his head. Tristan slowed in his run.

Suddenly, as the portal was about to close completely, the keep erupted in a massive explosion of fire and smoke. Large chunks of the wall landed in the courtyard and surrounding land. The Mage Killers who were chasing Tristan were now squashed under one of the towers. Colour drained from Tristan's face as he remembered Beverlin was still inside.

Beverlin!' He called but no reply came.

As the smoke cleared he could see that the centre of the blast was where Beverlin had been fighting the enemy. Tristan's chest clenched tight as the emotional loss hit him. Tears flowed freely and he mourned the only woman who had stirred his heart and awoken a love within him.

A horn rang outside the castle gates announcing the arrival of Durin. Not wanting to stay for a lifetime of torture, Tristan found a section of wall that had been destroyed in the blast and fled the keep.

'I will avenge you, Bev,' Tristan said. His mind was now solely locked on Genji, for if not for his betrayal, Beverlin's sacrifice may of held some meaning for their quest.

Chapter 14

A mix of emotions were churning inside Aski's mind. She couldn't think straight after watching Genji leave their friends behind. She bore holes with her eyes into Genji's back but it had little effect. There was no emotion in the Mage as he took unhesitating steps up the stairwell. He didn't even flinch when an explosion burst through the sliver of the portal that remained before it closed.

'Stop!' Aski screamed.

Genji turned back to look down at her, Eyebrow raised in question.

'We must go back. The explosion just now couldn't be anything good but it could mean they have a chance against all those knights.'

Genji shook his head. 'I have seen the remains of that Keep after the explosion. There is nothing left. In years to come the grounds will be taken back by nature and the Keep will become a distant memory. No one could have survived.'

'Tristan could have. He can't die by any natural means. He might be hurt and alone. If Beverlin was the one who crafted the attack she may have directed it away from herself. They could still be alive and you're just leaving them there.'

'As you say, they could be alive,' Genji said dryly. 'If they are then they have each other. Beverlin can use time magic so they will meet up with us later.' With that Genji turned and continued up the stairs. There was no empathy in his heart for Aski's worries as the safety of the sword was all that mattered.

A darkness crafted of fear and despair crossed the stairways like an evil mist. Aski trembled as the shadow circled around to stop at the edge of the railing. It's eyes like silver globes of emptiness locked to Aski's. She felt them eat deep into her soul as if reading her inner most thoughts. She was frozen, paralysed through fear with no way to break free and call for Genji to save her.

Paws read the situation and felt the intrusion of the

creature. Not only was it searching through Aski's mind but it was probing Genji's and his through their intricate links. With no hesitation Paws sunk his fangs deep into Aski's shoulder causing the girl to flinch back before letting out a shrill, high pitched cry.

Genji turned to find the dark entity floating before Aski. He recognized it as Aragaranatan, the one who would destroy the world as they knew it. He took two steps in retreat knowing he was no match for the creature and saw Paws hiss at him for his cowardice. Genji remembered his link to Aski. To allow the girl to die now would mean a harsh, almost detrimental severing of their link causing great pain that could last months, if not years. This was the risk any summoner took when summoning a creature. If it were to die the caster would be harmed also. Genji couldn't risk the severity of the pain he would feel when losing the link to Aski unnaturally after being joined for so long. With trembling hands he reached for the hilt of the sword. The sword was warm to the touch and Genji felt a soft humming vibration through the metal. As he drew the sword, light filled the area like a thousand candles.

Aragaranatan cried out like a hundred tortured souls wailing in the darkness. He broke off from Aski and circled outside the light of the sword. Genji could just see his misty form at the edge of the light circling backwards and forwards.

'Thank you, Genji, for this gift you have given me,' the evil spoke. It's voice scrapped at the soul causing goosebumps to rise and tremors to run up the spine.

'I give you nothing, foul creature,' Genji said, more confident now with the power of the sword to back him. Aski had raced up the stairs to stand at his side.

'But you have,' Aragaranatan replied. 'I travelled the girls mind, read her thoughts, saw the power that was in her soul. She is a gifted child who will accomplish great things in her time. Curiously, within her mind I found a doorway to your own. A link no normal human could share. Through this I travelled to your mind and read your memories. What I found there was invigorating. I saw my image in your mind time and again. You have shown me my heart's desire. I will be free of this wretched stairwell to cause destruction and havoc on the puny creatures that walk the lands. The time is not quite right but I need only be patient now.'

'You will never be free,' Aski yelled defiantly from the relative safety beside Genji. She felt the creature's eyes once more upon her.

'Dear child, you are but a pawn in the larger picture. You are a child of darkness and as such would make a powerful vessel for me,' Aragaranatan laughed. The reverberating sound was such that it leeched away happiness from all around. 'You would not even need the summoning mark to allow me access.'

Genji brow furrowed at the comment and he stuck out a protective arm. 'Get back, Aski. Make for the exit.' She hesitated. 'Now!' Genji yelled and Aski started to move. Holding up the sword, Genji made a slow retreat.

'You believe the sword will save you,' Aragaranatan laughed again. 'You spurned the creature that would have given you the ability to wield this weapons true potential. The creature of green mist had chosen you but you blocked it. Now, you can only harness a tenth of the swords power. Enough to irritate me but not enough to save yourself.'

Doubt rose in Genji's mind and as a show of power Aragaranatan slowly approached through the light. Swirls of dark mist vanished from his ephemeral body as if evaporating only to seemingly grow back again. Genji's mind started to race and his heart beat faster. Missing a step, Genji fell back upon the stairs and Aragaranatan swooped upon him. With a sweep of his hand, Genji cut into the dark creature's outstretched arm. With a cry, Aragaranatan reared back holding the stub of an arm that vanished into dark mist. Genji saw that the mist was swirling back and forming the arm once more. Taking the moment, he got to his feet and started running up the stairwell. He saw the exit still some distance away and could tell Aski was too slow to reach the door before Aragaranatan had recovered.

'Ody,' Genji said and a strong gust of wind picked Aski up and catapulted her from the stairwell into the world beyond. Feeling more than seeing, Genji knew the creature of darkness was in hot pursuit once more. Without looking back, Genji bolted for the exit, throwing himself through the doorway. He started closing it the moment he was clear.

'Your end is soon at hand, Genji Tsukasa. I shall be waiting for when you next enter the stairwell,' the grating voice of Aragaranatan said drifting through the portal.

Genji shivered at the use of his full name and knew he had lost his ability to time travel lest he wish to face the unnatural force once more. A cry brought him back to the present and he looked across to see Aski with cuts and abrasions over her skin after landing with force on a patch of gravel. A large gash could be seen across her forehead from where she had struck a rather large stone. With the sword sheathed and it's invisibility cloak in place, Genji moved to Aski. He placed both hands upon her and started the healing process. Warmth moved through Aski's body sealing the wounds and mending the skin. He found the gash in the forehead tricky as the blow also caused the brain to swell. Pouring healing energy into Aski's head, Genji worked the brain through the process of healing itself and returning to a normal state. It took a matter of moments and when Genji knew Aski was going to be okay, allowed himself to rest. The healing drained him beyond what he expected and needed a moment to catch his breath.

'Genji? Is that you?' A voice asked behind him.

Genji turned to see Gerard, his examiner, standing over him. Looking around, Genji took in the familiar sights of the Academy of Mage Craft and remembered this was the destination he chose. 'Gerard, I didn't expect a welcoming party.'

'I hadn't expected you at all. It's almost been a year since last you were here,' Gerard saw Aski coming to, his brows furrowing. 'Are you both okay?'

208

'We had a run in with the demon you would have found mention in the book on darkness while traversing the stairs,' Genji said. 'That though was the least of our troubles.'

'Beverlin and Tristan fell to a group of Mage Killers while trying to escape,' Aski said as she caught on to the conversation. Her eyes had become glassy and Genji thought any moment she would burst into tears.

Gerard nodded understanding. 'And the sword? Were you able to recover it?' Gerard caught the look of annoyance in Genji's expression before he hid it behind a fake pout.

'No,' Genji said with heavy sincerity. 'The blade was lost to a time loop. I cannot recover it without crossing my own physical self-multiple times.'

'Pity,' Gerard replied. He glanced down at Aski who had a rather confused look on her face. She was staring at Genji's hip as if something was there. Gerard smiled at the implications. 'Aski,' he got the young girls attention. 'Have you finally been released from the summoning so that you may attend the Academy of Mage Craft...? No, I think not.'

'She is still with me,' Genji stepped in front of Gerard. 'She will be the one to release the summoning when she is good and ready. Even then, she may not wish to attend this Academy.'

'I would like to attend,' Aski said.

Genji turned to look sternly at her. 'What?'

'One day when I'm able, I want to learn about magic here.'

'One day,' Genji pursed his lips before slowly looking back at Gerard who had a smile on his face. 'It was good to see you again but we had better be leaving now.' Taking Aski by the arm, Genji headed out the front of the Academy.

'Don't be a stranger,' Gerard called after him.

Genji ignored the man as he led Aski to the taxi rank close by. 'I'll take you to my home in the city. It may not have the same atmosphere as my forest cottage but it is comfortable.'

'Why did you lie about the sword?' Aski asked. 'You said you didn't find it but it's strapped to your belt.'

'I...' Genji thought quickly realizing Aski had been on the stairs when he had used it. 'I didn't find the real one. I only found a replica that works at half power. You saw the demon on the stairs. The real sword was designed to kill it but the demon wasn't worried by my imitation. It's a fake.' Genji saw Aski register this new information, her face showing her disappointment. With a smile Genji stepped into a cab that pulled up.

'Chirp, squeak,' Paws sounded.

Aski's expression grew dark. Paws had told her the sword was the true sword of power and that Genji didn't have the means to wield it to its full potential. Also that Genji knew this was the genuine blade. As Genji turned to look back at her, Aski's expression shifted once more hiding her true feelings. She jumped into the taxi. Placing her seatbelt on, Aski started to wonder just what had happened to Genji while he was searching for the sword on his own. He once stated that as family he would always be honest but right now lied to her. He was not as trustworthy as he had once been and Aski needed to watch out around him now.

Drops of water dripped from Genji as he turned the handle to off. The steamy shower was just what he needed after a long and surprisingly profitable venture. The King's sword was a lucky find for his magical ability and Genji didn't feel any remorse for what he had to do to Tristan to protect the weapon. For all he knew, the knight was dead and buried hundreds of years ago anyway and there was no harm done. He was sure the creature that possessed him would have used up its energy by now or jumped to a new host. It may have been worthwhile to mention to Tristan in the beginning that a spirit or demon will get tired of the body eventually and seek out a fresh host. It may have quelled some of Tristan's drive and allowed him to let nature take its course. In any case, Genji didn't see himself as the bad guy for what he'd done.

210

Not a thought was given to Beverlin who he had also been left behind.

Reaching for a towel, Genji decided to dry himself the old fashioned way. Also with the sword left safely on his bed in his invisibility cloak, he didn't care to draw the symbol to perform magic. It felt invigorating using magic through the sword that Genji never wanted to do spells without it again. There was so much raw energy that he felt like a lesser Mage to play with the basic forms of magic now. Genji thought of Gerard and laughed. The man was weak and had no right to bring Genji back down to his level. It was humorous that Aski would want to train in the use of Mage Craft at that place.

Reaching back, Genji wrestled his dark hair into a ponytail. At least Aski was innocent in her belief that the academy was all powerful. He would change her mind though. Genji would show her the things he could do and she would only want to be trained by him. After some time he would even let her see the sword and possibly use it once or twice for inspiration. Genji knew he lied to Aski about the sword but he was only trying to protect her. He knew she wasn't ready to feel this sort of power. Only a Mage of Genji's stature could hope to wield this beautifully crafted blade. Or at least someone trained by Genji. He couldn't risk just anyone touching the King's sword... No, the Mage's blade, Genji corrected himself nodding. He couldn't risk someone unworthy using the Mage's blade and damaging it.

Throwing on a robe, Genji left the bathroom and started making his way to his bedroom. He couldn't see signs of Aski in the living area and thought she must have been resting in her room. Genji glanced out over the city. From the vantage of the penthouse suite in such a tall building Genji could see everything the world below was doing. And with all the exterior walls made of glass, there was a 360 degree view. Genji rubbed his feet on the carpet as he walked. The grey material was ruffled in a way to resemble the feel of grass and Genji thought of his cabin. He considered all the magical items he'd left behind. Originally, he would have jumped back to a point in time he wasn't around and retrieved some things but with the sword in his possession he didn't care for second rate magical objects. Aragaranatan wasn't going to make use of the stairwells easy either.

A low humming caught Genji's ear and he turned to see the TV was left on. The sound was set just below what a person could hear clearly. Reaching for the remote, Genji pointed it at the screen and paused as he was about to hit the power button. On screen was a husband and wife talking to a reporter of some sort. The wife was clearly distressed with tears in her eyes and holding onto the husband letting him do all the talking. What caught Genji's attention, however, in the wife's hand was a picture of Aski. Genji turned the sound up.

'Please, if anyone has seen our Hazel we just want her to come home,' the husband said.

Genji sniggered at the TV hitting the power button. The man just wants his plaything back and the wife is too stupid to know any better, Genji thought. Genji made a mental note of the parents' features and stored it away for a time when he may come across them randomly, putting Aski in harm's way. He would kill these people before he let them touch another hair on Aski's head. Reaching for the handle to his room, Genji pushed open the door feeling good about himself.

'Genji this apartment is wonderful,' Aski told him. She was sitting on the bed with Paws perched in front of her.

Genji smiled at the girl making herself at home before spying the Mage's blade resting in Aski's lap. A sudden fear clenched at Genji's chest and his eyes bulged. 'What the hell are you doing, you stupid girl!' Genji screamed. Genji stormed towards the physically shocked girl. Aski's face had drained of all blood and she was paralysed having never seen Genji so angry even against an enemy. 'Give me my sword!' he screamed again. Without waiting for Aski, Genji reached down and snatched the Mage's blade from her lap.

With the hackles erect down Paws's spine the mouse leapt upon Genji's arm sinking his fangs deep into the skin. As Genji struck out, paws jumped back to the bed landing in front of Aski. He raised his hackles once more and hissed dangerously at the Mage.

Rubbing his arm Genji looked from Paws to Aski. The scowl etched into his face broke when he saw the terror evident in Aski's eyes. 'I'm sorry,' Genji's voice was still sharp and direct when he spoke. 'This sword is dangerous. It's a weapon and not a child's plaything. I don't want you to hurt yourself.'

'I was only resting it in my lap,' Aski said keeping her eyes low. There was a quiver in her voice as she spoke. 'I was being careful.'

'How did you find it? I had it cloaked in invisibility. Only I could see it.' Two bulging eyes starred back at him and Genji could see that he would be getting nowhere with her. After a long pause, he turned to walk out the door.'

'Maybe it's the link we share in our minds,' Aski said barely above a whisper.

Genji stopped for a moment realizing his stupidity. Of course Aski could see the sword. The bond they shared through the summoning spell meant that they would be sharing everything magical about themselves. A spell designed only for Genji would still allow Aski to utilize it. This was going to be a problem.

Glancing at the TV a thought occurred to him. Picking up the phone, Genji contacted the local station. 'Hi, yes, I need the address for the parents that were on air recently. I've seen their daughter, Hazel, and have a way of returning her to them.'

Her little head bobbed along to the music as the car weaved its way through city life. It had been too long since Aski felt the comfort and ease of traveling in a vehicle and she felt as if her very essence was melting into the soft leather seats. Looking around the interior Aski knew the car wasn't production made. For one, there weren't any seat belts. All the seats in the car could spin to face any direction the passenger wanted and on more than one occasion, Genji had left the driver's seat to retrieve something from the back storage compartments, leaving the car to drive itself. In the roof was a full-size TV that, with a little backwards pressure on the seat, a passenger could lay back and watch. In the doors, were menus for a range of food and drink. Aski had pressed a button for an orange juice and within moments a glass of sweetened, pulp free, juice arrived on a little conveyor belt below the armrest.

'Was this car your design or is it universal Mage transportation?' Aski asked Genji as she sipped her juice.

Genji narrowed his eyes considering the girl. 'You really have a keen eye when it comes to picking out magical objects. The car is my own design,' Genji said with a genuine superior air about him. 'No one else could conjure a car with such finely tuned attributes.'

'It's really comfortable,' Aski commented. She was becoming uncomfortable with how snobbish Genji had become recently. The comments were uncalled for and usually made him less of the person she had come to trust at the small cottage in the woods. She decided to change the subject. 'So where are we going today?'

'It's a secret,' Genji replied. He kept focus on the road, an odd expression crossing his face.

Aski decided not to push it. Whatever it was, it made Genji serious. When he woke her this morning Genji had entered her room without permission. It was only a foot in the door but it went against everything he promised her. With a deep monotone voice he commanded Aski out of bed and to get ready to go out for a drive before returning to the living area. It had been a shock but the idea of getting out of the apartment and possibly go shopping or some other fun activity excited her.

Shifting her attention to watch the world outside her window, Aski saw a little bakery that reminded her of one her brother used to buy treats from. They would walk down to a nearby park... Aski turned her head and there was the open green fields with the small pond from her memory in the middle. A sense of dread started to grow within Aski's gut as she began to recognize specific landmarks from her past. Please don't turn here, Aski begged in her mind right before the blinker came on.

'Genji... Genji where are we going?' her voice betrayed her face, trembling and frantic.

'Somewhere important. That's all I'll say,' Genji told her. Again, he wouldn't look at Aski.

Glancing at Paws, Aski expressed her concern. Immediately, Paws chirped back and Aski's face drained of all colour. Reaching for the door handle she tried to open the door but it wouldn't budge. She looked around desperately but couldn't see any other form of escape. Looking back at Genji, Aski suddenly lunged for the steering wheel to alter the course. Genji threw his arms up in the air as Aski wrenched the steering wheel violently... But the car didn't turn.

'Aski, sit down,' Genji instructed.

'No! Stop! Let me out! Leave me alone,' Aski screamed.

'You will be getting out soon enough,' Genji said calmly, lacking all emotion.

'No, you promised you would stop if I said so. I don't want to go back there.' Tears had started to form in Aski's eyes.

'I'm doing this for you, Aski. You will thank me one day,' Genji said.

Paws hissed and started chirping almost bird like. Hearing Genji's true intent from Paws, Aski was shocked he would go so far.

'Please Genji! I don't even want to touch the Mage's blade. It means nothing to me. Please don't take me back there.'

Genji looked at her sharply. Turning his seat, he faced Aski directly. 'Where did you hear that name?' Aski turned away. 'Aski, look at me when I'm talking to you... ASKI!' Genji reached out to pull Aski's face back into view but Aski struck his hand away. She finally turned back to look him straight in the face, her eyes burning with hatred.

'Don't you dare touch me,' Aski's voice was almost a whisper but the strength behind it was crushing. 'You took me in as family. Helped me choose a name. You showed me that life could be enjoyable even when the rest of the world was out to get you. As long as you had friends who watched your back nothing bad could go wrong. But you proved me wrong, Genji. Greed will always win out and you're going to abandon me to people who will hurt me just so I don't see your precious sword.'

'That's not the reason...' Genji stammered but Aski held up a finger.

'Don't lie to me. Paws is linked into your mind and has been telling me your thoughts, showing me your memories.' Genji's eyes bulged and he looked at the Lazurian Mouse. 'Paw Paw told me how to produce the barrier near the desert; he showed me the finer points of transmork...' Paws squeaked and Aski nodded. 'Transmuting objects and, while we were locked inside that dungeon hoping you would come and rescue your friends, Paws taught me how to summon a Salamander. The memories and feelings of your first summon in your room were all I needed.'

Genji let out a long, guttural laugh. 'Your story was almost believable, Aski, but you failed on one major point. You're too young to summon a being of any sort. And even if you had of somehow crafted the summoning circle perfectly and called forth a fire demon as you say, you would have lost control instantly. Your mind is too fragile, your body too weak.'

Aski smiled. 'Yes, I lost control of the Salamander and my brother paid the price for it, getting scorched

216

up one side. Still, I was able to hold the creature's soul captive behind a wall of will long enough to force it to melt the lock upon the door. How do you think we got out?'

Genji pursed his lips as he considered the possibility that what Aski said was true. He shook his head dismissing it. That wasn't important right now. 'It doesn't matter what you say. We are here and you will be released.'

Wide eyed, Aski looked around seeing the house in which she once lived looming over the vehicle. The harsh tones of the walls encroached upon her space suffocating her. Each breath came in short ragged bursts as her chest tightened. The door to the house started to open and Aski dropped to her knees just peering over the window sill. Her mother came out first and paused on the porch. She had her hands cupped together resting under her chin as if hoping for something to happen. Aski almost felt for the woman until her step dad walked out to stand beside her. The man with the sunken expression and perpetually dirty clothing. Her mother remained with him all this time. The feelings that almost grew when Aski saw her mother died instantly. Whatever the woman got she deserved for sticking with a man like that.

Hearing the car door open, Aski watched as Genji walked around the front of the vehicle to greet her mum, Jo, and step dad, Henry. As the car was sound proofed from the outside world, Aski relied on Paws to relay the conversation taken straight from Genji's mind. Seeing her mother slap Genji hard across the face, Aski waited impatiently to hear what was going on. With a chirp, Paws relayed the first few words.

'I'll make sure you rot in a prison for the rest of your life for what you have done to my family,' Jo spat.

The raw sting of the slap raged beneath Genji's skin as he took a step back. 'Ma'am, I have only tried to help your family. When I saw the intervi...'

'Liar!' Jo's eyes were wild. 'You've had that little slut for over a year now and didn't try to find us. What?

217

Have you grown tired of her now?'

'No..?' Genji hadn't predicted the reunion would go so wrong.

'Did you know she tried to steal Hank from me,' Jo said pointing at Henry. 'When he turned her down she would make up outrageous stories about him to try and break us up. She probably ran off with you because she couldn't get what she wanted from Hank.'

Every word was a knife in Aski's heart and she felt her cheeks grow damp from tears. She watched as Genji just stood mouth hanging low. Paws told her that Genji was starting to regret his decision and was contemplating walking away. Aski could only hope this would eventuate. At least there was a little humanity deep down in the Mage trying to break free.

'Calm down, Jo,' Henry said in a soothing voice. He'd stepped up behind her and was rubbing Jo's shoulders. 'We still want to get our daughter back.'

Genji shot the man a dark look and to his surprise it was returned by Henry behind Jo's back. Reaching down he grasped the invisible sword hanging at his side. A deep breath calmed Genji's thoughts and steeled his mind to the decision ahead. 'Your daughter has been in my care for the period she has been missing, I will not lie, but I had no clue to where she came from or who her parents were. For a time, I didn't even know her true name. When I saw the interview last night, I knew I needed to bring her back to you.'

Aski's heart sunk as it was only moments before her mother and that man knew she was there.

'And...?' Jo asked spreading her arms in front of her at elbow length, palms up.

Genji's brow furrowed. 'And what?'

'Where is she?'

'Your daughter's waiting for you in the car,' Genji replied.

Even before Paws had relayed Genji's words Aski could already see her mum pushing him aside and marching towards the vehicle. Aski felt her chest tighten even more and her heart raced as the imminent confrontation approached. She couldn't think straight. All she could picture in her mind was the fire burning behind her mother's eyes as the angry woman closed in. With a clenched fist, Aski pounded the lock in the lower frame of the window. From every side of the car, a satisfying click could be heard to indicate she was secure.

Jo tried the door handle and a look of frustration overwhelmed her when she found she couldn't get the door open. Turning around, she started flailing her arms at Genji pointing back at the door. Aski never heard what her mum said but her eyes opened wide in fear seeing the remote Genji held. On instinct, Aski drew a triangle face up. 'Krak,' she said. The rims of each door started to glow with an orange light. Heat emanated into the car but Aski ignored it. As long as the doors were now welded shut nothing else mattered.

Genji knew Aski would put up some type of fight using magic but with the sword at his side he was prepared for whatever happened. Reaching down, Genji took hold of the Mage's Blade and whispered the word of power for energy. In an instant one whole side of his car was ripped away by an invisible force. A shiver ran down his spine from the sheer power he now possessed in just a whisper.

Colour drained from Aski's face as she sat exposed to her parents. She saw Paws protecting her, hissing at Jo baring his small fangs. Turning to flee, Aski almost went head first into the cars remaining side. Trying desperately to open the handle, her instinctively driven mind couldn't process the fact she welded them shut moments earlier. Screaming in frustration and fear, Aski banged against the glass.

'No!' Aski cried as cold tentacle like claws wrapped around her ankle.

Pawing at the car door, Aski sought some leverage or protruding grip to hold herself back from the turbulence that had come to steal her away. As everything had shifted to become more streamline while the car was turned off, Aski could only desperately cling to the seats.

Jo's grip tightened around Aski's ankle and with a sudden surge of power, Aski was ripped from the vehicle. She landed with a thud on the polished stone driveway, a gasp escaping her mouth as pain shot through her muscles. Paws jumped down beside her hissing at Jo.

'Eww,' Jo said spying the large mouse. 'Why do you have that filthy creature?' Jo brought her shoes up to try and stomp on him but Paws kept jumping away.

On one attempt, Aski thrust her hand out to protect her friend and Jo stomped on her arm instead. With a cry, Aski retrieved her arm and cradled it as Jo was able to get a good kick in sending Paws flying into the bushes.

Jo looked at Aski with disdain. 'It's your own fault for sticking your arm out. The creature was disgusting and probably had diseases.' She produced an ugly smile when Aski didn't reply, curling up tighter into a ball. 'Are you going to come quietly now?'

Peeking out from under her sleeve, Aski saw Henry leaning against a side wall with arms crossed. He had a cruel smile slashed into his face and piercing eyes that hooked into Aski and didn't let go. She then glanced at Genji who was also leaning against the home but his head was bowed as if asleep. He wasn't paying any attention to what was happening.

Rolling to her belly, Aski started to crawl away but Jo was ready for this. Catching Aski by the ankle, she started to drag her up the driveway towards the house. With the awkward angle she found herself in, Aski could only cry and succumb to her current situation. She couldn't generate any momentum to get away.

For a brief instant, Aski saw the form of her brother, Tristan, across the street. He was bathed in golden light and had a soft smile that lifted her spirits. Aski calmed a little and her rational mind started to filter through. Wincing for a moment as a rock bit into her thigh, Aski looked back across the road to find the form was nothing more than an illusion. The uplifting affect however didn't leave her and Aski remembered the last words Tristan spoke to her.

'There is nothing to be frightened of little one. You have been gifted with such exceptional ability in life. Strong of heart, pure of soul, and wise beyond your years. You have saved us many times over. It's everyone else that should be scared to approach you.'

Every part of her being resonated with these words, building her courage, igniting the fire within. A perfect calm fell across her soul and for the first time since arriving at her old home, Aski was thinking clearly. 'Kaytsak,' Aski said with purpose, etching the symbol for lightning into the air.

'Quite mumbling and speak properl...' Jo started. A bolt of lightning rippled across Aski's skin and latched onto Jo's hand. In an instant the strength in the electrical force grew from a slight buzz to an explosive avalanche that burst into Jo catapulting her into the air. She landed with a thud against the Colorbond fence dinting it inward and rendering Jo unconscious.

Henry stood with his mouth hanging open for a moment before a burning rage started in his head. 'You bitch!' he growled. 'How dare you lay a hand on your mother.' Henry started to approach Aski, his hands set into fists so tight the colour was draining from his fingers. Whatever narcotics were coursing through his system kept Henry from realizing just how dangerous Aski had become. 'I'm going to beat you to within an inch of your life for the trouble you have put us through.'

'You will not touch me again,' Aski told Henry confidently. She drew a triangle face up. 'From this moment forward I am no longer yours or Jo's daughter. You are nothing to me.'

Henry genuinely laughed. 'You will do as you're told.' He reached out to grab her by the arm.

'Krak.' The word was so soft, so gentle and Aski scoffed as she spoke it. Henry had manipulated and crushed her tiny spirit in the time she had been with him just as he had done Jo's. Aski hadn't believed she could do anything to save herself from her entrapment. She didn't realize that all along she needed a single word, any word, to free her from the cage. Even without her magic, Aski could have talked to a school councillor, a policeman on the street, a store keep or even just a neighbour. She understood it would cause conflict but that was what she needed to escape. It would be enough to break the false love her parents preached and give her the life of freedom she deserved. One simple word. The magical outcome was just a bonus.

Henry froze mid movement. His eyes were fixed on the ball of fire floating in the space between them. He was having a hard time comprehending what was happening. 'Whaaa...' he mouthed.

'I've changed since you saw me last,' Aski told him. She looked straight into the eyes of the man who tortured her. 'This flame is a manifestation of my hatred for you. It will live within you feeding on your organs, causing you immense pain. Your skin will blister and melt away. Slowly, though, giving your body just enough time to replenish what was lost. No, you won't lose your life from this but for as long as you abused me the flame will eat at you. You will not know peace for years to come. You will feel everything I felt and more. Then it will end and you will have to pick up what is left of your life. I don't give you an end because I am weak or feel sorry for you. I give you an end to the pain because I need to forgive and forget. If I don't you will always have a hold on a small part of my soul.'

Fear was evident across Henry's face and as the flame started to approach him Henry began to retreat. Coming hard against something firm, Henry struggled to turn only to find he was held in place by Genji. 'What are you doing? Let me go,' Henry screamed struggling to break free. The flame entered his body disappearing below the surface of the skin with no pain. Genji let the man go. Henry dropped to his knees breathing heavily.

Placing a hand on his shoulder, Aski funnelled healing energy into Henry until he overflowed. 'And if you decided to end your life before your sentence has been complete your body will heal you instantly. Goodbye, Henry.' Aski took one last look at the insignificant human as he started screaming uncontrollably. Narrowing her eyes she glared at Genji. 'Now you get what you want. Do what you have to.'

'Emundetur a fluxi seminis,' Genji said raising an arm at Aski.

Shimmering for a moment, Aski disappeared into a ball of golden light. When she was able to see again, Aski found herself in her brother's room upstairs. The exact location she had been summoned from. A shiver ran up her spine as a strong sense of freedom fell upon her. True freedom with no attachments to anyone or anything. An image of Paw Paw lying in the garden crossed her mind.

'Paws!' Aski shouted racing down the stairs and out of the house. She saw Genji transmuting the vehicle to repair the damage but ignored him running to the garden bed. Inside she found Paws lying in a foetal position unmoving. Gently picking him up, Aski started stroking his fur pulsing healing energy into his body. Tears were flowing from her eyes as she tried to revive her friend. 'Please, please, please,' Aski said resting her forehead on Paws.

'Chirp,' came a soft noise from within her arms.

Aski pulled away, breath caught in her throat. 'Oh, Paws,' Aski cried relieved her friend was going to pull through. The joy was ruined by Genji's voice.

'Will you be coming with me?' He called from the car.

Aski just shook her head and ignored him.

'There is nowhere else you can go right now,' Genji reminded her.

Aski thought for a moment then turned to face the Summoner Mage. 'The next we go to the Academy of Mage Craft I will be leaving you.' Without another word she got into the car focusing on Paws recovery.

Chapter 15

Tristan watched from across the road as Aski went through her ordeal. So much did he want to race across and save her from those terrible people but Tristan knew that if he did this, she would always look for someone to save her in life. There was a deep well of strength within her and Tristan wanted nothing more than for Aski to access it. As the sun broke through a large cloud the light engulfed Tristan causing his invisibility illusion to shimmer and break for a moment. His eyes met Aski's and he gave her the proudest smile he could before recovering his illusion. And he was proud. Tristan watched Aski's strength recover and nodded at the way she handled the situation from that point.

For a year after his betrayal at Rolund's Keep, Tristan sought any sign he could of the Summoner Mage Genji or word of a powerful sword wielded by a Mage. To his surprise, stories from taverns and inns suggested that the Mage Killer Commander Durin was killed by just such a weapon at the Keep the day Tristan had fled. For a brief moment only, Tristan felt a small amount of guilt for the harsh thoughts he directed at Genji. This stopped when he heard the Mage was actually a woman and not Genji at all. How she had come by the sword was anyone's guess but Tristan started to believe with all his heart that Aski had recovered it at some point in the future and come back to save them all from their fate.

Following his original calling, Tristan spent his exceptionally long life hunting and killing Mages in response to the feelings burning inside him over Genji. Lost without their Commander, it wasn't long before the Mage Killers accepted Tristan once more into their ranks and even raised him to the new Commander position. Under his command, the Mage Killers fulfilled their mission in eradicating all the Mages and anyone who showed promise on the mainland.

For a long time, Tristan was happy and did everything he could to ensure the Magic never returned to the land. He knew he couldn't hold it back forever as Genji's very existence was evidence of this. When he finally failed and the Mage Killers were no more Tristan took a different tack and founded the Academy of Mage Craft. He even spent his time learning the craft so that when he once more came up against Genji, he would be ready in every way. He knew that even years of training and perfecting the art may not be enough to combat the power of the sword but he needed to try. It was a comfort to know that win or lose, the sword would still need to be used to stop him and end his life.

There was one person that never left Tristan's mind through all the years and that was Aski. He pledged himself to be her Knight and would honour that until the moment he passed from this world. Tristan always kept an eye out for a birth notice of a girl named Hazel with a brother named Tristan. It had been hard enough to find Aski's birth name and when a girl was finally born at the proper year with her name, Tristan couldn't be sure that it was Aski. For one, she was an only child. As time went by and no other child sharing her name was born Tristan decided to watch this Hazel. Soon, her father left and her mother met someone new. This man showed every sign of abusing Hazel and Tristan had to restrain himself from hurting Henry. He needed to allow the time to pass and Genji to bring Aski to him in the past. He couldn't alter anything before that point.

A thought came to Tristan and he smiled. He realised with a deep joy that he was Aski's true brother. Tristan used his ability with illusion to disguise his tortured body, wrapped in enchanted chain mail, in a cloak resembling his younger self. He planted memories into Aski, Jo and Henry of his existence as their son and brother then resumed this life. In this way he could stay close to Aski and give her the brother she always remembered. He could protect her against Henry and show her the love every child deserved in their life.

He couldn't stay forever though and soon the plans he set in motion decades before started to come to fruition. It was the hardest choice Tristan could make but knew he needed to leave Aski unguarded for a time. Henry couldn't wait to see the back of Tristan and on the day he left home, Henry took Tristan aside.

'If you ever come back to this house, I will make sure you never wake once you fall asleep,' Henry threatened.

Tristan just smiled walking out the door. To reply would be to set Aski up for a harder time then she was already destined to endure. To witness how mature she was in her revenge and the strength she showed brought a tear to his eye. She was now his sister in every way Aski thought of him as her brother. Now that she had no ties to Genji it wouldn't be long before Tristan could free her from his world also. He noticed she was already starting to be disillusioned by Genji's charms. It was bound to happen. She was an intelligent girl.

From the shadows, a dark hooded figure moved to within a metre of Tristan. He stood waiting for instructions keeping his hood low. There were no discernible marks or emblems around his figure.

After watching Aski leave with Genji, Tristan acknowledged the hooded figure. 'The time has come. Genji is in possession of the sword and the young girl has been released from their long-standing connection. It is time to strike.'

Without a word the hooded figure faded back into the shadows. Tristan continued to watch Genji's car until it was lost around a corner.

'You can't ignore me forever,' Genji said as he pulled the car into an empty park outside his apartment. Aski just rolled her eyes as she continued to gently stroke Paws' fur. 'I mean you're going to want something soon. Information, food, entertainment. You'll need to talk to me then. When you're ready, I'll be here to help.'

Pursing her lips, Aski locked her eyes onto Genji's.

She was struggling with a wave of emotions over what had just transpired but at the top of it all was a dark and churning rage. It wasn't the forced reunion with Jo and Henry that caused such heightened emotions; they were as nothing to her now. Rather, it was Genji's betrayal. From the moment he saved her from a harsh life, Aski had slowly grown fond of the man. She saw him as a distant uncle and with the rules and boundaries that they made together, Aski grew to trust him. It was all too late when she realized that Genji was only nice until the next new thing came along. Now, Genji was all about that stupid sword hanging invisible at his side. There was no thought or concern for Aski if it affected his relationship to the piece of metal. He wasn't the same person and Aski would now treat him as such.

'You don't need to answer,' Genji said after a moment of silence. 'Just keep it in mind.'

The fake compassion made things worse. 'The only help I need from you is to get me to the Academy of Mage Craft,' Aski said through clenched teeth.

Genji smiled feeling victorious having made her talk. 'It's going to be a while before I set foot in that place again. In fact, I hadn't intended to ever go back.'

'But you said you would take me there,' Aski's face dropped. Just another lie to add to the list.

'No, you stated you would be leaving me the next time we go there but I never responded either way,' Genji corrected opening the car door. 'I accept your decision, Aski, but it's not my fault you put outrageous expectations on the outcome.'

Aski became deflated and continued to sit in the car as Genji walked towards the entrance of the apartment. For a fraction of a second, Genji hesitated before continuing forward. Aski wouldn't have thought anything of it but for the fact Genji now gripped the hilt of his sword. Even then, she only believed he'd gone too long without touching the thing.

Reaching the entrance, Genji motioned for Aski to hurry. She was tempted to remain in the vehicle and let him wait a bit but with the way he had been lately, Aski couldn't safely say whether he would wait. Sliding off her seat with Paw Paw in her arms, Aski dragged her feet taking as long as she felt comfortable.

'Hurry, girl!' Genji shot at her.

'*Girl!*' That was enough to stop Aski in her tracks. 'How dare you belittle me so,' she growled. 'Even after everything you've done to me today you still find greater heights to insult me. I have a name. It's Aski. We picked it together a whole lifetime ago but you wouldn't know that would you? You aren't the Genji I once knew.'

'Aski, you don't understand,' Genji shot again. 'You need to get inside now.'

'No!' Aski snapped. 'I'm not going anywhere with you. You're just as bad as Henry was. You put me down, insult me, and force me to do things against my will. I'm leaving right...' Aski's eyes widened in fear as Genji's face grew dark and he pointed a finger in her direction. Could she have angered him enough for Genji to use Magic on her?

'Kaytsak,' Genji whispered.

Aski didn't have the chance to hear Genji speak as lightning sped from Genji's fingers towards her in a random pattern of twists and turns. As it was about to connect the lightning turned 45 degrees and flew just over Aski's shoulder. Connecting with something solid yet invisible behind her. The bolt of light exploded in a rain of sparks and a roar of incredible fury.

With her body catching up to what her eyes registered, Aski flinched away to the side, too late to have been any aid if the lightning didn't shift direction itself. She jumped again at the loud explosion before turning back. What Aski witnessed horrified her. Laying on the bonnet of the car with one leg dangling over the edge was a man. His chest had exploded inward from where Genji's Magic struck. The smell of burning flesh reached Aski's nose and she almost vomited, struggling at the last minute to swallow back a small amount of her breakfast. Tears came unbidden to

228

her eyes reacting to the horrific smell and Aski held her nose with one hand while carrying Paws far from the smell towards Genji. His eyes had started to glow a rich orange like a sunset.

'You may think you're clever with your little sight barriers but you're years away from getting the jump on me,' Genji said slowly looking from one side to the other. 'With these eyes I can see you all clearly so you may as well come out.'

From around the parking lot and hanging on the sides of the apartment building figures slowly shifted into view. Each was dressed in dark tactical gear like an army would use and at their sides they sported small automatic machine guns. Aski thought that it was an odd weapon to carry when they could clearly do magic. On their chest each sported the same blue ring like the Mage Killers of old. This worried Genji as the Mage Killers had been disbanded when magic returned to the world after the years of the lost era. Not only that but the fact the Mage Killers, if that's what they were, now used magic was also a concern. Genji was just happy they didn't have such grand abilities like he did.

'What is it you want here?' Genji asked.

'Your sword or your life,' the closest Mage Killer replied. 'And before you start to argue we've already confirmed you have the sword through conversations you've had with Aski driving to her parents' residence.'

Genji's eyes narrowed. 'Who sent you?'

'Our commander has searched a long time for you,' the Mage Killer told him.

'The name?'

The Mage Killer just smiled. 'Your sword or your life.'

Genji didn't give them the courtesy of another answer. They wouldn't have liked what he had to say anyway. With his hand on the hilt of the Mage's Blade he conjured a fireball using the word of power. Like an arrow the ball of flame sped towards the speaker. Genji decided this man must rank higher than the others as he took the initiative to speak. At the last moment the

Mage Killer dodged the magic attack. Genji could have sworn the fire had touched but there was no evidence. The Mage Killer just smiled, cruel and unyielding.

Taking Genji's lead Aski drew the triangle for fire. 'Krak,' she said focusing her will into the magic. She had come a long way since the orc caves and could perform magic with far greater ease. This was in part due to Paw Paw's instructions and advice on the best ways of Mage Craft. The constant practice helped as well. As she spoke a tornado of fire swept through the area. Many of the Mage Killers were unprepared for a child so young to perform magic and were caught up in the inferno. The twister burned wildly and petered out too quickly. A sudden dizziness took hold of Aski and it was everything she could do to stay upright. She felt as weak as she had after the night of magic keeping the orcs at bay.

Genji wasn't surprised when the fire tornado died off quickly. There wasn't any power backing the magic and all the Mage Killers that got caught up in the flames recovered with a few minor burns. Glancing at Aski, he could see she was already drained. Now that she wasn't borrowing Genji's energy, she really had a small well to dip into. Genji believed with the right guidance, his guidance, she could build up her stamina and magical endurance quickly. Knowing how to use magic was her greatest advantage.

Suddenly, the Mage Killers came in to attack. Holding the Mage's Blade, Genji used his free arm to sweep Aski back, lobbing her at the door to his building. 'Ody,' Genji whispered. Aski's form shifted into air flowing around the door frame. Once the particles were on the other side, she reformed into the girl he knew. To rearrange his own particles using the shadow discipline was one thing but to change a person using the elemental discipline was unheard of. Genji wasn't even sure he was going to succeed. Then again, why shouldn't he. He was the most powerful Summoner Mage there was. The success of the action only confirming this in his mind.

230

With Aski safe behind the barrier that Genji had placed on the building long ago, he returned his attention to the Mage Killers. After launching Aski, Genji continued his rotation bringing his arm around while speaking the word of power for air once more. A horizontal line of focused air, sharper than a razor blade, tore across the area at chest height. None of the Mage Killers dodged fast enough to get out of the way. Telegraph poles, a phone booth and some palm trees all separated top from bottom. The higher halves sliding to the ground below. A wicked grin crossed Genji's face and he looked to the Mage Killers to see what type of mess they would make. His smile died.

The Mage Killers were all standing with similar smiles to the one Genji just lost. No one was harmed or put out in any way. Slowly, each started approaching Genji once more with a terrifyingly determined look on their faces. Taking a step back Genji started to panic. He fired off electrical bolts at the enemy but each attack passed right through the intended Mage Killer. This caused Genji to fall further into his panicked state changing elements on a whim trying different attacks. Nothing was connecting and the Mage Killers were getting closer.

Suddenly, one rushed Genji pulling out a small dagger. 'Kaytsak,' Genji almost screamed. His mind was now working completely by instinct. From the clouds above, a bolt of crimson lightning exploded into the Mage Killers tearing flesh from bone. The clumps of body tissue, splintered bone, and boiling blood continued to move towards Genji, crashing against him. So they can die, he thought, too caught up in the battle to acknowledge the body parts dripping from his clothing and skin. His mind suddenly calmed and he started to think rationally.

'I see your little trick,' Genji said. He realised the Mage Killers were shifting into a temporal state the moment the attacks were about to hit. They could only do this while remaining still. The first Mage Killer had been caught off guard not expecting an attack and therefore had no chance to shift. The last Mage Killer was too committed to an attack that he also couldn't shift or dodge the attack. It was a difficult situation to overcome but Genji had a solution. Calling on the earthen element, Genji cast multiple tentacles in front of himself that would attack anyone who moved within a few metres. The attacks would surely connect as the Mage Killers couldn't shift and approach at the same time.

A physical force slid under Genji's left arm wrenching it into the air and breaking his contact with the Mage's Blade. His head was pulled to the side as Genji realised another arm wrapped around his throat and, locking to the first, pulled him into a choke hold. The Mage killers disappeared from the area as if they had never been. Even the blood and guts covering Genji vanished leaving him as clean as when he stepped from the car moments before. Genji felt the warm breath of someone close rush against his ear and smelt a heavy, sickly strong, garlic stench that caused his nose to scrunch up.

'Such a slow and pathetic mind you have,' a voice whispered in Genji's ear. 'To think a simple illusion could hold your attention while I strolled in behind you... Ha! If the commander didn't want you for himself, I would kill you where you stand.'

Genji tried to break free but was lifted slightly from the ground. Feet kicking back and free arm swinging around, Genji could get no power in his attacks. As the brain became starved of blood and oxygen, dizziness swept over Genji, his eyes swimming. Soon, the darkness rolled in stealing the light of the world and toppling Genji into unconsciousness.

Orange and black. The colours danced along his eyelids beckoning him to wake. A soft breeze tingled over the skin causing light bumps to rise. The mind sparked as thoughts, small at first, sprung into life. The most prominent was the building pain stabbing into

Genji's skull. Slowly, he pushed himself from the coarse cement, muscles protesting as they were put to work. Reaching a sitting position, Genji took in his surroundings. The car park of his apartment building was ringed by palm trees. Sun beams sprayed off window glass highlighting the position of a dying sun. It was now late afternoon when, moments before, he had only just reached mid-morning.

Shifting like a groggy sailor, Genji's eyes landed on Aski lying unconscious behind the glass door. Shards of memory filtered through. Lightning... blood rain... Mage Killers. Eyes flaring, Genji reached for the Mage's Blade, his fingers curling around emptiness. Frantically, he searched nearby hoping the sword had simply come loose somehow, all the while a deep sense of dread filled his panicked mind. *Such a slow and pathetic mind you have.* The words of the Mage Killer scraped across his thoughts sending a shiver through his body. Genji knew without a doubt the man had taken his prize. The thought of his impure fingers touching Genji's blade caused a new emotion, rage, to burn through Genji's veins.

Adrenalin feeding his starved muscles, Genji surged to his feet. He looked around for possible signs indicating where the Mage Killer may have fled but came up short. Forcing himself to calm, Genji racked his brain for a possible solution. It was a number of long, desperate heartbeats before an answer came. There was once a day in the academy when a student had lost a valuable gem. This gem was his catalyst to everything in the shadow discipline and without it the student would lose another year imbuing a new gem with his essence. Each gem only becoming alive when a Mage manages to pass along enough of their own limitless soul.

As he walked by, Genji laughed at this student, finding much humour in the situation before shaking his head as a faculty member turned up to help. Genji made note to never give someone a free ride out of a hard situation they had created for themselves. He knew they wouldn't learn anything from it. Even so, Genji watched on, curious as to how the elder Mage would act. Genji was surprised when the Mage started crafting the salt circle for a wind elemental summoning within the academy. All the creatures Genji could imagine would be hard to control and should the creature escape the Mage's hold many students could get hurt.

Making his way to the far side of the room where an easy escape could be made, Genji watched the summoning. Ripples of green air carved their way through the room as a tornado was born on the circle. Watching with great intrigue, Genji leaned forward to see the creature that would appear. He was disappointed to see that, as the tornado died away, there was nothing inside.

'Lucky the old man didn't conjure anything,' Genji thought. *'He has no talent and would never have held anything through his will.'*

As Genji turned to walk away a haze caught in his peripheral. It was as if the air in the room was catching sunlight and shimmering like a kaleidoscope. He focused closer on the haze trying to figure out what was going on but before Genji could make sense of anything the haze fled away. Moments later, it was back surrounding the old Mage. The haze was denser now and Genji could just make out the form of a wind sprite. There were no true arms or legs on the creature. With the body almost completely translucent, the lower half was a shifting whirl of air while the top half was the torso and head of a woman. Her body swaying like a snake.

The Mage stood as if listening for a moment then nodded dismissing the sprite. Genji got the feeling the Summoner Mage and wind sprite had a deep bond as if they had known each other for years but he never did get the answer to that. The Mage had died the following year when a magical experiment went wrong.

Genji dismissed the thought of the old Summoner,

not caring to dwell on others. He'd already taken away the information he needed. A wind sprite could find the Mage's Blade with no trouble. And because the weapon was an extremely powerful item the sprite would not only find it but be drawn to it. With a smile, Genji whispered the word of power for air. He braced his muscles, facing the open balcony hundreds of floors above that led to his apartment. When nothing happened, his face became terse and he grumbled a curse under his breath.

With great disdain, Genji brought a finger up to draw the power symbol of air and paused. His eyes caught Aski still passed out inside the entrance. He knew he should help her to somewhere more comfortable but his mind was screaming at him with impatience. Swearing once more, Genji entered and moved to where Aski lay. Warmth pulsed through Genji's hand as he touched Aski's brow. The healing energy passed into the little girl and the quick, sharp breaths that caused her body to shudder softened into a more relaxed and steady breath. Aski slipped from an unconscious tremble into a deep and enriching sleep. Genji was surprised he could smile so warmly just seeing his friend sleep.

The moment was fleeting as the push to recover his sword started to surface. With a quick flick of the wrist, Genji drew the symbol for air. 'Ody,' he said and Aski rose into the air. As Genji walked, the levitating girl followed until they were in the lift being taken to the top floor. When the doors opened, a familiar feeling washed over Genji causing him to hesitate just a moment. A wicked smile crossed his lips as he stepped into the apartment directing Aski to her bed and tucking her in. Genji recovered the large shaker of salt from his cupboard and proceeded to jump from his balcony calling on the wind element after drawing the symbol of power. Floating softly to the ground, Genji wasted no time in preparing a summoning circle, a swirling array of lines spiralling out from a circular centre. The tips ended in wisps that looked like the tops of feathers.

'*So, he is alive,*' was all that bounced around Genji's mind. '*Well, if he's here then the Mage's Blade is still safe.*' An almost hysterical laughter burst from Genji's lips as he called forth the wind sprite. His wits not about him, Genji was met by a terrible pain pushing at all corners of his mind. The creature of wind was fighting him and it was all Genji could do to hold it back. Suddenly serious, he brought all his will into the fore and after a horrible tug-o-war battle of power, Genji finally locked the creature's soul away and took control. He had no time to rest his battered mind as the sprite was still crashing into its confinements sending physical shudders out into the surrounding world cracking cement and shaking the palms.

Genji sent the physical wind sprite into the city to seek his sword. It was only moments before the creature was back but unlike with the older Mage, Genji had linked to the creature's mind seeing everything it did. The Mage's Blade was currently being held in a warehouse only a few blocks away. The Mage Killer who stole it was now showing off to his fellow Knights slashing the sword back and forward and strutting around like a peacock. Genji's face grew stern and he dismissed the wind sprite not wishing to deal with the explosive creature any longer. The pain in his mind forgotten, Genji boosted his speed with magic as he took off towards the Mage Killer den.

Chapter 16

High upon the balcony, Tristan watched Genji summon the wind sprite before heading out into the city towards the warehouse. Tristan believed Genji to have the skill to win back the sword and knew that it would be Genji who brought the sword to him. Aski was the only reason Tristan hadn't already used the sword on himself. He wanted to ensure that her life from this moment had promise and the future she wanted.

With no memory of the feeling of warmth on his tattered and numb body, Tristan breathed in the last of the dying sun. With no reason he could fathom, Tristan didn't understand why his body still responded to that glowing orb in the sky. Feeling the smile for want of a better sense, Tristan looked inward at the ancient being inhabiting his body. It'd been two centuries since he last felt the being awaken.

'You have something to say?' Tristan asked. He knew it would be of no substance as none of the handful of conversations he'd had with the being ever were. It was countless times Tristan tried to get a name from his passenger but never was one given.

'The sunlight is for me,' the ancient voice replied. *'You may not feel it on your skin anymore but it still penetrates deep inside where I can enjoy it.'*

'You haven't said a word all this time and you broke your silence to rub my face in my disabilities. Thank you,' Tristan said, the sarcasm dripping off his words.

'Most welcome,' the being replied unperturbed. *'What will you say to your young friend when she wakes?'*

'Heal me!' Tristan said suddenly.

'Not an ability she possesses.'

'I want you to heal me,' Tristan said almost pleading. 'You've done it before.'

'Why now?' The being asked. *'Last time you carried your head around for a month before asking.'*

'It's Aski. I don't want her to see me this way but I don't want to lie to her either by hiding behind an illusion. I want to be whole again. I don't want her to fear me.'

'*Is that all?*'

'What do you mean is that all?' Tristan growled. 'My body has been hideously deformed over time. She will flee from me.'

'*You have more to learn than I realised. She will see straight to the heart of you. You cannot hide from that.*'

And with that, the being's presence drifted away. Tristan knew the being had ignored his request and through countless attempts learned that the being wouldn't talk when it didn't want to no matter what Tristan tried. Tristan was drowning in anxiety. All the possible reactions Aski could have were bouncing around his mind and none were positive.

A moan came from behind and Tristan jumped thinking Aski had woken but when nothing more stirred decided she must have just made a noise in her sleep. Looking from her room to the Lift at the far end of the room, Tristan struggled to find the courage to venture forward. Allowing his mind to be distracted by thoughts of retreat, Tristan moved his body into Aski's room quickly before his head could object.

As the darkness of the room enveloped Tristan, he reacted by hitting the light switch. A move he regretted instantly as Aski's eyes shot open. Panicked, Tristan cast an illusion on himself hiding his tattered body behind that of Aski's brother's youthful body. He was ashamed to have done so but he didn't want to lose her after waiting so long to see the "aware" Aski once more who knew him and could talk to him like she had when they first met. Tristan felt an amused smirk emanate from within.

Tristan watched as awareness filtered into Aski's mind and she started to look around getting her bearings. The moment she realised Tristan was in the room he would never forget. Her eyes wide and mouth slightly ajar, Tristan held her shocked expression making the moment feel like a lifetime.

'Brother?' Aski broke the silence. Pausing a moment longer to confirm in herself he was really here, Aski dove from the bed into his arms. 'I knew you would find me. I tried to get Genji to save you from the keep too but he wouldn't listen.' Her eyes seemed to brighten a little as she started to look around. 'He said that Beverlin would be able to get you here with her magic...'

Tristan grew sad. 'Beverlin's not about to step out, little one,' Tristan said kneeling before Aski. He took her small hand in his own. 'An explosion took her life.' Tristan was caught unaware. Expressing for the first time across the centuries of Beverlin's passing, he wasn't ready for the pain those words held. Tristan thought he'd accepted Beverlin's fate but now he knew he had only buried it deep within. With the pressure finding a way to the surface, the volcano of feelings erupted in a waterfall of tears. Tristan's face crumpled into his hands and with no chance to hold back the deluge, cried uncontrollably. Memories of a stolen kiss, a warm embrace, a stern look, all came flooding back. She was the reason he hadn't been present at the Academy of Mage Craft these last few years. Tristan knew intuitively he couldn't survive even a glance of the girl who owned his heart. A heart he never recovered, burnt up in the explosion at Rolund's Keep.

A soft hand curled around his back and cradled his head. Tristan couldn't remember just when Aski had drew him close but the love he felt in that moment coming from her was warm and strong. He looked up and saw the tear lines down her cheeks and realised she was pushing to stay strong for him. 'I'm sorry I took so long to find you, Aski,' Tristan whispered.

With a tender smile, Aski shook her head. 'The handful of days didn't kill me,' Aski said. 'In fact, I have grown so much because of it.'

A strong, rumbling laugh rolled from Tristan as he

realised Aski had only lived a few days compared to the centuries he struggled through just to reach her. 'I saw you come into your own, little one. I hadn't wanted to let my presence known too soon but you saw me none the less. I'm proud of you for what you achieved.'

'I thought what I saw an illusion but, even so, it reminded me of the words you spoke at the keep,' Aski admitted. 'Of the strength I held and how others should be afraid of me. I understood at that moment the depth of character you saw in me. Even without magic to fall back on I would never have let those people care for me again. The strength was hiding there all along. Thank you.'

'It takes just as much strength to reach in and bring it out,' Tristan said with a smile. 'What you accomplished was all you, Aski.'

With a rose blush, Aski nodded. 'I'm glad your burns healed,' Aski said taking the focus from herself. 'When did the... he,' she pointed at Tristan's belly. 'Heal you?'

'I'm not pregnant,' Tristan commented. Aski knew he was trying to make a joke but it lacked feeling. Tristan seemed distant all of a sudden. 'The being healed me recently...'

It was there. That deep, fearful tone that Genji expressed so often lately had crawled into Tristan's voice. And now she heard it she could see it written across his face, dragging down his entire body. The lie. But where Genji thought he was getting away with his honeyed words, Tristan looked almost in pain. 'How bad is it?'

Tristan's eyes shot up registering what Aski referred to. 'It's... I'm fine,' Tristan replied.

'Ever since Genji found the sword the most important things in his world shifted to become solely that blade,' Aski spoke softly. 'Yes, I could see that somewhere in his fractured mind he still believed he cared for me and wanted the best for me but if my existence threatened his relationship to that sword, he would do everything he could to rectify my threat. His voice turned from speaking the truth to speaking half-

240

truths, from lying to my face to believing what he said to be absolute truth. Genji relished in the power he believed he had over me. I see your lies, Tristan, and your despair.'

Tristan looked away unable to hold Aski's gaze but Aski pulled him gently back to look at her once more. She waited until he found courage enough to hold her eyes in his own again.

'I despair, for these lies only succeed in hurting you,' Aski said with a sad smile. 'The lie you create is crafted for yourself alone. Show me who you truly are and let go your fears.'

'*Straight to the heart of you,*' sounded the familiar echo.

Tristan seemed truly scared and doubt crept into Aski's heart as to whether she was able to reach the man before her. Slowly she noticed a change as Tristan's features shimmered and started to fade. Tristan let his illusion fall revealing cuts and wounds across his tortured body that would have killed a normal man. And for all Aski saw she didn't see them. With a warm smile she only saw Tristan.

'You found your courage, Brother,' she said embracing him. 'It is good to finally see you again... And with Magic?'

'I needed something to do while I waited to see you,' Tristan replied. His chest tightened as he held back tears. He'd been so stupid to allow his fears to influence how he treated Aski.

A moment of clarity pierced Aski's mind. 'You lived across all those years!'

'I did. I have made so many terrible choices in my life. Taken many lives along the way. Some that didn't even deserve to be taken. Very few of my choices bettered mankind but opening the Academy of Mage Craft was one of my more favourable. I have studied the deep, dark secrets and soared the bright, warm heights of Magic with so many talented people. Even Genji had flourished in those halls. Maybe you would like to attend too? You could find a true home there.'

241

The new revelation floored Aski. She could not begin to fathom the kind of life Tristan had led. She was moved to be offered a home in the world Tristan created but a small thought niggled at her. 'And how long will you be accompanying me at the Academy?'

'You are wise beyond your years, little one,' Tristan smiled. 'It is true that I still seek the Sword of Power. My body has experienced pain beyond your darkest nightmares. Lived lifetime upon lifetime in this tortured state. Even now, I feel like a statue locked in time. Numb to the world I once knew. Trapped in the pain always present within even the smallest wound. My life has reached its final hours. I know I only got to spend a small time with you but I need Genji to bring me the sword and use it to take my life.'

'And having me come to the academy will spark Genji's new found ego causing him to feel slighted. He will seek to take me back just to sate his wounded pride?' Tristan was about to speak but Aski held up a hand. 'I know your intentions for me are not so sinister. It is a bonus to you for helping me. I told you I would help get you the sword and this hasn't changed. I accept your invitation to enter the Academy of Mage Craft.'

The tears didn't stay away. With a quavering lip Tristan nodded at this wonderful girl before him. 'Thank you.'

Aski didn't worry to give a reply, she just hugged him tightly. A weary squeak came from within Aski's clothing and she jumped back. 'Sorry, Paws,' she said pulling him out. Paws looked dreadfully tired barely able to stand.

Tristan saw the state Paws was in and held out a hand. 'Pass him to me.' Aski did as he bade and he placed his other hand over the top of the Lazurian Mouse. To Aski the air smelt of fresh autumn leaves just as they fell from their home tree. This was accompanied by a rich warmth and when Tristan pulled his hand away Paws was up and bouncing around on his hand. He danced up to Tristan's shoulders and snuggled around his neck. With a quick nuzzle of thanks, Paws escaped back down the other arm to pounce into Aski's embrace. Tristan smiled. "Your turn, Aski.'

'With the way my head feels, it would be most welcome.' Closing her eyes, Aski got the same draw upon her senses when Tristan placed his hands upon her. More than this, it was as if every fibre in her being was breaking down and regrowing young, fresh and full of vitality. She had never felt more refreshed in her life. 'Genji never had this kind of affect when he healed me.'

'That's because Genji doesn't know what he's doing,' Tristan said with a smirk. 'Yes, he went through the lessons at the academy and rose to pass all tests given but the academy is for beginners. It is the first level of training to see what a person will excel in. Genji believes that he now knows everything there is to know but the next level of training is done on one's personal journey. Everyone is different and not all we achieve a higher knowledge of Magic but those that do understand Genji is a beginner.'

'With the sword, I have seen him do things that are not supposed to be possible,' Aski argued.

'Like casting elemental magic without the use of symbols.' Tristan held his hand palm up and a small ball of fire came into life to float above it. The flames danced and swirled before they grew smaller and vanished within themselves. 'It took me 200 years before I didn't need the symbol and another 600 before I could cast without invoking the word of power. To begin with, a Mage needs the symbol and the word to focus their desire. In time with training, not so much. This is true in all disciplines.'

'My training has now begun,' Aski grinned broadly. 'Shall we go find me a room?'

'Let's,' Tristan said. 'I'll leave Genji a note to let him know you have departed.' Placing a note upon Genji's table Tristan turned back to find himself bathed in golden light. Warmth touched his skin once more and as it faded, he found his body was healed. Forgotten feelings he once knew blessed his renewed body and Tristan could only stand mouth agape.

'*A gift at the* 'final hours' *of your life.*'

'Oh, Brother, I am so happy for you,' Aski said witnessing the healing.

One last barrier stood between Tristan and Aski. Tristan had no fear anymore and with a swipe of his hand dismissed his spell. Memories disintegrated in Aski's mind opening the doorways to her true memories. She saw her life as an only child and then the day Tristan came into her life. She got to see it all without any illusion or spell that Tristan may have used when she was growing up and she smiled.

'Let's go, Brother,' Aski said, holding out a hand.

A distant rumble rolled across the city. There was electricity in the air as the darkening clouds gathered producing a powerful silence. Genji knew when the first branch of lightning parted the sky the waters would fall but in this strong, quiet moment at the beginning of the storm he was at peace. This was his most favourite elemental moment and he took it as a sign the coming struggle would go his way. He took a second to stand and feel the power of nature replenishing his own tender body. It was just the moment he needed.

A burst of light arced across the sky with a loud and instant boom. As expected, moments later the rain started to fall sending chills across the skin as it struck. Genji quickly flicked a plain circle and spoke the word Energia. Pure energy enveloped him so that no drop of rain could break through. Genji hurried forward, his destination only a couple more blocks away.

Reaching the final corner, Genji peered around to inspect the warehouse. It was a large hollow building built at the edge of a wharf. Gulls had painted the roof white, made permanent by age and a blaring sun. Three large roller doors gave access to the insides, all of which were closed. The recent rain now a blessing as all the guards, if any, were hiding away staying dry within. Whipping out his extendable staff, Genji focused. His eyes changed hue to a soft purple as the world around him changed to colours representing hot and cold areas. He scanned the front of the warehouse once more and found only one heat signature close to the doors. By the shape of it, he concluded whoever was inside was resting with back against the external wall. They wouldn't see his approach.

Dropping the magic and sheathing the retracted staff, Genji started across the road. Before he had gotten off the footpath a truck sped by splashing a large puddle in Genji's direction. The onslaught of water was too much for his barrier and engulfed Genji, soaking him from head to toe. A look of sheer hatred darkened his face as Genji glared at the truck.

'Krak,' Genji said focusing on the engine exploding and the tyres melting in an inferno. Reaching out with open palm, he squeezed dramatically, the truck disappearing behind his clenched fist. Nothing happened. 'Fuck,' Genji swore quickly tracing the sign for fire but the truck had already rounded a corner. Turning to face the warehouse where the heat signature was, Genji tried once more, his rage fuelling his imagery. 'Krak!' Genji said between clenched teeth.

White flames tore at the metal wall eating into it within seconds and melting it down. The lava like substance dripped and flowed onto the lookout and before he knew what was happening had become completely covered in the scorching fluid. Skin and muscle started to melt away to the man's anguished screams. Screams that died away as his voice box melted down into his chest. The flailing man gave one last twitch before his half-eaten body grew still.

Genji twisted his magic to pull the heat out of the metal and it instantly solidified creating an opening for him to enter. Inside, Genji could see small rooms and hallways that ran deep into the back area. The walls were only half the height of the room and he considered simply flying over it. This was in competition with continuing the pyromancy path and setting everything

245

to flame. Both of these options however were turned back in his mind. Should anyone inside be adept at magic and use the same types of tricks the first Mage Killer used it would cause some hassles. Genji wouldn't be tricked a second time but it was still something he didn't feel like dealing with at this moment.

Choosing the more sensible option, Genji proceeded cautiously into the hallways. He kept a wary eye down side passages as he passed. Mostly, they were just rows of random goods that Genji couldn't find common ground with any other item. He thought it wasn't a store warehouse as much as it was made to look like one. Coming to a dead end after taking a turn at a fork, Genji back tracked. As he reached the fork once more, he glanced back along the way he'd come and noted the shelves seemed to shimmer as if forcing themselves to hold shape.

Reaching out, Genji swiped at the walls of the corridor. As his hand passed through, he broke down into a hysterical laughter. 'You think you can fool me again,' he shouted. 'You are nothing... Dirt beneath my boots... You hear? I'm going to slaughter your little sect and when I'm through with you, I'll rip apart that half bit knight who leads you. I'll carve him into tiny chunks and he can live out the rest of his life being digested by the mongrel dogs that roam the city streets!' Genji's eyes looked maniacal as they darted this way and that looking for someone he could take his anger out on.

With no one in sight, Genji kicked at a sack on a lower shelf and expecting his foot to pass through, let out a sharp cry. His foot connected with something solid and now the contents were spilling out over the floor. Contents he was delighted to find being salt. The pain in his foot dried instantly and an evil smile slit his face in two. Wasting no time, Genji started to draw a circle with the salt in the pattern of darkness. The true darkness pattern and not the failure he designed at his exam all those months ago. This was his true test. His moment to prove to himself he deserved the title Summoner Mage and show he was the rightful wielder of the Mage's Blade.

And Genji knew the perfect creature to summon. White almost skeletal skin, shrouded in a dark mist like the deepest midnight. The skin only seen upon the two arms as all else was cloaked. Even the head was cloaked in such a thick darkness only two glowing, blue, spectral eyes could be seen. On the left arm from the elbow down, the limb was replaced with a curving blade wade of bone. The blade could be extended like a sword or retracted to look similar to a scythe. Those that saw this creature and lived would tell the story of a ghostlike skeleton in a dark cloak that takes lives with a scythe. Close like any legend was but still so far from the truth. This creature was the only one of its kind in existence and had lived nearly as long as the elder gods themselves. No one could kill this creature and very few could control it.

With the circle drawn, Genji concentrated on the creature to be summoned. 'Tenebris Adducere,' he said, arms extended upwards. 'Come forth, Death, and drink your fill of souls.'

The normal spectacle of twirling colour, rushing air and dredging energy was non-existent in this summon. Darkness filled the corners of the room and blurred the vision. A chill spilled across the floor biting at the legs and producing patches of slick ice. Death was always present just outside one's grasp, the summoning circle a tool to ensure you got an audience when you spoke to it.

Genji felt a shiver run up his spine and the curved bone, as sharp as any sword, edged around his throat. Unperturbed, Genji continued to look straight ahead for if he were to turn it would be his end. 'This warehouse is filled with souls to steal. Take all but the one who summoned you,' Genji commanded.

The dark mist swept around Genji and up over the shelves ahead of them. Almost instantly the first scream came up from somewhere near the back of the warehouse. Genji found it hard to pinpoint as the sound reverberated around the walls. Not wanting to miss the action, he drew the power symbol of air. 'Ody,' Genji said and gale force winds tore through the opening at the front of the warehouse to blow aside any solid matter. Most things blew aside but still more were in the way. 'Emundetur a fluxi seminis,' Genji said, dismissing the rest of the magic in the room and the shelving and items left over disintegrated into the air.

Near the rear of the now open space, a group of Mage Killers stood trembling in terror. They'd heard the rantings of an intruder and gathered their weapons but now stood facing a creature of fearsome carnage. Some tried to raise their weapons against it but crossbow bolts sung through the mist as if through empty air and swords bit into nothing of substance. These Mage Killers died first with terrible screams. The scythe arm slicing through body parts as if they two were made of mist. Other Mage Killers died just as easily with horrific fear frozen into their features. These men and women had not tried to resist.

Genji stood in appreciation of the work being done by the bringer of chaos until he saw him. Standing at the far end of the warehouse was the Mage Killer that stole Genji's sword. He stood there dressed in the black tabard of the Mage Killers with the almost glowing, blue circle on the chest. Genji's eyes narrowed dangerously when he saw how the Mage's Blade was being treated. The tip was resting on the cement, possibly dulling it, made worse by the weight of the Mage Killer's hands resting upon the pommel. The man had his eyes locked upon Genji adding to his frustration.

Genji saw that Death was devouring the last soul in the room leaving only the lead Mage Killer and his prize. Genji snickered at the man. 'Have you met Death?' Genji asked motioning towards the ephemeral being.

The Mage Killer smiled. 'Once or twice,' was the reply. He seemed unperturbed by the dark spirit hovering closer. When Death reached the man, it whisked around him, coiling up the body to look back at Genji with the icy blue stare. 'In fact, I called him forth only moments before you arrived.'

Eyes blaring wildly, Genji spied the salt of a recent summoning circle and his face drained of colour. When he found the words to talk, his voice was shaky and week. 'That's impossible,' If the creature was already summoned by you, I wouldn't have been able to.'

'Normally, a truth every Summoner Mage lived by,' the Mage Killer replied. 'But this creature is different. Special if you will. If allowed by the original Summoner, it can pass through any number of summoning circles.' The man smiled at the sheer terror now evident in Genji's whole manner. 'Would you care to become better acquainted?'

Death seemed to grow behind the Mage Killer in both size and the density of the dark mist forever swirling around it. The horrific killer moved only a foot towards Genji but it was enough for the Mage to fall back a few steps.

'No!' came the squeak of Genji.

'No?' the Mage Killer teased, holding up a hand to stop Death's advance. 'Then how about you and I get to know each other. My name is Rogan Daze. It is an honour to take the place of Death.' Without pause, Rogan charged Genji brandishing the Mage's Blade.

With little time to react and without knowing if his trembling body would respond, Genji forced himself to find something to stop the attack. His fingers wrapping around a hard wooden object at his belt, Genji wrenched it forward in front of himself in an attempt to block the sword edge now coming at his head. Clenching his eyes shut tight, Genji felt the wicked crack of an object hitting his forehead. It didn't bite like a sword would but rather felt solid.

Stumbling back from the force of the strike, Genji fell to the ground. Head reeling from the blow, he looked up with groggy eyes. The world was spinning but he had his wits about him to take note of Rogan's movements. He was circling Genji with sword raised but wasn't yet advancing. Looking down, Genji saw in

249

his hand the retractable staff he valued so dearly. Other, than the Mages Blade this was one of his most cherished instruments. Across the centre ran a large crack that cut deep down to the reinforced core. Genji realised this was where the Mages Blade struck. Genji raised a hand tenderly to his forehead. A large egg was forming and a deep throbbing had begun.

'Come on, Mage,' Rogan said. 'A little hit and you're already giving up. I may as well let him have you.'

Genji saw him gesture to Death floating around the walls, watching intimately. A shudder ran through Genji once more as he met Death's glare. The eyes were hungry like a lion's stalking its prey. Genji forced himself to look away and focus on Rogan. Though he'd proven himself to be a formidable opponent, Death would be unbeatable. 'You haven't beaten me yet,' Genji said. He was trying to buy himself a little time to allow his healing magic to take effect. The throbbing, pressure subsided, but he could still see the small bump protruding out just above his eyes.

Rogan smiled. 'A little healing on oneself feels nice but ultimately you will be weaker for it.'

'I don't need advice in Mage Craft from you,' Genji grumbled. 'If I had my sword you wouldn't have even lasted this long.'

'Do you want it?' Rogan asked. He extended the sword out for Genji pommel first.

'What is this?' Genji asked sceptically. 'No one would give away such a prize.'

'For the likes of you I don't need it.'

To Genji's great surprise and utter glee, Rogan slide the Mages Blade across the floor to bump into Genji's legs. Genji scooped it up quickly, cradling it to his chest. Rising to his feet with a surge of confidence, Genji pointed the Mages Blade at Rogan. 'You must have a death wish giving me this. You may have tricked me once but the abilities I can now bring forth, the height of Mage Craft I can reach is beyond anything you can do.'

250

'Hmph. You mean crafting magic without a power symbol?' Rogan said. 'Krak.'

A small fireball appeared above Rogan's head and rushed towards Genji. With little time to react, Genji was just able to swivel away. The fireball singed Genji's shirt, scoring the skin underneath. 'That's impossible!' Genji said. Looking down at the sword he held, a terrible realisation struck him. 'Is there no height to your deceit,' Genji said casting the sword across the room. 'You still have possession of my sword. Where is it?'

'Clearly you just cast it aside,' Rogan laughed. 'It's not deceit, Genji. I only use my opponent's weakness to my advantage. Yours is your insatiable lust for power. Krak.'

Another fireball flew at Genji causing him to dive to his left and to safety. 'You arrogant bastard. I'll kill you!' Genji screamed.

'Krak.'

Caught off balance, this fireball struck Genji's shoulder sending him spinning to the ground. When he picked himself back up, Genji's eyes were wild. His fingers quickly drew the symbol for air on the ground and then he waited. His eyes were locked on Rogan's as the Mage Killer's lips started to move.

'Krak...'

'...Ody,' Genji said quickly setting his magic in motion. Genji crafted an invisible ball of pure Oxygen in front of Rogan. As the Mage Killer sent his new fireball at Genji it connected with the oxygen and exploded. Rogan was sent flying across the room to land next to the Mages Blade. Genji rushed forward and leaping upon Rogan he scooped up the Sword and put it to Rogan's neck. 'It's time you shut up,' Genji whispered in his ear. As he was about to draw the blade across Rogan's throat he hesitated. Rogan, in his beaten state was laughing.

'Best be quick.'

Genji ignored the man's rambling and tensed to make the kill. Before he could strike, Genji froze. A shiver passed through his entire body as bony white fingers wrapped around his throat.

'Death will protect its original summoner, Genji,' Rogan smiled a crooked smile. A small trail of blood trickled from the side of his mouth. 'Any last words?' If the wicked light in Genji's eyes dimmed, Rogan didn't see it. What he did see was a maniac smiling back at him.

'Emundetur a fluxi seminis,' Genji said the words of release.

Rogan's eyes went wide with the implication of those words. Though Genji hadn't been the original summoner the same rules applied. Dismissing his summon would send it back to the location it was summoned from. For Death this was only 10 metres away. A short distance but Genji made use of that single moment sending a crimson line to streak across the warehouse floor as Rogan's throat was opened. His mouth opened and closed a few times as he tried to speak but the vocal chords were severed and the only sounds that came out were a guttural choking noise as his own blood blocked his airways.

Genji turned to face the approaching Death but to his relief Death had eyes only for Rogan. Reaching out with a cold misty hand, Death ripped the soul from Rogan's body. It was small, in the shape of a ball, but glowed with a brightness to rival the sun. Genji couldn't watch as Death devoured the orb. When he finally looked back, Death was gone.

Searching Rogan's body, Genji found no sign of the Mages Blade and he started to consider the blade in his hand. The blade he threw away.

'Kaytsak,' Genji tested the power word for lightning and electricity raced up the walls of the warehouse to reach a central point before striking the ground once more. 'Heh... Hehe...heheheh,' Genji started laughing uncontrollably realising he had the chance to enhance his skills in battle but threw it away and it almost cost him his life. 'Never again,' Genji said aloud clutching the blade close.

Leaving the warehouse refreshed from the healing arts, Genji utilised air magic. He rose into the sky and, breaking the sound barrier like a gunshot, Genji rocketed home in a matter of moments. He almost misjudged his landing but corrected at the last moment stumbling through his open balcony door. 'Are you, too, ready for your death, Tristan?' Genji yelled into the empty apartment. He raced from room to room looking this way and that but found no one inside. A note on a hall table caught his eye and Genji picked it up to read:

You have lost. I have the girl and am taking her to the Academy. Hide away in your little apartment and rot. I have plenty of time to take the King's Sword from your dead fingers.

Scrunching the paper in his fist, Genji looked to the balcony door with dread determination.

Chapter 17

'Excited?' Tristan asked as they approached the Academy of Mage Craft.

Aski flashed a beaming smile that warmed Tristan more than the sun had these last few centuries. She was almost skipping as she approached the front entrance to one of the eight disciplines in magic... Nine she corrected herself as she spied a smaller building tucked behind the furthest one. She theorised it belonged to the discipline of dispelling as there was only one important spell to learn. She wondered what the building they were about to enter was for. 'Yes, very excited,' Aski replied. 'And intrigued, scared and a little overwhelmed.'

'What is it you're worried about?' Tristan asked. 'From what I've seen, you are stronger than most of the Mages here and you have a personality that would fit in with so many different types of people.'

'Most of my power came from Genji. Now that we don't share a link to one another I am weak,' Aski admitted. She felt ashamed to admit this and was staring at the ground. She felt a hand gently take her chin and guide her eyes back to Tristan's.

'You would have me be strong and keep eye contact when I was fearful of your reaction yet you can't hold mine?' Tristan smiled which Aski caught and echoed as she thought of their reunion. 'You are not weak, Aski. The summoning link does allow for the sharing of ones potential magical abilities. From Genji you gained a greater stamina in casting. This you will achieve in your own in time. You're still young and your physical body can't keep up with the magic flowing through it.'

'So I am weak without Genji then.' Aski looked disappointed.

'Tell me about Genji. How strong was he before finding the sword?' Tristan asked.

Aski thought about the journey they undertook and all the impossible things Genji achieved. 'It was like he could do anything. I have not met many Mages but I can't begin to imagine a power that could be greater.'

'And how could this be if he was in turn sharing your weakness. Genji's magical ability would have been drastically compromised if your potential was weaker than his. If this were the case we would have definitely heard about it. Genji is the type of person to complain when things don't go his way.'

'But when we got back to the present he wasted no time severing the link between us. Why was that if not to gain back his power?'

Tristan was racking his brain trying to find the best possible reasons for Genji to dismiss Aski so soon when he heard a squeak from within Aski's hood. He saw Aski's lips purse. 'What did Paws say?'

'...Nothing.'

Tristan just shot Aski a look suggesting he would find out one way or another.

Aski caved. 'Genji severed the link between us so that I couldn't see the sword he cherished so much. He made it invisible to everyone but not to me.'

'A note that shoots true for his character,' Tristan smiled. 'It's a new life for you, Aski, and I would be surprised if you weren't a little anxious but don't stretch the truth to make up reasons to put yourself down. I can see the strength in you.'

Before Aski had a chance to reply Tristan opened the doors to the building and walked in. Aski followed him inside looking around. Ebony tiles covered the floor of the hallway. Doorways of the same dark colour could be found sporadically along the grey walls. Aski turned to Tristan.

'Wha...?' she started.

'...Tristan.'

Another voice cut in and Aski looked at the speaker striding down the hallway. An older man with a stern look on his face. He reminded her of a teacher at the school she once attended. Thinking of the man standing behind a lectern, mouthing off at a student who had been talking triggered a memory of a very different occasion. Aski remembered the man before her, sitting at a bench far above. The man was looking down at her with annoyance written across his face. Aski was able to place it at the moment her adventures started. The exam when Genji summoned her.

'And Aski. It is good to see you once more in these halls,' Gerard said giving an awkward smile. Aski thought it looked unnatural for the man but she nodded politely. Gerard directed his attention quickly back to Tristan. 'How did it go?'

'Genji will be bringing me the sword soon. We will need to prepare,' Tristan replied.

Catching the topic of conversation, Aski zoned out. She had had enough of Genji for a time and wanted to set her attention to other things. Hanging on a wall near the closest doorway was a poster of the time stairways. Walking up to get a closer look at the poster, Aski berated herself for not realising this building was for the time discipline. The amount of ebony tiles that matched the colour of the stairways should of been her biggest give away.

'Excuse me but what are you doing here? There are no children allowed in the main halls of the academy.'

Aski looked up to see a thick pair of glasses looking back at her from the now open doorway. The man behind them was thin and Aski realised he wasn't leaning over her to try and be dominative but because of his age had bent his back over the course of time. 'I'm here with my brother. I'm going to be going to this Academy.'

'Well I don't know who your brother is but he should know better than to let you wander alone in these halls.' Though he was old, or maybe because of, the man's voice was dripping with pomp. 'You may be going to attend the academy in the next few years but there is great danger here that you are yet aware of. You must always have a member of staff with you at all times. Tell me your brother's name and I'll be sure to have words with him.'

'Tristan,' Aski said in a soft voice.

The man's eyes shot up and found, across the hall,

Tristan was watching him out of the corner of his eye. Tristan gave the slightest of nods and without narrowing the older man's eyes came to rest upon Aski once more. 'My apologies. It is my duty to ensure that no one, student or outsider, comes to any harm. If you are Tristan's... ward, I will not bother you,' he couldn't bring himself to say sister having knowledge of Tristan's circumstances and knowing he could not have any siblings. 'My name is Burt.'

Aski found that he was waiting for her to respond. 'Aski.'

'I saw you were interested in my poster. Do you know what it's of?' Burt asked. Since finding out who Aski was his whole demeanour had changed. He was now treating her like any other student of his.

'They are the stairs you walk when you travel in time,' Aski replied cautiously. She didn't like Burt's change in attitude more than she didn't like his pompous self. At least the first personality didn't feel fake.

'Good work,' Burt smiled. 'I see you have been told a thing or two then. When you do attend the Academy you will be a little more prepared than most of the students who come here.'

Aski's eyes narrowed, the strength of self she found when standing up to her parents coming to the surface. 'I haven't been told anything. I walked those stairs a week ago. And again a few weeks before that. I walked these streets a thousand years ago when the deserts still held sway over the land. And I'm not *visiting* the academy. I just enrolled and am now a student of Mage Craft.'

'I'm sorry, my dear,' Burt said. He was trying to process everything Aski was saying before she suddenly raised a hand, palm out, in front of him.

'Let's start off on the right foot. I am not your dear,' Aski powered forward. 'Don't stand there and suck up to me now that you know my reasons for being here. You showed me a glimpse of your true personality. Give me that or nothing at all.'

Burt glanced at Tristan once more who was now standing solo watching the conversation. Tristan opened his hands and shrugged. Burt's brow furrowed. 'You, Aski, are a rude little girl. I think I'm about done talking to you'

'Good,' Aski replied. 'At least I know this isn't fake. I've had too many fake people in my life of late. If you are to teach me than treat me no differently to how you would treat people close to you.'

'Teach you? You're too young and naive to learn from me. Come back when you're fifteen or so and then maybe I'll let you squander over my secrets.' With that Burt turned to walk back into his classroom.

'Do you know how to use time magic?' Aski asked over her shoulder.

Burt's face contorted as if struck. He turned back to glare at Aski. 'Of course I...'

Aski flapped her hand for him to be quiet as she nudged her hood. Burt was feeling rather annoyed at how rude Aski was being but was curious as to who she was talking to.

A small squeak arose.

'Show me what you recovered before the link was lost.' Aski watched and felt exactly what Genji had on the number of times Paws was able to witness the time magic. She ran through the feelings of creating a multi-dimensional and omnipotent line of thought to run through her mind and found it wasn't anything difficult now she could see it being done. She closed her eyes thinking of Rolund's Keep. It was the last moment she knew of before coming back to this time and felt it was safe. The lines in her face contorted as she pushed her concentration.

'What are you doing?' Burt asked becoming more annoyed by the moment. 'You look like a constipated chicken.'

Aski ignored his words and continued. Sparks ran through the air as a small time portal opened. With mouth ajar, Burt went to inspect the window. It was big enough to put a notebook through but just opening anything was an incredible feat. Looking back, he saw Aski sway and Tristan stepped in before she lost her feet.

'That's enough now, Aski,' Tristan said. 'Sorry to be any trouble, Burt.'

'Not... Not at all,' Burt stammered. He was having trouble working out exactly what happened.

Aski felt herself being swept up into Tristan's arms as she found she could no longer stand herself. With the portal now dissipated, Tristan carried Aski back outside and towards the rear of the buildings. Here the grounds were littered with a number of smaller, single story buildings. Aski saw few people enter or exit.

'Dorm rooms,' Tristan said. 'There is enough room in each building for four bedrooms only. It allows the best use of space and gives each student a sanctuary with minimal distractions.'

Aski looked wearily at all the buildings. Each of the hundred or more dorm buildings were identical and as Tristan weaved through the rows she knew she would have trouble finding her way back to her room should she wander. 'I'm too tired to remember where my room is. How will I find my way back?'

Tristan looked at her and smiled. 'When you take a room as your own you will need to place a droplet of your soul in the room. The room will be powered by this and will forever more glow the colour of your soul. You will be the only person that can see it. When you leave the Academy grounds you will take back your soul and allow the room to be used by another.'

'And these rooms house all the students learning Mage Craft?'

'No,' Tristan said. 'Some students learn better with closer proximity to others and take up rooms in the main buildings. Others will live off campus in personal dwellings. Everyone learns differently and for now, you can have a room offering more peace and quiet until you settle in and work out what will best suit your needs.' Tristan came to a stop outside a door no different to any other. At the entrance were four touch pads. Three were glowing in a soft blue while the fourth remained empty. 'Here we are. Place your hand on the blank touch pad and ask to enter. This will light your room up and stop anyone from entering who isn't invited.'

Tristan leaned down and let Aski rest her hand against the small screen. 'May I enter?' Aski asked taking Tristan's instructions too literal. The pad started to glow softly under her hand and the doors opened allowing her access to the hallway. Four doors branched out of the hall at North, South, East and West, the rooms forming an 'X'.

'You will need to tell me which room is yours, Aski,' Tristan said.

Aski looked from doorway to doorway and as she assessed the southern door, Aski noted a deep purple aura. The colour swayed and swirled around the entrance and she found it to be a beautiful, almost, perfect display. 'That one there,' Aski said pointing. By this time she was having trouble keeping her eyes open. As Tristan walked her inside and placed her in the bed, Aski drifted off to sleep. The last thing she heard before the world faded away was Tristan's farewell. His voice sounded almost sad.

A picture of Genji crossed her mind. Aski realised that this may be the last moment she got to spend with Tristan and her eyes shot open. Though it felt as though only seconds had passed since she closed her eyes all around the room was dark. Aski catapulted to her feet, cursing herself for her weakened state and raced outside. Glancing back only once, Aski took note of the deep purple that filled the air above her room. She knew now what Tristan had meant with finding her way back. There would be almost no angle that would block her from seeing the colour in the sky as she walked through the dorm rooms.

An explosion caught Aski's attention and she saw smoke coming from the direction of the summoner buildings. She knew it could of been any number of students who had made one mistake or another but a deep dread sitting in the pit of her stomach said otherwise. Making for the building with haste, Aski realised Paws was running beside her. She could feel his unease as well and this made Aski all the more worried. 'Be ready for anything,' Aski said and Paws chirped back.

Finding the large, glass doors shattered, Aski stepped in cautiously looking for any signs of danger. She moved down the hallways, peering around corners and stepping lightly so as not to make too much noise. As she came upon the central hall, Aski was blocked by a wall of darkness. It filled the hallway from wall to wall; floor to ceiling and Aski couldn't see any way around. She knew with every fibre of her being that Tristan and Genji were inside. Picking up a small piece of debris, Aski lobbed it at the shadow wall. On impact the small granite stone was accelerated back in the direction of Aski missing her by millimetres. The debris continued into the side wall at great speed causing a small explosion of stone and granite to burst into the hall. Dust filled the area and Aski started coughing uncontrollably as she fought for fresh air.

Paws made a series of squeaks suggesting a new path had opened and Aski made her way to where he was. The wall had collapsed in every direction but on the other side was mostly clear of the engulfing dust. Aski took a few deep, relieving breaths as she worked out where she needed to go from there. Two directions opened up to her and as Aski decided on which path may work best she spied a third option. Behind a door that stood ajar was a set of stairs leading up. It looked to be in the general direction of the main hall and Aski hoped it opened up somewhere leading into a higher area of the hall.

Taking the staircase, Aski found the wall at the top had caved in from some form of magic. She could see it led into a large open space and rushed up the stairs two at a time. Reaching the top, her face dropped. The room beyond was in shambles with large chunks of stone and piles of debris filling the area. The roof was none existent and light from the half-moon flooded the area. What caused Aski the most grief was the figure of Genji standing above Tristan. He held the Mage's blade in hand above his head ready to strike and as the sword started to come down Aski saw a smile creep across Tristan's face.

'Nooo!' Aski screamed.

Tristan closed the book he'd been reading. A tear trailed over his cheek. So many times he had turned the pages of this book yet always the ending got to him. It was dark, beautiful and exceptionally flawed all at once leaving Tristan feeling things he had not experienced anywhere else. A perfect farewell to this life for tonight Genji would come.

With a sigh, Tristan rose from his deep reading chair and placed the leather bound book in its proper place. He stroked the spine one last time whispering his goodbye before moving away to stand by the window. From his vantage point high above the Academy, Tristan could view the whole ground. His tower-like room tucked away behind all the other buildings. His view tonight was not on the ground however, but the vast starlit sky. A half-moon hung low over the horizon threatening at any moment to plunge the world into complete darkness as it retired for the night. It would be this moment that Genji would choose to approach his home. Most Mages couldn't discern another Mage passing by while invisible when the world was this dark. Even Tristan had trouble at times but the Shadow discipline was never his strong suit.

Looking down at Aski's little room; he knew she was now safe. She could choose the path she wanted to walk from this moment onwards and had the strength and ability to enforce her own will. And when she finds the hidden, magical instruments the last Mage had left, Aski will get a massive head start in certain lessons.

Tristan chuckled as he thought back to the previous owner. A lazy, loner who spent more time trying to find shortcuts than actually putting in the effort. It would normally be a surprise that the Mage became anything more than a second rate drop out but Tristan knew better, the Mage being Genji. Tristan was only surprised he didn't take his remaining magical objects when he left.

Genji would have a fit if he knew it was actually Tristan that first brought him to his room and explained how to find it again. Tristan had personally greeted every Mage that had ever walked the Academy halls. Genji was no different. It was Genji's indifference to others and the simple fact he hadn't met Tristan before that allowed Tristan to get by unnoticed. Genji probably hadn't even given the Tristan from that day a second thought.

Movement caught Tristan's eye. It was slight, barely noticeable and should he have been looking even minutely to left or right he would have missed it. A leaf, falling in the soft breeze, struck something solid for a split second. This changed it's trajectory enough for Tristan to comprehend and alert him to the unnatural movement. He focused his eyes to magically change. He wasn't about to try and break the invisibility spell. Rather, Tristan gave himself the ability to see the wind. There was barely a wind blowing tonight but even still air had a substance to it with these eyes and Tristan soon saw what he was after. A large empty mass was passing through the open air making straight for the tower.

'You've finally arrived,' Tristan whispered and looked to Aski's room once more. 'Farewell, little one.'

Tristan moved back to his reading chair and made himself comfortable. It was facing the doorway so anyone coming in would be in full view of him. A large clock above the doorway created loud ticks that echoed around the room. Each one seemed slower than the last and Tristan started to grow impatient. He hadn't made the trek to his door difficult in any way and Genji should have made the distance by now. Likely, he was being over cautious for once in his life.

Tick...

Tick....

Tick.....

Ti BOOM! The door imploded in a rage of fire and smoke narrowly missing Tristan to crash into the wall behind. Having dropped his invisibility cloak, Genji rolled in and fired off two ice balls that were set to engulf and freeze anything they came in contact with. Genji had set the magic in motion before confirming Tristan's location but the split second he did directed the balls straight at him.

Tristan remained calm and as the ice balls were inches away, Tristan spoke. 'Ody,' he said and a gust of wind deflected the two balls in different directions. One collided with the busted door, extinguishing the flames and wrapping it in ice. The other hit the northern window bursting into hundreds of icicle shards as the glass gave way.

Genji spied the elemental power symbols etched into Tristan's chair. 'Only luck saved you then. Next time you won't be so lucky,' Genji said. 'It appals me to think this once prestigious Academy is being run by a Mage Killer turned Mage Touched Traitor. The world of magic deserves better than that,'

Tristan smiled at the comments. Genji's lust for power was all consuming and blinded him completely. 'And how will you stop an immortal such as I?'

'Your life essence may be prolonged but you aren't immortal, Tristan. This sword could end your life swiftly but that would be a blasphemous act. An act that would destroy the sword. The Mage's Blade is a gift to the world. Only the most elite of Mage's could wield it properly and to throw it away on one life would be a waste. You are more than simply selfish, Tristan. You are a self-centred, uncaring and manipulative person and your reign upon this world ends tonight.' Genji had grasped the sword hilt and wouldn't let go. Further needing a show of power, Genji drew the blade and lowered it on Tristan. 'The power held in this blade will kill you slowly. Painfully. I will funnel it through myself and in doing so will save the wondrous Blade. I will find peace once more and will save Aski from this prison you have brought her to.'

Tristan's face grew hard. 'I had contemplated letting you live, Genji. That maybe there was a good person inside you somewhere. There isn't. That you would distress that girl any more has made it clear you will need to die with me.'

A wicked gleam crossed Genji's eyes. His lips curled back into a dark smile as words dripped from his tongue. 'Krak. Energia.' Twin twisters of pure energy and fire burst from the tip of the sword and spread to encompass the room in its entirety. The powerful attack swirled for Tristan engulfing the area and tearing the walls away.

Genji pulsed power for a minute not leaving anything to chance. All he saw in front of himself was a swirling vortex of fire and white energy. He pictured a far more intricate pattern but the raw power took on a life of its own and not even Genji, who created it, could control it. As he allowed the attack to subside, more to let his arm rest from holding up the sword, the destruction was breath taking. Nothing remained of the room beyond. Stone walls, steel ornaments, jewellery, furniture had all melted away to coat the lower levels in molten material. Even the roof and floor boards that were made of hardwood could only be found in the ash falling like black snow from the sky. Of Tristan there was no sign.

'That's it?' Genji jeered. He couldn't hold back the laughter and ripples of over glorified spasms escaped Genji's throat. 'You boast of strength and within moments you are nothing?'

'Not quite accurate,' a voice reached his ears.

Genji turned sharply to see Tristan standing casually by the nearest of the student accommodation pods. A snarl crossed Genji's lips and he launched from the last remnants of the tower to land near Tristan. The control he felt flying through the air was almost second nature to him now.

'Shall we take this fight to a more secluded area?

The Academy learning centres are empty tonight. You need only pick a building,' Tristan said with a wave of his hand.

'I think this'll do just fine,' Genji replied. Raising the Mage's Blade once more, he tried the same fire energy beam as in the tower. Noticing a dark vortex opening in front of Tristan, Genji almost missed the second one that opened beside him. A swift dive to land hard on his shoulder was all that saved him from his own attack being diverted straight back at him to then pass safely behind the student rooms. 'You crazy bastard,' Genji screamed. 'Do you want to die or not.'

'There is a right and a wrong way to die and when I do, I will die knowing that Blade is no longer in existence. If I fail in killing you I will have at least taken your precious toy.' Tristan enjoyed toying with Genji almost a little too much. He knew he needed to keep things moving.

'Krak. Krak. KRAK!' A little insanity entered Genji's voice as he attacked.

Three balls of fire raced towards Tristan who just shook his head. As they connected with Tristan's chest they all fizzled out. 'You have little elemental power left. Shall we move to the summoner hall instead? Maybe you could find a creature of elemental nature to fight for you.' With that Tristan turned his back to Genji. He knew the move would infuriate the power hungry Mage. Having the fireballs be negated by the magic chainmail under his clothing could only fuel the flames now burning in Genji. Tristan was painfully aware how little time Genji spent at Rolund's Keep that he couldn't know about the chainmail and Tristan would exploit this to no end.

A scream erupted from Genji as he raced at Tristan sword raised. Tristan just turned, arms open, but the fatal strike never came. Genji caught himself and against all his instincts allowed Tristan his way. 'Lead on.'

Smiling inwardly, Tristan guided Genji to the halls of summoning. There was a lot at stake right now and part of his plans relied on the help of his celestial hitch hiker. Tristan shot out a probing thought to the being but got nothing in return. He wasn't worried though as this was normal. Reaching for the door Tristan felt a soft thump on his back. He turned to find Genji had tried his elemental magic again. The look on Genji's face could crumble holy relics.

'What trickery is this? You couldn't have blocked that attack.' Genji growled.

'There is no trickery. Your magic is just weak,' Tristan replied. He entered the building and, not waiting to see if Genji was following, made his way to the centre hall, a vast open area that had a glass ceiling. On the floor was the pattern of light summoning, though, as Genji had found, was also the summoning circle for darkness. This was the first room of the Academy Tristan had built and so it should be the last he saw.

Moving to the far side of the room, Tristan turned to wait patiently for Genji's arrival. He glanced to either side ensuring none of the bags of salt had been moved that day. A number of students finalizing their summoning techniques had grumbled and complained while leaving the building this morning. Tristan had closed the rooms for learning to prepare for this moment. He didn't want anything or anyone to get in the way. Now that it was here he could barely contain himself. His life had been too long and too full of pain.

'I'll see you soon, Beverlin,' Tristan whispered as Genji walked cautiously into the room. 'Genji, you have wielded the King's Sword for barely a week. You have been claimed by it while believing you claimed it as your own. Through your own vanity you have given the sword a new name. A name that denotes your own power and prestige as if the sword was made for you. Today, you will find out just how unworthy you are of that sword. Today, you will give up the power it shares in search of true strength. Today... you will kill me.'

Genji waited patiently, a smug smile curving his lips. It was true Tristan would die today but nothing else rung true. Genji knew the pure strength the Mage's Blade held and nothing could convince him otherwise. 'You are so naive, Tristan,' Genji said. His voice had found it's calm in the short walk to this final arena. He was ready for the showdown of Mage and Mage Killer. 'You think by stealing power over the Academy of Mage Craft, the school where I learned the disciplines of magic, would affect me in this battle. You believe finding a second rate understanding of the arts I have mastered would help persuade me to your desires. You have nothing, Tristan. I will kill you today but I won't destroy the sword doing so.'

Tristan laughed long and loud. 'Do you know what the first room was in the academy that was built?' Tristan asked.

'An irrelevant question,' Genji replied.

'There is great relevance in it as the room was built with you in mind,' Tristan said, amused with the confused expression that crossed Genji's face. 'This room with the functioning summoning circle and other hidden features was built for this battle alone.'

'That's impossible. I was yet to be born when the Academy was made,' Genji said. Uncertainty starting to grow as he looked around the room for other hidden mechanisms. 'And another thing. Many adept Summoners have tried using this circle to summon creatures and no one succeeded. Someone should have if this were a true circle.'

Tristan shook his head. 'To say you weren't born is immaterial. The moment you started traveling in time to moments before the Academy made it possible this room was created for you. To believe I somehow gained power over the Academy is a limiting line of thought. I was there when the Academy was built. I designed this learning environment and had it built from ground up with one purpose in mind. Tonight. The *Once prestigious Academy*' has always been my creation. I have personally welcomed every student in this school. Even yourself though you never realized. I have waited patiently for today. And the reason the summoning circle never worked for anyone... Well, I think you have the smarts enough to discern that. Emundetur a fluxi seminis,' Tristan invoked the words of dispel.

Colour drained from Genji's face upon hearing those final words. The circle could not be used by another while an active summon was in place. Genji couldn't imagine the strain holding a summon over the last few centuries would take. He wondered what sort of creature had been wandering the country side in the meantime when an even more chilling event happened. Tristan vanished for a moment to reappear at the very edge of the Summoning Circle. 'But summoning humans is impossible.' Genji stammered.

Tristan was incredulous that such a comment could come from Genji's mouth. 'And Aski? She wasn't part of the act of summoning a human? What you should be more surprised or curious about is how I summoned myself.' Tristan could see the words weren't sinking in and that Genji was about to flee as he always did when presented with a tough opponent. Tristan bent down to touch the edge of the summoning circle once more. 'Tenebris Adducere,' Tristan said calling upon a being of darkness.

Instantly dark smoke billowed into the room filling every nook and crevice. Genji made to flee but before he had moved more than a few feet smoke filled his lungs causing him to cough and splutter as he fought to get clean oxygen. It wasn't to last, however, as Tristan directed the smoke to cover all entrances and windows into the room cutting off a retreat.

Genji ran to the nearest doorway and crashed against the smoke as if it was cement, knocking him to the ground. He found his feet once more and ran his hand over the smoke. The surface was smooth and solid while moving as if insubstantial. 'What is this?' Genji said.

'I know you have certain tendencies to not hang around,' Tristan replied. 'When things don't go your way you become a scared little child prone to flee. Even with the sword you put so much faith in you are running because I managed to do something you didn't think I could. One way or another, Genji, this ends tonight.'

Genji turned to face Tristan, his lips pursed. There was a determined look upon his face. 'You don't know...'

'And if you say I don't know something again I will kill you right here and now and use the sword myself.' Tristan said. 'I know more than you could ever imagine. The only reason you are alive right now is because I am giving you one last chance of redemption. To honour the word you once gave and take my life using the Sword of Power. If you still want to run away place the sword on the ground and leave. Otherwise, fight me with all you have. Elemental magic, blood magic, shadow magic. I have even left bags of salt for you to summon,' Tristan waved a hand around the room. 'Make your choice.'

Genji held the sword before him watching the light bounce off the metal in tantalizing ways. He could feel the power tingling through his fingers where they touched the hilt. His whole being felt connected to this sword and he wasn't about to give that up. 'Ody,' Genji said.

'About time,' Tristan commented getting ready. He watched as bags of salt were picked up by invisible gusts of air and ripped apart, spilling the content. The air continued to manipulate the salt upon the ground until it formed into the circle for fire.

'Ignis Adducere,' Genji said as he touched the tip of the sword to the summoning circle. Flames spewed from the salt like a volcanic eruption forcing Tristan to fall back. Genji smiled for if the act of summoning was this strong then the creature he selected would put great fear into his enemy. As the flames died back a giant wolf like creature was standing before them. Its fur billowed smoke and wisps of fire escaped it's deadly maw.

Tristan took one look at the beast and laughed. 'That sword you crafted from my friends twin short swords.

270

This was the type of creature that killed him. The same type of creature I killed even without my immortality. You're gunna have to try harder than that."

Genji glowered. As if sensing the detest of its master the wolf leapt to the attack. Bouncing around the walls, the strong talons tore bricks and masonry away to fall into the room.

Tristan was impressed at the speed the creature possessed. He was having a hard time keeping track of the wolf's movements even for such a large creature. When the wolf attacked, Tristan had a fraction of a moment to twist away from the sharp talons. As he twisted the wolf flexed its monstrous paw causing the talons to extend a further inch. Tristan had no time to dodge and the force of the blow sent him spinning back into a wall.

Lungs convulsing, Tristan tried to draw in a breath but couldn't. Gasping, trying to get oxygen, the path to his lungs finally cleared and they started to operate properly. Tristan drew in three deep gulps before standing to stare at the wolf that hadn't advanced further. The snarl across its face a warning not to underestimate it again. Tristan was about to move when he felt a weight slide from his left shoulder to draw down on his right. Looking down, his chainmail armour was in shreds and across his chest were four red marks showing the path of the wolf's talons. The armour had protected him this last time but was now unwearable. With a shrug of his shoulder the shreds of armour fell to the ground.

'That armour had been priceless and reminded me of Beverlin.' Tristan bent down placing his hands upon the ground. 'You should have had your little pet continue the attack while I was still down. That chance won't come again.' Tristan concentrated and the ground started to glow a deep violet. The glow created a large ring upon the ground with symmetrical squares and circles inside. As Tristan pulled his hands back from the ground a sword and knife started to form out of the floor as if growing like two small trees. As the tips formed on each, Tristan grasped the hilts.

'To think an alchemy circle could be found below the floor. The fun the students would of had,' Genji remarked. He then recognised the sword Tristan held. 'Your little blades will prevail you not. Even if it is the sword I forged for you.'

Tristan ignored the comment and waited.

'Attack,' Genji ordered and the wolf leapt forward between him and Tristan. Genji's brow narrowed as the wolf slumped to the ground dead. 'What did you do?'

Tristan didn't answer but simply retrieved his dagger from the wolf's eye socket. Genji couldn't see Tristan used the simple manoeuvre he had so many years ago that allowed him to open the wolf's throat. These creatures never changed, Tristan knew, and with a steady hand could be taken down so easily. 'Your move again,' Tristan said.

Genji grunted but was already manipulating the salt into a new circle. The wolf, Genji left in place. The summoners link was already severed upon it's death and there were some valuable parts he could harvest from the creature later. The summoning circle finished moving and formed a simple circle. 'Energia Adducere,' Genji said touching the Mage's Blade to the salt once more.

Ripples of electricity crackled in the air. Where it hit the walls small explosions occurred sending chunks of masonry around the room. Tristan tried his best to dodge by them but electricity grazed his arm scorching it with a large red burn. The pain pulsed through Tristan's body like he hadn't felt in decades.

'*You wanted a fresh body. The pain will only intensify the more new the flesh,*' the ancient voice echoed inside Tristan's mind.

'Through gritted teeth he shot back. 'This will be the one. Whatever comes out of that circle, you will help me.'

'*That will be entirely up to you, Tristan. You need to allow me control of your body for this to work. You need to let me in charge.*'

'Why didn't you tell me this before?' Tristan asked. He thought for a moment. 'All this time, this has been your plan, hasn't it? The reason you didn't stop us finding the sword that could kill you. The suggestions and small persuasions. You want control, don't you?'

Before the ancient being could respond, a large energy blast exploded from the summoning circle. Tristan was forced back against the far wall. A rain of glass shards fell from the ceiling window and Tristan thought the pulse would've been big enough to shatter every window on campus.

'Fuck!' Tristan exclaimed as he focused on the creature summoned before becoming angry. 'You summoned a Titan into the Academy! He could kill everyone here, Aski included, with the swipe of his arm.'

Genji just smiled his wicked grin and gave a nod. The Titan, standing almost as high as the ceiling itself. It's large translucent form filled most of the room and as it moved, trails of energy crackled through the air. With one of its four open palms, the Titan moved to squash Tristan.

Its large, bulky form made movement slow but even so, Tristan only just rolled out of the way, slipping between two open fingers. Tristan noticed that where the hand touched his discarded chainmail, energy was seeped away and neutralized. The hand pulsed replenishing it's energy and Tristan's eyes widened looking back at the summoning circle. He swore again, realising the circle was open feeding the creature unlimited power from its homelands. Locking eyes with Genji once more, Tristan knew it was useless to try and reason with him. The Mage was psychotic.

A loud tearing noise like an earthquake ripping through streets and buildings sounded behind Tristan. Without wasting the time to look for the danger, Tristan used the elemental power for wind to launch into the air over the Titan's arm ripping up the floor as it raced towards him. Tristan couldn't clear the arm completely, his heel just grazing the energy force.

Immediately, Tristan wailed in pain as the flesh disintegrated back to the bone and he fell heavily holding his ankle.

Another hand attacked Tristan but this time he had no focus to avoid it. The hand engulfed Tristan completely melting the flesh from bone. Even as his form was reduced to a skeleton, Tristan's soul could not find freedom. Pain rippled through him as if the bone was still cocooned in flesh and his jaw hung in a soundless scream. Tristan couldn't believe there could be a pain worse than this but there was. Flesh started to grow back over his bones before melting away once more heightening his pain, keeping him locked in an eternal hell.

'STOP!' Tristan screamed, not at Genji, but the being possessing him, causing him to heal at this moment. 'Let me die! Let me go!' Tristan couldn't think straight as the pain ensnared his entire body with no release. He sought for any escape he could. 'Take it!' Tristan cried.

Immediately, Tristan's skeleton went limp. The flesh didn't grow back anymore and Genji believed he had won. Commanding the Titan back, Genji made to move over to Tristan but froze. 'How can you still be alive?' Genji said.

Within the skeleton's eyes a green glow grew in intensity. '*NO HUMAN CAN KILL ME WITH MAGIC ALONE. I WHO CREATED THE SUN AND THE SEAS, THE MOUNTAINS AND THE TREES. MY LIFE IS ETERNAL.*'

Genji had not been prepared for the deep booming voice that came from Tristan. With each syllable fear gripped his heart and as the flesh finally started to reform over Tristan making him whole, Genji ordered the Titan to attack once more. The Titan swung all four arms to come down upon Tristan's form but before they connected the green, glowing eyes in Tristan's skull locked onto the Titan, causing it to pause.

'*YOU ARE MINE, ARKANDO, LORD OF THE SILVER FLAMES,*' the ancient voice said speaking the

274

Titan's name. The Titan considered this little creature only a moment before seeing the one controlling it and relented. The Summoning link shifting to connect with Tristan's form.

Standing tall once more the Titan rounded on Genji who shrunk back in fear. 'It's not possible,' he said to the winds. The Titan's hand moved to squish Genji as it once did Tristan and Genji shot his arms up to protect himself. 'No!' he screamed.

As the massive hand of energy crackled into contact with Genji it withdrew in pain. Still held in Genji's clutches was the Mage's Blade. Contact with the Titan caused it to come alive and propel the hand backwards. The Titan seemed to become confused seeing the sword as if for the first time. And looked to Tristan's form for guidance. The ancient being nodded back allowing the Titan to step aside and return to its own plane. In a flash the Titan was gone.

Tristan had no memory of what occurred in the time he gave up his body. Now he found himself in full control again, the excruciating pain an unpleasant memory at the front of his mind.

'*It looks like you will get your wish,*' the ancient voice echoed in Tristan's mind.

'I will not be made a fool of,' Genji said.

Tristan barely heard him and as he looked over saw that Genji was looking downward. His shoulders moved in time with his breaths as if he was holding in a burning rage. His fingers gripped the hilt of the Mages Blade so tightly his knuckles were turning white.

'I will not be made a fool of,' Genji repeated a little louder. Head coming up, Genji locked burning eyes with Tristan's. 'I WILL NOT BE MADE A FOOL OF!' Genji screamed charging in and shoulder barging Tristan to the ground. Raising the sword above his head, Genji swung at Tristan to the sound of a cry behind him.

A touch of sadness entered Tristan at his final moment. He hadn't wanted Aski to witness this but would not stop it. Tristan's eyes widened as a small rift opened between Genji and himself the moment before the Blade connected. The sword vanished inside it and out of shock Genji let go essentially throwing the sword down the ebony staircase. The rift closed as fast as it opened with the sword inside.

Tristan and Genji's disbelief mirrored one another as they sought to make sense of what just happened. Tristan, recovering first, drew a dagger across Genji's throat. The Mage dropped silently, eyes still echoing a shattered world. Tristan had no need of the man anymore and to leave a man so broken like him alive no one would be safe. Tristan turned in time to see Aski tumble from one of the holes made by the wolf. Racing over he caught her at the last moment cradling her in his arms.

'Why, Aski?' Tristan said. Tears welled in his eyes seeking an answer for his broken dreams.

Aski was hovering on the brink of passing out. The energy exerted to open the small time rift taking its toll. 'I'm sorry,' she said softly. 'I just reacted. You are too speci...' Aski's eyes closed as she lost consciousness.

Tristan's tears ran freely.

Epilogue

As her consciousness grew sentient, pain coursed through her entire body. Beverlin gave a choking cough as her throat and lungs rebelled against the acrid smoke she had been breathing. All around her was darkness and there was a weight holding her pinned in place. Reaching back into her mind, Beverlin sought her last memories trying to solve her current predicament. She found it difficult to even bring up any memories at first but slowly they started to creep back. She remembered the college and the quest she started with Genji, Aski and Tristan. Thoughts of the knight started flooding her mind and she pushed them back. They were happy and full of love but brought her despair when she thought what Tristan's fate may be. Memories of her capture and the escape from the keep came back. When she reached the hall everything came flooding in as if a dam had burst.

Standing in a room full of Mage Killers, Beverlin had conjured walls of fire to hold the knights in place. She enjoyed listening to their taunts from the other side of the flames, unable to get to her. She enjoyed it even more as she maneuvered the flames to kill the knights one at a time, toying with them. She saw that some of the Mage Killers had retreated to find other paths so as to outflank her but Beverlin was too smart to let that happen. Turning she made to flee the area and reconnect with Tristan and Aski but an explosion sent her flying and into unconsciousness. She could only conclude that the rooms above were a storehouse for the explosive black powder the priests of the old religion used to craft and her flames had burnt hot enough to ignite them.

Feeling sorry for her predicament, Beverlin set about freeing herself from the crumbling tomb of debris. With each hand she traced the sign for earth onto the stones and simultaneously cast earth magic with each. 'Yerkiry,' Beverlin said. Power flowed through her into the rocks of the keep and soon they started to shift off of her giving passage to the surface only a foot above. With the weight off her chest, Beverlin found each breath to be more fulfilling than any she had taken since waking. Taking a moment longer to find some strength, Beverlin pulled herself from the hole and out into the wreckage of the keep. She stared in horror at the destruction she'd brought upon the ancient structure. Over half the keep was in pieces and a large, blackened circle was found at the centre of the blast.

'You're a rather pretty one,' a voice behind her said. 'Is this your doing?'

Beverlin turned and her heart dropped. In the courtyard and the now free spaces of the keep, Mage Killers had set up camp. A large group of them were gathering around Beverlin and she started to give up on everything.

'We don't interact with their kind,' said a large man with orange hair and beard.

Beverlin recognized him as Durin, commander of the Mage Killers, after he pursued them through Boerus. She remembered a Shade had possessed him and knew she was outmatched.

'Kill her slowly,' Durin commanded. The Mage Killers grinned and started to circle Beverlin with weapons drawn.

Beverlin just shook her head and with a shrug of her shoulders, gave up on life. Nothing she possessed was going to get her through this fight as she used the last of her mental strength to move the debris that buried her. Light filled the sky above and the Mage Killers stepped back, weary of what was to come. The light parted into a shimmering rift and Beverlin saw the ebony staircase beyond. A clatter echoed from within before a large object came spinning out embedding itself into the ground next to Beverlin.

The rift closed and Beverlin was left staring at a simple sword with elegant finery detailed into the hilt, crossbar, and blade. As she grasped at the hilt power flowed through her awakening the soul. She knew at

278

that moment what sword was in her possession. Looking at the Mage Killers, Beverlin gave a wicked smile.

~ End

Thank you and I hope to see you again soon.

Books currently in the Aether

Veritas Rerum novels
Pyre of Souls
Veritas Rerum

The Birth of Magic

The Elven King Trilogy

Mage Killer Trilogy

Sword of the Immortal Trilogy
Child of Darkness
The Immortal Knight

Novels of the Wandering Swordsman Kiyoshi
A Stolen Sword
Split Personality Swordsman

The Future Past

The Boatman – A book of short stories

Written in the Stars Trilogy
The Stars Above Us
The World Around Us